# NORTHANGER ABBEY AND ANGELS AND DRAGONS

## Jane Austen and Vera Nazarian

Cover Art Details: "St. George And The Dragon," Paolo Uccello, 1460; "Saint Michael and the Dragon," Raphael, c1505; "An Angel Playing a Flageolet," Edward Burne-Jones, 1878; "Angel (two details from the Linaioli Tabernacle)," Fra Angelico 1433; "Angel Annunciating," "Madonna and Child with Saints and an Angel," Lorenzo Lotto, 1527-1528; "Angel with the Flaming Sword," Franz von Stuck (1863-1928); "Dead Christ Attended By Two Angels," Alessandro Allori (1535-1607); "Angel," Georg Pencz, 1525-1530; "Angel," Abbott Handerson Thayer, c1889; "An Angel Awakens the Prophet Elijah," Juan Antonio Frias y Escalante, 1667; "How an Angel rowed Sir Galahad across the Dern Mere," Joseph Noel Paton, 1888; "The Violinist," Edward John Poynter, 1891.

Interior Illustrations: "Appendix," courtesy of Pearson Scott Foresman. All other interior illustrations Copyright © 2010 by Vera Nazarian

Cover Design Copyright © 2010 by Vera Nazarian

ISBN-13: 978-1-60762-058-7
ISBN-10: 1-60762-058-8

FIRST EDITION
Trade Paperback

December 5, 2010

A Publication of
Norilana Books
P. O. Box 2188
Winnetka, CA 91396
www.norilana.com

Printed in the United States of America

# Northanger Abbey
# and
# Angels and Dragons

Curiosities

an imprint of

Norilana Books

www.norilana.com

**The Collected Supernatural Jane Austen**
by Vera Nazarian

*(Series includes the following titles)*

**Mansfield Park and Mummies:**
*Monster Mayhem, Matrimony, Ancient Curses,
True Love, and Other Dire Delights*

**Northanger Abbey and Angels and Dragons**

*Forthcoming:*

**Pride and Platypus: Mr. Darcy's Dreadful Secret**

**Pagan Persuasion: All Olympus Descends on Regency**

**Emma Enchanted**

**Sense and Sanguine Sensibility**

**Lady Susan, Succubus**

# Northanger Abbey

and

# *Angels*

and

# Dragons

⚜

# Jane Austen

and

# Vera Nazarian

⚜

*With Scholarly Footnotes and Appendices*

## A Daring Dedication

To the Almighty
With profound gratitude for creating Satire
And being the only One
Consistently, eternally, unconditionally
Able to Appreciate it.

# Advertisement by the Authoress, to Northanger Abbey

This little work was finished in the year 1803, and intended for immediate publication. It was disposed of to a bookseller, it was even advertised, and why the business proceeded no farther, the author has never been able to learn. That any bookseller should think it worthwhile to purchase what he did not think it worthwhile to publish seems extraordinary. But with this, neither the author nor the public have any other concern than as some observation is necessary upon those parts of the work which thirteen years have made *supernaturally* obsolete. The public are entreated to bear in mind that thirteen years have passed since it was finished, many more since it was begun, and that during that period, places, manners, books, and opinions—indeed, the very fabric of the world itself!—have undergone considerable changes. . . .

Not the least of which is the sometime-tangible presence in nature of angels, demons, and the great winged dragons.

# Chapter 1

In the beginning was the Word—also known as a very *big bang* marvelous sort of Expletive—a circumstance wherein God created the universe.

He made light and stars and constellations and galaxies and planets, and a certain very particular lump of matter called earth, which He populated—heavens and firmament—with teeming curious creatures. These included, among others, trilobites and baboons, porcupines and ferrets, pigeons and bumblebees, manatees and kangaroo, the duck and the duckbill platypus, and of course, the upright great apes called humans.

The latter, created most in His Image, immediately proceeded to "ape" for all they were worth—in other words, to *create* in turn—and were directly responsible for the manufacture of virtue and taste, style and erudition, and henceforth the knowledge of Good and Evil as pertaining to fashionable trifles suitable for adornment during a preening exhibition called the London Season.

Also created were gossip and dowry, followed by courtship and matrimony, and then tedium and ennui. Last, and not least, came the acquired taste for trimming hedges in the French style, and the secret delight in sanguine scenes of murderous dread, gothic terrors, and dark rending romance, particularly in the young female of the species, as perpetuated by a certain literary female by the name of Mrs. Radcliffe.

To provide this teeming Creation with some modicum of order and supervision, God also created angels and demons and seraphim and nephilim, and occasional great serpents and dragons, all of which he initially imbued with common sense—the one precious and infinitely rare faculty that the rest of the Creation was sorely lacking.

For, what is order without common sense, but Bedlam's front parlor? What is imagination without common sense, but the aspiration to out-dandy Beau Brummell with nothing but a bit of faded muslin and a limp cravat? What is Creation without common sense, but a scandalous thing without form or function, like a matron with half a dozen unattached daughters?

And God looked upon the Creation in all its delightful multiplicity, and saw that, all in all, it was quite Amiable.

There was but one minor problem.

Common sense was not as common as the Deity might wish for. Indeed, not even angelic choirs were entirely free of a certain vice known as silliness.

And if the very angels were thus flawed, then what might one expect of innocent young ladies?

Speaking of innocent young ladies—behold our heroine, Catherine Morland. Admittedly, no one who had ever seen Catherine in her infancy would have supposed her born to be an heroine. Her situation in life, the character of her father and mother, her own person and disposition, were all equally against her.

In one inconsequential detail alone was she at all a standout—indeed, it was such a very peculiar and supernatural thing that some might venture to question its validity. For, not unlike the saintly Joan of Arc of old, our Catherine could hear the voices and speech of angels and demons, and had the innate ability to understand their language, both profane and divine. Furthermore, she was also able to see them as corporeal beings, in all their bright glory and terrifying aspect. Of course, for a very long time she was blessedly unaware of the fact.

But, gentle Reader, we are getting ahead of ourselves.

A s is rather appropriate for a young girl who was one day to commune with the otherworldly, her father was a clergyman. Without being neglected, or poor, he was a very respectable man, though his name was Richard[1]—and he had never been handsome. He had a considerable independence besides two good livings—and he was not in the least addicted to locking up his daughters.

Her mother was a woman of useful plain sense, with a good temper, and, what is more remarkable, with a good constitution. She had three sons before Catherine was born; and instead of dying in bringing the latter into the world, as anybody might expect, she still lived on—lived to have six children more—to see them growing up around her, and to enjoy excellent health herself. A family of ten children will be always called a fine family, where there are heads and arms and legs enough for the number; but the Morlands had little other right to the word, for they were in general very plain. And Catherine, for many years of her life, was as plain as any, not to mention, completely deaf to any dulcet tones of the angel choirs in the ether all around.

She had a thin awkward figure, a sallow skin without colour, dark lank hair, and strong features. Her eyes were not sapphire like the summer skies; nor her lips like ripe cherries (though occasionally this could be said of her nose after she had been outside on a particularly frosty winter day). Neither were her cheeks like roses (tea or floribunda), nor the tone of her voice like tinkling bells, but more often like a foghorn coming off a very distant waterway (their domicile being nowhere near

---

[1] Gentle Reader, not all Richards are "Poor" nor are they all "Dicks."

the coast) when she rolled about the grass screaming with rather gargantuan laughter among her younger siblings;—so much for her person; and not less unpropitious for heroism seemed her mind.

She was fond of all boy's plays, and greatly preferred cricket not merely to dolls, but to the more heroic enjoyments of infancy, nursing a dormouse,[2] feeding a canary-bird, or watering a rose-bush. Indeed she had no taste for a garden (nor had she any idea of the extent to which gardens were filled to bursting with all manner of angels, paunchy cherubs, and other metaphysical spirits and fae). And if she gathered flowers at all, it was chiefly for the pleasure of mischief (indeed, a mild bit of demonic inclination here—but, rest assured, dear Reader, quickly overcome and conquered as a youthful personality deficit)—at least so it was conjectured from her always preferring those which she was forbidden to take.

Such were her propensities. Her abilities were quite as extraordinary. She never could learn or understand anything before she was taught; and sometimes not even then, for she was often inattentive, and occasionally stupid. Her mother was three months in teaching her only to repeat the "Beggar's Petition"; and after all, her next sister, Sally, could say it better than she did. Not that Catherine was always stupid—by no means; she learnt the fable of "The Hare and Many Friends" as quickly as any girl in England (and since the days of her metaphysical ignorance were numbered, there was just a hint of Ancient Hebrew, hovering, one might say, at the tip of the tongue, and quite ready to be thoroughly absorbed and fathomed).

Her mother wished her to learn music; and Catherine was sure she should like it, for she was very fond of tinkling the keys of the old forlorn spinnet; so, at eight years old she began. She learnt a year, and could not bear it (and neither could most of the

---

[2] As opposed to a Windows mouse.

household angelic sprites who, upon the first tinkling sound, fled the music room in greater haste and dread than had they been chastised by the archangels themselves). Thankfully, Mrs. Morland, who did not insist on her daughters being accomplished in spite of incapacity or distaste, allowed her to leave off (for which, little did she know, but the good matron received a host of supernatural blessings, including a permanent guarantee against curdled milk on the premises). The day which dismissed the music-master was one of the happiest of Catherine's life. That same happy day was marked by hosannas and seraphim making particular celebratory music in the spheres.

Her taste for drawing was likewise not superior; though whenever she could obtain the outside of a letter from her mother or seize upon any other odd piece of paper, she did what she could in that way, by drawing houses and trees, hens and chickens, and an occasional monstrous duck, all very much like one another. Writing and accounts she was taught by her father; French by her mother: her proficiency in either was not remarkable, and she shirked her lessons in both whenever she could (for, as can be seen, there was as yet no dulcet angelic voice whispering in her ear and guiding her toward prudence).

What a strange, unaccountable character!—for with all these symptoms of profligacy at ten years old, she had neither a bad heart nor a bad temper, was seldom stubborn, scarcely ever quarrelsome, and very kind to the little ones, with few interruptions of tyranny. She was moreover noisy and wild, hated confinement and cleanliness, and loved nothing so well in the world as rolling down the green slope at the back of the house.

Such was Catherine Morland at ten. And precisely at such a youthful junction, an event of arcane magnitude occurred that, with a single blow of fate, transformed our mundane heroine into a metaphysical prodigy.

Catherine, merrily skipping down the above-mentioned green slope in the back, did not notice where her foot was placed. She tripped and fell; her head came in contact with a rocky lump of earth. And just as a freshly painful lump immediately appeared at the back of her head—a lump not unlike numerous other lumps she had received previously upon many similar circumstances—in that very same moment Catherine felt and heard a *crack* . . . It was as though her skull was curiously cracked open like a walnut, and *something opened* inside her head.

The next moment was a veritable flood of senses. Sight and sound were suddenly more pungent; colors rippled and doubled as though imbued with a secret rainbow; sunlight fractured into splinters of magical glass, and sweet music filled the air from all directions.

And then came the angel voices!

Oh, how they sang! Light, clean soprano and sweet alto, and all things in-between! How pure and far-ranging were their tones, how amazing the echoes of cathedral richness in the grand open expanse!

Catherine stood up, forgetting all about the painfully stinging lump in her head, the grass staining her knees, and merely lingered with wonder, taking it all in, listening, listening, *looking* . . .

And as she looked, she began to *see* the sources of the divine chorus, the many tiny figures of light, like distant fireflies, sparkling akin to disembodied candle flames among the grass and the flowers and among the leaves of the trees.

"Oh dear!" said Catherine. "What—who are you?"

In response, one tiny figure, radiating tangible warmth and kindness, sprang up like a shooting star, or possibly a dragonfly, and darted to hang in the air just an inch before Catherine's nose.

"Dearest child, we are angels, of course!" it replied, looking at her with infinite love.

Catherine blinked, and the next moment they came to her, shooting stars from all directions, a moving cloud of fiery hummingbirds—nay, tiny winged beings—and they exclaimed in sweet voices, "Behold! At last, she can see!"

From this remarkable point forward, things were rather different, for, wherever she went, Catherine was never again to be alone. Her world had shifted and expanded, she saw, and heard, and as a result *paid better attention,* and thus it was that her life had entered the next stage—which is inevitable when everything is to be accompanied by faithful commentary and a remarkable audience.

A t fifteen, appearances were mending, not only of the world around her, but also of Catherine herself.

Now that angels filled every nook and crevice and whispered perfectly reasonable and wise advice in her ear, it did not at all prevent her from beginning to curl her hair and longing for balls. Her complexion improved, her features were softened by plumpness and colour, her eyes gained more animation, and her figure more consequence. Her love of dirt gave way to an inclination for finery, and she grew clean as she grew smart. She had now the pleasure of sometimes hearing her father and mother remark on her personal improvement.

"Catherine grows quite a good-looking girl—she is almost pretty today," were words which caught her ears now and then, in addition to various angelic whispers and exclamations of delight as to her character growth as a heroine-to-be; and how welcome were the sounds of approval at last from both parents and seraphim!

To look almost pretty is an acquisition of higher delight to a girl who has been looking plain the first fifteen years of her life than a beauty from her cradle can ever receive. And to be almost perfectly good was the kind of heavenly approbation that had no earthly match of any kind.

Mrs. Morland was a very good woman in her turn, and wished to see her children everything they ought to be. But her time was so much occupied in lying-in and teaching the little ones, that her elder daughters were inevitably left to shift for themselves; and it was not very wonderful that Catherine, who had by nature nothing heroic about her (except for the arsenal of angels), should prefer cricket, baseball,[3] riding on horseback, and running about the country at the age of fourteen, to books— or at least books of information—for, provided that nothing like useful knowledge could be gained from them, provided they were all *story* and no reflection, she had never any objection to books at all. Whilst from ten onward she was in training for a mystical prodigy, from fifteen to seventeen she was in training for a heroine—reading all such works as heroines must to supply their memories with those quotations which are so serviceable and so soothing in the vicissitudes of their eventful lives.

From Pope, she learnt to censure those who

*"bear about the mockery of woe."*

From Gray, that

*"Many a flower is born to blush unseen,*
*"And waste its fragrance on the desert air."*

From Thompson, that—

*"It is a delightful task*
*"To teach the young idea how to shoot."*

---

[3] The Astute Reader is surely stunned! But yes indeed, *baseball* is known and acknowledged by the Esteemed Author—possibly its earliest literary mention ever!

And from Shakespeare she gained a great store of information—amongst the rest, that—

> *"Trifles light as air,*
> *"Are, to the jealous, confirmation strong,*
> *"As proofs of Holy Writ."*

That

> *"The poor beetle, which we tread upon,*
> *"In corporal sufferance feels a pang as great*
> *"As when a giant dies."*

And that a young woman in love always looks—

> *"like Patience on a monument*
> *"Smiling at Grief."*

Last but not least, it must be told that, from more than one angelic entity she heard—nay, was frequently instructed to

*Look where you step, dear child—careful, no! That is, Catherine, indeed, do, please look OUT—oh!*
*Oh dear . . .*

And

*You must always consider carefully before speaking your mind. Indeed, words in certain combinations have the curious power to affect others far more resoundingly than sticks and stones—That is, please, don't—WAIT—goodness, no!*
*Oh dear . . .*

Indeed, the angelic advice and commentary so very often began and ended with "Oh dear . . ." that Catherine took it as a habitual heavenly refrain, and with time unfortunately paid it even less attention—much to the frustration of the dear blessed ones who were tirelessly looking after the immortal soul of their young charge.

Since there were always at least one or two angels present within hearing distance (and somewhat less commonly within *sight*—which Catherine was rather thankful for, particularly in moments of necessary daily toilet and privacy), and sometimes there were three or four or even more, the advice given and received took on the form of animated conversation.

"Watch out, dear child! Draw the hair comb across just so—"

"Catherine, your left sleeve is a bit rumpled, do straighten it just a tad—"

"Yes, I know!" Catherine would exclaim, or, "Goodness, enough! I am about to do it myself, please. Would you mind terribly moving out of the way, for maybe a few moments?"

For anyone looking on, it appeared that Catherine was talking to herself—or arguing with herself, and sometimes even having a bit of a miff with herself—but her parents soon decided it was a charming, normal portion of growing up and becoming a young woman. "Look at the dear child declaim so well," her mother would say, "I do believe she is reciting a bit of Aristotle? No? What a nice change from running wild in the grass!" And as far as her siblings, they simply decided her apparent soliloquies were a thing that young ladies did when they thought themselves a bit smart.

As a result, Catherine's tendency to converse with herself was allowed to continue without the least bit of concern on anyone's part. And a good thing it was, too, since no one would have liked to bring in even the merest hint of Bedlam.

So far her general improvement was sufficient—and in many other points she came on exceedingly well; for though she could not write sonnets, she brought herself to read them (and recite a few of them out loud to throw off suspicion, in case of particularly pointed angelic argument). And though there seemed no chance of her throwing a whole party into raptures by a prelude on the pianoforte, she could listen to other people's performance with very little fatigue. Furthermore, an angel could always be relied upon if needed to pull open her drooping eyelids.

Her greatest deficiency was in the pencil—short of stick figures and monstrous ducks, she had no notion of drawing—not enough even to attempt a sketch of her lover's profile, that she might be detected in the design. There she fell miserably short of the true heroic height, and it was something for which no heavenly reinforcement could compensate. At present she did not know her own poverty, for she had no lover to portray. She had reached the age of seventeen, without having seen one amiable youth who could call forth her sensibility, without having inspired one real passion, and without having excited even any admiration but what was very moderate and very transient, much less gothic or medieval.

This was strange indeed! But strange things may be generally accounted for if their cause be fairly searched out. There was not one lord in the neighbourhood; no—not even a baronet. There was not one family among their acquaintance who had reared and supported a boy accidentally found at their door—not one young man whose origin was unknown. Her father had no ward, and the squire of the parish no children. Even the servants had no sufficiently ruddy cheeked and comely young son to mysteriously pass by her in the green, while leading a nobly saddled mare (nay, a proper stallion!) or carrying a mighty load of firewood worthy of someone endowed with Herculean or knightly upper limbs.

But when a young lady is to be an heroine, the perverseness of forty surrounding families cannot prevent her. Neither can large oceanic-bound landmasses, arid deserts or frightful moors. Indeed, not even Heaven itself. Something must and will happen to throw a hero in her way.

Mr. Allen, who owned the chief of the property about Fullerton, the village in Wiltshire where the Morlands lived, was ordered to Bath for the benefit of a gouty constitution—and his lady, a good-humoured woman, fond of Miss Morland, and probably aware that if adventures will not befall a young lady in her own village, she must seek them abroad, invited her to go with them. Mr. and Mrs. Morland were all compliance, and Catherine all happiness.

And the angels? For mysterious reasons they were in a bit of a tumult!

# Chapter 2

In addition to what has been already said of Catherine Morland's personal and mental endowments, when about to be launched into all the difficulties and dangers of a six weeks' residence in Bath (and a possible heroic grand adventure), it may be stated that her heart was affectionate; her disposition cheerful and open, and—discounting her tendency to "converse" out loud, without conceit or affectation of any kind. Her manners were just removed from the awkwardness and shyness of a girl; her person pleasing, and, when in good looks, pretty—and her mind about as ignorant and uninformed as the female (or for that matter, male) mind at seventeen usually is. In short, a mind ready to be molded by grander forces, be it of Heavenly, or, God forbid, of a rather *lower* variety.

But once again, dear Reader, we are getting somewhat ahead of ourselves. . . .

When the hour of departure drew near, the maternal anxiety of Mrs. Morland will be naturally supposed to be most severe. A thousand alarming presentiments of evil to her beloved Catherine from this terrific separation must oppress her heart and drown her in tears for the last days of their being together (while angels all over the domicile went into veritable flurries of sympathetic agitation, occasionally knocking down minor objects on shelves and raising inexplicable drafts in closed windowless rooms). And important advice must of course flow from wise maternal lips in their parting conference in her closet (closets being the obligatory locales for such). Cautions against the violence of noblemen who delight in forcing young ladies away to some remote farm-house, must, at such a moment, relieve the fullness of her heart. Who would not think so?

But Mrs. Morland knew so little of lords and baronets, that she entertained no notion of their general mischievousness, and was wholly unsuspicious of danger to her daughter from their machinations. Her cautions were confined to the following points. "I beg, Catherine, you will always wrap yourself up very warm about the throat, when you come from the rooms at night; and I wish you would try to keep some account of the money you spend; I will give you this little book on purpose—Pray, are you listening, child? You appear so distracted yet again. Were you just talking to the wardrobe chest? Oh dear . . ."

"Not at all, mama," replied Catherine reasonably, and avoided bestowing a glance at the three tiny angelic figures practically doing cartwheels on top of the chest, in their attempt to capture her attention.

Soon enough Mrs. Morland left the room for a moment, in order to fetch some pins that the maid apparently left in the parlor. And Catherine allowed herself to look directly at the heavenly beings. "Goodness, what is it?"

"Oh, Catherine!" exclaimed one tiny figure of light—tiny indeed, for he (or she?) was no greater than three inches in height, including folded wingspan. "Catherine, you are hereby placed in gravest danger!"

And the other two echoed him in tinkling voices, "Catherine, oh, Catherine, oh, woe! Danger!"

"What? What do you mean?"

"Oh!" cried another tiny angel. "Whatever you do, you must not go away!"

"No, dear child, you must not! This trip bodes dire and eternal misfortune!"

"But—" said Catherine, sitting down on the edge of her bed. "But, how awful! It is Bath! How can I *not* go? And it is to be with Mrs. Allen; she is so kind to have invited me, and—what in the world could be so horridly dangerous?"

In response the angels started flittering about terribly, their luminescent figures growing in brightness, which happened frequently when they were in a state of agitation.

Eventually one of them collided with a candlestick, and Catherine had to jump up in a hurry to catch the burning candle with amazing dexterity of one hand, while snatching a floundering winged being with another.

"Oh! Fire! Do be careful, Lawrence!" cried the other two, jumping up and down, then promptly collided with one another.

"Upon my word! This is quite ridiculous!" Catherine said, holding an angel in the palm of her hand and glaring at two more sliding around on her bedspread. "I insist you tell me what is the matter, at once! And for the hundredth time, keep away from burning flames!"

In her hand, the angel's golden glow dimmed a little to a warm peach and then soft mauve. The being settled firmly on her palm, and put its head between two tiny arms, in a gesture of infinite regret. "I am afraid, dear Catherine, I cannot."

"Cannot what?"

"He cannot speak, he may not answer," piped in the others. "Indeed, none of us can tell you. We can only warn you and entreat you not to go."

Catherine let out a long breath of frustration. "This is quite silly. How as I supposed to do or not do things, go or not go places, all without a good reason? And especially when you first frighten me to death and then refuse to explain?"

"We can only ask you to trust us—"

"Wait!" said Catherine, as though awakening out of an extended sleep. "And since when do you have given names? *Lawrence?*"

"It is indeed I," replied the little being on her palm.

"So you mean to tell me that for all these months I could have been referring to each one of you in a civil manner, instead of resorting to idiocy such as Splatterplop and Fumblehead—and—"

"I am Terence," said one of the two on her bed.

"And you may call me Clarence."

"Well, criminy!" said Catherine.

"Not Criminy, I am Cla—"

At which point Terence touched the other gently.

"We were not allowed to utter our names before this day," said Lawrence, folding his/her/its little hands together and fluttering its wings suddenly like a butterfly of pure light.

"Before this day? What changed? It is a Tuesday."

"Grave danger," said Clarence.

"Today we were instructed to guard you," said Terence.

"That is, we guard everyone, but from this point on we must guard *you* with particular care," added Lawrence.

"More than you already guard me, day and night?"

"More than imaginable," said Lawrence. "For today you are considering leaving home for the first time and venturing into the world, and when and once you do, it becomes inevitable that you will be assailed—"

"Attacked!"

"Besieged and sorely tempted!"

"Surrounded and stormed and thoroughly tested!"

"Fallen upon from all sides!"

"And for that reason we are given the sternest and most solemn instruction from On High, to watch over you and protect you with all our own strength!"

"All our fortitude!"

"Our loyalty!"

"Our love!"

"But—" said Catherine. "Yes, that is, I mean—thank you kindly from my heart, indeed—but, why? And who in the world will be attacking me? Why *me?* What is this dreadful danger?"

But all three angels hung their heads and would not speak. Several long moments passed, as Catherine considered this unbelievable turn of events while fiddling nervously with a bit of lace. Then, with a firm sense of resolve, she sat up straight, and announced, not unlike a proper heroine: "Since you will not explain, I am obviously meant to go and face this danger directly. Besides—it's adventure! It's Bath!"

One by one, the angels sadly looked up.

One nodded, whispering, "Oh dear . . . We knew you would decide thus."

"Please," tried Lawrence once again, glowing in the palm of her hand. "Catherine, oh, Catherine, mayhap you might still change your mind?"

But because the angel knew very well they were dealing with an heroine, it/she/he resigned himself to a heavenly sigh.

Meanwhile the trip preparations must but continue. Catherine's sibling Sally, or rather Sarah (for what young lady of common gentility will reach the age of sixteen without altering her name as far as she can?), must from situation be at this time the intimate friend and confidante of her sister. At least, such was the assumption (though Catherine already had a veritable regiment of heavenly confidants at her disposal). It is remarkable, however, that Sarah neither insisted on Catherine's writing by every post, nor exacted her promise of transmitting the character of every new acquaintance, every interesting conversation that Bath might produce. She did however request chartreuse ribbon, such as was rumored to be particularly fashionable.

Everything indeed, relative to this important journey, was done, on the part of the Morlands, with a degree of moderation and composure—excepting a few inexplicable flurries of drafts, moving curtains, and strangely teetering figurines on shelves and mantels. All preparation seemed more consistent with the common feelings of common life, than with the tender emotions which the first separation of an heroine from her family ought always to excite.

Her father, instead of giving her either nothing at all or an unlimited order on his banker, gave her only ten guineas, and promised her more when she wanted it.

Under these unpromising auspices, the parting took place, and the journey began. Catherine, with at least half a dozen glowing angelic figures hovering overhead, sat in the carriage seat near Mrs. Allen who, she noticed, had a few angels of her own (but was perfectly oblivious of them, as everyone else in the world but Catherine seemed to be). For hours Catherine dearly kept her eyes away from the supernatural presences and bravely ignored them practically crawling all over Mrs. Allen's bonnet, not to mention, their exclamations and sighs and repeated cries of "Beware! Oh, dear child, what frightful harm might befall you any moment!"

Their agitation got so dire and tedious at one point that Catherine had to mutter, "Shush!" and disguise it with a cleverly timed sneeze into a handkerchief (which sent Terence—or possibly Lawrence—flying into the brocade curtain).

But despite the warnings, the trip was performed with suitable quietness and uneventful safety. Neither robbers nor tempests befriended them, nor was there one lucky carriage overturn to introduce them to the hero. There were no romantic masked highwaymen in the moonlight (indeed, the moon itself was in a thin new crescent state, thus refusing to cooperate with a proper heroic scenario).

Nothing more alarming occurred than a fear, on Mrs. Allen's side, of having once left her clogs behind her at an inn (a fine establishment which was neither haunted nor occupied by a band of cutthroats—though there were rumors of a monstrous flying fowl observed in the neighborhood, pronounced in whisper to be none other than the Brighton Duck[4]), and that fortunately proved to be groundless.

They arrived at Bath. Catherine was all eager delight—her eyes were here, there, everywhere, for once naturally ignoring the heavenly host.

They approached Bath's fine and striking environs, and afterwards drove through those streets which conducted them to the hotel. She was come to be happy, regardless of angelic warnings of decidedly silly and unfounded doom, and she felt happy already.

They were soon settled in comfortable lodgings in Pulteney Street.

It is now expedient to give some description of Mrs. Allen, that the astute Reader may be able to judge in what manner her actions will hereafter tend to promote the general distress of the work, and how she will, probably, contribute to reduce poor Catherine to all the desperate wretchedness of which a last volume[5] is capable—whether by her imprudence, vulgarity, or jealousy—whether by intercepting her letters, ruining her character, or turning her out of doors. For, surely the angels cried such dire warning in regard to none other than Mrs. Allen?

---

[4] A creature of nightmares, rumored to be first observed and harbored at a certain fine estate called Mansfield Park.

[5] It must be noted that some "last" volumes work better than others that actually precede the first volume in an endless series of imperial space battle rehashes, cute stuffed creature aliens and brother-sister pairings, strange *forces* that may or may not be with one—that is, ahem! Upon my word, what was that all about?

Or, quite possibly, not. . . .

Mrs. Allen was one of that numerous class of females, whose society can raise no other emotion than surprise at there being any men in the world who could like them well enough to marry them. She had neither beauty, genius, accomplishment, nor manner. The air of a gentlewoman, a great deal of quiet, inactive good temper, and a trifling turn of mind were all that could account for her being the choice of a sensible, intelligent man like Mr. Allen.

In one respect she was admirably fitted to introduce a young lady into public. She was as fond of going everywhere and seeing everything herself as any young lady could be (only unhindered by *supernatural* awareness). Dress was her passion. She had a most harmless delight in being fine. And our heroine's entrée into life could not take place till after three or four days had been spent in learning what was mostly worn (not chartreuse, unfortunately for Sarah), and her chaperone was provided with a dress of the newest fashion. This was done to the accompaniment of angelic delight and running commentary in tinkling voices, on the fabric, pattern, and color—who could but imagine the angels were so well versed in style and decoration? Catherine could not help but smile when she saw Clarence—or possibly Terence—getting tangled in piles of muslin and ribbon at the shops they visited. Meanwhile, the poor shop girls and seamstresses nearly lost their minds at so much peculiar *displacement* of objects, bolts and skeins, at all the ceaseless fluttering and unraveling of thread that accompanied Catherine's visits to their fine establishments.

As for those frightful warnings of imminent danger? Blessedly, so far, none of it materialized.

Catherine too made some purchases herself (including a ribbon for Sarah—sunflower-golden, in place of out-of-vogue chartreuse), and when all these matters were arranged, the important evening came which was to usher her into the Upper Rooms.

Her hair was cut and dressed by the best hand, her clothes put on with care, and both Mrs. Allen and her maid declared she looked quite as she should do. The heavenly beings echoed them heartily. One of them exhibited enthusiastic approbation to the effect of falling into an open box of powder, fluttering its tiny wings and raising up such a puff-cloud that Mrs. Allen started to sneeze and had to be tended to by the maid all over again.

With such encouragement, Catherine hoped at least to pass uncensured through the crowd. As for admiration, it was always very welcome when it came, but she did not depend on it.

Mrs. Allen was so long in dressing that they did not enter the ballroom till late. The season was full, the room crowded, and the two ladies squeezed in as well as they could. As for Mr. Allen, he repaired directly to the card-room— accompanied by one solitary tiny glowing guardian angel hovering over his head like a determined personal hummingbird—and left them to enjoy a mob by themselves.

Two dozen or so tiny angelic figures fluttering above Catherine's impeccably sculpted hair, immediately dispersed about the large crowded expanse to scout and investigate all nooks for signs of menace. And yet, unless the threat came in the form and size of gnats or moths, Catherine wondered, what good did it do to check behind candelabras and curtain valances? She did note however that at least two angels remained in her vicinity at all times. Also, there were a number of other angels surrounding other persons in the room, in droves of varying number—angels that had already been present in the room before they arrived. (Sometimes Catherine forgot that other people, indeed everyone, had their own heavenly guardians. It is but that she seemed to attract and collect them inordinately, since they knew she could see them and it seemed to please them greatly.)

With more care for the safety of her new gown than for the comfort of her protégée, Mrs. Allen made her way through the throng of men by the door, as swiftly as the necessary caution would allow. Catherine kept close at her side, and linked her arm firmly within her friend's so as not to be separated. But to her utter amazement she found that to proceed along the room was by no means the way to disengage themselves from the crowd. It seemed rather to increase as they went on, whereas she had imagined that when once fairly within the door, they should easily find seats and be able to watch the dances with perfect convenience.

But this was far from being the case. Though by unwearied diligence they gained even the top of the room, their situation was just the same; they saw nothing of the dancers but the high feathers of some of the ladies (and Catherine noted angels perched on top of quite a few of them). Still they moved on— something better was yet in view; and by a continued exertion of strength and ingenuity they found themselves at last in the passage behind the highest bench. Here there was something less of crowd than below; and hence Miss Morland had a comprehensive view of all the company beneath her, and of all the dangers of her late passage through them.

It was a splendid sight, and she began, for the first time that evening, to feel herself at a ball. She longed to dance, but she had not an acquaintance in the room. Mrs. Allen did all that she could do in such a case by saying very placidly, every now and then, "I wish you could dance, my dear—I wish you could get a partner." For some time her young friend felt obliged to her for these wishes; but they were repeated so often, and proved so totally ineffectual, that Catherine grew tired at last, and would thank her no more.

A tiny voice sounded in her ear, "Dear child, be consoled by the fact that so far you have been unnoticed by any malevolent ones!" It was either Clarence or Lawrence, who found a sitting spot on one of her puffed sleeves. "Indeed, dancing, though pleasant, is far from being as universally enjoyable as one might suppose! Fie, dancing!"

"And how would one such as yourself know?" whispered Catherine at her sleeve, pretending to fan herself. "Isn't dancing a mundane frivolity?"

"Not in the least," said the angel. "For, we dance and rejoice when Good is accomplished, just as well as we weep and mourn when Evil is done."

"Then you must spend all your time waltzing and weeping simultaneously," mused Catherine. "What an oddity of existence!"

There was a tinkle of angelic laughter as another tiny being whispered in her other ear, "Oh goodness, no! Only the Almighty has that divine and paradox ability; we necessarily take turns doing one and then the other! For example, today, this moment, I am directed only to laugh and dance in joy at all the Goodness in the world. Lawrence, meanwhile, is away, doing his weekly share of mourning at the Suffering. But, fear not; he will return shortly, for a week's worth of mourning is but a blink of an eye in heavenly time."

"I thought you were Lawrence."

"Oh no, I am Terence."

"And I am Clarence," came from the other ear.

"Of course, I am sorry . . ." Catherine rushed to reply, though, to be honest, she mostly had no idea which of the angels she was talking to at any given moment.

"What was that, dear?" said Mrs. Allen. "Did you say something? No? Well indeed, I wish you could dance—I wish you could get a partner. Otherwise, you would not feel this regrettable need to hold discourse with your fan, you poor thing," she added to herself.

They were not long able, however, to enjoy the repose of the eminent spot they had so laboriously gained. Everybody was shortly in motion for tea, and they must squeeze out like the rest. Catherine began to feel something of disappointment. She was tired of being continually pressed against by people whose faces possessed nothing to interest, and with all of whom she was so wholly unacquainted that she could not relieve the irksomeness of imprisonment by the exchange of a syllable with any of her fellow captives.

When they at last arrived in the tea-room, she felt yet more the awkwardness of having no party to join, no acquaintance to claim, no gentleman to assist them (only angels peeking around teacups and saucers). They saw nothing of Mr. Allen; and after looking about them in vain for a more eligible situation, were obliged to sit down at the end of a table, at which a large party were already placed, without having anything to do there, or anybody to speak to, except each other.

And just for a single moment Catherine had an unsuitable thought—what if such pointed *lack of acquaintance* was the secret result of her heavenly guardians keeping them all away?

Mrs. Allen congratulated herself, as soon as they were seated, on having preserved her gown from injury. "It would have been very shocking to have it torn," said she, "would not it? It is such a delicate muslin. For my part I have not seen anything I like so well in the whole room, I assure you."

"How uncomfortable it is," whispered Catherine, "not to have a single acquaintance here!" And she moved her elbow slightly to push Terence, or Clarence, several inches away from the peril of falling onto a pastry dish.

"Try not to flap your wings so," she added, as the angel regained its balance on the gilded china rim.

"Yes, my dear," replied Mrs. Allen, with perfect serenity, "it is very uncomfortable indeed. That is, no—what was it that you said? Wings? Oh dear! Am I flapping something? Is something torn?"

"Nothing, I mean, *rings!* What lovely rings that lady has!" Catherine hurried to speak.

Mrs. Allen was mollified.

Catherine continued, steering the conversation further: "What shall we do? The gentlemen and ladies at this table look as if they wondered why we came here—we seem forcing ourselves into their party."

"Aye, so we do. That is very disagreeable. I wish we had a large acquaintance here."

"I wish we had *any*—it would be somebody to go to."

"Very true, my dear; and if we knew anybody we would join them directly. The Skinners were here last year—I wish they were here now."

"Had not we better go away as it is? Here are no tea-things for us, you see."

"No more there are, indeed. How very provoking! But I think we had better sit still, for one gets so tumbled in such a crowd! How is my head, my dear? Somebody gave me a push that has hurt it, I am afraid. Even now I feel something pulling, indeed—"

Catherine enacted a meaningful stare at the tiny glowing figure that managed to land on Mrs. Allen's feather-spangled crown and was duly caught on a hairpin.

"No, indeed, it looks very nice. But, dear Mrs. Allen, are you sure there is nobody you know in all this multitude of people? I think you must know somebody."

"I don't, upon my word—I wish I did. I wish I had a large acquaintance here with all my heart, and then I should get you a partner. I should be so glad to have you dance. There goes a strange-looking woman! What an odd gown she has got on! How old-fashioned it is! Look at the back."

After some time they received an offer of tea from one of their neighbours; it was thankfully accepted, and this introduced a light conversation with the gentleman who offered it, which was the only time that anybody spoke to them during the evening, till they were discovered and joined by Mr. Allen when the dance was over.

"Well, Miss Morland," said he, directly, "I hope you have had an agreeable ball."

"Very agreeable indeed," she replied, vainly endeavouring to hide a great yawn.

"I wish she had been able to dance," said his wife; "I wish we could have got a partner for her. I have been saying how glad I should be if the Skinners were here this winter instead of last; or if the Parrys had come, she might have danced with George Parry. I am so sorry she has not had a partner!"

"We shall do better another evening I hope," was Mr. Allen's consolation.

The company began to disperse when the dancing was over—enough to leave space for the remainder to walk about in some comfort; and now was the time for a heroine, who had not yet played a very distinguished part in the events of the evening, to be noticed and admired. Oh, if only they could see how many shining angels ringed her head in a joyful halo of brightness— but no, of course no one could see it, and thus the heroine continued to endure enforced anonymity.

Every five minutes, by removing some of the crowd, gave greater openings for her charms. She may not have been *observed,* but surely she was now *seen* by many young men who had not been near her before. Not one, however, started with rapturous wonder on beholding her. No whisper of eager inquiry ran round the room, nor was she even once called a divinity by anybody, despite the supreme irony of having so much *of the divine* fluttering about her. Yet Catherine was in very good looks, and had the company only seen her three years before, they would now have thought her exceedingly handsome.

She *was* looked at, however, and with some admiration; for, in her own hearing, two gentlemen pronounced her to be a pretty girl. Such words had their due effect; Catherine immediately thought the evening pleasanter than she had found it before—her humble vanity was contented. She felt more obliged to the two young men for this simple praise than a true-quality heroine would have been for fifteen sonnets in celebration of her charms, and went to her chair in good humour with everybody.

She was thus perfectly satisfied with her share of public attention, while the angels, of course, were perfectly satisfied with the fortunate lack of threat to her person.

All in all, things had gone tolerably well.

# Chapter 3

Every morning now brought its regular duties—shops were to be visited; some new part of the town to be looked at; and the pump-room to be attended, where they paraded up and down for an hour, looking at everybody and speaking to no one. Everywhere they went, the angels spread about like fireflies, winking among stylish scenery and even more stylishly attired pedestrians. Catherine heard their melodious voices declaring safety and pronouncing various unlikely spots such as flower vases and decorative marble pedestals to be free of malice.

The wish of a numerous acquaintance in Bath was still uppermost with Mrs. Allen, and she repeated it after every fresh proof, which every morning brought, of her knowing nobody at all. Catherine was beginning to think her unseemly idea about angelic intervention was not far off the mark.

They made their appearance in the Lower Rooms; and here fortune was more favourable to our heroine. The master of the ceremonies introduced to her a very gentlemanlike young man as a partner; his name was Tilney.

As soon as the introduction took place, in that exact moment, there was a minor commotion behind Catherine's ear, as Lawrence, or possibly Terence, exclaimed, "Oh dear! Oh, Catherine! Danger! Oh—"

But of course our heroine did not, and indeed could not—or possibly *would* not—pay any heed, since here was the dear opportunity, at last, to make a proper new acquaintance.

Mr. Tilney seemed to be about four or five and twenty, was rather tall, had a pleasing countenance, a very intelligent and lively eye, and, if not quite handsome, was very near it. His address was good, and Catherine felt herself in high luck. There was little leisure for speaking while they danced (and the angels—being at least half a dozen in number, on each side, and talking all at once in both of Catherine's ears—did present an inordinate aural challenge).

But when they were seated at tea, she found him as agreeable as she had already given him credit for being. He talked with fluency and spirit—and there was an archness and pleasantry in his manner which interested, though it was hardly understood by her.

"Be careful, oh, do be careful of this gentleman, dear child! You know nothing about him!" exclaimed one particularly noisome heavenly creature at some point, balancing on the handle end of a teaspoon, so that she had to press down the other end for balance or have it go flying across the room (and possibly into the eye of the dignified matron or any one of her three young daughters across the table).

"Shush! Enough!" said Catherine to the angel, whispering this admonition while moving her lips as little as possible. Then, bending forward, she pretended to blow on her tea.

Seeing Mr. Tilney's bemused attention to her mutterings and movements, she hurried to amend: "That is, I mean, cough! Cough!" And she politely cleared her throat to reinforce her point. "Goodness, the tea is rather hot."

But Mr. Tilney continued to observe her with an expression she could not fathom.

After chatting some time on such matters as naturally arose from the objects around them, he suddenly addressed her with—

"I have hitherto been very remiss, madam, in the proper attentions of a partner here; I have not yet asked you how long you have been in Bath; whether you were ever here before; whether you have been at the Upper Rooms, the theatre, and the concert; and how you like the place altogether. I have been very negligent—but are you now at leisure to satisfy me in these particulars? If you are I will begin directly."

"Tell him nothing!" exclaimed Clarence, or Terence.

"No indeed! you must remain very circumspect in what you say!" echoed Lawrence—or—or *someone* . . . Catherine was dearly annoyed at this point; she simply wanted to attend carefully to this pleasant gentleman.

"You need not give yourself that trouble, sir," she therefore said, flatly ignoring the angelic clamor.

"No trouble, I assure you, madam." Then forming his features into a set smile, and affectedly softening his voice, he added, with a simpering air, "Have you been long in Bath, madam?"

"About a week, sir," replied Catherine, trying not to laugh.

"Really!" with affected astonishment.

"Why should you be surprised, sir?"

"Why, indeed!" said he, in his natural tone. "But some emotion must appear to be raised by your reply, and surprise is more easily assumed, and not less reasonable than any other. Now let us go on. Were you never here before, madam?"

"Never, sir."

"Oh Catherine, you must not divulge—" But the angel was not allowed to finish, since our heroine's fingers moved a carafe of cream to block his/her/its view and simultaneously just slightly *shove* him out of the way.

"Indeed! Have you yet honoured the Upper Rooms?" continued Mr. Tilney.

"Yes, sir, I was there last Monday."

"Have you been to the theatre?"

*"No, she has not!"*

"Yes, sir, I was at the play on Tuesday."

"To the concert?"

"Yes, sir, on Wednesday."

"And are you altogether pleased with Bath?"

"Yes—I like it very well."

*"Fie! No, she does not!"*

"Now I must give one smirk, and then we may be rational again," said Mr. Tilney.

Catherine turned away her head, not knowing whether she might venture to laugh, and also because she was widening her eyes very fiercely at one particular tiny figure of divine light that was leaping with animation and soon likely to topple into her teacup.

"I see what you think of me," said the gentleman gravely—"I shall make but a poor figure in your journal tomorrow."

"My journal!"

"Yes, I know exactly what you will say: Friday, went to the Lower Rooms; wore my sprigged muslin robe with blue trimmings—plain black shoes—appeared to much advantage; but was strangely harassed by a queer, half-witted man, who would make me dance with him, and distressed me by his nonsense."

"Indeed I shall say no such thing," said Catherine, thankful he knew hardly anything really about the true extent of nonsense or oddity a person could harbor, else he would not be referring thus to himself. . . .

"Shall I tell you what you ought to say?"

"If you please."

"I danced with a very agreeable young man, introduced by Mr. King; had a great deal of conversation with him—seems a most extraordinary genius—hope I may know more of him. That, madam, is what I wish you to say."

"But, perhaps, I keep no journal."

"Perhaps you are balancing an angel on your shoulder"—
(Catherine nearly choked)—"while I have the coiled tail of a
serpent around mine—equally doubtful. Not keep a journal!
How are your absent cousins to understand the tenour of your
life in Bath without one? How are the civilities and compliments
of every day to be related, unless noted down every evening in a
journal? The various dresses to be remembered, the particular
state of your complexion, the curl of your hair? My dear madam,
I am not so ignorant of young ladies' ways as you wish to
believe me; it is this delightful habit of journaling which largely
contributes to form the easy style of writing for which ladies are
so generally celebrated. The talent of writing agreeable letters is
peculiarly female. Nature may have done something, but I am
sure it must be essentially assisted by the practice of keeping a
journal."

"Well! He is, mayhap, not such a fiendish fellow after all,"
whispered Terence, or possibly Clarence. "*Dangerous* in his
own way? Undoubtedly: anyone who ponders the craft of
writing must somehow wield the *potential,* in the least, if not the
secret power itself, to change the world. But malicious? Not this
one. Dear child, we declare him to be a suitable companion . . ."

But our heroine never heard this advantageous analysis, so
engrossed she was in the conversation of the moment.

"I have sometimes thought," said Catherine, doubtingly,
"whether ladies do write so much better letters than gentlemen!
That is—I should not think the superiority was always on our
side."

"As far as I have had opportunity of judging, it appears to
me that the usual style of letter-writing among women is
faultless, except in three particulars."

"And what are they?"

"A general deficiency of subject, a total inattention to stops,
and a very frequent ignorance of grammar."

"Upon my word! I need not have been afraid of disclaiming the compliment. You do not think too highly of us in that way," said Catherine, unwittingly focusing her gaze upon a trio of angels that settled upon Mr. Tilney's jacket lapel like a corsage of heavenly light.

"I should no more lay it down as a general rule that women write better letters than men, than that they sing better duets, or draw better landscapes. In every power, of which taste is the foundation, excellence is pretty fairly divided between the sexes."

Catherine was momentarily thankful Mr. Tilney had never seen her horrid scrawlings of stick figures and monstrous ducks, else he might form a different, less balanced opinion.

They were interrupted by Mrs. Allen: "My dear Catherine," said she, "do take this pin out of my sleeve; I am afraid it has torn a hole already; I shall be quite sorry if it has, for this is a favourite gown, though it cost but nine shillings a yard."

"That is exactly what I should have guessed it, madam," said Mr. Tilney, looking at the muslin, while Catherine fiddled with the pin in Mrs. Allen's attire, finding not only a hole but an angel inadvertently entangled in it by a bit of thread, which had caused additional tearing and unraveling.

The angel exclaimed in dulcet tones, "Oh dear, oh dear!" as Catherine set it loose.

"Do you understand muslins, sir?" said Mrs. Allen meanwhile.

"Particularly well; I always buy my own cravats, and am allowed to be an excellent judge; and my sister has often trusted me in the choice of a gown. I bought one for her the other day, and it was pronounced to be a prodigious bargain by every lady who saw it. I gave but five shillings a yard for it, and a true Indian muslin."

Mrs. Allen was quite struck by his genius. "Men commonly take so little notice of those things," said she; "I can never get

Mr. Allen to know one of my gowns from another. You must be a great comfort to your sister, sir."

"I hope I am, madam."

"And pray, sir, what do you think of Miss Morland's gown?"

"It is very pretty, madam," said he, gravely examining it; "but I do not think it will wash well; I am afraid it will fray."

"How can you," said Catherine, laughing, "be so—" She had almost said "strange," then thought better of it, all things considered.

"I am quite of your opinion, sir," replied Mrs. Allen; "and so I told Miss Morland when she bought it."

"But then you know, madam, muslin always turns to some account or other; Miss Morland will get enough out of it for a handkerchief, or a cap, or a cloak. Muslin can never be said to be wasted. I have heard my sister say so forty times, when she has been extravagant in buying more than she wanted, or careless in cutting it to pieces."

"Harrumph!" Catherine wanted to say, for no better reason than she felt she ought to—but held herself in check, due to the timely actions of an angel who lightly pinched her cheek before she could open her mouth and spoil the pleasantry.

Instead, it was Mrs. Allen who waxed eloquent: "Bath is a charming place, sir; there are so many good shops here. We are sadly off in the country; not but what we have very good shops in Salisbury, but it is so far to go—eight miles is a long way; Mr. Allen says it is nine, measured nine; but I am sure it cannot be more than eight; and it is such a fag[6]—I come back tired to death. Now, here one can step out of doors and get a thing in five minutes."

---

[6] Ahem! Gentle Reader, it is not what one thinks it is. Besides, there is nothing wrong with that.

Mr. Tilney was polite enough to seem interested in what she said; and she kept him on the subject of muslins till the dancing recommenced.

Catherine feared, as she listened to their discourse, that he indulged himself a little too much with the foibles of others.

"What are you thinking of so earnestly?" said he, as they walked back to the ballroom; "not of your partner, I hope, for, by that shake of the head, your meditations are not satisfactory."

Catherine coloured, and said, "I was not thinking of anything."

The angels never condoned her rare instances of uttering untruths; thus, it was a bit worrisome what they were likely to say—but for once Catherine was presented with complete angelic silence. Tiny glowing beings reposed on her sleeves, her shoulders, Mr. Tilney's shoulders and lapels . . . and they simply regarded the two of them.

"That is artful and deep, to be sure; but I had rather be told at once that you will not tell me," he persisted.

"Well then, I will not."

"Thank you; for now we shall soon be acquainted, as I am authorized to tease you on this subject whenever we meet, and nothing in the world advances intimacy so much."

They danced again, accompanied by a lovely whirling cloud of angels; and, when the assembly closed, parted, on the lady's side at least, with a strong inclination for continuing the acquaintance.

Whether she thought of him so much, while she drank her warm wine and water, and prepared herself for bed, among the gentle whispers of her divine guardians, as to dream of him when there, cannot be ascertained. But I hope it was no more than in a slight slumber, or a morning doze at most.

For if it be true, as a celebrated writer has maintained, that no young lady can be justified in falling in love before the gentleman's love is declared,[7] it must be very improper that a young lady should dream of a gentleman before the gentleman is first known to have dreamt of her.

How proper Mr. Tilney might be as a dreamer or a lover had not yet perhaps entered Mr. Allen's head. But that Mr. Tilney was not objectionable as a common acquaintance for his young charge he was on inquiry satisfied. Indeed, early in the evening Mr. Allen had taken pains to know who her partner was, and had been assured of Mr. Tilney's being a clergyman, and of a very respectable family in Gloucestershire.

However well that might be for Mr. Allen's peace of mind, our heroine's own was somewhat less secure. It is well known that pleasant twilight reveries are often followed by the coming of night and that which abides in it. And—dear Reader—in the darkness, dreams often turn to nightmares, just before the coming of the dance of thunder and lightning that accompanies heaven's storm. . . .

Things were about to become very heroic indeed.

---

[7] *Vide* a letter from Mr. Richardson, No. 97, Vol. ii, "Rambler." Verily dear Reader, young ladies in love must never divulge their delicate amorous state, for gentlemen are such flighty creatures, easily frightened out of their wits.

# Chapter 4

With more than usual eagerness did Catherine hasten to the pump-room the next day, secure within herself of seeing Mr. Tilney there before the morning were over. She was ready to meet him with a smile; but no smile was demanded—Mr. Tilney did not appear.

Instead, every creature in Bath, *except* himself, was to be seen in the room at different periods of the fashionable hours. Crowds of people and their guardian angels of every hue and brightness were every moment passing in and out, up the steps and down, and *hovering* overhead (the angels naturally performed the hovering, not the people). These were persons whom nobody cared about, and nobody wanted to see—and he only was absent. Even the everpresent heavenly glow appeared somewhat dimmer than usual—indeed, the familiar presence of the tiny beings seemed rather tedious, as was their constancy of attending her.

"What a delightful place Bath is," said Mrs. Allen (while Catherine was, in that moment, of another mind altogether) as they sat down near the great clock, after parading the room till they were tired; "and how pleasant it would be if we had any acquaintance here."

This sentiment had been uttered so often in vain that Mrs. Allen had no particular reason to hope it would be followed with more advantage now. But the unwearied diligence with which she had every day wished for the same thing was at length to have its just reward.

For hardly had she been seated ten minutes, before a lady of about her own age, who was sitting by her, and had been looking at her attentively for several minutes, addressed her with great complaisance in these words: "I think, madam, I cannot be mistaken; it is a long time since I had the pleasure of seeing you, but is not your name Allen?"

This question answered, as it readily was, the stranger pronounced hers to be Thorpe; and Mrs. Allen immediately recognized the features of a former schoolfellow and intimate, whom she had seen only once since their respective marriages, and that many years ago.

Their joy on this meeting was very great, as well it might be, since they had been contented to know nothing of each other for the last fifteen years. Compliments on good looks now passed; and, after observing how time had slipped away since they were last together, how little they had thought of meeting in Bath, and what a pleasure it was to see an old friend, they proceeded to make inquiries and give intelligence as to their families, sisters, and cousins, talking both together, far more ready to give than to receive information, and each hearing very little of what the other said. Catherine was reminded just a tad of the occasional angelic habit of imparting too much information all at once.

Mrs. Thorpe, however, had one great advantage as a talker, over Mrs. Allen, in a family of children. When she expatiated on the talents of her sons, and the beauty of her daughters, when she related their different situations and views—that John was at Oxford, Edward at Merchant Taylors', and William at sea—and all of them more beloved and respected in their different station than any other three beings ever were, Mrs. Allen had no similar information and triumphs to give, and was forced to sit and appear to listen to all these maternal effusions. She consoled herself, however, with the discovery, which her keen eye soon made, that the lace on Mrs. Thorpe's pelisse was not half so handsome as that on her own.

Catherine, sitting quietly, suddenly felt an odd difference in the atmosphere. It was as if the temperature plummeted a few degrees, and the brightness of the angels hovering about her head lost some of its luster.

"Here come my dear girls," cried Mrs. Thorpe, pointing at three smart-looking females who, arm in arm, were then moving towards her. And as they drew near, there was a very subtle stillness that came with them.

An inexplicable stillness in the air.

"My dear Mrs. Allen, I long to introduce them; they will be so delighted to see you: the tallest is Isabella, my eldest; is not she a fine young woman? The others are very much admired too, but I believe Isabella is the handsomest."

"Oh, Catherine! Beware! *Beware!*" came the usual angelic voices. But for some reason, it was as though they were receding in volume, or possibly coming from a great distance . . .

For whatever reason, Catherine could barely hear them, despite the fact that Clarence, or Terence, or Lawrence were all in great proximity, variously pulling at her earlobes, tweaking locks of her hair, and pinching her sleeves from all directions.

Indeed, it was rather easy to forget they were even there.

The Miss Thorpes were introduced; and Miss Morland, who had been for a short time forgotten (while she was engaged in her own peculiar manner of *forgetting*), was introduced likewise. The name seemed to strike them all. And, after speaking to her with great civility, the eldest young lady observed aloud to the rest, "How excessively like her brother Miss Morland is!"

"The very picture of him indeed!" cried the mother—and "I should have known her anywhere for his sister!" was repeated by them all, two or three times over (while the air in the room continued to grow curiously cold).

For a moment Catherine was surprised. No, it was not at the chill and the strange heavy stillness all around (if only she had been paying proper attention)—it was merely at the coincidence of such familiarity with her family.

Incidentally, the eldest Miss Thorpe—why, she was indeed so decidedly extraordinary, so remarkable looking, it occurred to Catherine. But in *what* manner exactly, she was uncertain.

But Mrs. Thorpe and her daughters had scarcely begun the history of their acquaintance with Mr. James Morland, before Catherine remembered that her eldest brother had lately formed an intimacy with a young man of his own college, of the name of Thorpe; and that he had spent Christmas vacation with his family, near London.

The whole being explained, many obliging things were said by the Miss Thorpes of their wish of being better acquainted with her; of being considered as already friends, through the friendship of their brothers, etc., which Catherine heard with pleasure, and answered with all the pretty expressions she could command.

Indeed, all this sudden pleasure was rather remarkable. Catherine was put in a wonderful, even giddy mood—especially the longer she looked upon the decidedly handsome eldest Miss Thorpe.

And, as the first proof of amity, she was soon invited to accept an arm of the same Miss Thorpe, and take a turn with her about the room. It hardly mattered that the arm Catherine touched sent an odd chill right through her gloves, and seemed to grow icy the longer they stayed in contact—Miss Isabella Thorpe radiated uncanny charm and amiability. And all other things and people and *temperatures* paled in comparison.

Catherine was so delighted with this extension of her Bath acquaintance, that she almost forgot Mr. Tilney while she talked to Miss Thorpe. Friendship is certainly the finest balm for the pangs of disappointed love.

Their conversation turned upon subjects which perfect a sudden intimacy between two young ladies: dress, balls, flirtations, and quizzes[8]. Miss Thorpe, being four years older, and at least four years better informed, had a very decided advantage in discussing such points. She could compare the balls of Bath with those of Tunbridge, its fashions with London. She could rectify the opinions of her new friend in many articles of tasteful attire; could discover a flirtation between any gentleman and lady who only smiled on each other; and point out a quiz through the thickness of a crowd.

These powers received due admiration from Catherine, to whom they were entirely new. And the respect which they naturally inspired might have been too great for familiarity, had not the easy gaiety of Miss Thorpe's manners, and her frequent expressions of delight on their acquaintance, softened down every feeling of awe, and left nothing but tender affection.

And an arm chilled to the bone . . .

Their increasing attachment was not to be satisfied with half a dozen turns in the pump-room, but required, when they all quitted it together, that Miss Thorpe should accompany Miss Morland to the very door of Mr. Allen's house; and that they should there part with a most affectionate and lengthened shake of hands, after learning, to their mutual relief, that they should see each other across the theatre at night, and say their prayers in the same chapel the next morning.

---

[8] Delightful pastime consisting of observing people and objects at a distance through a magnifying glass in order to generate better informed gossip, or plan a more effective courtship, or, in some instances, to quit the room in a hurry.

Catherine then ran directly upstairs, and watched Miss Thorpe's progress down the street from the drawing-room window; admired the graceful spirit of her walk, the fashionable air of her figure and dress; and felt grateful for the chance which had procured her such a friend.

It was only then that she felt the pulls and tugs on her lace and once more heard the chorus of angelic voices that bloomed into focus once more. Indeed they were teeming in an agitated cloud all about her.

"Dear child!" Terence was crying—or possibly Lawrence— "Oh, what a terrifying sorrow has come upon us!"

"Sorrow? Gracious, what is it?" said Catherine, feeling a tiny twinge of guilt for having genuinely *forgotten* all about her faithful companions for most of the afternoon.

"Why, it is witnessing you unable to hear us, and not paying any attention, as if you could no longer see us all around you!"

Catherine thought back for a moment. It was true, she did not recall any angels at all for the duration of her delightful new acquaintance. Possibly, they had been there as usual, but she simply did not *recall*.

"How odd!" admitted Catherine out loud. "I do not remember observing you, Terence—"

"Dear child, it is I, Clarence."

Catherine coughed.

"I wonder what happened?" she continued. "I must have been so engrossed with the sweet Miss Thorpe—"

"Sweet? Oh, no, you are sorely mistaken, dear Catherine! This *Miss Thorpe,* as you call her—she is not what she seems!"

"Oh?" Catherine grew more puzzled by the moment. "Whatever is she, then?"

"She is dangerous!"

"She is dark!"

"She is filled with deceit! Corruption!"

"She is wicked—"

"Oh, *stop it!*" Catherine exclaimed, unable to bear it any longer. "Please stop saying these terrible things! Miss Thorpe is amiable and charming, and she is now my friend!"

At that, the angels settled all around her in unhappy silence.

Mrs. Thorpe was a widow, and not a very rich one. She was a good-humoured, well-meaning woman, and a very indulgent mother. There was entirely nothing metaphysically out of the ordinary about her. But the same could not be said about her two eldest children.

Dear Reader, it must now be told—in her time, Mrs. Thorpe had unluckily given birth to two *nephilim*.

During her first lying in, a dark being—some might call him a demon of the highest ranks, or possibly a fallen angel— flew over their residence, sensed the quickening of new life and, on a whim, decided to pay an unwelcome visit. That first time he merely touched the sleeping mother's brow with his fiery breath, and slipped away. The resulting naphil child was a son, and scalding hellfires burned inside him.

The second time the dark being chose to return, a year later, on an equally wicked whim, he breathed an icy breath of the tomb over the mother-to-be, before disappearing. This time the resulting naphil issue was a daughter, with the coldest heart of hell instilled within her.

Poor Mrs. Thorpe! She had no idea. She bore both unknowingly, and all her other children since had been normal, amiable and human.

But the eldest, John and Isabella, were wicked fire and ice. And they had been instructed from *below* with a dark purpose.

Mrs. Thorpe's eldest daughter Isabella had great personal physical beauty, and—by virtue of her unnatural tainted bloodline—a great beguiling *attraction,* to all in general and to the members of the opposite sex in particular. The younger daughters, by pretending to be as handsome as their sister, imitating her air, and dressing in the same style, did very well.

This brief but accurate account of the family is intended to supersede the necessity of a long and minute detail from Mrs. Thorpe herself, of her past adventures and sufferings, which might otherwise occupy three or four tedious chapters while completely failing to mention the supernatural aspects.

Instead, the estimable Reader is forewarned to pay particular heed to the two unnatural children and their dark intentions—with Catherine Morland as their intended prize!

# Chapter 5

Catherine was not so engaged at the theatre that evening, in returning the nods and smiles of Miss Thorpe (though they certainly claimed much of her leisure, as did the immediate distracting angelic sighs and whispers in both her ears), as to forget to look inquiringly for Mr. Tilney in every box which her eye could reach.

But she looked in vain. Apparently Mr. Tilney was no fonder of the play than the pump-room.

She hoped to be more fortunate the next day. And when her wishes for fine weather were answered by seeing a beautiful morning, Catherine hardly felt a doubt of it—a fine Sunday in Bath empties every house of its inhabitants, and all the world appears to tell their acquaintance what a charming day it is.

As soon as divine service was over (the delightful angelic chorus following her out of the church for quite some time longer than necessary, so that Catherine had to engage in meaningful eye-widening grimaces and facial ticks which were thankfully and *mostly* unobserved by those in her vicinity), the Thorpes and Allens eagerly joined each other. In vain did Lawrence or Clarence attempt to lecture Catherine when Isabella drew near. Indeed, an angel's dulcet voice only grew thin and distant, while still saying: "Did you not wonder, dear child, why

Miss Thorpe sat at the farthest pew in the back, nearest the exit, and farthest from the sacred altar?"

But, with her ears still ringing from the volume of angelic hymn and therefore somewhat less amenable to their advice in general, Catherine chose to ignore the familiar heavenly admonition and the growing chill in the air. She instead returned her new friend's exceedingly *charming* and vibrant smile.

The families stayed long enough in the pump-room to discover that the crowd was insupportable, with not a genteel face to be seen. And so they hastened away to the Crescent, to breathe the fresh air of better company.

Here Catherine and Isabella, arm in arm (Catherine's going numb from the cold, and yet unheeded), again tasted the sweets of friendship in an unreserved conversation. They talked with much enjoyment; but again was Catherine disappointed in her hope of catching sight of her gentleman partner.

He was nowhere to be met with; neither in morning lounges nor evening assemblies. Neither was he at the Upper nor Lower Rooms, at dressed or undressed balls; nor among the walkers, horsemen, or curricle-drivers. His name was not in the pump-room book, and curiosity could do no more. He must be gone from Bath.

Yet he had not mentioned that his stay would be so short! This sort of mysteriousness, always so becoming in a hero, threw a fresh grace in Catherine's imagination around his person, and increased her anxiety to know more of him.

From the Thorpes she could learn nothing, for they had been only two days in Bath before they met with Mrs. Allen.

It was a subject, however, in which Catherine often indulged with her fair friend, from whom she received every possible encouragement to continue to think of him. Thus, his impression on her fancy was not to weaken.

Isabella was very sure that he must be a charming young man, and was equally sure that he must have been delighted with her dear Catherine, and would therefore shortly return. She liked him the better for being a clergyman, "for she must confess herself very partial to the profession"; and something like a *sigh* escaped her as she said it.

Perhaps Catherine was wrong in not demanding the cause of that gentle emotion—but she was not experienced enough in the finesse of love, or the duties of friendship, to know when delicate raillery was properly called for, or when a confidence should be forced. And at that moment there were no angelic voices within *awareness* to offer the sort of guidance she was willing to hear.

Meanwhile, Mrs. Allen was now quite happy—quite satisfied with Bath. She had at last found some acquaintance in the family of a most worthy old friend; and furthermore had found these friends by no means so expensively dressed as herself. Her previous sad daily expressions were changed into, "How glad I am we have met with Mrs. Thorpe!" and she was as eager in promoting the intercourse[9] of the two families, as her young charge and Isabella themselves could be; spending the chief of each day by the side of Mrs. Thorpe, in what they called *conversation* (scarcely any exchange of opinion, and hardly any resemblance of subject), for Mrs. Thorpe talked of her children, and Mrs. Allen of her gowns.

Contrary to angelic warning, the progress of the friendship between Catherine and Isabella was quick, as its beginning had been warm (at least in the figurative sense—without admitting it even to herself, Catherine resorted to wearing additional wraps in her friend's chill-inducing presence; even Mrs. Allen started to notice the *cold* and complain about it, without clearly knowing its cause).

The two friends passed rapidly through every gradation of increasing tenderness. They called each other by their Christian name, were always arm in (frozen) arm when they walked,

---

[9] Goodness, how thoroughly unseemly!

pinned up each other's train for the dance, and were not to be divided in the set. And if a rainy morning deprived them of other enjoyments, they were still resolute in meeting, and shut themselves up, to read novels together.

Yes, *novels*. For I will not adopt that ungenerous custom so common with novel-writers, of degrading by their contemptuous censure the very things which they are producing—and scarcely ever permitting them to be read by their own heroine. If she is to accidentally take up a novel[10], she must turn over its insipid pages with disgust.[11]

Alas! If the heroine of one novel be not patronized by the heroine of another, from whom can she expect protection and regard? I cannot approve of it. Let us leave it to the reviewers[12] to abuse such effusions of fancy at their leisure, and over every new novel to talk in threadbare strains of the trash with which the press now groans.[13]

Let us not desert one another; we are an injured body. Although our productions have afforded more extensive and unaffected pleasure than those of any other literary corporation in the world, no species of composition has been so much decried.[14]

---

[10] A Novel is a metaphysical Object of great power, capable of Changing Minds and Creating Worlds of untold wonder. It is also a secret means of universal travel.

[11] Be warned, O Fair Reader, this is an Authorial Aside, and as such, a measure of passion on the part of the humble Author must be excused, for she speaks from the heart, and Knows what she Speaketh.

[12] A Reviewer is a metaphysical Being for whom there are no proper earthly terms, O Blessed Reader; verily, neither angel, nor demon, nor dragon, nor even a monstrous duck. And yet, all that can be said is, Thou must Fear and Tremble!

[13] Ahem!

From pride, ignorance, or fashion, our foes are almost as many as our readers.[15] There seems almost a general wish of decrying the capacity and undervaluing the labour of the novelist,[16] and of slighting the performances which have only genius, wit, and taste to recommend them.

"I am no novel-reader—I seldom look into novels—Do not imagine that I often read novels—It is really very well for a novel." Such is the common cant.

"And what are you reading, Miss—?"

"Oh! It is only a novel!" replies the young lady, while she lays down her book with affected indifference, or momentary shame. "It is only *Cecilia,* or *Camilla,* or *Belinda*"—only some work in which the greatest powers of the mind are displayed, in which the most thorough knowledge of human nature, the happiest delineation of its varieties, the liveliest effusions of wit and humour, are conveyed to the world in the best-chosen language. Now, had the same young lady been engaged with a volume of the *Spectator,*[17] instead of such a work, how proudly would she have produced the book!

Thus ends the Authorial Aside, and we may now proceed with the Story.

---

[14] One begs to differ—there is that fiendish Thing that rhymes, commonly found inside a greeting card.

[15] A Reader! A most happy breed of all, for Thou art Blessed and Wanted and Worshiped and Adored! Ahem! (The Author must hereby be pardoned for going into these warmest effusions of sentiment.)

[16] A Novelist is a metaphysical Being who has taken it upon her sorry shoulders to carry the burden of conscience of the entire modern civilization, while being paid less than minimum wage, working three or more additional jobs to avoid homelessness and starvation, and having no personal life to speak of, all in exchange for the privilege of speaking the Truth clad in Story.

[17] A forgotten periodical, gentle Reader, which finely illustrates the argument.

# Chapter 6

The following *momentous* conversation, which took place between the two friends in the pump-room one morning, after an acquaintance of eight or nine days, is given as a specimen of their very warm attachment, of delicacy, originality of thought, of literary taste . . . and of the dreadful danger in which our heroine was about to find herself.

They met by appointment; and as Isabella had arrived nearly five minutes before her friend, her first address naturally was, "My dearest creature, what can have made you so late? I have been waiting for you at least this age!"

Catherine, who had been making haste but was being invariably detained by trifles of suspiciously angelic origin—such as her gown catching on stationary objects every few steps, her lace and ribbons pulled and tweaked by invisible breezes, her sash nearly getting pulled by a closing door, and her bonnet swept sideways by a particularly ferocious gust in an otherwise calm day—could only respond with apologies.

"Have you, indeed! I am very sorry for it; but really I thought I was in very good time. It is but just one. I hope you have not been here long?"

"Oh! These ten ages at least. I am sure I have been here this half hour," said Isabella, smiling in delightful honeyed reproach.

Catherine felt the familiar gathering of cold as she found herself standing at her dear friend's side, and resolutely ignoring the drop in degrees. A few gentlemen passerby threw them curious glances, lingering in particular on irresistible Miss Thorpe despite her arctic clime.

"But now, let us go and sit down at the other end of the room, and enjoy ourselves." Isabella continued, taking Catherine by the arm and leading her along (it occurred to Catherine yet again she might consider bringing along a fur muff, just for that arm). "I have an hundred things to say to you. In the first place, I was so afraid it would rain this morning, and that would have thrown me into agonies! Do you know, I saw the prettiest hat in a shop window in Milsom Street just now—very like yours; I quite longed for it. But, my dearest Catherine, what have you been doing with yourself all this morning? Have you gone on with *Udolpho?*"

She was referring, of course, to the dire and dreadful and wonderful novel—the one that Catherine had been reading with passionate horror before bed the previous eve, and the one which several angels attempted to hide from her nightstand, locking it in a commode.

"Yes, I have been reading it ever since I woke; and I am got to the black veil." Catherine was not the least bit ashamed to admit her engrossed interest in Mrs. Radcliffe's creation of wild fancy.

Isabella's lovely eyes seemed brighter than usual in response. Or possibly they changed hue to a peculiar *yellowish* tinge—that could not be, of course, it was just a trick of the morning light . . .

"Are you, indeed? How delightful! Oh! I would not tell you what is behind the black veil for the world! Are not you wild to know?"

*"No, dear child! You must not be tricked into agreeing!"*

The words came as though from a great distance, then grew louder—Angels! Her familiar angels were clamoring all around, and suddenly once again Catherine could hear them all; and she blinked, as though coming awake.

"Catherine!" exclaimed a tiny being of light, darting just below her ear. "Believe us! This is the moment of truth! If you reply in agreement to her innocently veiled question—nay, a secret request to claim your soul—you are in fact agreeing to her dark influence! Her query is a trick!'

"Huh? What?" said Catherine, and then immediately pretended to cough into her palm.

But the angels were satisfied she was at last paying attention to them.

Isabella meanwhile watched her friend's odd extended pause and coughing fit, with her smile frozen in place, and poised for her answer.

Catherine was feeling a strange ringing sensation—very similar to her moment of metaphysical awakening several years ago when she first began to hear heavenly voices—only this time it was different, even more profound. It was as though an additional layer before her perception was stripped away, and suddenly Catherine could *see* in twice-as-sharp focus. The angels, in a cloud of fireflies, were fiercely bright as candles! And the charming young Miss Thorpe before her—

*Oh . . . Oh dear,* thought Catherine, verily staring.

Because the previously delightful Isabella now appeared very swarthy and strange and not at all charming. Instead of being a blooming beauty, somehow she was sallow, rather angular of feature, and there was an unhealthy greenish tint to her previously peach-perfect complexion. Isabella looked decidedly ghastly! And, as for her youthful vivacity, why she seemed dreadfully worn out, as though a thousand balls and seasons were behind her, and the *ennui* of the world settled under her eyes in ugly circles. Oh, and the *cold!* The dire bone-deep cold that was emanating from her in palpable waves!

"*Oh, yes, you see her as she* is, *at last! Her true visage has been revealed to you, and you are no longer deceived by her outer beauty. Indeed, the real Black Veil has been lifted.*"

And then an angel added softly, "*Behold! You are seeing her* inside out, *Catherine.*"

Catherine was stunned.

In that moment, Isabella, who had been patiently waiting for her response but finding none forthcoming, gently prompted her friend, in what Catherine now heard as a sickly-sweet unnatural, grating voice: "What is it, my sweet? I said, *are not you wild to know what is behind the black veil?*"

And Catherine watched as Isabella's eyes *glowed* yellow.

"No!" blurted Catherine, and then amended, "that is, not wild, no; not at all, for I am still reading, and it is such a pleasure to discover for oneself, no spoiling surprises, please, my dear Isabella—"

She could almost hear multiple angelic sighs of relief coming from all directions.

"*Well done, child, well done! Never agree directly to anything she asks of you, always, circumspectly deny!*"

For a moment it seemed that Isabella's eyes flashed a frustrated spark of red, like distant hellfire, but oh-so-cold . . .

Catherine proceeded to carry on somewhat, to disguise the strange turn of conversation and her own unnerved state. "*Udolpho* is marvelous! Pray, excuse my excitement, of course, but I am very particular in these things. So, do not tell me—I would not be told upon any account. I know it must be a skeleton, I am sure it is Laurentina's skeleton. Oh! I am delighted with the book! I should like to spend my whole life in reading it. I assure you, if it had not been to meet you, I would not have come away from it for all the world."

The demonic cold billowed about them and for once Catherine was so direly aware of it that her teeth were on the verge of chattering. But she braced them in a smile, and watched

the angels come to surround her with a barrier of warming light
that eased the wintry sensation.

Isabella appeared mollified for the moment. "Dear creature!
How much I am obliged to you; and when you have finished
*Udolpho*, we will read *The Italian* together; and I have made out
a list of ten or twelve more of the same kind for you."

"Have you, indeed! How glad I am! What are they all?"

"I will read you their names directly; here they are, in my
pocketbook. *Castle of Wolfenbach, Clermont, Mysterious
Warnings, Necromancer of the Black Forest, Midnight Bell,
Orphan of the Rhine,* and *Horrid Mysteries*. Those will last us
some time."

"Yes, pretty well; but are they all horrid, are you sure they
are all horrid?" Catherine pretended she was eager for a good
literary fright, but for once she was not in the mood—not with
Isabella and her true *horrid* visage directly at her side. With all
that, who needed Mrs. Radcliffe or her ilk?

But the tedious charade must now be maintained.

"Yes, quite sure; for a particular friend of mine, a Miss
Andrews, one of the sweetest creatures in the world, has read
every one of them. I wish you knew Miss Andrews, you would
be delighted with her. I think her as beautiful as an angel, and I
am so vexed with the men for not admiring her! I scold them all
amazingly about it."

"Scold them! Do you scold them for not admiring her?"
Catherine could not help saying earnestly, though she now knew
very well that all manner of *peculiar* things were to be expected
from this abominable Isabella.

"Yes, that I do. There is nothing I would not do for those
who are really my *friends*," said Isabella meaningfully.

And then Miss Thorpe went on, in a preening, unnaturally
modulating voice (that now sounded to Catherine a bit like the
clucking of a hen, followed by the honking of a rather large and
ghastly duck): "I have no notion of *loving* people by *halves;* it is

not my *nature*. My attachments are always excessively strong. I told a certain Captain Hunt I would not dance with him, unless he would allow Miss Andrews to be as beautiful as an angel—"

"Fie! *She* has no notion of angelic beauty!" whispered one of those very beings into Catherine's right ear.

*Indeed,* our heroine thought, *if this Miss Andrews properly looked like an angel, she would also be winged and about three inches tall.*

"The men think us incapable of real friendship, you know, and I am determined to show them the difference. Now, if I were to hear anybody speak slightingly of you, dearest Catherine, I should fire up in a moment: but that is not at all likely, for you are just the kind of girl to be a great favourite with the men."

"Oh dear!" cried Catherine, colouring. "How can you say so?"

"I know you very well; you have so much animation, which is exactly what Miss Andrews lacks, for I must confess there is something amazingly *insipid* about her. Oh! I must tell you, that just after we parted yesterday, I saw a young man looking at you so earnestly—I am sure he is in love with you."

Catherine coloured, and disclaimed again, wondering meanwhile where all this was leading. What kind of verbal trap was this *creature* laying out for her?

Isabella laughed (sounding to the world like a dulcet proper lady and to Catherine like a much-pained horse). "It is very true, upon my honour, but I see how it is; you are indifferent to everybody's admiration, *except* that of one gentleman, who shall be nameless. Nay, I cannot blame you"—speaking more seriously—"once the heart is really attached, it cannot be pleased with the attention of anybody else. Everything is so insipid, so uninteresting, that does not relate to the beloved object! I perfectly comprehend your feelings."

"But you should not persuade me that I think so very much about Mr. Tilney, for perhaps I may never see him again."

"Not see him again! My dearest creature, do not talk of it. I am sure you would be miserable if you thought so!"

"*No,* indeed, I should *not.*" Catherine made a point of saying "no" and "not" very succinctly this time. "I do not pretend to say that I was not very much pleased with him . . . But while I have *Udolpho* to read, I feel as if nobody could make me miserable. Oh! The dreadful black veil! I am sure there must be Laurentina's skeleton behind it." Catherine almost forgot with whom she was conversing, so caught up she was again in recalling the story . . . For a moment, the horrors of *Udolpho* reasserted their compelling power, even in face of the dire reality before her—ah, such is the power of the novel in the heroic imagination!

"It is so odd to me, that you should never have read *Udolpho* before; but I suppose Mrs. Morland objects to novels."

"*No,* she does *not.* She very often reads *Sir Charles Grandison* herself; but new books do not fall in our way."

"*Sir Charles Grandison!* That is an amazing horrid book, is it not? I remember Miss Andrews could not get through the first volume," said Isabella, glancing sweetly at a gentleman walking by and observing him suddenly grow daft and run into a potted planter, due to fixing his sights exclusively on her.

"It is *not* like *Udolpho* at all; but yet I think it is very entertaining." Catherine said, noting with amazement how easily mesmerized gentlemen appeared to become, in the presence of this Isabella creature. And while their guardian angels became greatly distressed, they always went unheeded.

"Do you indeed! You surprise me; I thought it had not been readable. But, my dearest Catherine, have you settled what to wear on your head tonight? I am determined at all events to be dressed exactly like you. The men take notice."

"But it does not signify if they do," said Catherine, very innocently, observing to herself that men taking notice was the last thing Isabella needed.

"Signify! Oh, heavens! I make it a rule never to mind what they say. They are amazingly impertinent if you do not treat them with spirit, and make them keep their distance."

"Are they? Well, I never observed that. They always behave very well to me. And they certainly seem *aware* of you."

"Oh! They give themselves such airs. They are the most conceited, self-important creatures in the world! By the by, what is your favourite complexion in a man? Do you like them best dark or fair?"

"I hardly know. I never much thought about it. Something between both, I think. Brown—not fair, and—not very dark."

"Very well, Catherine. That is exactly he. I have not forgot your description of Mr. Tilney—'a brown skin, with dark eyes, and rather dark hair.' Well, my taste is different. I prefer light eyes, and as to complexion—do you know—I like a sallow better than any other. You must not betray me, if you should ever meet with *one of your acquaintance* answering that description."

"Betray you! What do you mean?"

"Nay, do not distress me. I believe I have said too much. Let us drop the subject."

Appearing to better comprehend what was implied, the angels circled Catherine in a fiercely protective twinkling cloud.

Catherine, in some amazement, complied. After remaining a few moments silent, she was on the point of reverting to discussing Laurentina's skeleton . . .

But her unnatural friend prevented her, by saying, "For heaven's sake! Let us move away from this end of the room. Do you know, there are two odious young men who have been staring at me this half hour! Let us go and look at the arrivals. They will hardly follow us there."

Away they walked to the book—one in a cloud of bitter cold air, the other in a cloud of angels. And while Isabella

examined the names, it was Catherine's employment to watch
the proceedings of these alarming young men.

"They are not coming this way, are they?" said Isabella,
meanwhile making bold eye contact with the selfsame distant
creatures of the masculine persuasion. "I hope they are not so
impertinent as to follow us. Pray let me know if they are coming.
I am determined I will not look up."

In a few moments Catherine, with unaffected pleasure,
assured her that she need not be longer uneasy, as the gentlemen
had just left the pump-room.

"And which way are they gone?" said Isabella in a squeak
voice, turning hastily round (and briefly scattering Catherine's
cloud of angels). "One was a very good-looking young man."

"They went towards the church-yard."

"Well, I am amazingly glad I have got rid of them! And
now, what say you to going to Edgar's Buildings with me, and
looking at my new hat?"

Catherine readily agreed. "Only," she added, "perhaps we
may overtake the two young men. Would it not appear we are
following them?"

"Oh! Never mind that. If we make haste, we shall pass by
them presently, and I am dying to show you my hat."

"But if we only wait a few minutes, there will be no danger
of our seeing them at all."

"I shall not pay them any such compliment, I assure you. I
have no notion of treating men with such respect. *That* is the
way to spoil them."

Catherine had nothing to contradict such reasoning.
Therefore, to show the independence of Miss Thorpe, and her
resolution of humbling the sex, they set off immediately as fast
as they could walk, in pursuit of the two young men.

# Chapter 7

Half a minute conducted them through the pump-yard to the archway, opposite Union Passage. But here they were stopped. Anyone acquainted with Bath may remember the difficulties of crossing Cheap Street at this point—a street of so much traffic, that a day never passes in which parties of ladies in quest of pastry, millinery, or young men, are not detained on one side or other by carriages, horsemen, or carts.

This evil had been felt and lamented, at least three times a day, by Isabella since her residence in Bath; and she was now fated to lament it once more. For at the very moment of coming opposite to Union Passage, and within view of the two gentlemen, they were prevented crossing by the approach of a gig, driven by a most knowing-looking coachman with all the vehemence that could endanger the lives of himself, his companion, and his horse . . .

And with it came a blast of *infernal* uncanny *heat*.

"Oh, these odious gigs!" said Isabella, looking up. "How I detest them." But this detestation, though so just, was of short duration, for she looked again and exclaimed, "Delightful! Mr. Morland and my brother!"

"Good heaven! 'Tis James!" was uttered at the same moment by Catherine. Simultaneously, the wave of unseasonal heat reached her, momentarily dispelling the cold atmosphere of her companion.

*"Beware, oh, twice beware, dear child!"* came the voices of the angels. "It is the *other* one that you must now beware, he is here! Infernal nephilim, demon children of the fallen ones, both are here to claim you, and you must resist—"

"Oh, criminy, no!" muttered Catherine. "I still don't understand, why me?" And she hid her whisperings in a series of coughs.

As soon as the young ladies caught the young men's eyes, the horse was immediately checked—with a violence which almost threw him on his haunches. The servant scampered up, the gentlemen jumped out, and the equipage was delivered to his care.

Catherine, by whom this meeting was wholly unexpected, received her brother with the liveliest pleasure. She noted, his one angelic guardian flew bright and eager to join her own heavenly cloud of at least a dozen (and she could distinctly hear his dulcet voice complaining not-so-dulcetly about "having to endure the constant proximity of the *infernal one* and his *infernal heat,* and oh, poor James—").

James, being of a very amiable disposition, and sincerely attached to his sister, gave every proof on his side of equal satisfaction at seeing Catherine.

Meanwhile the searing-bright decidedly *yellowish* eyes of Miss Thorpe were incessantly challenging his notice. And to her his devoirs were speedily paid, with a mixture of joy and embarrassment which might have informed Catherine—had she been more expert in the development of other people's feelings, and less simply engrossed by her own—that her brother thought her friend quite as pretty as she herself initially did. That is, until the second metaphysical veil of *vision* parted and she could see the horrid creature for what she truly was.

John Thorpe, who in the meantime had been giving orders about the horses, soon joined them.

Preceding him came the heat of a furnace. But even before it struck full force, Catherine *saw* him, and muttered, "Oh dear, he is an ogre!"

It was indeed the frightful truth. Seen with the clarity of supernatural vision that Catherine now enjoyed, he was a large bulky gentleman with limbs like trunks and a torso like a barrel of old port. His skin was coarse and elephantine, swarthier than his sister's, and with an even more greenish tint—a few degrees more and his complexion might have rivaled a toad. His hair stuck out like dry straw from underneath the edges of his otherwise stylish top hat, and had a suspiciously fire-tinged ruddy tint, as though it's been though a curtain of flames. And when he grinned, his teeth were simply enormous—

*Oh dear,* Catherine thought. Indeed, she was so struck by the oddity before her that she forgot to be properly frightened or alarmed, and unabashedly stared in amazement (a behavior which later she comprehended to be hardly appropriate on her part; no wonder the gentleman may have gotten certain ideas).

Possibly as a result of her particularly fixed examination, she directly received from him the amends which were her due. For while he slightly and carelessly touched the hand of Isabella—causing a strong hiss of steam in the atmosphere as hellish heat met sepulchral cold and issued forth precipitation—on *her* he bestowed a whole scrape and half a short bow.

Angels immediately rose in glorious motion to hover in the air between Catherine and him in a translucent wall of glittering light, and managed to alleviate the furnace blasts that threatened to overbear Catherine, into reasonable summer mid-noon levels.

But nature was less tolerant. It started to rain overhead, big sloppy droplets, but only in their immediate vicinity of about five feet. However, this being England, no one was particularly flummoxed even by such a particularly localized, extraordinarily *specific* example of maudlin weather.

It must be said that, to anyone else who did not have the metaphysical visual acuity of Catherine, this is what they saw when they observed John Thorpe—a stout young man of middling height, who, with a plain face and ungraceful form, seemed fearful of being too handsome unless he wore the dress of a groom, and too much like a gentleman unless he were easy where he ought to be civil, and impudent where he might be allowed to be easy.

He took out his watch: "How long do you think we have been running it from Tetbury, Miss Morland?"

Catherine still recovering from the amazement, took several additional moments to gather her mind in reply. "I do not know the distance."

Her brother—flushed in the face as though he'd been working a smithy's bellows—told her that it was twenty-three miles.

"Three and twenty!" cried Thorpe—and his voice sounded like a foghorn to Catherine. "Five and twenty if it is an inch."

And then the two gentlemen meaningfully argued meaningless distances. "I defy any man in England to make my horse go less than ten miles an hour in harness," ended Thorpe on an uproar.

"You have lost an hour," said Morland; "it was only ten o'clock when we came from Tetbury."

"Ten o'clock! It was eleven, upon my soul! This brother of yours would persuade me out of my senses, Miss Morland; do but look at my horse; did you ever see an animal so made for speed in your life?" (The servant, also red in the face from being in the *scalding* gentleman's company had just mounted the carriage and was driving off.)

"He *does* look very *hot,* to be sure," said Catherine, glancing in their wake, feeling rather heated herself (and in a not-so-good way), in John Thorpe's proximity. She wondered about the poor horse having had to endure such ghastly atmosphere for so many miles. Not to mention, her poor brother!

James did appear to be sweating at the temples, and his pleasant countenance was ruddier than usual—but was cooling down rapidly in the icy proximity of arctic Isabella.

In all this, the angels were making haste in moving back and forth between their Morland sibling charges, in some distress, trying to cool one down and warm the other by fanning the air with their bright wings, this way and that way . . . and this way and that way . . . and—

"Hot!" exclaimed Thorpe meanwhile, unable to forget his horse. "Why, he had not turned a hair till we came to Walcot Church; but look at his forehand! Look at his loins!"

"Dearest John, there is hardly any need for Miss Morland to look at his loins," put in Isabella.

"—only see how he moves; that horse cannot go less than ten miles an hour: tie his legs and he will get on—" John Thorpe was not to be silenced. That is until he himself changed the topic: "What do you think of my gig, Miss Morland? A neat one, is not it? Well hung; town-built—" his voice roared and ripped the air, modulating in ogrish crescendos, and would have been audible as a hellish monstrosity far across Cheap Street to anyone who was as metaphysically attuned as Catherine (all others merely heard a horrid foghorn).

"And how much do you think he asked for it, Miss Morland?" he finished at last, after describing a tedious purchase transaction.

"I am sure I cannot guess at all."

"He asked fifty guineas; I threw down the money, and the carriage was mine!"

"And I am sure," said Catherine, "I know so little of such things that I cannot judge whether it was cheap or dear."

"Neither one nor t'other; I might have got it for less; but I hate haggling, and the poor fellow wanted cash."

"That was very good-natured of you," said Catherine, quite pleased to be able to say something relevant and even minimally positive in light of so much *heat*.

"Oh! D—— it, when one has the means of doing a kind thing by a friend, I hate to be pitiful."

*"Do not believe it, Catherine!"* the angels clamored. "All kindness of *his* kind has ulterior motives!"

"Yes, I am not all daft, thank you!" she replied smartly, rather aggrieved by the heat and the cold in the vicinity, and then coughed profusely to make up for her mumble.

"Gracious! My sweet, I do hope you are not developing a sore throat," announced Isabella, in her honey intonations, but with just a hint of solemn *meaning*. "Or was it something you said? I did not quite catch, with all your coughing."

"Oh no, I am quite fine—that is, 'tis nothing, cough cough!" said Catherine, while a chill of another sort came to her. What if horrid Isabella and her dreadful ogre brother—being what they were, *unnatural*—could see the angels too? Or at least be aware of them somehow?

Did they know what *she* could see? And did they perchance know she could *see them?*

While our heroine was beset by these new alarms, it was decided that the gentlemen should accompany the young ladies to Edgar's Buildings, and pay their respects to Mrs. Thorpe.

James and Isabella led the way, moving along the street like an arctic cold front. And so well satisfied was Isabella with her lot, so content to ensure a pleasant walk for her brother's friend, and her friend's brother, so pure and uncoquettish were her feelings, that—though they passed certain two young men—she paid them no notice whatsoever and looked back at them only three times.

John Thorpe kept of course with Catherine, following up the cold front with a major heat wave. After a few minutes' silence, he renewed the conversation about his gig. "Miss Morland, it would be reckoned a cheap thing by some. I might have sold it for ten guineas more the next day! Morland was with me at the time."

"Yes," said Morland, who overheard this; "but you forget that your horse was included."

"My horse! Oh, d—— it! I would not sell my horse for a hundred. Are you fond of an open carriage, Miss Morland?"

Catherine spoke, glancing as little as possible at the lumbering ogre at her side. "Yes, very; I have hardly ever an opportunity of being in one; but I am particularly fond of it."

"I am glad of it; I will drive you out in mine every day."

"Thank you," said Catherine, in some distress, from a doubt of the propriety of accepting such an offer, and from the small matter of *whom* the offer came from.

"I will drive you up Lansdown Hill tomorrow."

*"No! No! No!"*

The angelic chorus of protest was so loud that it eclipsed all other street noises.

"Oh, hush!—choo!" sneezed Catherine, and widened her eyes meaningfully at the darting figures of Lawrence, inches from her nose, and Clarence and Terence at both her ears, plus a dozen or so unnamed seraphs pulling at her hair and bonnet and petticoats.

"Thank you; but will not your horse want rest?" she then managed to utter.

"Rest! He has only come three and twenty miles today; all nonsense; nothing ruins horses so much as rest; nothing knocks them up so soon. No, no; I shall exercise mine at the average of four hours every day while I am here." As Thorpe spoke with animation, the heat in his immediate vicinity shot up at least five more degrees.

"Shall you indeed!" said Catherine very seriously, removing a handkerchief to wipe her brow and the tip of her nose. "That will be forty miles a day."

"Forty! Aye, fifty, for what I care. Maybe even sixty! Nay, why stop there—seventy! Well, I will drive you up Lansdown tomorrow; mind, I am engaged."

"How delightful that will be!" cried Isabella, turning round, and bringing a much-needed cooling weather front, which Catherine momentarily appreciated—that is, before she felt her moist brow start to rime over. "My dearest Catherine, I quite envy you; but I am afraid, brother, you will not have room for a third."

"A third indeed! No, no; I did not come to Bath to drive my sisters about; that would be a good joke, faith! Morland must take care of you."

Angels were verily colliding in the air between them all.

James Morland, meanwhile, pulled out his own handkerchief, and started to mutter about blasted unseasonable cold and rotten heat at this time of the year, and how, dare say, one could hardly keep up with the flux of it all, in the span of minutes, it seemed . . .

This was followed by a dialogue of civilities between James and Isabella, as they now all milled about in one grouping. And it started to rain yet again, so that even the passerby stared at the precipitation of about three feet in diameter, as if a single watering pail was being emptied from far up in the heavens directly over their spot. One matron stopped, saying, "Upon my word, one sees it all in Bath!" and graciously offered them her umbrella.

But Catherine heard neither the particulars nor the result. As they resumed walking, distancing the two nephilim from each other, the rain ceased. And Catherine's brutish companion's discourse now sunk from its hitherto animated thunder-and-brimstone pitch to nothing more than grunts of praise or condemnation on the face of every woman they met.

And Catherine—after listening and agreeing as long as she could, with all the civil deference of the youthful female mind, fearful of hazarding an opposite opinion to a large-toothed ogre—ventured at last to vary the tedious subject to one uppermost in her thoughts: "Have you ever read *Udolpho,* Mr. Thorpe?"

"*Udolpho!* Oh, Lord! Not I; I never read novels; I have something else to do."

Catherine, humbled and ashamed, was going to apologize for her question, but she received angelic succor.

"Fie! One might wonder, dear child, if this one ever reads at all!" said Clarence, or maybe Terence.

And Thorpe prevented her by saying, "Novels are all so full of nonsense and stuff; there has not been a tolerably decent one come out since *Tom Jones,* except *The Monk;* I read that t'other day; but as for all the others, they are the stupidest things in creation."

"I think you must like *Udolpho,* if you were to read it; it is so very interesting." Catherine was emboldened by her favorite subject.

"Not I, faith! No, if I read any, it shall be Mrs. Radcliffe's; her novels are amusing enough; they are worth reading. Some fun and nature in them, not to mention, the secret to hidden treasure—"

"Ahem!" came a loud meaningful cough from Isabella up ahead.

"*Udolpho* was written by Mrs. Radcliffe," said Catherine, with some hesitation, from fear of mortifying him into raising the immediate temperature even further.

"Not sure; was it? Aye, I remember, so it was. I was thinking of that other stupid book, written by that woman who married the French emigrant."

"I suppose you mean *Camilla?*"

"Yes, that's the book; such unnatural stuff! An old man playing at see-saw."

"I have never read it."

"You had no loss, I assure you; the horridest nonsense you can imagine; nothing but an old man's playing at see-saw and learning Latin; upon my soul there is not . . ."

Catherine wiped her brow and wisely endured.

This brought them to the door of Mrs. Thorpe's lodgings. "Ah, Mother! How do you do?" said the dutiful and affectionate son, giving her a hearty shake of the hand (and possibly some heat blisters, but the dear mother was surely used to it). "Where did you get that quiz of a hat? It makes you look like an old witch." And a wicked yellowish glow came to the monstrous creature's eyes.

Poor Mrs. Thorpe, thought Catherine, surely did not deserve such unfounded commentary, in light of having borne such offspring and thus performed her required Herculean Labors upon this earth.

The offspring continued: "Here is Morland and I come to stay a few days with you, so you must look out for a couple of good beds somewhere near."

And this address seemed to satisfy all the fondest wishes of the mother's heart, for she received him with the most delighted and exulting affection. It occurred to Catherine that Mrs. Thorpe had *no idea*—which was surely for the best.

On his two younger sisters Thorpe bestowed an equal portion of his fraternal tenderness. He asked each of them how they did, and observed that they both looked very ugly.

Such manners heartily repulsed Catherine; but he was James's friend—she could not very well tell her brother she routinely witnessed angels, and now—demonic ogres.

Her judgment was further confounded by Isabella's assuring her, when they withdrew to see the new hat, that John thought her the most charming girl in the world. And before they parted, John engaged her to dance with him that evening.

Had Catherine been older or vainer, such attacks might have done little. But youth requires uncommon steadiness to resist the attraction of being called the most charming girl in the world—even by demonic nephilim with large carnivore teeth—and of being so very early engaged as a partner.

As a consequence, when the two Morlands, after sitting an hour with the Thorpes, set off to walk together to Mr. Allen's, and James said, "Well, Catherine, how do you like my friend Thorpe?" instead of answering plainly, *"I do not like him at all, he is a drooling ogre, and his sister a man-luring harpy,"* she carefully replied, "I like him very much; he seems very agreeable."

This made some of the angels weep, and James's own heavenly guardian bawled outright, shedding great diamond-bright tears to scatter on the ground as lovely sparkles.

"Oh dear . . ." whispered Catherine, biting her lip in regret. "I can hardly tell him the truth, can I?" And she coughed as usual, muttering the rest of the sentence in her sleeve.

But James was exceedingly gladdened. "He is as good-natured a fellow as ever lived; a little of a rattle, but—And how do you like the rest of the family?"

Once placed on a path of minor deception, what could Catherine say?

"Very, very much indeed: Isabella—uhm—particularly."

"I am very glad to hear you say so; she is just the kind of young woman I could wish to see you attached to. So much good sense! So thoroughly unaffected and amiable! So *lovely!*—ahem. I always wanted you to know her; and she seems very fond of you. She said the highest things in your praise; and the praise of such a girl as Miss Thorpe even you, Catherine," taking her hand with affection, "may be proud of."

"Indeed I am," she replied (while angels sobbed all around); "I—ahem—*like* her exceedingly—that is, well—yes, I am delighted that you like her too. You hardly mentioned anything of her when you wrote to me after your visit there."

Catherine wanted to rend her handkerchief in horrid guilt and agitation at her own untrue words, but her brother was still holding her hand. . . .

"Because I thought I should soon see you myself," said James warmly. "I hope you will be a great deal together while you are in Bath. She is a most amiable girl; such a superior understanding! How fond all the family are of her! And how she must be admired in such a place as this—is not she?"

"Oh, *yes.* Very much indeed, I fancy; Mr. Allen thinks her the prettiest girl in Bath." *And so does every other gentleman.*

"I dare say he does; and I do not know any man who is a better judge of beauty than Mr. Allen. I need not ask you whether you are happy here, my dear Catherine; with such a companion and friend as Isabella Thorpe, it would be impossible to be otherwise. And the Allens are very kind to you?"

"Yes, very kind; I never was so happy before; and now you are come it will be more delightful than ever. How good of you to come so far on purpose to see me."

James accepted this tribute of gratitude, and qualified his conscience for accepting it too, by saying with perfect sincerity, "Indeed, Catherine, I love you dearly."

He then added, "But there is one more reason for my arrival, I admit. It might be complete nonsense, but it is amusing to imagine . . . There was talk, I must say, among the Thorpes when I was there, of *hidden treasure.* From what I understand, there is a grand ancient hoard of gold—or diamonds, sapphires, rubies, and emeralds!—or other some such, buried or otherwise hidden away in Bath, or its whereabouts. Maybe in the pump-room! Or *underneath* the pump-room, in deep secret corridors! Or maybe even right underneath our feet! And there are Secret

Clues! They are supposedly concealed all about, leading to horrid places just like in Mrs. Radcliffe's novels. All very gothic and sanguine and mysterious!"

Catherine froze and listened, her imagination immediately and fiercely engaged. *Dark gothic mysteries! Treasure! Here in Bath! Dark gothic mysteries beyond a black veil! Udolpho!*

But the fascinating subject was far too quickly changed.

Inquiries and communications concerning brothers and sisters, followed. Family matters passed between them, and continued (with only one digression on James's part, in praise of the beauties of Miss Thorpe), till they reached Pulteney Street.

Here he was welcomed with great kindness by Mr. and Mrs. Allen, and invited to dine with them. A pre-engagement in Edgar's Buildings prevented his accepting the invitation and obliged him to hurry away.

Until the time of the two parties uniting in the Octagon Room, Catherine was left to the company of dear, familiar fluttering angels whom she largely ignored, and the luxury of a raised, restless, and frightened imagination, in near darkness, over the pages of *Udolpho*—lost from all worldly concerns of dressing (and Mrs. Allen's late-running dressmaker) and dinner, and taking only a minute to reflect upon her own felicity in being already engaged for the evening.

**Catherine reads** *The Mysteries of Udolpho.*

# Chapter 8

In spite of *Udolpho* and the dressmaker, however, the party from Pulteney Street reached the Upper Rooms in very good time.

The Thorpes and James Morland were there only two minutes before them. Catherine observed James's angelic guardian soar nervously over the top of his head and rapidly beat his tiny glittering wings in an attempt to fan away the scalding air radiated by John Thorpe. The other household angels—likely in charge of Mrs. Thorpe and her younger daughters—were making every effort to assist, but keeping well away from both John and Isabella.

"Upon my word! It only now occurs to me," whispered Catherine to Lawrence who perched on one of her sleeves, "that neither of these . . . nephilim have angels to watch over them!"

"Indeed, not," the angel replied. "The nephilim are most often watched over by beings of another kind."

"You do not perchance mean—*demons?* Oh dear!"

The angel sadly nodded, adding, "But, it *is* their choice. Nephilim—even though they are children of the fallen ones—are fundamentally *neutral,* poised on the brink of Good and Evil, and gifted with human free will. They are able to take either fork in the road. Sadly, they most often choose the non-human side of their blood, which is tainted by the dark."

"Are their—demons—*here,* then? Should I somehow see them also?"

"Blessedly, they are not," replied Lawrence, unfurling his wings, and starting to fan Catherine gently as the Thorpes closed the distance enough to make John Thorpe's heat palpable. "You will indeed *know* them if you see them, dear child, and I hope you never have to . . . But, by Heavenly Decree, demons are not permitted to appear in the flesh, or be fully tangible, before midnight, and not after three in the morning when the rooster crows. So, they are not here . . . *yet.*"

And Catherine realized in that chilling moment that she had never up to that point had the pleasure of being in Isabella's company at an evening event that carried on past midnight— either one or the other of them had been elsewhere, or had left early.

She was fortunate all this time—indeed, all her life! To have never seen a demon! And, most recently, to have avoided being in the presence of Isabella's demonic guardian! As if Isabella herself was not dire enough!

*But, oh dear, tonight was going to be horridly different . . . Although, I did long for frightful Udolpho excitement, did I not?*

Catherine's eager yet terrified anticipation of horrid events was momentarily lessened as the two parties came together. Isabella went through the usual ceremony of meeting her friend with the most smiling and affectionate haste, admiring her gown, and envying the curl of her hair. Catherine felt only mildly doubtful about reciprocating, even though to her true sight Isabella appeared to be a scarecrow attired in finery.

They followed their chaperones, arm in (thoroughly chilled) arm, into the ballroom, whispering to each other whenever a thought occurred, and supplying the place of many ideas by a squeeze of the hand or a smile of sometimes forced affection.

The dancing began within a few minutes after they were seated. Catherine stared in open wonder at the sea of dancers and, directly overhead, a blazing cloud of their angels, brighter than candlelight—oh, so many glorious angels!—all whirling in time to the music, above and below. An impossible, beautiful sight!

James, who had been engaged quite as far in advance for dancing as his sister, was very importunate with Isabella to stand up. However, John had gone into the card-room to speak to a friend (*hidden clues* and *treasure* was overheard by Catherine despite all the best efforts on the gentleman's part to keep his roar down) and taken the infernal heat wave with him and away from the proximity of his sister's cold front—thus assuring there would be neither dance partner nor indoor precipitation.

As a result, Isabella declared that nothing should induce her to join the set before her dear Catherine could join it too. "I assure you," said she to enraptured James, "I would not stand up without your dear sister for all the world; or we should certainly be separated the whole evening."

Catherine gratefully accepted this kindness, and they continued as they were for three minutes longer. Isabella, talking to James, turned again to his sister and whispered in her honeyed shrill tone, audible as such to no one but Catherine, "My dear creature, I am afraid I must leave you, your brother is so amazingly impatient to begin; I know you will not mind, and I dare say John will be back in a moment."

Catherine, though a little disappointed, had too much good nature to make any opposition in a friendly situation even to a naphil. And Isabella had only time to press her friend's hand long enough to make it thoroughly ice-numb, and say, "Good-bye, my dear love," before they hurried off in a wintry whiff.

The younger Miss Thorpes also away dancing, Catherine was left to the mercy of Mrs. Thorpe and Mrs. Allen. She could not help being vexed at the non-appearance of Mr. Thorpe, even though he was a large-toothed ogre with foul breath, for she not only longed to be dancing, but was, to her discredit, revealing the *want of a partner*.

However, to be disgraced in the eye of the world due to the misconduct of another, is one of those fortitude-building circumstances which belong to the heroine's life. Catherine had fortitude too; she suffered, but no murmur passed her lips—only several angels, and one right near her nose, as they were guarding her.

From this state of humiliation, she was soon roused to a pleasanter feeling, by seeing, not Mr. Thorpe, but Mr. Tilney, within yards of where they sat.

He seemed to be moving her way, but did not see her. Thus, the smile and the blush, which his sudden reappearance raised in Catherine, both passed without sullying her heroic gravity.

"Look, dear child, there, at last, is your *good* friend!" whispered Clarence, and Catherine felt another flush of warmth.

Mr. Tilney looked as handsome and as lively as ever, and was talking with interest to a fashionable and pleasing-looking young woman on his arm, and whom Catherine immediately guessed to be his sister (unthinkingly *not* considering him lost to her forever on the arm of another female). It had never entered her head that Mr. Tilney could be married. He had certainly not behaved like a married man, and he *had* acknowledged a sister. Thus, instead of turning deathly pale and fainting on Mrs. Allen's bosom, Catherine remained perfectly upright and sensible, and with cheeks only a little redder than usual.

Mr. Tilney and his companion eventually approached, preceded by a lady acquaintance of Mrs. Thorpe. And Catherine, catching Mr. Tilney's eye, instantly received from him the smiling tribute of recognition.

Directly overhead, angelic guardians of the Tilneys happily fluttered to mingle with Catherine's own grand aerial crowd. Mr.

Tilney's angel in particular seemed to regard her with a glorious smile.

She returned both smiles of the man and his angel with pleasure. Then, advancing nearer, Mr. Tilney spoke both to her and Mrs. Allen, by whom he was very civilly acknowledged.

"I am very happy to see you again, sir, indeed; I was afraid you had left Bath." Mrs. Allen was eager to share her most recent textile purchases with a well-versed fellow connoisseur.

He thanked her for her fears, and said that he had quitted it for a week, on the very morning after his having had the pleasure of seeing her.

*Gone for a week! That explains it!* thought Catherine.

"Well, sir, and I dare say you are not sorry to be back again, for it is the most agreeable place for young people, and everybody else too. I tell Mr. Allen, when he talks of being sick of it, that he should not complain. Much better to be here than at home at this dull time of year. He is lucky to be sent here for his health."

"And I hope, madam, that Mr. Allen will be obliged to like the place, from finding it of service to him."

"Thank you, sir. I have no doubt that he will. A neighbour of ours was here for his health last winter, and came away quite stout."

"That circumstance must give great encouragement."

"Yes, sir—he and his family were here three months; so I tell Mr. Allen he must not be in a hurry to get away."

Here they were interrupted by a request from Mrs. Thorpe to Mrs. Allen, that she would move a little to accommodate Mrs. Hughes and Miss Tilney with seats, as they had agreed to join their party. This was accordingly done, Mr. Tilney still continuing standing before them. And after a few minutes' consideration, he asked Catherine to dance with him.

This compliment, delightful as it was, produced severe mortification to the lady. Having promised the dancing to

Thorpe and still waiting for her original partner, inferno and all, Catherine gave Tilney her denial and expressed such sorrow on the occasion that there could be no doubt she really felt it.

Thorpe joined her just afterwards, preceded by warping desert-hot air, so that the seated ladies in the vicinity all started fluttering their fans, and Mrs. Allen thought she saw a *mirage* of the exact dress of particular fine mulberry brocade and satin she had once encountered in London and had never forgotten. . . .

The very easy manner in which John Thorpe then told Catherine that he had kept her waiting did not by any means reconcile her more to her lot. Nor did the particulars which he entered into while they were standing up—horses, dogs, the friend he had just left, a proposed exchange of terriers between them—interest her enough to prevent her from looking very overheated, and looking very often towards that part of the room where she had left Mr. Tilney.

However, there was one item that caused her to listen closely, and even venture to look directly at the hideous large-toothed gentleman. At one point Thorpe mentioned that his terrier-propagating friend was also a 'fine thinker,' and a clever fellow, and that he was superbly versed with *decryption* of clandestine papers, including pedigrees of horses and other such well-guarded *secret documents*. It was the manner in which he pronounced the words 'secret documents' that gave Catherine pause. In addition, there was a corner of an old yellowing and thoroughly folded piece of parchment sticking from the top pocket of Thorpe's evening jacket. Had this something to do with hidden treasure? Or *Udolpho?*

And then Catherine had a truly awful thought. What if *The Mysteries of Udolpho* held the key to the treasure? What if, somehow, it contained secret clues and arcane code? What if—

"Miss Morland! I say, Miss Morland!"

Her thoughts were interrupted by a strong whiff of oven heat and John Thorpe nearly barking in her ear, in an attempt to engage her lost attention and simultaneously toast her collar lace.

"Oh dear, I am very sorry, Mr. Thorpe," said Catherine, while two angels fluttered their wings at extraordinary speed in front of her cheeks, in an attempt to dissipate the scalding air. "I was just thinking, if there is indeed secret treasure hidden somewhere in Bath, as I heard it rumored—"

"What?" John Thorpe's bellow was sufficient to carry across the room, but thankfully was ignored by all less supernaturally attuned. "Wherever did you hear that rumor, Miss Morland? Who told you? Why, was it that sister of mine, so easy with her tongue, even when I tell her to keep the lid on it— ahem, that is, what treasure? What do you know of it?"

Catherine was not at all good at deception. But here, she had the good sense to at least not give her brother away. "I don't exactly remember," she said, turning somewhat pink. "It must have been someone talking in—in the pump-room."

"In the pump-room! By Jove! Do you suppose—" And then Thorpe decided for some reason it was of little use to withhold this confidence from the lovely Miss Morland after all, since for all practical purposes they were getting so well and charmingly acquainted, all of them. And so he pulled her unceremoniously a few steps, almost breaking up their dance set, and proceeded to tell her his suspicions every time the music put them in proximity.

Apparently, Thorpe told her, there was a grand hoard of gold, jewels, and other amazing valuables stashed away somewhere in this very town, very possibly under their noses, and the value of this stash was, to put it bluntly, extraordinary. Gold bullion, jewels, *mountains* of coin; John Thorpe painted a stupendous picture, so that Catherine momentarily wondered if so much treasure was to be found only in the royal treasury in London, and whether such hills of jewels and valleys of precious stones could even fit a single building.

**Mrs. Allen sees a mirage.**

"In short, Miss Morland, it is all here," he ended. "And before the fortnight is over, I dare say it will be all ours, all in our hands."

"Oh. And how do you propose to accomplish the discovery of this amazing hoard?"

"The Code, Miss Morland! Why, stupendously simple, I say! We must crack the Code!"

"What code?"

For a moment it seemed Thorpe was regretting having said all that much to her. But then with a minor roar and a blast of heat, he gave in, and allowed himself to disclose the rest of his suspicions to his fair companion.

"None other than the Code hidden in the novels of Mrs. Radcliffe! Why do you think Isabella and I have been reading them? Do you suppose I would otherwise waste my time with such drabble and stupid stuff?"

"But you did say the other day that Mrs. Radcliffe's novels are 'amusing enough' and 'worth reading.'"

"Ah, dear Miss Morland, that was just to throw off suspicion, to keep the wolves at bay, so to speak, to slay the jackals and jackrabbits, and pry off the scent from the prancing elephants and galloping ponies! And it was all before I had any mind to trust you with this—you must forgive me of course, but one must be careful, you know, what with so much treasure at stake, enough to fill two palaces, and three treasuries!"

"Oh dear, I suppose, though you did say there was a large amount of it, but—*three* treasuries?"

"Three? Nonsense, there is at least enough for four, and very likely five!"

"Treasuries?"

"Mountains!"

"Oh, gracious goodness!"

This went on for quite some time, until Catherine suddenly recalled that Mr. Tilney was on the other side of the room. And she wondered what *he* would say to all this talk of treasure.

Of her "dear" Isabella, to whom she particularly longed to point out that gentleman, she could see nothing. They were in different sets.

Indeed, Catherine was separated from all her party, and away from all her acquaintance. One mortification succeeded another, accompanied by blasts of scalding nephilim heat which were—to be truthful—rather direly annoying at this time of night in an already overheated ballroom.

From the whole she deduced this useful lesson, that to go previously engaged to a ball does not necessarily increase either the dignity or enjoyment of a young lady. Eventually the dance ended, Thorpe pronounced the urgent need to procure them drinks, and disappeared in the crowd, taking the Sahara with him.

Catherine was suddenly roused by a touch on the shoulder, and turning round, perceived Mrs. Hughes directly behind her, attended by Miss Tilney and a gentleman.

"I beg your pardon, Miss Morland," said she, "for this liberty—but Mrs. Thorpe said she was sure you would not have the least objection to letting in this young lady by you."

Catherine was overjoyed to oblige. The young ladies were introduced to each other, with proper exchanges of goodness and delicacy; and Mrs. Hughes returned to her party.

Miss Tilney had a good figure, a pretty face, and a very agreeable countenance. She was accompanied by a very lovely angel who soared overhead and nodded to Catherine with delight.

Furthermore, Miss Tilney had neither pretension, nor the resolute stylishness of Miss Thorpe's, but far more real elegance, good sense, and good breeding. Neither shy nor affectedly open, she seemed capable of being young, attractive, and at a ball without wanting to fix the attention of every man near her. She expressed no exaggerated feelings of ecstatic delight or inconceivable vexation on every little trifling occurrence.

Catherine, interested at once by her appearance and her relationship to Mr. Tilney, was desirous of being further acquainted with her. But without embarking on a speedy intimacy, they could do little more than inform themselves how well the other liked Bath, whether she drew, or played, or sang, and whether she was fond of riding on horseback.

The two dances were scarcely concluded before Catherine experienced the delicate flapping breezes of angels fleeing and scattering every which way, felt a blast of arctic cold, and then found her arm gently seized by her faithful Isabella, who in great spirits exclaimed, "At last! My *dearest* creature, I have been looking for you this hour. What could induce you to come into this set, when you knew I was in the other? I have been quite wretched without you."

"My *dear* Isabella, how was it possible for me to get at you? I could not even see where you were."

"So I told your brother all the time—but he would not believe me. Do go and find her, Mr. Morland, said I—in vain— he would not stir an inch. Was not it so, Mr. Morland? But you men are all so immoderately lazy! I have been scolding him to such a degree, I never stand upon ceremony with such people."

"Look at that young lady with the white beads round her head," whispered Catherine, detaching her friend from James. "It is Mr. Tilney's sister."

"Oh! Heavens! You don't say so! Let me look at her this moment. What a delightful girl! I never saw anything half so beautiful! But where is her all-conquering brother? Is he in the room? Point him out to me this instant, I die to see him—Mr. Morland, you are not to listen. We are not talking about you."

"But what is all this whispering about? What is going on?" said James, shivering slightly in his jacket (the collar of which was developing a fine dusting of unseasonal icy rime), but observing Isabella as though bewitched. He was then regaled with commonplace chatter, which lasted some time, the original subject entirely forgotten.

Catherine was pleased to have it dropped for a while. But the total suspension of all Isabella's impatient desire to see Mr. Tilney seemed a bit odd.

When the orchestra struck up a fresh dance, James would have led his fair partner away, but Isabella resisted. "I tell you, Mr. Morland," she cried, sending up curling vapors from her icy breath in a complete reverse of natural law, "I would not do such a thing for all the world. My dear Catherine, your brother wants me to dance with him again, though it is a most improper thing, entirely against the rules. It would make us the talk of the place, if we were not to change partners."

"Upon my honour," said James, "in these public assemblies, it is as often done as not."

"Nonsense, how can you say so? But when you men have a point to carry, you never stick at anything. My sweet Catherine, do support me; persuade your brother how impossible it is. Tell him that it would quite shock you to see me do such a thing; now would not it?"

"No, not at all; but if you think it wrong, you had much better change." Catherine said absently, glancing around with some concern for a sight of Mr. Tilney.

"There," cried Isabella, "you hear what your sister says, and yet you will not mind her. Well, remember that it is not my fault, if we set all the old ladies in Bath in a bustle. Come along, my dearest Catherine, for heaven's sake, and stand by me." And off they went, to regain their former place.

John Thorpe, in the meanwhile, had walked away in search of their drinks and never actually made it back. Thus, Catherine was happily willing to give Mr. Tilney an opportunity of repeating the agreeable and flattering dance request. She made her way to Mrs. Allen and Mrs. Thorpe as fast as she could, followed by a cloud of bright twinkling angels floating overhead like a sizeable candelabra. She hoped to find him still with them—but the hope proved to be fruitless.

"Well, my dear," said Mrs. Thorpe, impatient for praise of her son, "I hope you have had an agreeable partner."

"Very agreeable, madam," replied Catherine politely, recalling excessive heat and secret codes.

"I am glad of it. John has charming spirits, has not he?"

The angels made flutterings of alarm, reminding Catherine she was never good at deception, nor should she aspire to be.

"Did you meet Mr. Tilney, my dear?" said Mrs. Allen, opportunely changing the subject.

"No, where is he?"

"He was with us just now, and said he was so tired of lounging about, that he was resolved to go and dance; so I thought perhaps he would ask you, if he met with you."

"Where can he be?" said Catherine, looking round; but she had not looked round long before she saw him leading a young lady to the dance. At this sight, Catherine felt something that was quite possibly a bit of discomfort, or maybe a little twinge in her heart.

*"Oh, dear child, take cheer! Surely the gentleman will make his way here eventually and ask you!"* It was Terence, or possibly Clarence, expressing sympathy from a sleeve near her right ear.

"Then you decidedly approve of this gentleman?" whispered Catherine, glad to have at least someone to share her observations of Mr. Tilney, and hiding her animated outburst under the flutterings of her fan. "Admit it, you do *approve!*"

The angel responded with a happiest nod.

"A prune, my dear?" meanwhile said Mrs. Allen. "What prune? Oh, I dare say, yes, I do recall that one terribly overcooked prune in the plum pudding we dined on earlier, was it not? I even mentioned to Mr. Allen, I did, how overcooked it was."

"Yes, yes, that is exactly what I was saying." Catherine hurriedly coughed for good measure.

And then Mrs. Allen noticed Mr. Tilney dancing. "Ah! He has got a partner; I wish he had asked you." And after a short silence, she added, "he is a very agreeable young man."

"Indeed he is, Mrs. Allen," said Mrs. Thorpe, smiling complacently; "I must say it, though I am his mother, that there is not a more agreeable young man in the world."

This inapplicable answer might have been too much for the comprehension of many; but it did not puzzle Mrs. Allen, for after only a moment's consideration, she whispered to Catherine, "I dare say she thought I was speaking of her son!"

Recalling inferno, Catherine politely remained silent.

Indeed, she was disappointed and vexed. She seemed to have missed by so little the very object she had had in view. And Catherine was not inclined to a very gracious reply, when a heat wave and John Thorpe came up to her soon afterwards and said (that is, John Thorpe spoke; the heat wave merely scalded everything around them in a thoroughly disagreeable manner), "Well, Miss Morland, I suppose you and I are to stand up and jig it together again."

"Oh, no; I am much obliged to you, our two dances are over; and, besides, I am tired, and do not mean to dance any more." Catherine spoke thus not only because she remembered the angelic instruction never to agree directly with anything the two nephilim asked of her, but also because she was peeved.

"Do not you? Then let us walk about *decrypting secret locations* of certain *secret valuable items* and quiz people. Come along with me, and I will show you the four greatest quizzers in the room; my two younger sisters and their partners. I have been laughing at them this half hour. And I do believe I have arrived at a certain *derivation* of occult *meaning* from a *grand clue*—"

Again Catherine excused herself. And at last he walked off to quiz his sisters by himself and mutter in a roar about hidden treasure. Catherine was still quite piqued by the notion of *Udolpho* and treasure being somehow connected, and all these wonderful secrets. But she was overheated and sorely inclined to tell John Thorpe he was being tediously monstrous, and she just wished he would go away and stand next to a thoroughly drafty window open to the chill night breeze—which was not at all a charitable thing to say, nor particularly polite. She even wished Isabella would come by and bring some cooling relief.

The rest of the evening she found very dull, despite the many sympathetic whispers of angels in both her ears. Mr. Tilney was drawn away from their party at tea, to attend that of his partner. Miss Tilney, though belonging to it, did not sit near her. And James and Isabella were so much engaged in conversing together that the latter had no leisure to bestow more on her friend than one smile, one icy squeeze, and one "dearest Catherine."

And yet—before the end of the evening, dullness was promptly dispelled, to be replaced by something truly horrific. For, soon enough, it was midnight, and Catherine was suddenly reminded of the angelic warning . . .

At the striking of the clock, Isabella momentarily paused and oddly flexed her shoulders, as though a strange invisible weight had settled on her. And, as Catherine continued to observe, she began to *see* that there was indeed a *shadow*, a shape forming near Isabella—verily, *out of* Isabella.

The air itself seemed to fill with despair.

The shape—at first only a grotesque distortion of Isabella's own shadow cast by candlelight—in a matter of seconds took on a life of its own, a dark unnatural *animation* and existence. It wavered, it moved; it stretched and reformed and thickened into an ugly thing, remotely human, with blunt limbs, glowing slits of coal-red eyes, scaly and elephantine hide, a darting forked tongue, and a pair of prominent horns.

Isabella's demon was here.

And while Isabella chattered on about trifles, and James watched her with oblivious impossible fascination (meanwhile turning blue from the cold), Isabella's demon stretched and looked around, and hissed like a serpent at the cloud of angels.

And then *it* looked directly at Catherine.

And it belched, in the *filthiest* manner possible.

# Chapter 9

The progress of Catherine's unhappiness from the events of the evening was as follows:

First, she had been deprived, multiple times, and in the most disagreeable ways imaginable, of Mr. Tilney's company.

Second, she had seen a *demon*. Her first ever, horrid, impossible, putrid demon.

Third, the demon had seen *her*. And although it did not particularly do anything but grossly breathe through its mouth, or say anything, Catherine had a firm suspicion that it had said plenty to Isabella, whispering inside her head and making the naphil of ice even colder and darker than she already was.

Next, Catherine experienced a general dissatisfaction with everybody about her—with the people who were so clearly oblivious to the putrid demon in their midst—and the fact that she could only mutter her complaints to the angels while pretending to cough yet for the hundredth time, else she would be overheard by the seated company all around them, taken for a ninny, and that simply would not do.

While she remained in the rooms, observing the disgusting demon skulking near Isabella (and curdling the drinks and the refreshment plates with its ghastly breath, and being an absolute toad with the angels all around, who, it must be said, swarmed between them in a wall of protection, the dears), she speedily felt considerable weariness and a violent desire to go home.

Then, on arriving in Pulteney Street, Catherine's suffering took the direction of extraordinary hunger (since she could not allow herself even a bite to eat back in the Upper Rooms, considering the rotten demon breath and the ensuing vapors), and when that was appeased, her misery changed into an earnest longing to be in bed. The angels crooned to her soothingly, and in her heroic distress she immediately fell into a sound sleep, and awoke nine hours later perfectly revived, in excellent spirits.

The first wish of her heart was to improve her acquaintance with Miss Tilney, and to seek her for that purpose, in the pump-room at noon.

In the pump-room, everyone so newly arrived in Bath must be met with. That building was so conducive to the discovery of female excellence, intimacy, secret discourses, and unlimited confidence, that she most reasonably expected another friend from within its walls—indeed, a friend rather more suitable to the true subjects of the heart. Her plan for the morning thus settled, she sat quietly down to her book after breakfast, resolving to be occupied till the clock struck one, reading about lurid horrors, drawing comparisons between the demon from the previous night to whatever monstrosities were described by Mrs. Radcliffe, and wondering about secrets of hidden treasure and mysterious arcane codes . . .

Meanwhile, Mrs. Allen, whose vacancy of mind and incapacity for thinking ensured that she could never be entirely silent, sat nearby at her work and observed aloud upon lost needles, broken thread, carriages in the street, specks upon her gown, while the angels danced in brightness over their heads.

At about half past twelve, a remarkably loud rap drew Catherine in haste to the window. Mrs. Allen scarcely had time to inform Catherine of there being two open carriages at the door—in the first only a servant, her brother driving Miss

Thorpe in the second—before the surge of heat signaled advance warning . . .

John Thorpe came running upstairs, calling out in a quiet roar, "Well, Miss Morland, here I am. Have you been waiting long? We could not come before; blame the old devil of a coachmaker. How do you do, Mrs. Allen? A famous ball last night! Come, Miss Morland, be quick, for the others are in a confounded hurry to be off."

"What do you mean?" said Catherine, starting to fan herself with the palm of her hand. "Where are you all going to?"

"Going to? Why, you have not forgot our engagement! Did not we agree together to take a drive this morning? What a head you have! We are going up Claverton Down. There are mysteries afoot! Clandestine signs to be decrypted! Rare *valuables* lying in wait, mountains of 'em—"

"Something was said about it, I remember," said Catherine, looking at Mrs. Allen; "but really I did not expect you."

"Not expect me! That's a good one! And what a dust you would have made, if I had not come."

Catherine's silent appeal to her friend, meanwhile, was entirely thrown away; Mrs. Allen was oblivious. And while Catherine preferred to see Miss Tilney, she was not sufficiently put off by a delay in favour of a drive. Indeed, there could be no impropriety in going with toothy Mr. Thorpe, since Isabella was going at the same time with James (to ensure if not propriety then at least a reasonably clement temperature).

She was therefore obliged to speak plainer. "Well, ma'am, what do you say to it? Can you spare me for an hour or two?"

"Do just as you please, my dear," replied Mrs. Allen, with the most placid indifference, while her own angelic guardian waved languidly.

Catherine took the advice, and ran off to get ready. In a very few minutes she reappeared, in record time, while Thorpe procured Mrs. Allen's admiration of his gig. With her parting good wishes, they both hurried downstairs.

"My dearest creature," cried Isabella, voice rising in shrill modulations, before she could get into the carriage, "you have been at least *three hours* getting ready. I was afraid you were ill. What a delightful ball last night! I have a thousand things to say; but make haste and get in, for I long to be off."

Catherine followed her orders, hearing her exclaim aloud to James, "What a sweet girl she is! I quite dote on her."

Meanwhile, the angels moved in position overhead, starting up their customary air-circulating efforts to fan Isabella's cold atmosphere in the direction of John's inferno and ensure a moderately temperate zone for Catherine and James, at least within a close distance of their carriages. Some of the angels' long-suffering sighs could be heard periodically . . .

*Upon my word, at least it is daytime, and no demons present,* thought Catherine, thankful for small blessings.

"You will not be frightened, Miss Morland," said Thorpe with scalding breath, as he handed her in, "if my horse should dance about a little at first setting off. He will, most likely, give a fierce plunge or two, but he will soon know his master. He is full of spirits, playful as can be, but there is no vice in him."

Catherine did not think the portrait a very inviting one, but it was too late to retreat or be frightened. So, resigning herself to her fate, and to the animal's boasted knowledge of its owner, she sat peaceably down, and saw Thorpe sit down by her.

Everything being then arranged, the servant who stood at the horse's head was bid in an important voice "to let him go," and off they went in the quietest manner imaginable, without a plunge or a caper. Catherine, delighted at such plodding calm, expressed her grateful surprise. Her companion immediately made the matter perfectly simple—it was entirely owing to the judicious manner in which he controlled the reins, and his singular discernment and dexterity with the whip.

Catherine could not help wondering why he felt it necessary to alarm her in the first place, but was glad to be under the care of such an apparently excellent coachman even though he were a hulking ogre. Perceiving that the animal continued in the same safe and quiet manner, its frisky pace being ten miles an hour, she gave herself up to all the enjoyment of invigorating air and exercise, in a fine mild day of February.

A silence of several minutes was broken by Thorpe's saying very abruptly, "Old Allen is as rich as a prince—is not he?"

Catherine did not understand him—and he repeated his question, adding in explanation, "Old Allen, the man you are with."

"Oh! Mr. Allen, you mean. Yes, I believe, he is very rich."

"And no children at all?"

"No—not any."

"A famous thing for his next heirs. He is your godfather, is not he?" Thorpe continued, his voice modulating from a low rumble to a pleased steady roar. The radiant heat around him had grown even more palpable—thank goodness for a steady breeze.

"My godfather! No." Catherine felt droplets of sweat gather on her brow. She ignored it politely, and soon enough all was dried by the scalding air, followed by gusts of normal wind around them that penetrated the inferno when it could.

"But you are always very much with them."

"Yes, very much."

"Aye, that is what I meant. He seems a good kind of old fellow enough, and has lived very well in his time, I dare say; he is not gouty for nothing. Does he drink his bottle a day now?"

"His bottle a day! No. Why should you think of such a thing? He is a very temperate man, and you could not fancy him in liquor last night?"

"Lord help you! You women are always thinking of men's being in liquor. Why, you do not suppose a man is overset by a bottle? If everybody was to drink their bottle a day, there would not be half the disorders in the world—a good thing for us all!"

"I cannot believe it," said Catherine, observing with some alarm the hideously exultant ogre face of the gentleman as he visualized the state of the world after its daily bottle.

"Oh! Lord, it would be the saving of thousands. Tens of thousands! Millions! There is not the hundredth part of the wine consumed in this kingdom that there ought to be. Our foggy climate wants help."

Catherine lingered wistfully on the delightful notion of *foggy climate*. "And yet I have heard that there is a great deal of wine drunk in Oxford."

"Oxford! There is no drinking at Oxford now, I assure you. Nobody drinks there. Hardly a man goes beyond his four pints at the utmost. Now, it was reckoned a remarkable thing, at the last party in my rooms, that upon an average we cleared about five pints a head. Mine is famous good stuff, to be sure. Not often anything like it in Oxford—and that may account for it. But this will give you a notion of the general rate of drinking there."

"Yes, it does give a notion," said Catherine warmly, "that you all drink a great deal more wine than I thought you did. However, I am sure James does not drink so much."

This brought on a loud roar and an overpowering reply, of which no part was very distinct, except the frequent exclamations, amounting almost to oaths, adorned with gusts of locomotive heat. The frightful gentleman was acting exceedingly like his nephilim self, and angels rose up in a flock all about Catherine at each of his infernal outbursts.

When it ended, Catherine was left with a strengthened belief of Oxford practically drowning in wine, tempered only by a happy conviction of her brother's comparative sobriety.

Thorpe's ideas then all reverted to the merits of his own equipage. She was called on to admire the spirit and freedom with which his horse moved along, the ease of his paces, the excellence of the springs in the motion of the carriage.

She followed him in all his admiration as well as she could. To go before or beyond him was impossible. His knowledge and her ignorance, his rapidity of expression, and her diffidence of herself put that out of her power. She was left to echo whatever he chose to assert. It was settled—his equipage was altogether the most complete of its kind in England, his carriage the neatest, his horse the best goer, and himself the best coachman.

"You do not really think, Mr. Thorpe," said Catherine, dabbing her brow with a handkerchief, and venturing after some time to offer some little variation on the subject, "that James's gig will break down?"

"Break down! Oh! Lord! Did you ever see such a little tittuppy thing in your life? There is not a sound piece of iron about it. The wheels, fairly worn out these ten years at least, nay, twenty years, possibly thirty—and as for the body! Upon my soul, you might shake it to pieces yourself with a touch, or most likely a breath. It is the most devilish little rickety business I ever beheld! Thank God! we have got a better. I would not be bound to go two miles in it for fifty thousand pounds. For that matter, not even a mile for a hundred!"

"Good heavens!" cried Catherine, quite frightened. "Then pray let us turn back; they will certainly meet with an accident if we go on. Do let us turn back, Mr. Thorpe; stop and speak to my brother, and tell him how very unsafe it is."

Catherine was so agitated that the angels began to fly about in sympathetic extraordinary clamor, some of them colliding with each other, and one landing distastefully on top of Thorpe's rakish yet clod-like hat.

"Unsafe! Oh, lord! What is there in that? They will only get a roll if it does break down; and there is plenty of dirt; it will be excellent falling. Oh, curse it! The carriage is safe enough, if a man knows how to drive it. A thing of that sort in good hands will last above twenty years after it is fairly worn out. Lord bless you! I would undertake for five pounds to drive it to York and back again, without losing a nail."

Catherine listened with astonishment. She knew not how to reconcile two such very different accounts of the same thing. She had not been brought up to understand the propensities of such a vain rattle for idle assertions and impudent falsehoods.

Her own family were plain, matter-of-fact people who seldom aimed at wit of any kind. Her father was content with a pun, her mother with a proverb. Neither were in the habit of telling lies to increase their importance, or of asserting at one moment what they would contradict the next.

Catherine reflected on all this in much perplexity, and was on the point of requesting from Mr. Thorpe a clarification of his real opinion on the subject. But she checked herself—clearly he did not excel in being plain. And surely he would not suffer his sister and his friend to be exposed to the dangers of an unsafe carriage. There was decidedly no need to be alarmed.

In that exact same moment, an event took place, which no one could have predicted on such a fine mild day in February.

They were passing a copse of trees, and suddenly a dark, large, swiftly moving *object* came hurtling down upon them— seemingly from out of nowhere, possibly from the branches or possibly even from heaven itself.

There were no words to properly describe it. Fairly, it was winged, with a great wide wingspan, silhouetted black against the sky, and it made loud horrifying thunderous noises, not unlike honks, and very similar to a foghorn, yet more sonorous, and altogether dreadful.

The *creature,* flapping wildly, screeching like a flock of banshees (and nearly as terribly as Isabella), lunged directly at the carriage driven by Thorpe.

While Thorpe had one hand on the reins, the other clutching the whip, he could not very well do anything appropriate to defend himself or his fair passenger, except roar.

Catherine squeaked only once, briefly, in horror. She naturally shrank away from the beating wings, then grew instantly silent. Because what followed was a truly heart-stopping, intestine-curdling *shriek* from the other carriage—worthy of *Udolpho* and Mrs. Radcliffe's darkest sanguined nightmare.

It was Isabella—who had seen the thing attacking them and reacted as was expected of a lady.

"Ah! Heaven help us!" cried James next to her, jumping in sudden terror and nearly losing control of his carriage (and lord knows what else).

"What in blazes is this? *What?*" exclaimed Thorpe, baring his long yellow ogre teeth which only Catherine could see. He then brandished his whip in an attempt to fight off the thing attacking him in the face with its powerful wings, beating at him, clawing at his hat, his nose—

And not even once touching Catherine.

Therefore our heroine remained silent, shocked into horrified amazement, but not particularly alarmed for her own safety. Even the angels nearest to her were surprisingly unresponsive, as they soared gently in the vicinity, watching also it seemed, as John Thorpe was being thoroughly mauled and assailed.

Isabella shrieked again, and Catherine almost reacted by stopping her ears with her fingers, but held herself back from such an unseemly, rudely inappropriate action.

"What is this, oh lord! What is this?" she finally exclaimed, blinking from the feathers flying in every direction, into her face, as Thorpe was snarling, huffing and puffing, and wallowing in his seat, while the horse blessedly stood in place.

"Some kind of horrid bird!" shrieked Isabella.

"Is that a wild . . . *chicken?* A pheasant, mayhap?" Catherine was not sure what it could possibly be, considering its white-tipped grayish feathers. "Could it perchance be *rabid?*" she ventured.

"No! This is no blasted rabbit!" roared Thorpe. "Lord help you! whoever heard of a flying rabbit? What kind of blazing nonsense do they teach the ladies these days—"

"Oh, I know it, wait, I know it!" James attempted to calm his own horse, as he yelled out. "It's that famous *duck,* is it not? What is it called again? You know, the horrid one, the Bath Duck? No—the Brighton Duck!"

"By Jove, yes! The monster!" cried John Thorpe, as the flying thing swooped away, then came back for another pass. "That's it, yes! It has to be! It's none other than the Brighton Duck! Just look at the size of it!"

Catherine recalled the frightful stories told of a monstrous, decidedly *unnatural* duck terrorizing various neighborhoods, mostly in the county of Northampton, but seen also in Portsmouth and London and various other locales. Supposedly it originally hailed from Peking, then was purchased by a gentleman in Brighton and raised by that same gentleman, an heir to a baronetcy, to be a *killer*. The duck escaped, and had been blamed in the death of a prominent dowager—indeed, a half a dozen ladies of rank—and the collapse of an admiral and several otherwise valiant gentlemen . . .

*What horrors, worthy of Udolpho!*

Catherine shivered despite the waves of heat streaming from her carriage companion, and observed the duck continue to assault the gentleman at her side.

"But is it not nocturnal, then?" she ventured once more. "Why is it out and about now? And why attack us?—or, attack Mr. Thorpe, to be precise?"

"No one knows the ways of such abominations, my dearest!" screeched Isabella from the other carriage. "You must remain brave, my sweet Catherine, my dearest friend! For I cannot bear to lose you! No, I cannot! Not to this horrid creature! And you, John, you must stand firm against it! Fight, fight valiantly, and we shall venture to get help!" And with those loyal words of friendship and sisterly concern, she turned to James, exclaiming, "Drive on, Mr. Morland, this instant! You must not sit still here another moment, we must flee!"

Before James could make any reasonable decision related to the situation, the duck abruptly gave one truly horrible screech-honk. It then rose high overhead and suddenly let go of some goodly amount of an unmentionable but completely natural *material* which landed precisely with a filthy plop on top of Thorpe's hat.

John Thorpe roared like a herd of elephants, and spun around with the whip, missing everything thankfully, including Catherine, the carriage, and the long-suffering horse.

The Brighton Duck trumpeted its victory, circled once more, higher, and then took off, unscathed, wings beating rapidly, somewhere into the trees.

It was gone.

For a long moment everyone remained motionless and silent. And then Thorpe removed his hat, shook it out over the side of the carriage (not particularly taking care not to splatter Catherine), spat unceremoniously, said a few dire oaths, and then put the hat back on his frightful head.

"Hah!" he then cried. "I taught that monster a lesson, did I not? Hah!" And he brandished his whip for good measure.

"Are you well, Catherine, dearest?" Isabella intoned from the other carriage. "I was just telling Mr. Morland, he is to come to your rescue immediately, but men are such slow-witted creatures—"

"I am quite well," Catherine reassured her friend. "But I am concerned, is Mr. Thorpe in any way hurt? Are you, sir?"

"Hurt? *Me*, Miss Morland, hurt? Hah!" roared Thorpe. "I just drove off a giant of a monster, did I not? As everyone is my witness, it was the size of a goat at least, nay, a bullock! I showed it who is master, it was thoroughly thrashed by my whip, and will never venture to harm anyone again!"

"But," Catherine said, "it appeared to fly off on its own."

"On its own? By heaven, what nonsense! I drove it away, wounding it, and it is even now suffering from a mortal blow to itself! It slunk away to expire, Miss Morland, did not you see? Even now it probably staggers somewhere in the shrubbery, croaking its last unholy breath! Mark my words, the monster will be found legs up and stiff as a board, upon the morrow!"

Catherine wisely decided not to say another word. Meanwhile, James and Thorpe conversed briefly, and it was mutually decided that everyone was sufficiently well and unperturbed to continue their excursion.

The carriages thus resumed motion, and John Thorpe periodically roared out "Hah!" every several paces, for at least a quarter of an hour.

Soon enough the details of the whole matter seemed entirely forgotten by him. All the rest of his talk covered his usual concerns—horses bought for a trifle and sold for incredible sums; racing matches, in which he infallibly foretold the winner; shooting parties, in which he had killed more birds than all his companions together (and each bird twice the size of that Brighton Duck!); and some famous day's sport with the fox-hounds, in which his skill had surmounted that of the most experienced huntsman, and the boldness of his riding, though never endangering his own life for a moment—he calmly concluded—had broken the necks of many.

Catherine was not in the habit of judging others, and her general notions were unfixed. But while she endured his endless conceit, she could not repress a sense that John Thorpe was altogether completely and hopelessly *disagreeable*. Yes, he was a naphil, a strange unnatural creature, and rather a frightful ogre with large yellow teeth, but up to this moment she had done him the honor of keeping a charitable open mind.

But, as of now, the gentleman had crossed the line of all good breeding, manners, and charity.

It was a bold surmise. For he was Isabella's brother; and she had been assured by James that his manners would recommend him to all her sex. But in spite of this, the increasingly oppressive weariness of Thorpe's company—from the beginning till they stopped in Pulteney Street again— induced Catherine to resist such high fraternal authority. After all, James *had* been bewitched by Isabella! Catherine was yet to have a painful discussion with him about *that* unfortunate circumstance.

When they arrived at Mrs. Allen's door, Isabella was suddenly astonished to find that it was too late in the day for them to attend her friend into the house: "Past three o'clock!" Isabella refused to believe any watch, but could only protest that no two hours and a half had ever gone off so swiftly before, as Catherine was called on to confirm.

Catherine could not tell such a blunt falsehood even to please Isabella; but, happily, the latter did not wait for her answer. She was wretchedly obliged to go directly home. It was ages since she had had a moment's conversation with her dearest Catherine; with thousands of things to say, yet apparently they were never to be together again. So, with smiles of most exquisite misery, and the laughing eye of utter despondency, Isabella rushed away.

Catherine found Mrs. Allen just returned from all the busy morning idleness, and was greeted with, "Well, my dear, here you are, and I hope you have had a pleasant airing?"

"Yes, ma'am, we could not have had a nicer day." As she spoke thus, Catherine glanced at the dear angels all around her with a measure of guilt, recalling infernal heat, horrid tedious ogre Mr. Thorpe, and the frightful *duck.*

"Mrs. Thorpe was vastly pleased at your all going."

"You have seen Mrs. Thorpe, then?"

"Yes, I went to the pump-room as soon as you were gone, and there I met her, and we had a great deal of talk together."

"Did you see anybody else of our acquaintance?"

"Yes; we agreed to take a turn in the Crescent, and there we met Mrs. Hughes, and Mr. and Miss Tilney walking with her."

"Did you indeed? And did they speak to you?"

"Yes, we walked along the Crescent together for half an hour. They seem very agreeable people. Miss Tilney was in a very pretty spotted muslin, and I fancy, she always dresses very handsomely. Mrs. Hughes talked a great deal about the family."

"And what did she tell you of them?"

"Oh! A vast deal indeed; she hardly talked of anything else. That is, also something about *treasure,* rumored to be in Bath. Upon my word, she says there is a secret hoard of immense riches fit for a king, hidden somewhere hereabouts—"

"Did she tell you what part of Gloucestershire they come from?"

"Yes, she did; but I cannot recollect now; all that talk of *secret clues* and treasure had me all agitated and inclined to quiz everyone passing by—But yes, they are very good people, and very rich. Mrs. Hughes and Mrs. Tilney were schoolfellows. Back then Mrs. Tilney was a Miss Drummond with a very large fortune. When she married, her father gave her twenty thousand pounds, and five hundred to buy wedding-clothes."

"And are Mr. and Mrs. Tilney in Bath?"

"Yes, I fancy they are, but I am not quite certain. Or, I have a notion they are both dead; at least the mother is. Yes, I am sure Mrs. Tilney is dead. Mrs. Hughes told me that Mr. Drummond gave his daughter very beautiful pearls on her wedding-day, and

Miss Tilney has them now, for they were to be hers when her mother died."

"And is Mr. Tilney, my dancing partner, the only son?"

"I cannot be quite positive about that, my dear; I have some idea he is. A very fine young man, and likely to do very well."

Catherine inquired no further; Mrs. Allen had no real intelligence to give. Catherine had missed a delightful meeting with both brother and sister.

Could she have foreseen such a circumstance, nothing should have persuaded her to go out with the others. She could only lament her ill luck, and think over what she had lost in exchange for a disagreeable drive with a gentleman ogre.

# Chapter 10

The Allens, Thorpes, and Morlands all met in the evening at the theatre. As Catherine and Isabella sat together, here was an opportunity for the latter to utter the many thousand things which had been collecting within her.

"Oh, heavens! My beloved Catherine, have I got you at last?" was her address on Catherine's entering the box and sitting by her. "Now, Mr. Morland," for he was close to her on the other side, "I shall not speak another word to you all the rest of the evening."

And then Isabella proceeded to regale Catherine with inquiry-styled commentary that neither begged nor allowed a response, but consisted of gusts of ice-cold air and screeching praise of her hairstyle, dress and appearance, insinuations that John Thorpe was besotted with her, and inquiries as to the whereabouts of the elusive Mr. Tilney who was obviously the most delightful man in the world and perfectly attached to Catherine, and where in the world was he, and could Catherine see him in the theatre?

"No," said Catherine, shivering, "he is not here; I cannot see him anywhere."

"Oh, horrid! Am I never to be acquainted with him? How do you like my gown?" And Isabella raised her voice in amazing modulations distinguished only by Catherine and the angels in the vicinity who rose up in startled flocks with great frequency whenever she reached a certain pitch.

"Do you know, I get so immoderately sick of Bath; your brother and I were agreeing this morning that, though it is vastly well to be here for a few weeks, we would not live here for millions."

"But what about the secret hidden treasure? Do you not want to say here long enough to discover it?" Catherine artlessly spoke her mind, while pulling her wrap closer about her for desperate warmth against the polar freezing atmosphere. "I thought that was the primary object of your visit here? That is, Mr. Thorpe mentioned that there were hidden clues—"

"Oh heavens! Whatever do you mean, dearest? However did you hear that? What has my very *silly* brother said to you?" Isabella's voice went from screeching to hollow and scraping, and her sallow countenance turned even more unhealthy and possibly bluish-green, while her yellow eyes glowed a veritable chartreuse.

"Oh! Well, I simply inquired what he was going on about at the ball the other day—I overheard Mr. Thorpe conversing *with himself,* and he admitted he was apparently very interested in discovering the whereabouts of this treasure; and for that matter James was too—"

"James! Goodness, how does James know about it? Could it be possible, has John told this silly *nonsense* to everyone in Bath?"

"Well, apparently so, for it is spoken of plainly on the streets, and Mrs. Allen mentioned it; I believe Mrs. Hughes talked about it the other day; or maybe not—"

Isabella looked as if she were about to collapse in a faint, or usc her rapidly fluttering fan as an implement of murder.

"Well!" she said after a few moments, seeming to recover. "Upon my word, this is indeed an interesting development. My *dearest* brother has been very loose with his tongue, and we must now make the best of it."

"I am sorry if it were intended to be a great secret," said Catherine. "But I truly could not help overhearing—"

"Oh, my darling, never mind, and it *is* perfectly dear of you to be intrigued with this. Indeed, now that you know about this silly little secret, we can speak of it freely, and—" here Isabella's voice rose into a particularly high screech— "perchance you can even help me discover the secret clues! Yes! We will have a splendid time!"

Catherine was somewhat relieved that she did not have to withhold her awareness of this particular subject from Isabella any longer, for she had felt dreadfully uncomfortable when Thorpe had divulged it under such dire threats to secrecy.

"Since it is not such a secret any longer," said Catherine, "maybe we will indeed discover it and decrypt the clues. Mr. Thorpe did say that it had something to do with *Udolpho* or Mrs. Radcliffe's other novels?"

Isabella's yellow eyes were lit with greedy excitement. "Why yes, dear Catherine! We—John and I that is, no one else knows about it—we believe the clues lie within the novels, possibly in the titles of the novels themselves! Remember I had given you a list of those titles that absolutely must be read? They are in fact not written by Mrs. Radcliffe (which John constantly forgets), but they are all the same kind of novel."

"Yes, I remember avidly! I adore *Udolpho* and all the horrid things described, the black veil—oh!"

Catherine stopped, remembering the angels' warning.

"So you *do* want to know what is on the other side of the black veil?" said Isabella with a crafty wicked gleam.

"No! That is, I think I can tell you, I am certain I can, but— oh! Do remind me of the titles again!" Catherine had enough presence of mind to redirect the question.

"Why yes, I do have them memorized at this point." Isabella was quickly engaged and began to recite: "They are: *The Mysteries of Udolpho, Castle of Wolfenbach, Clermont, Mysterious Warnings, Necromancer of the Black Forest, Midnight Bell, Orphan of the Rhine,* and *Horrid Mysteries.*"

"Thank you. Now let me think upon them a bit," said Catherine. "Perchance indeed I will come upon the unraveling of this—this *Udolpho Code.*"

"Ah, you are a wonder, my dearest Catherine, and what a splendid name for it too, 'The Udolpho Code!' It has such a fierce horrid ring to it!"

And Isabella—having delegated this fierce and immense responsibility for a labor of thought to her dearest friend— smiled, radiated a strong puff of freezing air, and then turned around and talked the rest of the evening to James.

Catherine's resolution of endeavouring to meet Miss Tilney again continued in full force the next morning. And till the usual moment of going to the pump-room, she felt some alarm from the dread of a second prevention.

But nothing of that kind occurred, no visitors appeared to delay them, and they all three set off in good time for the pump-room, where the ordinary course of events took place.

Mr. Allen, after drinking his glass of water, joined some gentlemen to talk over the politics of the day, compare the accounts of their newspapers, and remark upon the rumors of some kind of monstrous creature that had assailed *someone* on a drive, supposedly some gentlemen and ladies out on a pleasure excursion. There was mention of a certain infernal thing known as the Brighton Duck; and then it was concluded absolutely inconceivable, to have such an attack in broad daylight. Besides—a gentleman imparted additional facts—the creature seen had been at least the size of a bullock, or maybe even an elephant, or quite possibly larger. . . .

It was at such juncture that another gentleman suggested an even more inconceivable option—that the creature, airborne as it was, was none other than a *dragon;* likely an African dragon, or possibly hailing from the Australian continent. Obviously it was not native and had flown all across the ocean and arrived in haste here in Bath, possibly due to inclement weather, or—

And in that moment everyone had ceased wondering. For it came to all that the single best *reason* why a semi-legendary, nearly extinct, and altogether foreign creature such as a dragon might show up here in Bath was to uncover and appropriate a hoard of treasure.

*By Jove, that had to be it!* It was common speculation that dragons sniffed out treasure, collected it, and fervently guarded it whenever possible.

"Bah! I knew it; we have got us a hoard somewhere!" an elderly gentleman exclaimed, brandishing his walking stick. And immediately all political discussion expired and there was only talk of *secret clues.*

In the meantime, the ladies walked about together, noticing every new face, and almost every new bonnet in the room. The female part of the Thorpe family, attended by James Morland, appeared among the crowd in less than a quarter of an hour, and Catherine immediately took her usual place by the side of her ice-bearing friend. James, who was now in constant attendance, maintained a similar position on the other side.

Separating themselves from the rest of their party, they walked in that manner for some time. Catherine began to sense that being confined entirely to her friend and brother, gave her very little share in the notice of either. They were always engaged in some sentimental discussion or lively dispute, with such whispering voices and laughter (undeterred by the arctic cold that surrounded Miss Thorpe), that Catherine's opinion was not heeded, though frequently called for by one or the other.

At length however she was empowered to disengage herself from her friend, by the avowed necessity of speaking to Miss Tilney, whom she most joyfully saw just entering the room with Mrs. Hughes, and whom she instantly joined.

Miss Tilney met her with great civility, returned her advances with equal goodwill, and angels soared from one to the other with an abundance of brightness. They continued talking together as long as both parties remained in the room, speaking nothing new, yet with uncommon simplicity and truth, and without personal conceit.

"How well your brother dances!" Catherine artlessly exclaimed, surprising and amusing her companion.

"Henry!" she replied with a smile. "Yes, he does dance very well."

"He must have thought it very odd to hear me say I was engaged the other evening, when he saw me sitting down. But I really *had* been engaged the whole day to Mr. Thorpe."

Miss Tilney could only bow.

"You cannot think," added Catherine after a moment's silence, "how surprised I was to see him again. I felt so sure of his being quite gone away."

"When Henry had the pleasure of seeing you before, he was in Bath briefly, only to engage lodgings for us."

"That never occurred to me; and of course, not seeing him anywhere, I thought he must be gone."

And then Catherine and Miss Tilney shared a few more pleasant comments.

"He never comes to the pump-room, I suppose?"

"Yes, sometimes; but he has rid out this morning with my father."

Mrs. Hughes now joined them, and asked Miss Tilney if she was ready to go. "I hope I shall have the pleasure of seeing you again soon," said Catherine. "Shall you be at the cotillion ball tomorrow?"

"Perhaps we—Yes, I think we certainly shall."

"I am glad of it, for we shall all be there." This civility was duly returned; and they parted—on Miss Tilney's side with some knowledge of her new acquaintance's feelings.

Catherine went home very happy. The morning had answered all her hopes, and the evening of the following day was now the object of expectation. Thoughts of reading *Udolpho* or decrypting secret clues were farther from her mind than usual (though occasionally she did allow the *titles* of the other horrid novels to sliver into her imagination, whirl around briefly, and rise up as delightful specters to engage her).

What gown and what head-dress she should wear on the occasion became her chief concern. Catherine knew very well it was frivolous; and yet she lay awake ten minutes on Wednesday night debating between her spotted and her tamboured muslin, and only time prevented her buying a new one for the evening.

This would have been an error in judgment, from which someone of the opposite sex might have warned her—for man only can be aware of the insensibility of man towards a new gown. The heart of man is little affected by fashion.[18] Woman is finely attired for her own satisfaction alone.

She entered the rooms on Thursday evening with feelings very different from the Monday before. She had then been exulting in her engagement to Thorpe, and was now chiefly anxious to avoid him, lest he should engage her again—even if he *were* to mumble tantalizing hints about treasure and clues.

For though she dared not expect that Mr. Tilney should ask her a third time to dance, her wishes, hopes, and plans all centered in nothing less.

Every young lady may feel for my heroine in this critical moment, for every young lady has at some time or other known the same agitation. All have been, or believed themselves to be,

---

[18] Unless the gentleman is Beau Brummell or Oscar Wilde, in which case fashion moves the heart with Swiss precision.

in danger from the pursuit of someone *ogre-like* whom they wished to avoid. And all have been anxious for the attentions of someone *amiable* whom they wished to please.

As soon as they were joined by the Thorpes, Catherine's agony began. She fidgeted about and hid herself as much as possible from John Thorpe's *infernal* view, and, when he spoke to her, pretended not to hear him. The cotillions were over, the country-dancing beginning, and she saw nothing of the Tilneys.

Even the several angels she daringly sent on a mission of discovery soon flitted back to inform her that Mr. Tilney was not directly in sight. Catherine could only sigh in regret and gently thank the heavenly beings while coughing into her fan.

"Do not be frightened, my dear Catherine," whispered Isabella, "but I am really going to dance with your brother again. I declare positively it is quite shocking. You and John must keep us in view. Make haste, my dear creature, come! John is just walked off, something to do with *treasure*, I dare say, but he will be back in a moment."

Catherine had neither time nor inclination to answer. The others walked away, horrid John Thorpe was still in view, and she gave herself up for lost.

However, she kept her eyes intently fixed on her fan, making no eye contact with a certain brutish heat-radiating gentleman. It was folly in supposing that among such a crowd they should even meet with the Tilneys . . .

And yet she suddenly found herself addressed and again solicited to dance, by none other than Mr. Tilney himself!

With what sparkling eyes and ready motion she granted his request, and with how pleasing a flutter of heart she went with him to the set! To so narrowly escape John Thorpe, and to be asked—so immediately—by Mr. Tilney, as if he had sought her on purpose! Verily, life could not supply any greater felicity.

Scarcely had they worked themselves into the quiet possession of a place, however, when her attention was claimed by John Thorpe, who stood behind her, together with a blast of oven heat which caused even Mr. Tilney to blink momentarily.

"Heyday, Miss Morland!" bellowed Thorpe, in his gentlest voice. "What is the meaning of this? I thought you and I were to dance together."

"I wonder you should think so, for you never asked me."

"That is a good one, by Jove! I asked you as soon as I came into the room, and I was just going to ask you again, but when I turned round, you were gone! This is a cursed shabby trick! I only came for the sake of dancing with you—well, and a bit of talk as to those rare dratted Clues; we may be up to something there—and I firmly believe you were engaged to me ever since Monday. And here have I been telling all my acquaintance that I was going to dance with the prettiest girl in the room; and when they see you standing up with somebody else, they will quiz me famously."

"Oh, no; they will never think of me, after such a description as that."

"By heavens, if they do not, I will kick them out of the room for blockheads." But the compliment was lost on Catherine, who was beginning to feel the familiar moisture on her brow from the inferno. A lady nearest her in the set pointed worriedly at what looked to be the beginnings of a particularly well-formed mirage of the supper table, wavering in the middle of the dance floor (the original, of course, was set up many paces away, against the distant wall). . . .

Thorpe continued: "What chap have you there?"

Catherine satisfied his curiosity.

"Tilney," he repeated. "Hum—I do not know him. A good figure of a man; well put together. Does he want a horse? A friend of mine, Sam Fletcher, has got one to sell. A famous clever animal—only forty guineas. I had fifty minds to buy it myself—" And then Thorpe roared for several excruciating minutes about horses, hunting, more secret clues, and buying a house in Leicestershire next season.

But before he could weary Catherine's attention any longer, he was borne off by the resistless pressure of a long string of passing ladies. Heat dissipated, and at last bright angels could soar gently overhead without needing to fan their wings for ventilation.

Her partner now drew near, and said, "That gentleman would have put me out of patience, had he stayed with you half a minute longer. He has no business to withdraw the attention of my partner from me."

And as Catherine smiled radiantly at him with all her being, yet registering the smile merely with her eyes, Mr. Tilney continued: "We have entered into a contract of mutual agreeableness for the space of an evening, and all of it belongs solely to each other for that time. Nobody can fasten themselves on the notice of one, without injuring the rights of the other. I consider a country-dance as an emblem of marriage. Fidelity and complaisance are the principal duties of both. Those men who themselves do not choose to dance or marry, have no business with the partners or wives of their neighbours."

"But they are such very different things!" Catherine wanted to laugh and sing and jump in place, just hearing Mr. Tilney speak. Good thing they were already dancing, else she may have been moved to something rather more silly than was suitable for an heroic young lady watched over by a cadre of angels.

"—That you think they cannot be compared together."

"To be sure not. People that marry can never part, but must go and keep house together. People that dance only stand opposite each other in a long room for half an hour."

"And such is your definition of matrimony and dancing. You will allow, that in both, man has the advantage of choice, woman only the power of refusal. Both constitute an exclusive engagement formed for mutual advantage, till the moment of its dissolution. The duty of both is to give the other no cause for wishing themselves elsewhere. You will allow all this?"

"Yes, all this sounds very well; but still they are so very different. I cannot look upon them at all in the same light or concerning the same duties." Catherine mused lightly, watching angels perch all over Mr. Tilney's coat sleeves and hide in his cravat.

"In one respect, there certainly is a difference. In marriage, the man is supposed to provide for the support of the woman, the woman to make the home agreeable to the man. He is to purvey, and she is to smile. But in dancing, their duties are reversed. The agreeableness, the compliance are expected from him, while she furnishes the fan and the lavender water. That, I suppose, was the difference of duties which struck you, as rendering the conditions incapable of comparison."

"No, indeed, I never thought of that. Though—it seems somewhat unfair, does it not, to expect the woman to take on a lifelong duty of compliance, while the man merely supplies agreeable smiles for the duration of a dance—"

"Then I am quite at a loss. One alarming thing, however, I must observe. You disallow any similarity in the obligations. May I thence infer that your notions of the duties of dance are not so strict? Ought I fear that if the gentleman who spoke to you just now—or any other gentleman—were to return to address you—there would be nothing to restrain you from conversing with him as long as you choose?"

"Mr. Thorpe is such a very *particular* friend of my brother's, that if he talks to me, I must talk to him again. But there are hardly three young men in the room that I have any acquaintance with."

"And is that to be my only security? Alas, alas!"

"Nay, I am sure you cannot have a better; for if I do not know anybody, it is impossible for me to talk to them. Besides, I do not want to talk to anybody."

"Now you have given me a security worth having. I proceed with courage. Do you find Bath as agreeable as when I had the honour of making the inquiry before?"

"Yes, quite—more so, indeed."

"More so! Take care, or you will forget to be tired of it at the proper time: at the end of six weeks."

"I do not think I should be tired, if I were to stay here six months. There is so much that is *secret* and delightful to discover here!"

"Bath, compared with London, has little variety, and so everybody finds out every year. But now I am curious—whatever can be so secret and delightful?"

And Catherine told Mr. Tilney of the wonderful rumors of the secret hoard of hidden treasure, hidden right here, somewhere in Bath. Upon hearing the words "secret treasure," Mr. Tilney's expression became rather hard to describe. And then he started to laugh.

"So this is what everyone is talking about!" he said with a measure of amusement and not a little surprise. "Whether one goes to the Theatre, the Upper Rooms, to the pump-room, the dining halls, all one hears, it seems, are secret whisperings—and not of the usual gossip or amorous kind! And as to *why,* at last everything is clear as day. Now, Miss Morland, have you any notion to whom do we owe the honor of this fantastic rumor?"

"I have more than a notion," said Catherine, surprising Mr. Tilney yet again. "Indeed, I have the utmost certainty that it was all initiated by none other than the very gentleman you observed talking to me a few moments ago, Mr. Thorpe. He is the one searching most earnestly for various secret clues, as he calls them, believing them to be *encrypted* in some portions of Mrs. Radcliffe's novels. And he does speak somewhat boisterously and indeed rather loudly so that he is often overheard—"

"I see," said Mr. Tilney. "And pray, might you be so kind as to divulge to me your own mind? Do you give credence to this truly delightful rumor? Should it be taken in all seriousness, or is this but nonsensical stuff that one is best allowed to ignore?"

"Oh, no, I think it must be quite true!" Catherine exclaimed. "Why else would Mr. Thorpe be so intent on discovering all of it? I am even now wondering myself as to the hidden secrets in this place. Could there be clues, for example, in this very ballroom?"

"Why else indeed. I have no answer to that," replied Mr. Tilney, observing her with a very peculiar and close expression, and the barest hint of a smile.

"These horrid and wonderful clues, why they could be *anywhere!* Just observe the walls, sir! Note the shape of the room, the lovely parquet floor. Indeed, could the floor itself conceal a mystery underneath?"

"Good heavens, you really *do* find Bath wondrous in every detail, do you not?"

Catherine blushed, and the angels closest to her rose up to gently fan her cheeks. "Well, other people must judge for themselves, and those who go to London may think nothing of Bath. But I, who live in a small retired village in the country, find it a wonder even without secrets or hidden treasure. For here are a variety of amusements, of things to be seen and done all day long, which I can know nothing of at home."

"You are not fond of the country."

"Yes, I am. I have always lived there, and always been very happy. But one day in the country is exactly like another."

"But then you spend your time so much more rationally in the country."

"Do I?"

"Do you not? For example, do you at any point spend even a moment looking for nonexistent treasure or secret clues?"

"I have been, upon occasion, accused of things far worse . . . such as running around in the grass. And—and talking to myself, which is only *partially* true, because I often recite lessons out loud . . . for memorization purposes." Catherine decided to include that last point just in case Mr. Tilney had observed her muttering with certain angelic beings and was getting the wrong idea.

"Ah, well then. Very industrious. Whereas *here* you are in pursuit only of amusement all day long."

"And so I am at home—only I do not find so much of it. Walking here I see a variety of people in every street. There I can only call on Mrs. Allen."

Mr. Tilney was very much amused. "What a picture of intellectual poverty! However, the next time you call on Mrs. Allen in the country, you will be able to talk of all that you did here in Bath."

"Oh! Yes. I shall never be in want of something to talk of again. If I could but have Papa and Mamma, and the rest of them here, I should be too happy! James's coming (my eldest brother) is quite delightful—especially as it turns out that the very family we are just got so intimate with are his intimate friends already. Oh! Who can ever be tired of Bath?"

"Not those who bring such fresh feelings to it as you do. But to most of the frequenters of Bath, the honest relish of balls, plays, and everyday sights, is long past. It is why they suddenly need secrets and clues to keep them occupied."

Here, the demands of the dance overtook their conversation.

Soon after their reaching the bottom of the set, Catherine perceived herself to be earnestly regarded by a gentleman who stood among the lookers-on, immediately behind her partner.

The angels flew up in a turbulent cloud, as though to signal by their very maneuverings his *importance*.

He was a very handsome man, of a commanding aspect, great and regal in a manner difficult to describe. He was past the bloom, but not past the vigour of life. And with his dragon eye still directed towards her, she saw him address Mr. Tilney in a familiar whisper.

Confused by his notice, and blushing from the fear of something being wrong with her appearance, she turned away. But the gentleman retreated, and her partner, returning, said, "That gentleman knows your name, and you have a right to know his. It is General Tilney, my father."

Catherine's answer was only "Oh!"—but it was an "Oh!" expressing every attention to his words, and perfect reliance on their truth. With interest and admiration did she now observe the general, as he moved through the crowd, thinking, "How handsome a family they are!"

In chatting with Miss Tilney before the evening concluded, a new source of felicity arose. Catherine had never taken a country walk since her arrival in Bath. Miss Tilney, familiar with all the commonly frequented environs, spoke of them in terms that made Catherine only too eager. It was then proposed by the brother and sister that they should join in a morning walk.

"I shall like it," she cried, "beyond anything in the world; and let us not put it off—let us go tomorrow."

This was readily agreed to, providing it did not rain, which Catherine was sure it would not. At twelve o'clock, they were to call for her in Pulteney Street; and "Remember—twelve o'clock," was her parting speech to her new friend.

Her other, more established, and more arctic friend, Isabella, whose fidelity she had enjoyed a fortnight, Catherine scarcely saw at all during the evening. Instead, she cheerfully submitted to the wish of Mr. Allen to leave well before midnight and the *demon* hour, which took them rather early away.

Catherine's spirits danced within her, the angels danced above, and she danced in her chair all the way home.

# Chapter 11

The morrow brought a very sober-looking morning, the sun making only a few efforts to appear—yet, to Catherine, a most favourable portent. A bright morning so early in the year would turn to rain, but a cloudy one foretold improvement as the day advanced.

Catherine applied to Mr. Allen for confirmation of her hopes of sunshine, then to Mrs. Allen, whose opinion was a veritable echo of one's hopes.

At about eleven o'clock, however, there were a few specks of small rain upon the windows. "Oh! dear, I do believe it will be wet," said Catherine in a most desponding tone.

Mrs. Allen could only echo her.

Two dear angels, possibly Lawrence or maybe Terence, or Clarence—oh, for heaven's sake, Catherine had no idea—settled on the nearest windowsill and attempted to console her with their dulcet voices. "A rainy day is a lovely time for thought and for reading, dear child—though maybe not necessarily those frightful books—Why not instead peruse the writings of a certain Miss Austen?"

Catherine sighed, ignoring heavenly wisdom. "No walk for me today," she said wistfully. "But perhaps it may come to nothing, or it may hold up before twelve."

"Perhaps it may, but then, my dear, it will be so *dirty*." Mrs. Allen mused in genteel despair, foreseeing soggy muslin, ruined gowns and shoes.

"Oh! That will not signify; I never mind dirt."

"No," replied her friend very placidly, "I know you never mind dirt."

After a short pause, it became apparent that the rain only increased. Catherine stood watching it at a window.

"Oh! There are four umbrellas up already. How I hate the sight of an umbrella! It *was* such a nice-looking morning!"

"There will be very few people in the pump-room, if it rains all the morning," said Mrs. Allen. "I hope Mr. Allen will put on his greatcoat when he goes. A gentleman had informed him that a *greatcoat* might indeed be the key to some secret clue—Oh dear, no; maybe he was talking about a great boat? Or was it a castle moat?"

"Goodness, what is it?" said Catherine, for the words "secret" and "clue" and "castle" drew her immediate attention.

But Mrs. Allen has absolutely forgotten what it is she was saying.

Meanwhile the rain continued—fast, though not heavy. Catherine went every five minutes to the clock. Eventually the clock struck twelve, and it still rained.

"You will not be able to go, my dear."

"I do not quite despair yet. I shall not give it up till a quarter after twelve. This is just the time of day for it to clear up, and I do think it looks a little lighter. There, it is twenty minutes after twelve, and now I shall give it up entirely. Oh! That we had such weather here as they had at Udolpho, or at least in Tuscany and the south of France!—the night that poor St. Aubin died!—such beautiful weather!"

And resigned to a gloomy day and no walk, Catherine sat down with *Udolpho* and attempted to read. But instead of losing herself in the gothic terrors, the *titles* of the other seven horrid novels tumbled in her mind.

"Upon my word!" Catherine decided. "If there is to be no walk, and no *Udolpho,* then at least I might use this tedious time to think upon the secret clues and the mysteries of the treasure!"

And so Catherine recited the novels in her mind . . .

*Castle of Wolfenbach . . . Clermont . . . Mysterious Warnings . . . Necromancer of the Black Forest . . . Midnight Bell . . . Orphan of the Rhine . . . Horrid Mysteries . . .*

Oh, criminy! What dark occult impossibilities were hidden in this Udolpho Code?

Maybe it had something to do with the first letters of each title? As in, a clever cryptic, formed as the result of considering only the capitals?

*"Perhaps,"* mused Catherine, *"if one is to take the capital letters of 'Castle of Wolfenbach', it spells the word 'cow.' Hence, could it be a Clue, and is a bovine involved? Possibly even an entire herd of them?"*

But then it occurred to her, maybe the titles themselves presented the secrets in the very images they formed, such as "Necromancer of the Black Forest"—who was surely none other than a wicked magician hiding away in a dark wooden glade, possibly masked and wearing a long black *greatcoat . . .* Possibly even ogre-shaped, and belching odious heat, not unlike a certain gentleman she knew . . .

*Oh dear! Could it be—Was John Thorpe* himself *a Clue?*

At half past twelve—when Catherine's anxious attention to the weather had been replaced with anxious muddled thoughts and feverish decrypting of horrid secrets—the sky began voluntarily to clear.

A gleam of sunshine took her quite by surprise. She looked round; the clouds were parting, and she instantly returned to the window. Ten minutes more made it certain that a bright afternoon would succeed. But whether Catherine might still expect her friends, or whether there had been too much rain for Miss Tilney to venture, was still a question.

It was too dirty for Mrs. Allen to accompany her husband to the pump-room. He accordingly set off by himself. Catherine had barely watched him down the street when she noticed the approach of the same two open carriages, containing the same three people that had surprised her a few mornings back.

"Isabella, my brother, and Mr. Thorpe, I declare!" exclaimed Catherine, unsuitably reminded of a certain encounter with a horrid flying *duck.* At present, thankfully, two angels fluttered overhead. "They are coming for me perhaps—but I shall not go—I *cannot,* indeed! For, Miss Tilney may still call."

Mrs. Allen echoed placid agreement.

But then the weather in the room changed to the Tropics, then the African Continent, all in a span of a few breaths. John Thorpe was soon with them—and his voice was with them yet sooner, for on the stairs he was bellowing out to Miss Morland to be quick.

"Make haste! Make haste!" He threw open the door. "Put on your hat this moment—there is no time to be lost—we are going to Bristol. How d'ye do, Mrs. Allen?"

"To Bristol! Is not that a great way off? Regardless, I cannot go with you today, because I am engaged; I expect some friends every moment." Catherine spoke bravely.

This was of course vehemently talked down as no reason at all. Mrs. Allen was called on to second him, and under the onslaught of such heat—both tangible and metaphoric—she wilted—both literally and figuratively.

The two others walked in, to give their assistance—and to return to this spot of nature a proper temperate climate.

"My sweetest Catherine, is not this delightful? We shall have a most heavenly drive!" screeched and cooed Isabella. "You are to thank your brother and me for the scheme, conceived at breakfast-time. We should have been off two hours ago if it had not been for this detestable rain. But it does not signify! Oh! I am in such ecstasies at the thoughts of a little country air and quiet! So much better than going to the Lower Rooms. We shall drive directly to Clifton and dine there; and then, on to Kingsweston."

"I doubt our being able to do so much," said Morland.

"You croaking fellow!" roared Thorpe. "We shall be able to do ten times more. Kingsweston! Aye, and Blaize Castle too, and anything else we can hear of, maybe even London itself and back! But here is your sister, says she will not go."

"Blaize Castle!" cried Catherine. "What is *that?*"

"The finest place in England—worth going fifty miles at any time to see."

"What, is it really a castle, an old castle?"

"The oldest in the kingdom. Maybe the entire Europe. Oh, all right, the civilized world, blast it!"

"But is it like what one reads of?"

"Exactly—the very same. Mrs. Radcliffe must have copied it word for word. Aye, letter to letter."

"But now really—are there towers and long galleries?"

"By dozens. Or twice that. All in all, a reeking bucket of secret Clues, ready to be popped."

"Then I should like to see it; but Oh! I cannot—I cannot go.

"Not go! My beloved creature, what do you mean?" interrupted Isabella in a delicate screech, training her sickly yellow eyes and an icy breath upon her dearest friend.

"I cannot go, because—" Catherine looked down, fearful of Isabella's treacle smile—"I expect Miss Tilney and her brother to call on me to take a country walk. They promised to come at twelve, only it rained. Now, I imagine they will be here soon."

"Not they indeed," growled Thorpe; "for, as we turned into Broad Street, I saw them—does he not drive a phaeton with bright chestnuts?"

"I do not know indeed."

"Yes, I know he does; I saw him. You are talking of the man you danced with last night, are not you?"

"Yes."

*The angels around Catherine signaled warning, but she knew not at what.*

"Well, I saw him at that moment turn up the Lansdown Road, driving a smart-looking girl."

"It is very odd! But I suppose they thought it would be too dirty for a walk."

"And well they might, for I never saw so much dirt in my life. Walk! You could no more walk than you could fly! It is ankle-deep everywhere. And some places, up to the waist."

Isabella corroborated it: "My dearest Catherine, you cannot form an idea of the dirt; come, you cannot refuse going now."

Catherine was truly torn . . .

"I should like to see the castle; but may we go all over it? May we go up every staircase, and into every suite of rooms?"

"Yes, yes, every hole and corner, and dig around aplenty."

"But what if they are only out for an hour, and then call?"

"Nay, there is no danger of that—I heard Tilney hallooing to a passerby, that they were going as far as Wick Rocks."

"Then—I suppose I will. Shall I go, Mrs. Allen?"

"Just as you please, my dear," was Mrs. Allen's echo reply.

And in two minutes they were off.

Catherine's feelings, as she got into the carriage, were in a very unsettled state; divided between hope and regret.

She could not think the Tilneys had acted quite well by her, in so readily giving up their engagement, without notice. It was now but an hour later, and—in spite of what she had heard of the prodigious accumulation of amazing dirt in the course of that entirely miraculous meteorological hour—she could not help observing they might have gone walking with very little inconvenience.

To feel herself slighted by them was very painful.

On the other hand, the delight of exploring an edifice like Udolpho—as her fancy represented Blaize Castle to be—was sufficient compensation for almost anything.

And thus, Catherine could not help but muse out loud, continuing the exciting mental calisthenics of earlier that morning, when gloom and rain had revealed in her a considerable sleuthing talent.

"I was pondering earlier upon the mysteries of Mrs. Radcliffe and other horrid novel authors, and what might constitute the Udolpho Code," she said. And she immediately received the full attention of the Thorpes and her brother.

"It seems to me," she continued, "that, as one possible solution, the various novels are to be considered as puzzles, by taking the first capital letter of each word in the title, and then arranging them, or perhaps *rearranging* them as needed to form other words! And the words themselves are grand Clues as to the secret location of the hidden treasure."

"Oh, is that so? Hum!" said Thorpe, thinking with such concentration that he almost released the reins of the horse. "How would that be then, exactly?"

"Well," said Catherine. "It came to me that if one were to take the first letters of 'Castle of Wolfenbach', it spells 'cow.'"

"Cow! By Jove, what brilliant thinking, Miss Morland! 'Tis so! A cow, indeed!"

"But what does it *mean?*" hissed Isabella, serpentine-sweet.

"Well, I venture it could be a cow one might look for to obtain a meaningful clue. Maybe a field of cows, grazing gently, and one might see a splendid landmark; or one might be required to dig in a spot where a cow—"

"—Where a cow made its dump!" finished Thorpe with a roar. "Exactly so! My deduction exactly! Aye, what a fine mind you have indeed, much like mine, I dare say!"

"*Oh dear . . .*" Clarence sighed into Catherine's right ear.

Catherine began to cough.

"But it is not all," she said, recovering. "There is another possible method of decrypting the code—the novel titles themselves could be descriptive clues to things, for example, 'Midnight Bell' may indicate an actual mysterious bell somewhere in Bath that either rings at a certain very *particular* time or is located *near* the treasure, or is a clue leading *to* it—"

"That's it! The bell tower! Blazes, yes! It could be the place to go look, first!" Thorpe was at this point roaring so loudly that on the sidewalk passerby turned to look in their direction.

"Now, some of these are more obscure than others," said Catherine. "Indeed, I am not entirely certain of 'Clermont'—"

"Clermont? Nonsense, I am certain as all Hades!" interrupted Thorpe. "It is none other than Mrs. Clermont and her daughters! You know the family, Isabella, father's an older daft fellow; daughters are passable—"

"There is—uhm—'Necromancer of the Black Forest'—" James dared to join the decryption discourse for the first time.

"N-O-T-B-F," muttered Isabella in a modulating voice, pronouncing each capital letter in a higher tone.

"N-O-T-B-F!" repeated Thorpe, bellowing in return. "That one is easy! The easiest ever! NOT BF! Who is BF? That's 'Not Beatrice Foster!' Lady Beatrice Foster it is!"

"But it is *'not'*," said Catherine.

"Well of course it is *not,* that is—it *is,* I mean, blazes!"

"But if it is *not* Lady Foster, then why mention her in a Clue in the first place?"

"Aha, but I have it all here, Miss Morland!—the Clue clearly states that it is not Beatrice Foster because it simply has to be in fact *her brother,* the baronet! The Clue points at him, verily screams! I am willing to bet fifty pounds on it!"

"Well, I dare say it is possible."

"Not just possible, but very likely, and a firm guarantee! As plain as day! Absolutely sterling to the pound!"

"Then how would you solve 'Orphan of the Rhine'?"

"Same exact way! Not some poor beady-eyed waif, I say, but O-O-T-R—"

"Wait, I have it! You must move the letters around for this one," Catherine interrupted him in turn. "Surely it must then be 'R-O-O-T'?"

"Yes! A *root* vegetable! Verily a potato, Miss Morland!"

"And why not a carrot or a turnip?" considered Isabella.

"Who says not?" Thorpe roared. "It is clearly all root vegetables! Every one of them, roots! Potatoes, turnips, carrots, rutabagas, horseradishes! What else is there, help me out, Bella, Morland, Miss Morland!"

At that point the conversation deteriorated even further into monosyllabic spellings out of various combinations of arcane first letters, with Thorpe yelling out new possible Clues every few seconds and waving his whip about with one hand, while narrowly missing the horse and his own sister at least upon two occasions.

They passed briskly down Pulteney Street, and through Laura Place, without ceasing this exchange. Thorpe talked to his fair companion, his sister, her partner, even his horse. And Catherine eventually ceased listening and meditated, by turns, on broken promises and broken arches, phaetons and false hangings, Tilneys and trap-doors. Clues of her own—marvelous, arcane, perfectly sensible yet utterly romantic—danced in her imagination to shape her own private version of the true Udolpho Code. . . .

As they entered Argyle Buildings, however, she was roused by this address from her companion, "Who is that girl who looked at you so hard as she went by?"

"Who? Where?"

"On the right—she is almost out of sight now."

Catherine looked round and saw Miss Tilney leaning on her brother's arm, walking slowly down the street. She saw them both looking back at her!

"Stop, stop, Mr. Thorpe," she impatiently cried; "it is Miss Tilney! How could you tell me they were gone? Stop, stop, I will get out this moment and go to them."

But Thorpe only lashed his horse into a brisker trot. The Tilneys, who had soon ceased to look after her, were in a moment out of sight round the corner of Laura Place.

During the length of several streets, Catherine entreated him continually to stop. But Mr. Thorpe only laughed in a subdued roar, smacked his whip, encouraged his horse, made odd noises even for an ogre, and drove on. Catherine, angry and vexed, had no means of escape, and was obliged to give up.

Her reproaches, however, were not spared. "How *could* you deceive me so, Mr. Thorpe? How could you say that you saw them driving up the Lansdown Road? I would not have had it happen so for the world. They must think it so strange, so rude of me! To go by them, too, without saying a word! You do not know how vexed I am; I shall have no pleasure at Clifton, nor in anything else. I would ten thousand times rather get out and walk back to them! How could you say you saw them driving out in a phaeton?"

Thorpe defended himself very stoutly, declared he had never seen two men so much alike in his life.

But now their drive was entirely disagreeable. Catherine listened reluctantly, and her replies were short. Blaize Castle remained her only comfort towards which she still looked with pleasure. Though, she would willingly have given up all its imagined delights—a long suite of lofty rooms, the remains of magnificent furniture, for many years deserted; narrow, winding vaults; low, grated doors; even having their *only* lamp extinguished by a sudden gust of wind, and being left in total darkness—eschew all of this to regain the Tilneys' approbation.

In the meanwhile, they proceeded on their journey, and were within view of the town of Keynsham, when a halloo from Morland behind them, made Thorpe pull up.

Morland said, "We had better go back, Thorpe; it is too late to go on today; your sister thinks so as well. We have been exactly an hour coming from Pulteney Street, little more than seven miles, with at least eight more to go. We set out too late. Best to put it off till another day, and turn round."

"It is all one to me," bellowed Thorpe rather angrily; and instantly turning his horse, they were on their way back to Bath.

"If your brother had not got such a d——d beast to drive," said he in a blast of heat, "we might have done it very well. My horse would have trotted to Clifton within the hour. Morland is a fool for not keeping a horse and gig of his own."

"No, he is not," said Catherine warmly (while the angels rejoiced), "for I am sure he could not afford it."

"And why cannot he afford it?"

"Because he has not money enough."

"And whose fault is that?"

"Nobody's, that I know of."

Thorpe then said something in his usual loud, incoherent roar, about its being a d—— thing to be miserly; *that if people who rolled in money could not afford things, he did not know who could*, which Catherine did not even endeavour to understand. Indeed, she was beginning to wonder if he were rather out of his mind from all the preoccupation with *treasure* and henceforth, money and costs and being able to afford or not afford things—

Furthermore, deprived of her only remaining consolation, Blaize Castle, Catherine was even less disposed to be agreeable. And they returned to Pulteney Street without her speaking twenty words.

As she entered the house, the footman told her that a gentleman and lady had called and inquired for her a few minutes after her setting off. When he told them she was gone out with Mr. Thorpe, the lady had asked whether any message had been left for her. On his saying no, she did not leave a card.

Pondering over these heart-rending tidings, Catherine walked slowly upstairs, accompanied by tender consolatory firefly lights of the angels. She was met by Mr. Allen, who said, "I am glad your brother had the sense to have you all come back. It was a strange, wild scheme."

They all spent the evening together at Thorpe's. Catherine was disturbed and out of spirits.

But Isabella seemed to find private partnership with Morland a very good equivalent for the quiet country air of Clifton, and satisfaction in not being at the Lower Rooms.

"How I pity the poor creatures that are going there! How glad I am that I am not amongst them! I wonder whether it will be a full ball or not!" And Isabella went on delightfully to charge James with longing to attend—no one here was preventing him!—in the shrillest and yet most dulcet tones imaginable.

Catherine could have accused Isabella in turn, of being wanting in sympathies towards herself and her sorrows. But then, oh dear, whatever *was* she expecting? This was a heartless naphil!

Why was it so easy for Catherine to forget all the time? Prehaps it was indeed a supernaturally difficult matter to maintain this clear true *vision*, to unwaveringly continue to *see* Isabella's true inner self. Was Catherine faltering in her sight? Or was she simply unwilling to continuously think ill of someone she knew as a friend, for the first time in her life?

"Oh, do not be so dull, my dearest creature," Isabella whispered meanwhile. "You will quite break my heart. It was amazingly shocking, to be sure; but the Tilneys were *entirely* to blame. Why were not they more punctual? It was dirty, but I am sure John and I should not have minded it for the sake of dear friends. Oh! Good heavens! What a delightful hand of cards you have got!"

Catherine was out and away from their residence well before midnight, once again cleverly avoiding any horrible encounter with not one but two nephilim guardian demons.

But at Pulteney Street, the only thing awaiting our heroine was the sleepless couch—the true heroine's portion—and a pillow strewed with thorns and, possibly, wet with tears . . .

Oh, for heaven's sake! In truth, there were no thorns, but a goodly number of angels who perched in the curtains and on the dresser, and softly sang our entirely tearless heroine into a sound sleep.

# Chapter 12

"Mrs. Allen," said Catherine the next morning, "will there be any harm in my calling on Miss Tilney today? I shall not be easy till I have explained everything."

"Go, by all means, my dear; only put on a white gown; Miss Tilney always wears white. Also, Mrs. Hughes says that *white muslin* is also a clue to that hidden treasure—at least according to Lady Raleigh, who was informed by Mrs. Sands—"

Catherine cheerfully complied, and being properly equipped, hurried to be at the pump-room, in order to ascertain General Tilney's lodgings.

To Milsom Street she was directed, and hastened away with an eager beating heart to pay her visit, explain her conduct, and be forgiven. She practically flew through the church-yard, resolutely turning away her eyes so as not to be obliged to see her beloved Isabella and her dear family, freezing a shop nearby.

She reached the house without any impediment, looked at the number, knocked at the door, and inquired for Miss Tilney.

She was told Miss Tilney *might* be at home. Would she be pleased to send up her name? She gave her card.

In a few minutes the servant returned, with a strange look and said he had been mistaken—Miss Tilney was out.

Catherine left, with a blush of mortification. She felt almost certain that Miss Tilney *was* at home, but too much offended to admit her.

As she retired down the street, she looked back at the house. And then she saw Miss Tilney herself issuing from the door, followed by a gentleman, whom Catherine believed to be her father. They turned up towards Edgar's Buildings.

Catherine, in deep mortification, proceeded on her way. She was almost angry herself at such incivility; but checked her resentment, aware only of her own profound ignorance of the laws of worldly politeness.

*"Take heart, dear child! Courage!"* the angels whispered.

Dejected and humbled, she considered not going with the others to the theatre that night, but soon recollected there was no real excuse for staying at home. And, besides, it was a play she wanted very much to see.

To the theatre accordingly they all went. No Tilneys appeared to plague or please her, only crowds of theatre-goers all speaking rather volubly of *secret clues* and *hidden treasure.*

*Oh dear,* thought Catherine.

In addition, she feared that, amongst the many perfections of the Tilney family, a fondness for plays was not to be ranked. Perhaps it was because they were used to the finer performances of the London stage, which—on Isabella's authority—rendered everything else of the kind "quite horrid"—though, not in the delightful Udolpho sense.

Catherine was not deceived in her own expectation of pleasure. Indeed, the theatre was a wonder, and oh! there were so many angels! As thousands of golden candle flames they floated in the dark expanse over everyone's heads, even after the lights dimmed—a heavenly wonder to which no one but Catherine was witness. And the comedy itself so well suspended her care that no one, observing her during the first four acts, would have supposed she had any wretchedness about her.

On the beginning of the fifth, however, the sudden view of Mr. Henry Tilney and his father, joining a party in the opposite box, recalled her to anxiety and distress.

The stage could no longer excite genuine merriment or keep her whole attention. Every other look was directed towards the opposite box. For the space of two entire scenes, she thus watched Henry Tilney, without being once able to catch his eye.

No longer could he be suspected of indifference for a play. His notice was never withdrawn from the stage during two whole scenes.

At length, however, he did look towards her, and he bowed—but such a bow! No smile, no continued observance attended it. His eyes immediately turned away.

Catherine was restlessly miserable. She almost ran to his box and forced him to hear her out. Feelings rather un-heroic possessed her. Instead of considering her own dignity injured, proudly resolving to show her resentment, leaving him to seek *her,* and meanwhile flirting with somebody else—she took upon herself all the shame of apparent misconduct, eager only for an opportunity to offer an explanation.

The play concluded—the curtain fell—Henry Tilney was no longer to be seen where he had hitherto sat. But his father remained.

Perhaps he might be now coming round to their box? Good heavens! She was right! In a few minutes he appeared, and, making his way through the thinning rows, spoke with calm politeness to Mrs. Allen and her young friend.

Not with such calmness was he answered by the latter: "Oh! Mr. Tilney, I have been quite wild to speak to you, and make my apologies. You must have thought me so rude! But indeed it was not my own fault, was it, Mrs. Allen? Did not they tell me that Mr. Tilney and his sister were gone out in a phaeton together? And then what could I do? But I had ten thousand times rather have been with you; now had not I, Mrs. Allen?"

"My dear, you tumble my gown," was Mrs. Allen's reply.

Her assurance, however, was not thrown away. It brought a more cordial, natural smile into his countenance, and Mr. Tilney replied in a tone which retained only a little affected reserve: "We were much obliged to you at any rate for wishing us a pleasant walk after our passing you in Argyle Street: you were so kind as to look back on purpose."

"But indeed I *did not* wish you a pleasant walk! I never thought of such a thing; but I begged Mr. Thorpe so earnestly to *stop!* I called out to him as soon as I saw you! And, if Mr. Thorpe would only have *stopped,* I would have jumped out and run after you!"

Is there a Henry in the world who could be insensible to such a declaration? Is there indeed an angel who could be?

Henry Tilney at least was not. With a yet sweeter smile, he said everything that need be said of his sister's concern, regret, and dependence on Catherine's honour.

"Oh! Do not say Miss Tilney was not angry," cried Catherine, "because I *know* she was; for she would not see me this morning when I called. I saw her walk out of the house the next minute after my leaving it! I was hurt, but I was not affronted. Perhaps you did not know I had been there."

"I was not within at the time. But I heard of it from Eleanor, and she has been wishing ever since to see you, to explain. It was nothing more than that my father made a point of her being denied—they were just preparing to walk out, and he was hurried for time. That was all, I assure you. She was very much vexed, and meant to make her apology as soon as possible."

Catherine's mind was greatly eased by this information. Yet she could not help the following artless question, rather distressing to the gentleman: "But, Mr. Tilney, why were *you* less generous than your sister? If she felt such confidence in my good intentions, and could suppose it to be only a mistake, why should you be so ready to take offence?"

"Me! I take offence!"

"Nay, I am sure by your look, when you came into the box, you were angry."

"I angry! I could have no right."

"Well, nobody would have thought you had no right who saw your face."

He replied by asking her to make room for him, and talking of the play. Their angels radiantly mingled overhead, then settled about gently among the folds of their clothing.

Mr. Tilney remained with them some time, and was only too agreeable for Catherine to be contented when he went away. Before they parted, however, it was agreed that their missed walk should be taken as soon as possible. And, setting aside the misery of his quitting their box, she was left one of the happiest creatures in the world.

While still talking to Mr. Tilney, she had observed with some surprise that John Thorpe—who was never in the same part of the house for ten minutes together, and was heard bellowing all about the theatre, either about "little wee Orphans of the Rhine," or "in the Rye," or herds of cows, or possibly cow *bells* around Mrs. *Clermont's* neck, in some *midnight black forest,* or possibly in a *black dress*—was now engaged in conversation with General Tilney.

Catherine felt more than surprise when she thought herself the object of their attention and discourse. What could they have to say of her?

She feared General Tilney did not like her appearance. Surely it was implied in his preventing her admittance to his daughter, rather than postpone his own walk a few minutes.

"How came Mr. Thorpe to know your father?" was her anxious inquiry, as she pointed them out to her companion.

Mr. Tilney knew nothing about it. But his father, like every military man, had a very large acquaintance, and that included, no doubt, some lumbering *infernal* gentlemen.

When the entertainment was over, Thorpe came to scorch the premises in their vicinity and assist them in getting out, causing at least two mirages to appear in the hallway—one of a kneeling footman, and the other of a portly dowager with tall ostrich feathers in her hat—both of which elicited gasps from occasional persons walking around and once *through* them, until the hot air was sufficiently dissipated.

Catherine was the immediate object of his gallantry. And, while they waited in the sweltering lobby for a chair, he prevented her unvoiced inquiry by asking, in a consequential manner, whether she had *seen him* talking with General Tilney: "He is a fine old fellow, upon my soul! Stout as a dragon, active—looks as young as his son. I have a great regard for him, I assure you: a gentleman-like, good sort of fellow as ever lived."

"But how came you to know him?" asked Catherine, fanning herself as rapidly as possible in the usual heat.

"Know him! There are few people much about town that I do not know. Indeed, likely there are none! I have met him forever at the Bedford; and I knew his face again today the moment he came into the billiard-room. One of the best players we have, by the by; and we had a little touch together, though I was almost *afraid of him* at first: the odds were five to four against me; and, if I had not made one of the cleanest strokes that perhaps ever was made in this world—" Thorpe rambled on at length about billiards, then concluded, "However, I did beat him. A very fine fellow; as rich as Croesus. I should like to dine with him; I dare say he gives famous dinners. But what do you think we have been talking of? *You.* Yes, by heavens! And the general thinks you the finest girl in Bath."

"Oh! Nonsense! How can you say so?"

"And what do you think I said?"—lowering his voice—"well done, general, said I; I am quite of your mind."

Here Catherine, who was much less gratified by his admiration than by General Tilney's, was not sorry to be called away by Mr. Allen. It was getting rather late, dangerously close to midnight, and she truly did not want to meet Thorpe's demon.

Thorpe, however, would see her to her chair, and, till she entered it, continued roaring the same kind of delicate mutton flattery, in spite of her entreating him to desist.

That General Tilney, instead of disliking, should admire her, was very delightful. And she joyfully thought that there was not one of the family whom she need now fear to meet.

The evening had done much more for her than expected.

Unfortunately in that moment from the distant bell tower sounded the *Midnight Bell*.

And there was Thorpe's *demon,* solidifying from his lumbering shadow like an evil genie detaching itself from a potbellied bottle. . . .

Standing up, it leered at her—twice the size of Isabella's own fiend, and twice as putrid. Its horns were bullish; its eyes were crimson-red infernal coals, burning with such heat that Catherine might have had to take a step back, had she not been safely ensconced in the chair, about to embark home.

The demon muttered something filthy in her wake. Catherine shuddered—for once she was truly glad that her loyal angels never for a moment left her side.

And then she glanced back at the demon and, without it seeing her, stuck out her tongue.

# Chapter 13

Monday, Tuesday, Wednesday, Thursday, Friday, and Saturday have now passed in review before the esteemed Reader, together with amazing events. Sunday only now remains to be described, to close the week.

The Clifton scheme had been deferred, not relinquished, and that afternoon, it was brought forward again. Isabella's iceberg heart was obviously set on going, and James, entirely besotted with the beauteous harpy, was anxious to please her. It was agreed that on the following morning they were to set off very early, in order to be at home in good time.

The affair thus determined, and Thorpe's fiery approbation secured, Catherine only remained to be apprised of it.

She had left them for a few minutes to speak to Miss Tilney. In that interval the dastardly plan was completed, and as soon as she returned, her agreement was demanded.

But instead of gay[19] acquiescence Catherine looked grave, was very sorry, but could not go. She had a firm engagement with Miss Tilney to take their proposed walk tomorrow—it was quite determined, and she would not, upon any account, retract.

---

[19] Oh dear! This is not in any way intended to remind the gentle reader of a certain Oscar Wilde, but rather of a happy butterfly, fluttering in the breeze.

*"Well done, Catherine!"* cried angels in both of her ears.

But oh, what an outcry issued forth from both the Thorpes! They must go to Clifton tomorrow, they would not go without her, it would be nothing to put off a mere walk for one day longer, and they would not hear of a refusal.

Catherine was distressed, but not subdued. "Do not urge me, Isabella. I am engaged to Miss Tilney. I cannot go."

This availed nothing. The same arguments assailed her again, like freezing hail beating against a shuttered window, followed by a blast of desert heat. "So easy to tell Miss Tilney that you had just been reminded of a prior engagement! Do put off the walk till Tuesday!"

"No," said Catherine.

"Yes!" screeched Isabella.

"No!" repeated Catherine, for the hundredth time.

*"Beware, stay strong!"* whispered the angels.

"By all galloping horses of Solomon! Yes!" roared Thorpe.

The air in the vicinity filled with such a charge of electricity—first from heat then from lashing cold—that Catherine wanted to run from the room. James Morland looked on dumbfounded as hissing droplets of water started to rain from the parlor ceiling, and muttered about Bath and its unbelievable *indoor* weather, no wonder its dratted name.

Isabella switched from yellow-eyed attacks to whining to weeping and cajoling, to attempts to hug and kiss her dearest best friend to convince her.

But all in vain; Catherine felt herself to be in the right, and was not to be influenced.

Isabella then tried another method. She reproached her with having more affection for Miss Tilney, than for her best and oldest friends. "I cannot help being jealous, Catherine, when I see myself slighted for strangers, I, who love you so excessively! To see myself supplanted in your friendship by strangers cuts me to the quick! These Tilneys!"

Catherine thought this reproach equally strange and unkind. Clearly, Isabella was not only a frightful unnatural scarecrow of a creature, with horrid glowing eyes, sallow sunken skin, and a putrid demon guardian, to boot—she was also *ungenerous* and *selfish*, thinking only of her own gratification.

These painful and reasonable ideas crossed Catherine's mind, though she said nothing.

Isabella, in the meanwhile, held her handkerchief to her eyes. Morland, miserable at such a sight, could not help saying, "Nay, Catherine, you cannot refuse. The sacrifice is not much; and to oblige such a friend—quite unkind, if you still refuse."

This was the first time her brother openly sided against her. Unhappy, Catherine proposed a compromise. If they would only put off their scheme till Tuesday, she could go with them, and everybody might then be satisfied.

But "No, no, no!" was the immediate answer, followed by inane, decidedly selfish reasons and some rapidly cooling dew.

Catherine was sorry, but adamant. A short silence ensued, broken by Isabella, who, in a voice of arctic-cold resentment, said, "Very well, then there is an end of the party. If Catherine does not go, I cannot. I cannot be the only woman. I would not, upon any account in the world, do so improper a thing."

"Catherine, you must go," begged James.

"But why cannot Mr. Thorpe drive one of his other sisters?"

"Thank ye," bellowed Thorpe, "but I did *not* come to Bath to drive my sisters about, and look like a fool. No, if you do not go, d—— me if I do. I only go for the sake of driving you."

"That is a compliment which gives me no pleasure." But her words were lost on Thorpe, who had turned abruptly away and lumbered off somewhere.

The three others still continued together, walking in silence, then with supplications, or reproaches. Catherine's extra-numbed and now entirely senseless arm was still linked within Isabella's, though their hearts were at war.

"I did not think you could be so obstinate, Catherine," said James; "you were once not so hard to persuade, but the kindest, best-tempered of my sisters."

"I hope I am not less so now," she replied, very feelingly; "but indeed I cannot go. I am doing what I believe to be right."

And the way around her seemed brighter indeed, from the heightened radiance coming from the many blazing angels. . . .

"I suspect," hissed Isabella, "there is no great struggle."

Catherine's heart swelled. She drew away her arm, and Isabella made no opposition. Thus passed a long ten minutes, till they were again joined by Thorpe, who, coming to them with a gayer look, said, "Well, I have settled the matter, and now we may all go tomorrow with a safe conscience. I have been to Miss Tilney, and made your excuses."

"*What?* You have not!" cried Catherine.

"I have, upon my soul. Left her this moment. Told her you had sent me to say that, having just recollected a prior engagement of going to Clifton with us tomorrow, you could not have the pleasure of walking with her till Tuesday. She said very well, Tuesday was just as convenient to her; so there is an end of all our difficulties. A pretty good thought of mine—hey?"

Isabella's frightful countenance was once more all honey smiles and good humour, and James too looked happy again.

"Heavenly indeed! Now, my sweet Catherine, all our distresses are over and we shall have a most delightful party."

"This will not do," said Catherine; "I cannot submit to this. I must run after Miss Tilney directly and set her right."

Isabella, however, caught hold of one hand, Thorpe of the other—so that Catherine was simultaneously freezing and burning; *oh, how exceedingly tiresome this was becoming!*—and remonstrances poured in from all three. Even James was quite angry, not to mention, starting to freeze around the forehead that had broken out in sweat just minutes earlier. Surely, if Miss

Tilney herself said that Tuesday would suit her as well, it was quite absurd to make any further objection.

"*I do not care.* Mr. Thorpe had no business to invent any such message. If I had thought it right to put it off, I could have spoken to Miss Tilney myself. This is only doing it in a ruder way. Now, let me go, Mr. Thorpe! Isabella, *do not* hold me."

The two nephilim momentarily stared at her in veritable amazement. *Then everything started all over again.*

Catherine wanted to beat her head against a hard *surface,* and, short of a hard surface, visualized a hard *object* she might brandish at these two. Something hefty, such as a couple of Mrs. Radcliffe's novels tied together into a brick ... She even wistfully thought of a certain monstrous *duck.*

Thorpe told her it would be in vain to go after the Tilneys; they were turning the corner into Brock Street when he had overtaken them, and were at home by this time.

"Then I will go after them," said Catherine; "wherever they are, I will go after them. If I could not be *persuaded* into doing what I thought wrong, I never will be *tricked* into it."

And with these words she broke away and hurried off.

Thorpe would have darted after her, but Morland held him.

"Fine! Let her go, if she will. She is as obstinate as—" Thorpe never finished the simile, for it could hardly have been a proper one.

Away walked Catherine in great agitation, as fast as the crowd would permit her, afraid of pursuit, yet determined to persevere.

As she walked, she reflected on what had passed. It was painful to her to disappoint *anyone,* particularly her brother. But she could not repent her resistance. To have failed Miss Tilney a second time—to have retracted a promise made only minutes before, and under false pretences—was abysmally wrong.

She was not being selfishly principled, only true to her conviction. And until she had spoken to Miss Tilney she could not be at ease.

Quickening her pace when she got clear of the Crescent, Catherine almost ran over the remaining ground till she gained the top of Milsom Street. So rapid had been her movements that, in spite of the Tilneys' head-start, they were but just turning into their lodgings as she came within view of them.

To the servant at the door she cried in passing that she must speak with Miss Tilney that moment, and hurrying by him proceeded upstairs. Then, opening the first door before her, she immediately found herself in the drawing-room with General Tilney, his son, and daughter.

*Oh, dear . . .*

Her explanation, full of nerves and dire shortness of breath, was instantly given. "I am come in a great hurry—It was all a mistake—I never promised to go—I told them from the first I could not go.—I ran away in a great hurry to explain it.—I did not care what you thought of me.—I would not stay for the servant!"

The situation however soon ceased to be a puzzle. Catherine found that John Thorpe had given the message; and Miss Tilney was greatly surprised by it. But whether Mr. Tilney had harbored resentment, Catherine—though she instinctively addressed both of them in her vindication—had no means of knowing. Whatever might have been felt before her arrival, her eager declarations immediately restored friendship.

The affair thus happily settled, Catherine was introduced by Miss Tilney to her father, and received by him with ready, solicitous politeness. This recalled Thorpe's information to her mind, and made her think with pleasure that even an ogre with a putrid guardian demon might be *sometimes* depended on.

To such anxious attention was the general's civility carried, that—unaware of her extraordinary swiftness in entering the house—he was quite angry with the servant who neglected his door duties. But Catherine most warmly asserted his innocence.

After sitting with them a quarter of an hour, she rose to take leave, and was then most agreeably surprised by General Tilney's asking her if she would do his daughter the honour of dining and spending the rest of the day with her.

Miss Tilney added her own wishes. Catherine was greatly obliged; but it was quite out of her power. Mr. and Mrs. Allen would expect her back every moment.

The general declared he could say no more; the claims of Mr. and Mrs. Allen were not to be superseded. But on some other day he trusted, they would not refuse to spare her.

Catherine was sure they would not have the least objection, and she should have great pleasure in coming. The general attended her himself to the street-door, saying everything gallant as they went downstairs, admiring the *elasticity* of her walk, which corresponded exactly with the spirit of her dancing, and making her one of the most graceful bows she had ever beheld, when they parted.

Catherine, delighted by all that had passed, proceeded gaily to Pulteney Street, walking with great *elasticity* (though she had never thought of it before). She reached home without seeing anything more of the offended party. And now that she had been triumphant throughout, she began (as the flutter of her spirits subsided, to be replaced by the usual soothing flutter of angelic wings) to doubt whether she had been perfectly right. She now had a friend displeased, a brother angry, and an ogre thwarted.

To ease her mind, she mentioned to Mr. Allen the half-settled scheme of her brother and the Thorpes for the following day. "Well," said Mr. Allen, "and do you think of going too?"

"No; I had just engaged to walk with Miss Tilney before they told me of it; therefore I could not go with them, could I?"

"No, certainly not. Young men and women driving about the country in open carriages! Going to inns and public places together! It is not right. I wonder Mrs. Thorpe should allow it. I am glad you do not think of going; Mrs. Morland would not be pleased. Mrs. Allen, are not you of my way of thinking?"

"Yes, very much so indeed. Open carriages are nasty things. A clean gown is not five minutes' wear in them. You get splashed; the wind takes your hair and your bonnet in every direction. I hate an open carriage myself."

"I know you do; but that is not the question. Do not you think it has an odd appearance, if young ladies are frequently driven about by young men, to whom they are not even related?"

"Yes, my dear, very odd indeed. I cannot bear to see it."

"Dear madam," cried Catherine, "then why did not you tell me so before? I am sure if I had known it to be improper, I would not have gone with Mr. Thorpe at all; but I always hoped you would tell me, if you thought I was doing wrong."

"And so I should, my dear, you may depend on it. As I told Mrs. Morland at parting, I would always do the best for you. But young people do not like to be always thwarted."

"So far, no harm done," said Mr. Allen; "I would only advise you, my dear, not to go out with Mr. Thorpe any more."

"That is just what I was going to say," echoed his wife.

Catherine was personally relieved, but felt uneasy for Isabella's reputation. She wondered whether she need warn Miss Thorpe, and explain the monstrous indecorum.

Mr. Allen, however, wisely discouraged her from doing any such thing. "You had better leave her alone, my dear. She is old enough to know better, and has a mother to advise her; you will be only getting ill-will."

# Chapter 14

The next morning was fair, and Catherine almost expected another attack from the assembled party. With Mr. Allen to support her, she felt no dread of the event: but she would gladly be spared a confrontation. She heartily rejoiced therefore at neither seeing nor hearing anything of them.

The Tilneys called for her at the appointed time. And no new difficulty arising, our heroine was most unnaturally able to fulfill her engagement, though it was made with the hero himself. They determined on walking round Beechen Cliff, that noble hill whose beautiful verdure and hanging coppice render it so striking an object from almost every opening in Bath.

"I never look at it," said Catherine, as they walked along the side of the river, "without thinking of the south of France."

"You have been abroad then?" said Henry, a little surprised.

"Oh! No, I only mean what I have read about. It always puts me in mind of the country that Emily and her father travelled through, in *The Mysteries of Udolpho*. But you never read novels, I dare say?"

"Why not?"

"Because they are not clever enough for you—gentlemen read better books."

"These days, gentlemen, at least here in Bath, read nothing *but* novels—the more frightful, the better. Apparently, such books seem to be practically imbued with occult secrets and encrypted clues that map not only the psyche, but actual topographical locations, no doubt down to the exact latitude and longitude. I do believe we've brought up the *treasure* subject previously. Who knew that fiction was such a literal roadmap? Who might have imagined Mrs. Radcliffe for a master cryptographer? Indeed the books should be bound together with maps and sold each with a pocket compass and slide rule. Maybe we need make such a suggestion to the publishers?"

"Oh! What a notion," said Catherine, smiling.

Mr. Tilney continued: "However, all treasure seeking aside, the person, be it gentleman or lady, who has not pleasure in a good novel, must be intolerably stupid. I have read all Mrs. Radcliffe's works, and most of them with great pleasure. *The Mysteries of Udolpho,* when I had once begun it, I could not lay down again; I remember finishing it in two days—my hair standing on end the whole time, though never from valiant attempts at code-breaking. Regretfully indeed, I found no cryptic clues, only a delightful sensation of wonder."

"Yes," added Miss Tilney, "and I remember you undertook to read it aloud to me, but when I was called away for only five minutes, instead of waiting for me, you took the volume into the Hermitage Walk. I was obliged to stay till you had finished it."

"Thank you, Eleanor—a most honourable testimony. You see, Miss Morland, the injustice of your suspicions. In my eagerness to read on, I refused to wait only five minutes for my sister. Breaking the promise of reading it aloud, I kept her in suspense at a most interesting part. And yes, I ran away with her very own volume! I am proud when I reflect on it—I think it must establish me in your good opinion."

"I am very glad to hear it indeed, and now I shall never be ashamed of liking *Udolpho* myself. But I really thought before, young men despised novels *amazingly*—that is, except when the novels provided specific decryption clues."

"Amazingly it may very well be—for they read nearly as many as women. I myself have read hundreds and hundreds. Do not imagine that you can cope with me in a knowledge of Julias and Louisas." And Mr. Tilney went on to demonstrate a truly formidable acquaintance with fictional names and places. "Consider how many years I have had the start of you. I had entered on my studies at Oxford, while you were a good little girl working your sampler at home!"

"Not very good, I am afraid. But now really, do not you think *Udolpho* the nicest book in the world?"

"The nicest—by which I suppose you mean the neatest. That must depend upon the binding."

"Henry," said Miss Tilney, "you are very impertinent. Miss Morland, he is treating you exactly as he does his sister. He is forever finding fault with me, for some incorrectness of language, and now he is taking the same liberty with you. The word 'nicest,' as you used it, did not suit him. You had better change it as soon as you can, or we shall be overpowered."

"I am sure," cried Catherine, "I did not mean to say anything wrong; but it *is* a nice book; why not call it so?"

"Very true," said Henry, "and this is a very *nice* day, and we are taking a very *nice* walk, and you are two very *nice* young ladies. A very nice word indeed, for now it does for everything."

"While, in fact," cried his sister, "it ought only to be applied to *you*, who are more nice than wise. Come, Miss Morland, let us leave him to meditate over our faults of diction, while we praise *Udolpho* in whatever terms we like best. It is a most interesting work. You are fond of that kind of reading?"

"To say the truth, I do not much like any other."

"Indeed!"

"That is, I can read poetry and plays, and things of that sort, and do not dislike travels. But history, real solemn history, I cannot be interested in. Can you?"

"Yes, I am fond of history."

"I wish I were too. I read it a little as a duty, but it tells me nothing that does not either vex or weary me. The quarrels of popes and kings, wars or pestilences in every page; the men all so good for nothing, and hardly any *women* at all—indeed, it is very tiresome to find that women and their brave acts are so gravely overlooked in those venerable pages, except when they are beauteous as Cleopatra!" Catherine paused, watching Lawrence or maybe Terence fly back and forth from her own bonnet to gently land on that of Miss Tilney.

"And yet," she went on, "I often think it odd that it should be so *dull*, for a great deal of it must be invention. The speeches of the heroes, much of their thoughts and intentions must be invention, and *invention* is what delights me in other books."

"Historians, you think," said Miss Tilney, "display imagination without raising interest. I am fond of history—and am well contented to take the false with the true. The principal facts have sources in reliable former histories and records. And as for the little embellishments, I rather like them as such."

"You are fond of history! And so are Mr. Allen and my father; and my two brothers do not dislike it. At this rate, I shall not pity the writers of history any longer. If people like to read their books, it is all very well. I used to think, nobody would willingly ever look into such lengthy volumes. The torment of little boys and girls, always struck me as a hard fate. And though I know it is all very necessary, I have often wondered . . ."

"That little boys and girls should be tormented," said Henry, "no one can deny. But historians might well be offended at being supposed to have no higher aim. Indeed, they are equally well qualified to torment the most advanced readers. As you say 'to torment,' instead of 'to instruct,' it is now admitted as synonymous."

"You think me foolish to call instruction a torment. But if you had observed, as I have, poor little children first learning their letters and how stupid they can be for a whole morning together, and how tired my poor mother, you would allow that 'to torment' and 'to instruct' might sometimes be synonymous."

"Very probably. But historians are not accountable for the difficulty of learning to read. And you might acknowledge that it is worthwhile to be tormented for two or three years of one's life, for the sake of being able to read all the rest of it. Consider—if reading had not been taught, Mrs. Radcliffe would have written in vain—or perhaps might not have written at all."

Catherine assented—and a very warm panegyric from her on that lady's merits closed the subject, at least for the moment.

The Tilneys were soon engaged in another on which she had nothing to say. They were viewing the country with the eyes of persons of real taste accustomed to drawing.

Here Catherine was quite lost. She knew nothing of drawing (except for stick figures and monstrous ducks)—nothing of taste. She listened to them with pointless attention, for they talked in phrases which conveyed scarcely any idea to her.

The little which she *could* understand, however, appeared to contradict the very few notions she *had*. It seemed "a good view" were no longer to be taken from the top of a hill, and "a clear blue sky" was no longer a proof of a fine day.

She was heartily ashamed of her ignorance. And yet—a well-informed mind harbors an inability of administering to the vanity of others. This, a sensible person would always wish to avoid. And a sensible *lady* should conceal it as well as she can.

But Catherine did not know her own advantages. A good-looking girl, with an affectionate heart and a very ignorant mind—except when it came to perceiving things *metaphysical*—cannot fail to attract a clever young man.

In the present instance, she confessed and lamented her want of knowledge. She declared that she would give anything in the world to be able to draw. And a lecture on the picturesque immediately followed, in which his instructions were so clear that she soon began to see beauty in everything admired by him, and her attention was so earnest that he became perfectly satisfied of her having a great deal of natural taste.

He talked of foregrounds, distances, and second distances—side-screens and perspectives—lights and shades. And Catherine—though still mostly seeing stick figures and ducks—was so hopeful a scholar that when they gained the top of Beechen Cliff, she voluntarily rejected the whole city of Bath as unworthy to make part of a landscape.

Delighted with her progress, and fearful of wearying her with too much wisdom at once, Henry suffered the subject to decline. And by an easy transition from a rock and withered oak near its summit, to oaks in general, to forests, wastelands, crown lands and government, he shortly found himself arrived at politics. And from politics, it was an easy step to silence—at which point all the angels in the vicinity circling them like gentle butterflies, sighed in relief.

The general pause was put an end to by Catherine, who suddenly pointed upwards at a distant black speck moving rapidly in the blue sky.

"Oh goodness, look! What manner of bird is that?"

The Tilneys raised their heads and suddenly there was a different kind of silence.

"What is it?" pressed Catherine.

The dark bird, at first a tiny shadow silhouetted against the bright heavens, rapidly grew in size as it approached, and in definition—so that Catherine could see the pronounced angular shape of its large, peculiar, almost *reptilian* wings.

If Catherine had learned anything from the landscape and drawing lesson she had just been given, it was that distances were to be judged by relative motion and comparison to other objects in the landscape. And as such, the approaching bird was to be judged *immense.*

Indeed, it could not be judged a bird at all . . .

It had to be a *dragon.*

Catherine recalled her torments in natural history and the instructions that accompanied her discovery of various flora and fauna, and the rare creatures found to be mostly native to the African and Australian continents.

Creatures, indeed, half-way out of legend! Creatures nearly extinct, extraordinary in their ancient, hoary origins, and imbued with almost supernatural abilities.

Indeed, this was one of the few bright sparks of what appeared to be glorious *invention* in a world of solid, dull, natural facts, that Catherine recalled from all her lessons. Even though invention it was not, she very well knew. But oh, it was so full of wonder!

Dragons had existed in hidden wild places of the world, verily since the beginnings of time, claimed modern science. They were as rare as the most precious natural resources, raw diamonds, emeralds, rubies; or great, uncultured pearls. They were intelligent, indeed, remarkably *sentient*—preternaturally so for what otherwise appeared to be wild beasts—and like the great whales and creatures of the deep they were said to hold in them the beginnings of original wisdom.

In modern times, they were either very well hidden, or they genuinely had become extinct in most places, never venturing out of Africa or Australia. The last living dragon had been observed briefly in the skies over an uncommonly stilled and becalmed Pacific Ocean, by Magellan sailing en route to the Spice Islands or the New World; and before that, an African dragon was captured and presented to the great Frankish monarch Charlemagne who, legend has it, tamed and kept the mystic creature as a powerful symbol of his reign, until the dragon either died or broke its chains and mysteriously disappeared.

But not since the darkest ages was there any truly verifiable scientific account of a dragon venturing as far as the Isles of Britain!

The creature in the sky continued its approach. As it neared, it was a thing of beauty—smooth leathery skin with a metallic tinge of gold as the sun struck the edges of its scaled wings, unfurled like sails, a strange serpentine neck and elegant head, and the wingspan of a grand cathedral. It cast a long giant shadow upon the ground, like a ghostly floating road, and Catherine stared at it in mesmerized fearless amazement. Then she finally said: "Oh, Mr. Tilney, you who know so much more than I do—oh, do tell me, I beg you, if this is a dragon; and if so, whence could it have come?"

But Mr. Tilney in turn surprised her. He threw his sister one long intense look, then turned around with abrupt motion, saying in an unusually cool manner, "Miss Morland, it is nothing, surely. And overgrown hawk, it is all. Do let us proceed onward—"

"A hawk?" Catherine cried. "My dear Mr. Tilney, please do not confound me so! You have just paid me the marvelous honour of providing a landscape drawing lesson, a lesson in beauty, and a lesson in *perception!* And if, according to anything you said about objects and the nature of relative perspective, if I am to look properly and judge what it is I see, why, the thing is monstrous! It is not a bird! And, believe me, I have seen giant monstrous ducks to make your heart stop! Why, the other day when Mr. Thorpe had driven me and—oh, yes, there was James with Miss Thorpe; we were in open carriages—a certain Brighton Duck attacked us, and—Mr. Tilney, I dare say it was not one hundredth the size of this giant flying creature!"

"Henry—" said Miss Tilney in a strange voice.

"A dragon is nonsense," he replied firmly, looking ahead of them. "The creatures do not exist. They are gone, all of them, even if they had walked the earth once, in distant places—but again, this is all nonsense. Think, Miss Morland—what in the world would a practically mythic dragon be doing here in Bath?"

But Catherine responded with animation. "Now that is one thing I can surely answer! If it *is* a true dragon, it is here seeking treasure, just as everyone else is! Why, it is plain as day! All accounts of dragons end in fabulous treasure hoards. And now, this is perfect absolute proof of it; this hidden wonder of infinite riches is somewhere here, nearby! Maybe right under our noses! To be sure, when I first heard talk in the pump-room the other day about a dragon sighting, I thought it was but silliness propagated by Mr. Thorpe who is always going on about everything very loudly—and I had thought he had exaggerated a large duck encounter into a giant dragon attack. So of course I gave none of it credit; though, some of the gentlemen discussing it were sensible, and friends of Mr. Allen. But now I see it is an entirely different matter!"

While Catherine continued to make her point, the great dragon soared closer and closer. And then suddenly the heavens went momentarily dark as it passed directly overhead, eclipsing the sun like a giant sky leviathan of the deep, pouring its immense shadow over them from the height equivalent of a tall edifice, such as a large church.

And in a blink it was racing on, and away—though Catherine imagined she had seen its great fiery eye upon her.

"I dare say, that was *not* a duck," admitted Miss Tilney with a sigh. "Come, Henry, it is no use denying."

For a moment Mr. Tilney continued his unusually obstinate silence. And then he threw one glance to the once more receding dark speck of fluid motion in the distant skies. "If you insist, it was indeed something other than a hawk, but I refuse to concede

"I dare say, that was *not* a duck," admitted Miss Tilney with a sigh.

that it was anything remotely like a dragon—not until there is adequate scientific proof from a qualified party, and a reasonable explanation."

"Is the presence of treasure not reasonable enough?"

"My dear Miss Morland," he retorted. "And now, in addition to all my other intimate faults of character to which you are being exposed, I must admit to being rather more pedantic than you are. Unlike those who spread or concede to rumor, I require tangible proof. But—until such sufficiently documented material proof is in our grasp, let us speak of something more pleasant."

There was a long pause of silence as they resumed their stroll, and Catherine attempted to compose her thoughts and feelings. It was only then she realized that the angels had either been very quiet throughout the incident or she had *momentarily stopped hearing or being aware of them.*

And that notion was more bothersome than anything else.

But soon enough a more casual and pleasant mood was restored. Since there was no more sign of the dragon, the conversation picked up.

"Well then," Catherine uttered, in rather a solemn tone of voice, "I have heard that something very shocking indeed will soon come out in London."

Miss Tilney was startled, and hastily replied, "Indeed! And of what nature?"

"That I do not know, nor who is the author. I have only heard that it is to be more horrible than anything we have met with yet. More terrifying than any mysterious flying creature!"

"Good heaven! Where could you hear of such a thing?"

"A particular friend of mine had an account of it in a letter from London yesterday. It is to be uncommonly dreadful. I shall expect murder and everything of the kind."

"You speak with astonishing composure! But I hope your friend's accounts have been exaggerated; and proper measures will undoubtedly be taken by government to prevent it."

"Government," said Henry, still in a bit of a serious mood, but now endeavouring not to smile, "neither desires nor dares to interfere in such matters. There must be murder; and government cares not how much."

The ladies stared. This time Catherine was aware of the angels moving in the ether around them, but altogether calmly.

Mr. Tilney laughed, and added, "Come, shall I assist your understanding, or leave you to puzzle out an explanation? Perhaps the abilities of women are neither sound nor acute—"

"Miss Morland, do not mind what he says; but have the goodness to satisfy me as to this dreadful riot."

"Riot! What riot?"

"My dear Eleanor, the riot is only in your own brain. The confusion there is scandalous. Miss Morland has been talking of nothing more dreadful than a new horror publication. And you, Miss Morland—my sister has pictured a mob of three thousand men, London flowing with blood, the 12th Light Dragoons called up, and the gallant Captain Frederick Tilney knocked off his horse by a brickbat from an upper window. Forgive her stupidity. She is by no means a simpleton in general."

Catherine looked grave.

"And now, Henry," said Miss Tilney, "that you have made us both feel very inferior, you may as well make Miss Morland understand yourself—unless you mean to have her think you intolerably rude to your sister, and a great brute in your opinion of women in general. She is not used to your odd ways."

"I shall be happy to make her better acquainted with them."

"No doubt; but that is no explanation of the present."

"What am I to do?"

"You know what you ought to do. Clear your character handsomely before her. Tell her that you think very highly of the understanding of women."

"Miss Morland, I think very highly of the understanding of all the women in the world—especially the present company."

And then Mr. Tilney proceeded to shock and invoke smiles simultaneously by his wit and contrary banter.

"We shall get nothing more serious from him now, Miss Morland," said Miss Tilney. "But I do assure you, he never says an unjust thing of any woman at all, nor an unkind one of me."

It was no effort to Catherine to believe that Henry Tilney could never be wrong. His mercurial manner might sometimes surprise, but his meaning must always be just. And what she did not understand, she was willing to admire.

The whole walk ended on a delightful note. Her friends attended her into the house, and Miss Tilney respectfully addressed Mrs. Allen and Catherine, petitioning for the pleasure of Catherine's dinner company another day. The latter could hardly conceal her pleasure.

The morning had passed away so charmingly that no thought of Isabella or James had crossed her during their walk. When the Tilneys were gone, memory returned, but Mrs. Allen had no intelligence to give that could relieve her anxiety—she had heard nothing of any of them.

Towards the end of the morning, however, Catherine, walked out into the town (in search of ribbon), and in Bond Street overtook the second Miss Thorpe as she was loitering towards Edgar's Buildings between two of the sweetest girls in the world, who had been her dear friends all morning. They were all bearing baskets full of *bells* of various shapes and sizes.

From her, she soon learned that the party to Clifton had taken place. "They set off at eight this morning," said Miss Anne, "and I am sure I do not envy them their drive. It must be the dullest thing in the world, for there is not a soul at Clifton at this time of year. Belle went with your brother, and John drove Maria. And here we are, looking for secret Clues to the treasure! They say a *dragon* has been sighted over Beechen Cliff this morning!"

Pretending to ignore the dragon comment, while her heart skipped a beat, Catherine inquired as to the specific arrangement of the drive.

"Oh, yes!" rejoined the other. "Maria is gone. She was quite wild to go. For my part, I was determined *not* to go, even if pressed. Instead, we have spent hours decrypting 'Mysterious Warnings'—why, it is none other than 'MW' or 'Mrs. Walter!'"

Catherine, a little doubtful of this, could not help saying, "But *what* or *who* is 'Mrs. Walter'? What does it all mean? Really, I wish you could have gone instead. A pity you did not."

"Thank you; but it is quite a matter of indifference to me. This treasure hunt is so much more amiable! Indeed, I was saying so to Emily and Sophia when you overtook us, that there was a *significance* to be found in *cow bells* at *midnight*, and are there any cow establishments in Bath?"

"If you mean steak or dairy, then, likely yes. Otherwise—"

Catherine was getting distracted with all this *decryption,* and still unconvinced; but glad that Anne should have the friendship of an Emily and a Sophia to console her.

She wished them luck with the bovine pursuits, bade her adieu, and returned home with the procured ribbon, pleased that James and Isabella managed their excursion successfully without her.

# Chapter 15

Early the next day, a note from Isabella—filled with peace and tenderness, and entreating the immediate presence of her friend on a matter of the utmost importance—hastened Catherine, in happy curiosity, to Edgar's Buildings.

The two youngest Miss Thorpes were by themselves in the parlour, sorting cowbells, dinner bells, sleigh bells, and tiny Christmas tree bells in various piles of cryptic relevance.

Anne left her task to call her sister, and Catherine took the opportunity to ask the other for particulars of yesterday's party. Maria—apparently not entirely interested in bells—eagerly paused her occupation to speak of it.

The angels floated about the room, and gently moved among the piles of bells. Presently, there arose a constant inexplicable general *tinkling* sound that was of course accounted for by drafts and breezes.

Catherine was informed by Maria that it had been altogether the most delightful scheme in the world—they had driven directly to the York Hotel, ate some soup, bespoke an early dinner, walked down to the pump-room, tasted the water, laid out some shillings in purses and spars; ate ice at a pastry-cook's, swallowed their dinner in haste back at the hotel; then had a delightful drive back, only the moon was not up, it rained a little, and Mr. Morland's horse was so tired he could hardly get it along . . .

Catherine listened with satisfaction. It appeared that a visit to Blaize Castle had never even been thought of. As for the rest, there was nothing to regret for half an instant. Maria ended with an effusion of pity for her sister Anne, for missing the party.

"She will never forgive me, I am sure. But John vowed he would not drive her, because she had such thick ankles—"

Isabella now entered the room with an eager step, a northern ice-wind, and a look of happy importance, engaging all notice. Maria was without ceremony sent away and told to take some of those *tedious tinkling things* with her.

Isabella, embracing Catherine, thus began: "Yes, my dear Catherine, it is so indeed! You see through everything!"

Catherine thought it was certainly a curious turn of phrase, all things considered, but replied only by a look of wondering ignorance.

"Nay, my beloved, sweetest friend," continued the other, starting her familiar shrill, "compose yourself. I am amazingly agitated, as you perceive. Let us sit down and talk in comfort. Surely you guessed it the moment you had my note? Sly creature! Oh! My dear Catherine, you alone, who know my heart, can judge of my present happiness. *Your brother is the most charming of men.* I only wish I were more worthy of him. But what will your excellent father and mother say? Oh! Heavens! I am so agitated!"

Catherine's understanding began to awake. A terrifying idea of the truth suddenly darted into her mind. Blushing, she cried out, "Good heaven! My dear Isabella, what do you mean? Can you—can you really be in love with James?"

*Oh, angels! Oh, dear God in Heaven!* she meanwhile thought in veritable panic. *No, no, she cannot! This frightening harpy scarecrow demonic dried out stick-creature with yellow eyes and freezing weather cannot think to love my poor brother!*

This, however was soon revealed to be only half the dreaded news. Apparently, in the course of their yesterday's party, Isabella received the delightful confession of an equal love from James.

Her heart and faith were alike *engaged to James.*

Never had Catherine listened to anything so full of interest, wonder, and terror. Her brother and her monstrous friend engaged!

*Oh, dear God in Heaven!*

The most impossible thing about this was that now Catherine instantly considered herself to be entirely at fault for allowing this to go on. To be frank, she had never in her wildest sanguined nightmare—direct out of Mrs. Radcliffe's complete works—could have imagined that James would be so enchanted, bewitched, and befuddled, as to take his unnatural attraction to this female *fiend* thus far!

For days now Catherine had been meaning to sit him down and divulge certain things about the beauteous Miss Isabella Thorpe—naturally without revealing the full horror of her nephilim origin. The difficulty of explaining herself to her brother (and possibly the rest of her family), of having to possibly reveal her *own* metaphysical ability to see certain supernatural things, held her back from having this painful conversation. Catherine held on to a vain hope that James was simply having a pleasant but casual flirtation; and surely with time he too would notice the yellow avaricious eyes, the shrill harpy voice, and oh, the beastly arctic cold. . . !

Even the dear angels had been patient with her, agreeing that it will be done "all in good time;" that truth will be established, and Catherine will eventually make her warnings to her brother, without unduly enraging the nephilim brother and sister in the process. For, according to the angels, there was still *great danger* in her path.

Thus, our heroine had to be on her guard. And although never untruthful, *for the present* she had to remain as friendly as possible with Isabella—at least until she could properly warn her brother (who in turn would artfully, carefully extricate himself from the engagement without having to explain the whole underlying *supernatural* aspect of it to their parents—or so Catherine dearly hoped would happen).

And so Catherine took a deep breath, and while the angels settled around her, she returned her attention full of seeming delight to her friend. The happiness of having such a sister would have been a natural first effusion (had it been genuine on Catherine's part), and thus the fair ladies mingled in embraces and tears of joy.

Though Catherine made the sincerest attempt at rejoicing, Isabella far surpassed her. "You will be so infinitely dearer to me, my Catherine, than either Anne or Maria: I shall be so much more attached to my dear Morland's family than to my own."

This was far beyond Catherine's ability to emulate.

"You are so like your dear brother," continued Isabella, "that I quite doted on you the first moment I saw you. The very first day that Morland came to us last Christmas—" And she tenderly screeched at length about how she had worn a yellow gown and thought him so handsome.

Here Catherine secretly acknowledged the power of love, even in *unnatural* creatures; for, though exceedingly fond of her brother, she had never in her life thought him handsome.

The lovelorn monstrous shrilling went on for some time, and, "Oh! Catherine, the many sleepless nights I have had on your brother's account! I am grown *wretchedly thin;* I have betrayed myself in my *partiality!* But my secret I was always sure would be safe with you."

Catherine could not imagine how much more *thinner* spindly "inner vision Isabella" could become, and likewise felt that no secret had been safer, considering her complete ignorance.

Meanwhile, her brother, she found, was preparing to set off with all speed to Fullerton, to make known his situation and ask for parental consent. Here was a source of some real agitation to Isabella.

Catherine did not endeavour to persuade that her parents would never oppose their son's wishes. But she readily vouched that they were kind and desirous of their children's happiness.

"Morland says exactly the same," replied Isabella; "and yet, my fortune will be so small; they never can consent to it. Your brother, who might marry anybody!"

Here Catherine again discerned the *abysmal* force of love, and could only respond in jest. "Indeed, Isabella, you are too humble. The difference of fortune signifies nothing. Not to mention, any one of us, at any instant, might stumble upon hidden treasure!"

"Oh! My sweet Catherine, and your generous heart!" The squealing cries from Isabella resounded to the ceiling. "I know it would signify nothing! I only wish our situations were reversed. Had I the command of millions, were I mistress of the whole world, your brother would be my only choice."

The notion of a "command of millions" gave Catherine tiny pause. But having not the foggiest notion of how to respond, she only smiled her best.

"For my own part," said Isabella, "the smallest income in nature would be enough for me. Where people are really attached, poverty itself is wealth; grandeur I detest: I would not settle in London for the universe. A cottage in some retired village would be ecstasy—Now, my dear, remind me again of some of your brilliant Udolpho Code significant Clues."

Catherine was glad to change this controversial subject, and the next few minutes were spent in discussion of whether

"Orphans of the Rhine" and O-O-T-R referred to little children or turnips and potatoes.

Then Isabella once again said, with a deathly-frozen sigh, "Oh! I will not allow myself to rest, till we have your father's answer. Morland says that by sending it tonight to Salisbury, we may have it tomorrow. Tomorrow? I know I shall never have courage to open the letter. It will be the death of me!"

Catherine attempted to interest her in guessing whether "Necromancer of the Black Forest" was indeed a *black magician* or merely *not Beatrice Foster*. But it was in vain. A brief reverie succeeded—and when Isabella spoke again, it was on the quality of her wedding-gown.

Their conference was put an end to by the anxious young lover himself. James came to breathe his parting sigh before he set off for Wiltshire.

Catherine wished to congratulate and *warn* him in one breath, but instead knew not what to say, and her anxious eloquence was only in her eyes.

Meanwhile James said his hundredth tender adieus, while frequently *detained* by the urgent entreaties of his fair one that he *go,* in order to hurry the inevitable. Twice was he called back almost from the door by her eagerness to have him gone. "Indeed, Morland, I must drive you away. Consider how far you have to ride. For heaven's sake, waste no more time, my love!"

The two friends, with hearts now "united" in schemes of sisterly happiness, were inseparable for the day.

Mrs. Thorpe and her son—acquainted with everything, and only waiting for Mr. Morland's consent—considered Isabella's engagement as the most fortunate circumstance imaginable for their family. But until the happiness was made formal, Anne and Maria were not informed. They however engaged in much whispering and giggling; and it remained only an affected secret.

Catherine was with her friend again the next day, supporting her spirits, and to while away the many tedious hours of distress before the delivery of the letters.

But when it did come, "I have had no difficulty in gaining the consent of my kind parents," were the first lines—and in one moment all was joyful security.

Isabella's spirits became almost too high for control. She screeched, she sang, she cooed and hallooed, and caused flurries of snow to appear—verily, Catherine had to blink it away—and she called herself the happiest of mortals.

*Are nephilim mortal?* Catherine pondered momentarily, then had to remind herself that *yes, indeed they were.*

Mrs. Thorpe, with tears of joy, embraced her daughter, her son, her visitor, and could have embraced half the inhabitants of Bath. Her heart was overflowing with tenderness.

Even the angels in the room could not help smiling and circled around energetically, narrowly avoiding the two nephilim, while greater light than usual streamed from their wings. Terence, or possibly Clarence, collided with each other in mid-flight and both landed on top of Mrs. Thorpe's bonnet.

John himself was no skulker in joy. He named Mr. Morland one of the finest fellows in the world. Bellowing, he swore off many sentences in his praise, sending waves of infernal heat about the room. At some point near the middle, and just beneath a chandelier, Isabella's cold front and the heat wave met . . .

Catherine sensed that, at some precarious point, and soon, indoor precipitation was entirely inevitable.

Meanwhile, the happy letter from James was short. But for the details Isabella could well afford to wait. By what means their income was to be formed, whether landed property were to be resigned, or funded money made over, was a matter in which her *disinterested* spirit took no concern.

It was enough to feel secure. Her imagination took flight; and she saw herself admired and envied, by friends old and new, at Fullerton and in Putney—a carriage at her command, a new name on her tickets, a brilliant exhibition of hoop rings on her finger.

John Thorpe, who had only waited for the momentous letter's arrival, now prepared to set off to London. "Well, Miss Morland," said he, on finding her alone in the parlour, "I am come to bid you good-bye."

Catherine wished him a good journey.

Without appearing to hear her, he walked to the window, fidgeted about, hummed a tune in a tender roar, and seemed wholly self-occupied.

"Shall not you be late?" said Catherine, wishing the inferno gone.

He made no answer; but after a minute's silence burst out with, "A famous good thing this marrying scheme, upon my soul! A clever fancy of Morland's and Belle's. What do you think of it, Miss Morland? I say it is no bad notion."

"I am sure I think it a very good one."

"Do you? That's honest, by heavens! I am glad you are no enemy to matrimony. Did you ever hear the old song 'Going to One Wedding Brings on Another?'" And Thorpe muttered self-indulgently, in a most delicate ogre rumble, about something—but Catherine was unsure what it was exactly.

"Well, I wish you a good journey. I dine with Miss Tilney today, and must now be going home."

"Nay, but there is no such confounded hurry. Who knows when we may be together again? A devilish long fortnight it will appear to me."

"Then why stay away so long?" replied Catherine tiredly.

"That is kind of you—and good-natured. I shall not forget it. But you have more good nature than anybody living. A monstrous deal of good nature! And not only that, you have such good brains for those *secret clues,* I say, and you have such—upon my soul, I do not know anybody like you."

"Oh, dear! There are a great many people like me."

"Miss Morland, I shall come and pay my respects at Fullerton before it is long, if not disagreeable."

"Pray do. My father and mother will be glad to see you."

"And I hope—I hope, Miss Morland, you will not be sorry to see me."

"Oh, dear, not at all. There are very few people I am sorry to see. Company is always cheerful."

"That is just my way of thinking. And I am heartily glad to hear you say the same. Blast it, Miss Morland! You and I think pretty much alike upon most matters."

"Perhaps; but it is more than I ever thought of."

"By Jove, no more do I. It is not my way to bother my brains with what does not concern me. Let me only have the girl I like, with a comfortable house over my head, and what care I for all the rest? Fortune is nothing. I am sure of a good income of my own. If she had not a penny, why, so much the better."

"Very true. I think like you there. If there is a good fortune on one side, there can be no occasion for any on the other. No matter which has it, so that there is enough. I hate the idea of one great fortune looking out for another. And to marry for money I think the wickedest thing in existence. Good day. We shall be very glad to see you at Fullerton, whenever it is convenient."

And away she went. It was not in the power of all his ogre gallantry to detain her longer.

Surprisingly, when Mr. and Mrs. Allen heard the news of the engagement, they observed to Catherine it had been foreseen by them both, ever since her brother's arrival. They expressed a placid wish for the young people's happiness—with a remark, on the gentleman's side, in favour of Isabella's beauty, and on the lady's, of her great good luck.

The only emotion raised was upon the disclosure of James's going to Fullerton the day before. Mrs. Allen repeatedly wished she could have seen him before he went, to offer her best regards to his father and mother, and compliments to all the neighbors.

Oh—and he simply *must* pass on to Mrs. Skinner the startling news about the frequent *dragon* sightings—a veritable *flock* of dragons has been observed here in Bath!

# Chapter 16

Catherine's expectations of pleasure from her visit in Milsom Street were so very high that disappointment was inevitable.

She was most politely received by General Tilney, kindly welcomed by his daughter; and even Henry was at home. Yet she found, on her return, that she had expected a happiness beyond reach.

Instead of finding herself improved in acquaintance with Miss Tilney, from the intercourse[20] of the day, she seemed hardly so intimate with her as before. Instead of seeing Henry Tilney to greater advantage than ever, in the ease of a family party, he had never said so little, nor been so little agreeable.

And, in spite of their father's great civilities to her—in spite of his thanks, invitations, and compliments—it had been a release to get away from him.

Indeed, it puzzled her to account for all this. It could not be General Tilney's fault. That he was perfectly agreeable and good-natured, and altogether a very charming man, did not admit of a doubt, for he was tall and handsome, and Henry's father.

---

[20] Gentle Reader, this Author is duly shocked. Whatever gutter filth must be passing through your thoughts! Oh dear! You must hasten to procure good soap and use it!

It was just that there was something heavy and odd in the atmosphere whenever he was in the room, and the sense of oppression was almost supernatural.

The angels were undeniably present, and Catherine could *hear* and *sense* and *see* them as they moved about like brilliant fireflies in the dining room and parlor, alighting upon mantelpieces and shelves, and occasionally upon the sleeves of *most* of those present. But sometimes, if she glanced at the general too closely, she could see the angels' brightness grow somewhat dimmer, more remote.

She blinked it away.

"What is it, dear Catherine?" asked an angel softly. "Are you afraid?"

"Should I be?" she replied, coughing into a napkin.

But the angel's whispered answer was somehow lost when in the very same moment the general inquired about some trifle and she had to address him directly.

Catherine pondered this. In short, he could not be accountable for his children's want of spirits, or for her want of enjoyment in his company. The former she hoped at last might have been accidental. And the latter she could only attribute to her own stupidity.

Isabella, on hearing the particulars of the visit, gave a different explanation, while freezing the contents of a teacup in her hand: "It was all insufferable haughtiness and pride! She had long suspected the family to be very high. Such insolence of behaviour as Miss Tilney's she had never heard of in her life! To behave to her guest with such superciliousness! Hardly even to speak to her!"

"But it was not so bad as that, Isabella; there was no superciliousness; she was very civil." Under the guise of wanting to examine the pattern on her friend's teacup, Catherine casually removed it from Isabella's fingers in exchange for her own so as to cool the tea down a bit, then retrieved it back, delightfully fit to sip.

"Oh! Don't defend her! Nor the brother, who had appeared so attached to you! Good heavens! And so he hardly looked once at you the whole day?"

"I do not say so; but he did not seem in good spirits."

"How contemptible! Let me entreat you never to think of him again, my dear Catherine; indeed he is unworthy of you."

"Unworthy! I do not suppose he ever thinks of me."

"That is exactly what I say. Such fickleness! How different to our own brothers! Indeed, John has the most constant heart."

"But as for General Tilney, there was great, most attentive civility. His only care was to entertain and make me happy."

"Oh! I know no harm of him; I do not suspect him of pride. I believe he is a very gentleman-like man. John thinks very well of him, and John's judgment—"

"Well, I shall see how they behave to me this evening; we shall meet them at the rooms."

"And must I go?" Isabella sighed, and made it briefly snow directly overhead—quite discreetly, just for the two of them.

"Do not you intend it? I thought it was all settled." Catherine politely dabbed at the snowflakes on her nose with her handkerchief, and a dear angel fanned its wings at several more.

"Nay, since you make such a point of it, I can refuse you nothing. But do not insist upon my being very agreeable, for my heart, you know, will be some forty miles off, with James. And as for dancing, do not mention it, I beg; that is quite out of the question—" And Isabella catalogued the various dance suitors she was now dearly anxious to refuse.

Fortunately, Isabella's opinion of the Tilneys did not influence her friend. Catherine was sure there had been neither insolence nor pride in their hearts.

The evening rewarded her confidence. She was met with the same kindness and attention, as heretofore: Miss Tilney took pains to be near her, and Henry asked her to dance.

And oh, the room then practically swelled with tiny whirling golden stars! The angelic host brought more brilliance to the air than all the candles ever could muster. . . .

Having heard the day before in Milsom Street that their elder brother, Captain Tilney, was expected almost every hour, she could easily name the very fashionable-looking, handsome young man, whom she had never seen before, and who now evidently belonged to their party.

She looked at him with great admiration. It was possible he was even handsomer than his brother—though, in her eyes, his air was more assuming, and his countenance less prepossessing. His taste and manners however were decidedly inferior. For, within her hearing, he protested against every thought of dancing and laughed openly at Henry for finding it possible.

*Such dragon pride, such superciliousness!*

It may be presumed that, whatever might be our heroine's opinion of him, his any possible admiration of her was in no danger of producing animosities between the brothers, nor dire romantic *persecutions* to the lady.

But Catherine could not help herself; she began visualizing possible Udolpho clues . . . Oh dear, he cannot be the *"Necromancer of the Black Forest,"* here in the flesh? He cannot be the instigator of the three villains in horsemen's greatcoats, by whom she will hereafter be forced into a traveling-chaise and four, which will drive off with incredible speed, bound toward some dire *"Horrid Mysteries"* . . .

Catherine abruptly forced herself not to pursue such grave and silly thoughts, and rather to remain undisturbed by presentiments of such an evil—or of any evil at all, except that of having but a short set to dance down. Indeed, she need but look at the dear angels; they appeared entirely untroubled. . . .

Thus, Catherine enjoyed her usual happiness with Henry Tilney, listening with sparkling eyes to everything he said. And, in finding him irresistible, she became so herself.

At the end of the first dance, Captain Tilney came towards them again, and, much to Catherine's dissatisfaction, pulled his brother away.

They retired whispering together. And, though she was not immediately alarmed that Captain Tilney must have heard some *malevolent misrepresentation of her,* which he now communicated to his brother (no doubt, in hopes of separating them forever), she did experience uneasy sensations.

"Fear not, dear Catherine," consoled a bright angel at her shoulder, at the same time adjusting the ribbon there that she had negligently forgotten to turn out. "There is no danger here; at least not quite."

Her suspense was of full five minutes' duration (though it did feel like a quarter of an hour), when they both returned, and an explanation was given. Henry inquired if she thought her friend, Miss Thorpe, would have any objection to dancing—his brother would be most happy to be introduced to her.

Catherine wondered at Captain Tilney's amazing change of heart as far as dancing, but without hesitation replied that she was very sure Miss Thorpe did not mean to dance at all. The cruel reply was passed on to the other, and he immediately walked away.

"Your brother will not mind it," said she, "because I heard him say before that he *hated dancing;* but it was very good-natured for him to think of it. I suppose he saw Isabella sitting down, and fancied she might wish for a partner. But he is quite mistaken—she would not dance upon any account in the world."

Henry smiled, and said, "How very little trouble it can give you to understand the motive of other people's actions."

"Why? What do you mean?"

"With you, it is not a matter of another person's exact feelings, age, particulars, habits, nature—but of your own choices; how *you* yourself would behave in a given situation."

"I do not understand you."

"Then we are on very unequal terms, for I understand you perfectly well," said he, with a faint smile.

At least three angels circled Mr. Tilney at that point, and Catherine could not help wondering it was somehow significant.

"Me? Yes; I cannot speak well enough to be unintelligible."

"Bravo! An excellent satire on modern language."

"It was decidedly not an intentional one," admitted she. "But pray tell me what you mean."

"Shall I indeed? Do you really desire it? But it will likely involve you in a very cruel embarrassment, and certainly bring on a disagreement between us.

"No, no; it shall not do either; I am not afraid."

"Well, then, I only meant that your attributing my brother's wish of dancing with Miss Thorpe to *good nature alone* convinced me of your being superior in good nature yourself to all the rest of the world."

Catherine blushed and disclaimed, and the gentleman's predictions were verified, while their immediate space grew bright with angelic light. . . .

There was a *something* in his words, which repaid her for the pain of confusion. And that something occupied her mind so much, that for some time she forgot to speak, listen, or indeed where she was—till, roused by the sweetly shrill voice of Isabella and the familiar northern clime, she looked up and saw her with Captain Tilney preparing to give them hands across.

Isabella shrugged her shoulders and smiled; moved away in the dance. But it was insufficient explanation for Catherine, and she spoke her astonishment in very plain terms to her partner.

"I cannot think how it could happen! Isabella was so determined not to dance."

"And did Isabella never change her mind before?"

"Oh! But, because—And your brother! After what you told him from me, how could he think of going to ask her?"

"I cannot be surprised completely. You bid me be surprised on your friend's account, and therefore I am. But as for my brother, his conduct has been no more than usual. The lovely fairness of your friend was an open attraction; her resolute firmness, on the other hand, could only be understood by you."

"You are laughing; but, I assure you, Isabella is very firm in general; rather icy, frequently. Indeed, I often require a wrap."

"It is as much as should be said of anyone—though, I do admit, the exceeding *cold* air in her immediate location is rather an oddity. Now, to be always firm is to be often obstinate. Without reference to my brother, I really think Miss Thorpe has by no means chosen ill in fixing on the present hour."

The friends were not able to get together for any confidential discourse till all the dancing was over.

Then, as they walked about the room arm in (petrified-frozen) arm, Isabella thus explained herself: "I do not wonder at your surprise; and I am really fatigued to death. He is such a rattle! Amusing enough, if my mind had been *disengaged;* but I would have given the world to sit still."

"Then why did not you?" Catherine asked plainly.

"Oh! My dear! It would have looked so particular; and you know how I abhor doing that. I refused him as long as I possibly could, but he would take no denial—" And Isabella proceeded to describe the shameless pressing, begging, compliments and wild inducements that verily forced her against all nature to concede.

She added: "And your dear brother would have been miserable if I had sat down the whole evening. I am so glad it is over! My spirits are jaded, listening to his nonsense—though, being such a smart young fellow, *every eye* was upon us."

"He is very handsome indeed."

"Handsome! Yes, I suppose he may. I dare say people would admire him in general; but he is not at all in my style of beauty. I hate a florid complexion and dark dragon eyes in a man. However, he is very well. Amazingly conceited, I am sure. I took him down several times, you know, in my way."

When the young ladies next met, they had a far more interesting subject to discuss.

James Morland's second letter was then received, and the kind intentions of his father fully explained. A living, of which Mr. Morland was himself patron and incumbent, of about *four hundred pounds* yearly value, was to be given to his son. It was no trifling deduction from the family income, no miserly assignment to one of ten children. Moreover, an estate of at least equal value was assured as his future inheritance.

James expressed himself on the occasion with becoming gratitude. And the necessity of waiting two or three years before they could marry was no more than expected, and borne by him without discontent.

Catherine, whose expectations, ideas of her father's income, and judgment was entirely led by her brother, felt well satisfied. While perfectly aware of the deeply unpleasant *conversation* she was yet to have with James about *his bride,* she heartily congratulated Isabella on having things so pleasantly settled.

"It is very charming indeed," said Isabella, with a grave face. There was a particularly fierce yellowish cast to her eyes. And the ice! Oh, the ice came from her in arctic waves. . . .

"Mr. Morland has behaved vastly handsome indeed," said the gentle Mrs. Thorpe, looking anxiously at her daughter. "I only wish I could do as much. One could not expect more from him, you know. If he finds he *can* do more by and by, I dare say he will, for I am sure he must be an excellent good-hearted man. Four hundred is but a small income to begin on indeed. But your wishes, my dear Isabella, are so moderate."

"It is not on my own account I wish for more. But I cannot bear to be the means of injuring my dear Morland, making him sit down upon an income hardly enough to supply the common necessaries of life. For myself, nothing; I never think of myself."

"I know you never do, my dear. And you will always find your reward in the affection everybody feels for you. I dare say when Mr. Morland sees you, my dear child—but do not let us distress our dear Catherine by talking of such things. Mr. Morland has behaved so very handsome. I always heard he was a most excellent man; and, suppose if you had had a suitable fortune, he would have come down with something more."

"Nobody can think better of Mr. Morland than I do," cooed and hissed Isabella. "But everybody has their failing, you know. And everybody has a right to do what they like with their own money."

Catherine was hurt by these insinuations. "I am very sure," said she, no longer bothering to be particularly gentle, "that my father has promised to do as much as he can afford."

Isabella recollected herself. "As to that, my sweet, there cannot be a doubt! Fie! A much smaller income would satisfy me. It is not the *desire* of more money that makes me just at present a little out of spirits—I hate money; if our union produced only fifty pounds a year, I should be satisfied. Ah! my Catherine, it is the long, endless *wait* of two and a half years before your brother can hold the living, that breaks my heart."

"Yes, my darling Isabella," said Mrs. Thorpe, "we perfectly see into your heart and understand the present vexation. All must love you the better for such a noble honest affection."

Catherine's discomfort continued. James soon followed his letter, and was received with the most gratifying kindness—and a terror on Catherine's part, due to what she had yet to divulge to him. How will she ever find the courage and the proper moment to break his heart with the truth?

# Chapter 17

The Allens had now entered on the sixth week of their stay in Bath. And whether it should be the last, was a question to which Catherine listened with a beating heart.

To have her acquaintance with the Tilneys end so soon was an evil which nothing could counterbalance.

Her whole happiness seemed at stake while the decision to return or stay was in suspense. And everything good in the world was secured when it was determined that the lodgings should be taken for another fortnight.

The happy reasons for this extended stay were manifold—first and foremost, Bath had become a delightful place to be this season; in particular, most recently. According to Mr. and Mrs. Allen, all fine society was engrossed in the pursuit of discovering fantastic and mysterious clues to that fantastic and mysterious treasure hoard that was now rumored to equal the value of several royal state treasuries, and to contain the world's supply of either sapphires or rubies, or possibly both. Eager parties of ladies and gentlemen eschewed balls and other usual entertainments in favor of being engaged in daily scavenger hunts in the Upper and Lower Rooms, in the pump-room, the Edgar's Buildings, the theatre, the markets, and on practically every street corner and storefront. Even the Regent had been rumored to have been notified and was secretly intending to pay a visit *incognito.* . . .

In the meantime, the town bookshops had been stripped of every copy of every volume ever written by Mrs. Radcliffe and her literary colleagues, and the lending libraries had a run on all her works by patrons swiftly reserving and withdrawing all editions—with one location witnessing an unfortunate incident that concluded in a duel of honor between a marquis and a baronet, all because of a single remaining unreserved volume of *The Mysteries of Udolpho* which was considered the masterwork and the key to the decryption of the entire grand mystery.

Wherever one went in Bath, quizzing glasses were pointed at inanimate objects on street corners, and erudite gentlemen and ladies wisely commented on every street sign, every statue of a saint, angel, and classical or historic personage, frozen in aspects that were somehow deigned *meaningful.* That figure had its upraised arm pointing at the bell tower; this was surely inclined to the right to indicate the theatre; that one bowing to the ground to suggest, "Dig here!"

And thus they dug—here, there, and everywhere—in planters, around columns and posts, in backyard gardens (cultivating meaningful *root* vegetables—and then simply any roots of any plant that appeared in the least bit guilty of secrets) underneath every spot where a pick or shovel could be made to disturb the earth in response to "Mysterious Warnings." Gentlemen walking the street no longer carried walking sticks but cleverly designed shovels they could unfold at any opportunity of impending Clue, like an umbrella for sudden precipitation. Ladies were equipped with small hand baskets, and wild random trinkets filled them; "Midnight Bells" being most common, followed closely by turnips, potatoes, carrots, or other edible *roots.*

Mrs. "Clermont" and her daughters were subjected to more daily visitors than they could handle—indeed, a steady relentless stream of perfect strangers coming to call, often at scandalous hours. They were constantly stopped on the streets or interviewed in their own parlor as to the significance of this or that, and their opinion on practically everything. They were introduced to orphans and presented with discreet cowbells. In addition, they each received several dozen marriage proposals, which Mrs. Clermont, an impoverished but genteel widow, found extremely gratifying for all (indeed, she and her spinster daughters were now suddenly all settled in way of impending matrimony to gentlemen of excellent connections, and all within one remarkable season).

A similar wave of attention plagued every lady and gentleman with the initials MW, and in some cases merely with the surname W. And oh, poor Beatrice Foster! How many times must the dear lady prove to practical strangers that she was *not* something or another; and if she was *not,* then surely she must know someone who *was,* or *is*—whatever *that* is or is not, or was or was not[21]. In particular had she resisted being thought the "Necromancer of the Black Forest" which, to put it plain, was entirely unseemly.

Two local orphanages became exceedingly popular, and the children were quizzed and examined, and inquiries were made as far as their Germanic origin. Indeed, the headmasters and proprietors soon recognized the advantage, and suddenly every darling child was discovered to be an "Orphan of the Rhine."

One gentleman of poor hearing took the above notion to an unfortunate extreme, and made relentless inquiries at the selfsame orphanages, as to whether there were any rye fields in the neighborhood, and if any of the dear orphans had been discovered "in the rye."

A certain Lord Wolfe was driven to distraction by inquiries as to whether he had the right to an ancestral title of

---

[21] Gentle Reader, pray, do not attempt to make sense of this.

"Wolfenbach"—and if so, if it had for its symbol a toothy grand wolf—and whether he owned a hoary castle somewhere in Austria; and if so, if it was called the "Castle of Wolfenbach." Meanwhile, various fine dining establishments made a point of emphasizing that they served *cow*, and fresh *milk*, and that the beef and dairy had indeed come from the grassy *cow*-teeming fields and green *cow*-overrun glades surrounding the "Castle of Wolfenbach"—with or without the blessing of Lord Wolfe and his supposed bovine-or-wolf-infested family.

A clever lady proposed that "Horrid Mysteries" indicated HM and was a secret royal treasure designator. An overly clever gentleman insisted that MB, the initials of "Midnight Bell," were to be reversed as BM, which indicated a certain bodily function not to be mentioned in polite society (but eagerly to be analyzed and poked and prodded—to pardon the putrid pun—in less sensitive company at the private clubs).

Indeed, things had generated to the point of being delightful to the extreme, and Mr. Allen and Mrs. Allen both had acquired a new fascination with all of it.

Thus, they all had to stay in Bath. How could they *not* stay, when the whole world was now *here*, running around in search of wonderfully amusing secret clues, or looking overhead to quiz the heavens for a glimpse of flying dragons?

*Oh dear! And all of it is my fault*, thought Catherine. *If only I had not divulged my silly thoughts on those horrid clues to Mr. Thorpe who then shared them with so many—*

In that additional time allotted to their visit here, our heroine herself had other more serious intentions. Secrets of the Udolpho Code to be unraveled were splendid in themselves. But Catherine was also hoping to gather enough courage to address her brother and have a discussion about certain *unnatural* and dangerous cold-front-inducing females who in reality were not lovely beauties but leathery stick-like scarecrows, with hay for hair, angular frightful countenances and bright yellow eyes—not to mention, with infernal ogre brothers. . . .

But every time Catherine found herself alone with James, she felt tongue-tied, and no words would come out. How to even begin to describe her reasons for the evil of this engagement without describing her ability to *see* angels and demons and everything else? In addition, despite everything wicked she knew about the naphil, she genuinely pitied Isabella. And so Catherine experienced agonies of guilt with every passing day.

What this additional fortnight was to produce to her beyond the fright of talking to James and the pleasure of sometimes seeing Henry Tilney made but a small part of Catherine's speculation. Once or twice indeed, since James's engagement had given her certain *notions,* she had got so far as to indulge in a secret "perhaps." But in general, the felicity of being with Mr. Tilney for the present bounded her views—the present was now comprised in another three weeks of happiness, while the future was too remote to excite interest.

In the course of the morning, she visited Miss Tilney, and poured forth her joyful feelings. But no sooner had she expressed her delight in Mr. Allen's lengthened stay than Miss Tilney told her of her father's having just determined upon quitting Bath by the end of another week.

Here was a blow! Catherine's countenance fell. In a small voice she echoed Miss Tilney, "By the end of another week!"

"Yes, my father can seldom be prevailed on to give the waters a fair trial. He is now in a hurry to get home."

"I am very sorry for it," said Catherine dejectedly; "if I had known this before—"

"Perhaps," said Miss Tilney in an embarrassed manner, "you would be so good—it would make me very happy if—"

The entrance of her father put a stop to the civility, which Catherine hoped might introduce a desire of their corresponding. After addressing her with his usual politeness, he turned to his daughter and said, "Well, Eleanor, may I congratulate you on being successful in your application to your fair friend?"

"I was just beginning to make the request, sir, as you came in."

"Well, proceed by all means. I know how much your heart is in it. My daughter, Miss Morland," he continued, without leaving his daughter time to speak, "has been forming a very bold wish. We leave Bath, as she has perhaps told you, on Saturday. My presence is wanted at home; and disappointed in my hope of seeing some of my very old friends, there is nothing to detain me longer in Bath. And but for you, we should leave it without regret. Can you, in short, be prevailed on to quit this scene of public triumph and *treasure* hunting and oblige your friend Eleanor with your company in Gloucestershire?"

The general then added, "I am almost ashamed to make the request, though its presumption would certainly appear greater to every creature in Bath than yourself. Modesty such as yours—If you can be induced to honour us with a visit, you will make us happy beyond expression. 'Tis true, we can offer you nothing like the gaieties of this lively place; neither amusement nor splendour, for our mode of living, as you see, is plain and unpretending. Yet nothing shall be wanting on our side to make Northanger Abbey not wholly disagreeable."

Northanger Abbey! These were thrilling words, and wound up Catherine's feelings to the highest point of ecstasy.

Her grateful and gratified heart could hardly restrain its expressions. To receive so flattering an invitation! To have her company so warmly solicited! Everything honourable and wonderful was generously implied. And her acceptance, hinging only on parental approbation, was eagerly given. "I will write home directly," said she, "I dare say they will not object—"

Meanwhile, General Tilney had already waited on her excellent friends in Pulteney Street, and obtained their sanction.

"Since they can consent to part with you," said he, "we may expect success."

Miss Tilney was gently earnest in her secondary civilities, and in a few minutes the affair became nearly settled.

Catherine's morning had started with uncertainty but now was safely lodged in perfect bliss. With spirits elated to rapture, with Henry at her heart, and Northanger Abbey on her lips, she hurried home to write her letter.

Mr. and Mrs. Morland felt no doubt of the propriety of entrusting their daughter on this new fine acquaintance; and their ready consent to her visit in Gloucestershire was sent by return post. This indulgence completed her conviction of being *favoured* beyond every other human creature, in friends and fortune, circumstance and chance—and of course angelic oversight and guidance.

Everything seemed to cooperate for her advantage. By the kindness of the Allens she had been introduced into scenes where pleasures of every kind had met her. Her feelings and preferences were reciprocated. Wherever she felt attachment, she had been able to create it.

There was even the unnatural *affection* of a naphil, Isabella, who apparently had every sincere intent to be her dearest sister.

The Tilneys—they, by whom, above all, she desired to be favourably thought of—outstripped even her wishes in the flattering measures by which their intimacy was to be continued. She was to be their chosen visitor! She was to be for weeks under the same roof with the person whose society she mostly prized—and, in addition, this *roof* was to be the roof of an abbey!

Her passion for ancient edifices was next in degree to her passion for Henry Tilney—and castles and abbeys made usually the charm of those reveries which his image did not fill. To see and explore either the ramparts and keep of the one, or the cloisters of the other, had been for many weeks a darling wish.

And now, this was to happen. Verily, Udolpho itself was to be before her, unraveling in all its occult glory!

*"Take care, dear child!"* whispered the angels. *"There is indeed danger to be found here!"*

"Criminy! Danger abides everywhere, including Bath, and I dare say, Fullerton!" replied Catherine, emboldened by the near fulfillment of her oldest desire.

With all the chances against her of house, hall, place, park, court, and cottage, Northanger turned up an *abbey*—a glorious haunted, ancient, twisted, menacing, drafty (the draftier the better) horrid delight of an abbey!—and she was to be its inhabitant!

Oh, its long, damp passages! Oh, its narrow cells and ruined chapel; oh, its dark, wicked, accursed, thoroughly sanguined, goodness-knows-whatsits!—All were to be within her daily reach! Who needed silly hidden *treasure* hoards (and strange, unidentified, and not-sufficiently-determined-to-be-real airborne dragons), when there was to be metaphysical ancient mystery? And she could not entirely subdue the hope of some traditional legends, some awful memorials of an injured and ill-fated *nun*. Or several nuns! Fie, an entire abbey of them!

And in all this, it was a wonder that her friends should seem so little elated by the possession of such a home. The power of early habit only could account for it. A distinction to which they had been born gave no pride. Their superiority of horrid abode was no more to them than their superiority of person.

Many were the inquiries that Catherine was eager to make of Miss Tilney. But so active were her thoughts, that when these inquiries were answered, she was hardly more assured than before—of Northanger Abbey having been a richly endowed convent at the time of the Reformation, of its having *fallen* into the hands of an ancestor of the Tilneys on its *dissolution,* of a large portion of the *ancient* building still making a part of the present dwelling although the rest was *decayed,* or of its standing low in a valley, *sheltered* from the north and east by rising woods of oak.

Catherine listened pointedly but heard mostly words such as "fallen . . . dissolution . . . ancient . . . decayed . . . sheltered . . ."

And oh, it was all such horrid Udolpho-worthy delight!

# Chapter 18

With a mind thus full of happiness, Catherine was hardly aware that two or three days had passed away, without her seeing Isabella for more than a few minutes together.

She began first to be sensible of this, and to almost miss her conversation, as she walked along the pump-room one morning, by Mrs. Allen's side, without anything to say or to hear, and feeling not even a twinge of icy Isabella-air to give her an invigorating chill. Scarcely had she felt a five minutes' longing of friendship and climate adjustment before the frost-bearing creature herself appeared, and inviting her to a secret conference, led the way to a seat.

"This is my favourite place," said Isabella as they sat down on a bench between the doors, which commanded a tolerable view of everybody entering at either; "it is so out of the way."

Catherine, observing that Isabella's eyes were continually bent towards one door or the other, as in eager expectation, gaily said, "Do not be uneasy, Isabella, James will soon be here."

"Psha! My dear creature," she replied in a gentle screech, "do not think me such a simpleton as to be always wanting to confine him to my elbow. It would be hideous to be always together; we should be the jest of the place. And so you are going to Northanger! I am amazingly glad of it. It is one of the finest old places in England, I understand. I shall depend upon a most particular description of it."

"You shall certainly have the best in my power to give. But who are you looking for? Are your sisters coming? Was that Maria over there, quizzing a statue with a bell, next to that gentleman with a walking-shovel?"

"I dare say not; they are off near the markets, collecting orphans or turnips—I forget which. And—I am not looking for anybody. One's eyes must be somewhere, and you know what a foolish trick I have of fixing mine, when my thoughts are an hundred miles off. I am amazingly absent—the most absent creature in the world. *Tilney* says it is always the case with minds of a certain stamp."

"But I thought, Isabella, you had something in particular to tell me?"

"Oh! Yes, and so I have. But here is a proof of what I was saying. My poor head, I had quite forgot it. Well, the thing is this: I have just had a letter from John; you can guess the contents."

"No, indeed, I cannot." Catherine rather felt her forehead requiring a handkerchief, just remembering that certain inferno.

"My sweet love, do not be so abominably affected. What can he write about, but yourself? You know he is over head and ears in love with you."

"With *me*, dear Isabella!"

"Nay, my sweetest Catherine, this is being quite absurd! Modesty is very well in its way, but really! His attentions were such as a child must have noticed. And it was but half an hour before he left Bath that you gave him the most positive encouragement. He says so in this letter—says that he as good as made you an offer, and that you received his advances in the kindest way. And now he wants me to urge his suit."

Catherine, with all earnestness, expressed her astonishment at such a charge. She protested her innocence of any thought of

Mr. Thorpe's being in love with her, and it was impossible she had ever encouraged him. "As to any attentions on his side, I do declare, upon my honour, I never was sensible of them for a moment—except just his asking me to dance the first day of his coming. And as to making me an offer, or anything like it, there must be some unaccountable mistake. I could not have misunderstood a thing of that kind! Indeed, I did not see him once that whole morning."

"But that you certainly did, for you spent the whole morning in Edgar's Buildings—it was the day your father's consent came; mother and Mrs. Allen had gone somewhere in search of muslin, or cows, or both. You and John were alone in the parlour some time—I venture, not discussing secret Clues!"

"Well, if you say it, it was so, I dare say—but for the life of me, I cannot recollect it. I do remember now being with you, and seeing him as well as the rest—but that we were ever alone for five minutes—However, it is not worth arguing about. You must be convinced that I never thought, nor expected, nor wished for anything of the kind from him. I am excessively concerned that he should have any regard for me. Pray undeceive him, and tell him I beg his pardon—that is—I do not know what I ought to say—but make him understand what I mean. I would not speak disrespectfully of a brother of yours, Isabella, I am sure; but you know very well that if I could think of *one man* more than another—he is *not* the person."

Isabella was silent like an iceberg floating in the Arctic.

Catherine shivered, while an angel began to fan the warmer air from the other side in her direction. "My dear Isabella, you must not be angry with me. I cannot suppose your brother cares so very much about me. And we shall still be sisters."

"Yes, yes" (with a blush and a screech), "there are more ways than one of our being sisters. But where am I wandering to? Well, my dear Catherine, the case seems to be that you are determined against poor John—is not it so?"

**The gentlemen and their walking-shovels.**

"I certainly cannot return his affection, and as certainly never meant to encourage it."

"Since that is the case, I am sure I shall not tease you any further. John desired me to speak to you on the subject, and I have. But I confess, as soon as I read his letter, I thought it a very foolish, imprudent business. For what were you to live upon, supposing you came together?" And Isabella went on for several ear-rending moments about the pitiful lack of money.

"You do acquit me, then, of anything wrong?—You are convinced that I never meant to deceive your brother?"

"Oh! As to that," Isabella shrilled laughingly, "I do not pretend to determine what your thoughts and designs in time past may have been. Little harmless flirtations will occur, and one is often drawn on to give more encouragement than one wishes. But you may be assured that I am the last person in the world to judge youth and high spirits. What is meant one day, may not be the next. Circumstances change, opinions alter."

"But my opinion of your brother never did alter; it was always the same. You are describing what never happened."

"My dearest Catherine," continued the other without at all listening to her, "I would not for all the world be the means of hurrying you into an engagement before you knew what you were about. Nothing would justify me in wishing you to sacrifice all your happiness merely to oblige my brother. Perhaps he might be just as happy without you, for people seldom know, young men especially—they are so amazingly changeable and inconstant. Why should a brother's happiness be dearer to me than a friend's? But, above all things, my dear, do not be in a hurry, or you will certainly live to repent it. *Tilney* says people are most deceived as to the state of their own affections, and I believe he is very right. Ah! Here he comes! Never mind, he will not see us, I am sure."

Catherine, looking up, perceived Captain Tilney. Isabella, earnestly fixing her blazing yellow eye on him as she spoke,

202      Jane Austen and Vera Nazarian

soon caught his notice. He approached immediately, enthralled, and took the seat to which her movements invited him.

His first address made Catherine start, and sent two angels tumbling from her shoulder. Though spoken low, she could distinguish, "What! Always to be watched, in person or by proxy!"

"Psha, nonsense!" was Isabella's answer in a cooing screech, interpreted by the gentleman as a similar delicate half-whisper. "Why do you put such things into my head?"

And then for several minutes they engaged in a flirtation that included references to *hearts, eyes,* and *torment.*

Catherine heard all this, and, quite out of countenance, could listen no longer. Amazed that Isabella could endure it, and jealous for her brother—though, *why,* she had no idea! Indeed, did she not *want* this fiendish engagement to be over?—she rose up, and saying she should join Mrs. Allen, proposed their walking.

But for this Isabella showed no inclination. She was so amazingly tired, and it was so odious to parade about the pump-room with the other silly treasure seekers; and if she moved from her seat she should miss her sisters who were out foraging for that orphaned turnip nonsense. Dearest Catherine must excuse her, and must sit quietly down again.

But Catherine could be stubborn too; and Mrs. Allen just then coming up to propose their returning home, she joined her and walked out of the pump-room, leaving Isabella still sitting with Captain Tilney.

Mrs. Allen went on at length about having seen a real *dragon* fly over the millinery shop minutes ago, and, she dared declare, it was *unbelievable*—but Catherine's mind was filled with too much contradictory uneasiness and outrage to properly respond.

It seemed to her that Captain Tilney was falling in love with Isabella, and Isabella unconsciously encouraging him.

Unconsciously it must be—for Isabella's attachment to James was as certain as her engagement. To doubt her good *intentions* was impossible. Even though, it occurred to Catherine, wasn't this possible disloyalty exactly what she was dearly hoping for—considering that she *wanted* the engagement between her brother and the frightful naphil to be dissolved?

Oh dear, didn't Catherine know her own mind any longer? Or maybe she was just getting used to it, to her horrid, unnatural female friend *being with* James?

And then . . . oh, the horrid ogre being in love with *her!*

But enough!—Her mind returned to her fiendish friend and Captain Tilney. During the whole of their conversation Isabella's manner had been odd. Catherine even wished Isabella had talked more like her usual gaily confident, screeching scarecrow self, and not so much about *money,* and had not looked so *well pleased* at the sight of Captain Tilney. How strange that she should not perceive his admiration! Catherine longed to give her a hint of it—*oh dear, there she was again, thinking along the lines of keeping her brother and his infernal bride together!* What in all heaven was she thinking? Yes, there would be pain for her brother, but it was for the best, surely!

Maybe it was because of the so-called "compliment" in the form of John Thorpe's horrid affection that made her mind decidedly not its own. She felt unmentionable revulsion and fright, merely at the thought.

Though, she was almost disbelieving of it. For she had not forgotten that the ogre frequently made glaring, blunt mistakes. His assertion of the offer and of her encouragement convinced her that his misunderstandings were indeed very egregious.

That he should think it worth his while to fancy himself in love with her was a matter of lively astonishment. Maybe he had been impressed by her *decryption* skills and enamored with her for the sake of the Udolpho Code?

Isabella talked of his attentions, but—upon her word, Isabella had said many things before which were frankly idiotic.

# Chapter 19

A few days passed, and Catherine, could not help watching Isabella closely. The result of her observations was not agreeable. Isabella seemed an altered creature.

Catherine knew that she alone was *seeing* her same, true, frightful monster self where others could only see an enchanted delightful veneer (the men, in particular). And yet, even the usual sallow stick-scarecrow at the heart of the *illusion* was now different somehow—more inward drawn, more emaciated perhaps?

When she saw Isabella, indeed, surrounded only by their immediate friends in Edgar's Buildings or Pulteney Street, her change of manners was so *subtle,* so trifling that, had it gone no farther, it might have passed unnoticed. A languid indifference, an absence of mind, would occasionally come across her.

But when Catherine saw her in public, admitting Captain Tilney's attentions as readily as they were offered, and according him almost an equal share of her notice and smiles as James, the alteration became undeniable. What could be meant by such unsteady conduct? Isabella could not be aware of the pain she was inflicting—granted, Catherine *wanted* this pain, did she not?—but James was the sufferer. Oh, it was unbearable!

She saw him grave and uneasy. For poor Captain Tilney too she was greatly concerned. For the sake of Henry, his better brother, she thought with sincere compassion of his approaching disappointment.

For, in spite of what she had believed herself to overhear in the pump-room, his behaviour was so incompatible with a knowledge of Isabella's engagement that she could not imagine him aware of it. He might be jealous of her brother as a rival, but anything more was her misapprehension.

Catherine was determined to at least remind Isabella of her engaged situation for propriety's sake (at least for now—no commitment must be broken until she had her fateful revelation talk with James), but seemed to find no opportunity for it either. Isabella appeared impervious to hints.

In this distress, the intended departure of the Tilney family became our heroine's chief consolation. Their journey into Gloucestershire was to take place within a few days, and Captain Tilney's removal would at least restore peace to every heart but his own.

But Captain Tilney had at present no intention of removing. He was not to accompany them to Northanger, he was to continue at Bath. When Catherine learned this, her resolution was directly made. She spoke to Henry Tilney on the subject, regretting his brother's evident partiality for Miss Thorpe, and entreating him to make known her prior engagement.

"My brother does know it," was Henry's answer.

"Does he? Then why does he stay here?"

He made no reply, and was beginning to talk of something else; but she eagerly continued, "Why do not you persuade him to go away? The longer he stays, the worse it will be for him at last. Pray advise him for everybody's sake, to leave Bath directly."

Henry smiled. "I am sure my brother would not wish it."

"Then you will persuade him to go away?"

"I cannot even endeavour to persuade him. I have myself told him that Miss Thorpe is engaged. He knows what he is about, and must be his own master."

"No, he does *not* know what he is about!" cried Catherine, while at least three angels rose up in anxious flurries of light and moved from her to Mr. Tilney, then back again. "He does not know the pain he is giving my brother. I *know* James is very uncomfortable."

"And are you sure it is my brother's doing?"

"Yes, very sure."

"Is it my brother's attentions to Miss Thorpe, or Miss Thorpe's admission of them, that gives the pain?"

"Is not it the same thing?"

"I think Mr. Morland would acknowledge a difference. No man is offended by another man's admiration of the woman he loves. It is the woman only who can make it a torment."

Catherine blushed for her *unnatural* so-called friend, and said, "Isabella is wrong. But I am sure she cannot mean to torment—well, not exactly, that is, considering what she *is,* she *could*—I mean, oh dear—" Catherine stopped, realizing in alarm that she almost confessed Isabella's true nature to Mr. Tilney—a notion rather disastrous since it would have certainly led her to divulge certain other supernatural things to him, including things about *herself.* And she was not ready to do such a thing at all.

Changing her words, she continued, "Isabella is very much attached to my brother. She has been in love with him ever since they first met, always at his side—"

"I understand: she is in love with James, and flirts with Frederick."

"Oh, no, not flirts. A woman in love with one man cannot flirt with another—could she?"

Henry's look was again rather unfathomable. "It is probable that she will neither love so well, nor flirt so well, as she might do either singly. The gentlemen must each give up a little."

After a short pause, Catherine resumed with, "Then you do not believe Isabella so very much attached to my brother?"

"I can have no opinion on that subject."

"But what can your brother mean? If he knows her engagement, what can he *mean* by his *behaviour?*"

"You are a very close questioner."

"Am I? I only ask what I want to be told."

"But do you only ask what I can be expected to tell?"

"Yes, I think so; for you must know your brother's heart."

"My brother's heart, I assure you I can only guess at."

This oddly compelling exchange continued until Henry admitted to his brother being upon occasion thoughtless, and Catherine inquired why General Tilney did not intervene.

"My dear Miss Morland," said Henry at last, "this solicitude for your brother's comfort is amiable. But, are you not carried a little too far? Would he thank you for supposing her affection, or good behaviour, is only to be secured by her never seeing Captain Tilney? Is he safe only in solitude? Is her heart constant to him only when unsolicited by anyone else?"

Perceiving her still doubtful and grave, he added, "Though Frederick does not leave Bath with us, he will remain but a very short time, only a few days behind us. His leave of absence will soon expire, and he must return to his regiment. There, all will be forgotten."

Catherine was at last comforted. Henry Tilney must know best. She blamed herself for her fears, and resolved not to think on it again until she and James had occasion to have the *talk*.

Her resolution was supported by Isabella's behaviour in their parting. The Thorpes spent the last evening of Catherine's stay in Pulteney Street, and nothing passed between the lovers to excite her uneasiness. James was in excellent spirits; Isabella engagingly placid, and only as chill as a summer day along one of the Poles. The heartfelt embraces, tears, and promises of their parting may only be imagined.

# Chapter 20

Mr. and Mrs. Allen were sorry to lose their young friend, whose good humour and cheerfulness had made her a valuable companion, and in the promotion of whose enjoyment their own had been rather unwittingly increased—in chief, the blame for the delightful condition of Bath society given over to the pursuit of *secrets* and *treasure* could be laid at her feet (by way of a rather industrious tongue of John Thorpe).

Her happiness in going with Miss Tilney, however, prevented their wishing it otherwise. They were to remain only one more week in Bath themselves, despite the charm of dragon sightings, cryptic root vegetables, quaint tinkling bells—some of the latter even recovered from the very water itself in the pump-room, etc. Her quitting them now would not long be felt.

Mr. Allen attended her to Milsom Street, where she was to breakfast, and saw her seated with the kindest welcome among her new friends.

But so great was Catherine's happy agitation in finding herself as one of the family, and so fearful was she of not doing exactly what was right, or losing their good opinion, that, in the embarrassment of the first five minutes, she could almost have wished to return with Mr. Allen to Pulteney Street.

Catherine refrained from talking to angels out of sheer nerves, even though they settled among the table settings, and soared from dish to dish in her vicinity, making gentle suggestions to compose her manners. *"You are managing wonderfully well, dear child, only do watch that sauce dish directly above your elbow—oh dear . . ."*

Miss Tilney's manners and Henry's smile soon did away some of her unpleasant feelings (and guilt over spilled sauce). But still she was far from being at ease.

Nor could the incessant attentions of the general himself entirely reassure her. Nay, perverse as it seemed, she might have felt *less* discomposure had she been less attended to by such an *imposing* man as himself. His anxiety for her comfort—continual solicitations that she eat, often-expressed fears of her seeing nothing to her taste—though never in her life before had she beheld half such variety on a breakfast-table—made it impossible for her to forget for a moment that she was a visitor.

Catherine felt utterly unworthy of such respect, and knew not how to reply to it. She nervously voiced inanities to Lawrence or Clarence, belatedly coughed into a napkin to disguise her mutterings, and was in such poor form that even Miss Tilney gave her comforting looks.

Her tranquility was not improved by the general's impatience for the appearance of his eldest son—nor by his displeasure at Captain Tilney's laziness when he at last came down. The severity of fatherly reproof seemed disproportionate to the offence. Her concern deepened when she found herself the principal cause of the lecture; his tardiness, a sign of disrespect to her. This placed her in a very uncomfortable situation. Soon, she felt great sympathy for Captain Tilney.

He listened to his father in silence, attempting no defense. Catherine feared this was an inquietude of his mind on Isabella's account; sleeplessness over her being the cause of his rising late.

It was the first time she found herself in his company (as opposed to being an observer in passing), and now she hoped to be able to form her opinion of him. But she scarcely heard his voice while his father remained in the room. Even afterwards, so much were his spirits affected, she could distinguish only his whisper to Eleanor, "How glad I shall be when you are all off."

The bustle of going was not pleasant. The clock struck ten while the trunks were carrying down, and the general had fixed to be out of Milsom Street by that hour.

His greatcoat, instead of being brought for him to put on directly, was spread out in the curricle in which he was to accompany his son. Catherine glanced at it in passing, oddly reminded of a grand wingspan of an ancient airborne *creature,* and thought for a moment that she saw a glitter of metallic scales. . . .

*Upon my word,* said Catherine to herself, *now I am being entirely nonsensical. And we have not even embarked to Udolpho yet—that is, to Northanger . . .*

The middle seat of the chaise was not drawn out, though there were three people to go in it, and his daughter's maid had so crowded it with parcels that Miss Morland would not have room to sit. So much was the general influenced by this apprehension when he handed her in, that she had some difficulty in saving her own new writing-desk from being thrown out into the street.

At last, however, the door was closed upon the three females. They set off at the sober pace in which the handsome, highly fed four horses of a gentleman usually perform a journey of thirty miles—such was the distance of Northanger from Bath, to be divided into two equal stages.

Catherine's spirits revived as they drove from the door. For, with Miss Tilney she felt no restraint. And, with the interest of a road entirely new to her, of an abbey before, and a curricle behind, she caught the last view of Bath without any regret of any of its hidden treasures, and only anticipation of horrid wonders ahead.

The tediousness of a two hours' wait at Petty France, in which there was nothing to be done but to eat without being hungry, and loiter about without anything to see or even *decrypt*, next followed. Her admiration of their travel style; the fashionable chaise and four—postilions handsomely liveried, rising so regularly in their stirrups, numerous outriders properly mounted—sunk a little under this consequent inconvenience.

Had their party been perfectly agreeable, the delay would have been nothing. But General Tilney, though so charming a man, seemed always a check upon his children's spirits. Scarcely anything was said but by himself. His discontent at whatever the inn afforded, his angry impatience at the waiters, made Catherine grow every moment more in awe of him, and appeared to lengthen the two hours into a horrid four (though, horrid not in the happy Udolpho sense).

At last, however, the order of release was given. Catherine was then much surprised by the general's proposal of her taking *his place* in his son's curricle for the rest of the journey: "the day was fine, and he was anxious for her seeing as much of the country as possible."

The remembrance of Mr. Allen's opinion in regard to young men's open carriages, made her blush at the mention of such a plan, and her first thought was to decline it. But her second deferred to General Tilney's judgment—he could not propose anything improper for her. For that matter, the angels surrounding her loudly rejoiced, and their suddenly iridescent wings glowed visibly brighter even in the sunlight.

Thus, she found herself with Henry in the curricle, as happy a being as ever existed. Soon she was convinced that a curricle was the prettiest equipage in the world. The chaise and four had grandeur, but it had stopped like a troll for two hours at Petty

France. Half the time would have been enough for the curricle. So nimble were the horses that they could have passed the general's carriage in half a minute.

But the merit of the curricle did not all belong to the horses; Henry drove so well—so *quietly*—without making any *ogre* disturbance, without an infernal attendant climate, without parading to her while also muttering about hidden Clues, or swearing at them in a roar, or needing to beat off any monstrous *ducks* . . . In short—so different from the only other gentleman-coachman whom she could compare him with!

And then his hat sat so well, and the innumerable capes of his greatcoat looked so becomingly important! Indeed, there was a sense of leashed wondrous *power* emanating from him; of mystery even. . . .

To be driven by him, next to dancing with him, was certainly the greatest happiness in the world.

In addition to every other delight, she was now listening to her own praise; was being thanked (on his sister's account) for her kindness in becoming her visitor; hearing it ranked as real friendship creating real gratitude. His sister, he said, was uncomfortably circumstanced—she had no female companion—and, in the frequent absence of her father, was sometimes without any companion at all.

"But how can that be?" said Catherine. "Are not you with her?"

"Northanger is only half my home; I have an establishment at my own house in Woodston, which is nearly twenty miles from my father's. Some of my time is necessarily spent there."

"How sorry you must be for that!"

"I am always sorry to leave Eleanor."

"Yes; but besides your affection for her, you must be so fond of the abbey! After being used to such a home as the abbey, an ordinary parsonage-house must be very disagreeable."

He smiled, and said, "You have formed a very favourable idea of the abbey."

"To be sure, I have. Is not it a fine old place, just like what one reads about?"

"Aha! And so we come at last to Udolpho! Well then, are you prepared to encounter all the horrors that a building such as 'what one reads about' may produce? Have you a stout heart? Nerves fit for sliding panels and tapestry? A mind steadfast and clear enough to decrypt sanguine *terror* from arcane clues?"

Catherine held back an imminent exclamation of utter delight.

"What," he continued, "think you only Bath has dire secrets to unravel, its carrots and cowbells at midnight? Wait till you see the abbey!"

"Oh! yes—that is, no! I do not think I should be easily frightened, because there would be so many people in the house—and besides, it has never been uninhabited and left deserted for years, and then the family come back to it unawares, without giving any notice, as generally happens."

"No, certainly. We shall not have to explore our way into a hall dimly lighted by the expiring embers of a wood fire—nor be obliged to spread our beds on the floor of a room without windows, doors, or furniture. But you must be aware that when a young lady is introduced into such a dwelling, she is always lodged apart from the rest of the family. While they snugly repair to their own end of the house, she is formally conducted by Dorothy, the ancient housekeeper, up a different staircase, and along many gloomy passages, thick with ghosts, into an apartment never used since some cousin or kin died in it about twenty years before—under *unspeakable* circumstances. Can you stand such a ceremony as this? Will not your mind misgive you when you find yourself in this gloomy chamber—too lofty and extensive for you, with only the feeble rays of a single lamp to take in its size—its walls hung with tapestry exhibiting figures as large as life, and the bed, of dark green stuff or purple velvet, presenting even a *funereal* appearance? Will not your heart sink within you?"

"Oh! But this will not happen to me, I am sure," said Catherine, breathlessly imagining things even more dreadful.

"How fearfully will you examine the furniture of your apartment! And what will you discern? Not tables, toilettes, wardrobes, or drawers, but on one side perhaps the remains of a broken lute, on the other a ponderous chest which *no efforts can open,* and over the fireplace the portrait of some handsome warrior, whose features will so incomprehensibly strike you, that you will not be able to withdraw your eyes from it. Dorothy, meanwhile, no less struck by your appearance, gazes on you in great *agitation,* and drops a few unintelligible *hints* (entirely more dire than turnips). To raise your spirits, moreover, she gives you reason to suppose that the part of the abbey you inhabit is undoubtedly *haunted,* and informs you that you will not have a single domestic within call. With this parting cordial she curtsies off—you listen to the sound of her receding footsteps as long as the last echo can reach you, not unlike *midnight bells*—and when, with fainting spirits, you attempt to fasten your door, you discover, with increased alarm, that it has *no lock.*"

"Oh! Mr. Tilney, how frightful! This is just like a book! But it cannot really happen to me. I am sure your housekeeper is not really Dorothy. Well, what then?"

"Nothing further to alarm perhaps may occur the *first* night. After surmounting your unconquerable horror of the bed, you will retire to rest, and get a few hours' unquiet slumber. But on the second, or at farthest the *third* night after your arrival, you will probably have a violent *storm.* Peals of thunder so loud as to seem to shake the edifice to its foundation will roll round the neighbouring mountains—and during the frightful gusts of wind you will probably discern (for your lamp is not extinguished) one part of the hanging more violently agitated than the rest. Unable of course to repress your curiosity in so favourable a moment for indulging it, you will instantly arise, throwing your dressing-gown around you, and examine this mystery. After a very short search, you will discover a *division* in the tapestry so artfully constructed as to defy the minutest inspection, and on opening it, a *door* will immediately appear—being only secured by massy bars and a padlock, you will succeed in opening it— and, with your lamp in your hand, will pass through it into a small vaulted room."

"No, indeed; I should be too much frightened to do any such thing. Heaven be praised there are dear angels to protect us—" Catherine was once again about to say too much.

Fortunately he seemed to overlook that portion of her utterance. "What! Not when Dorothy has given you to understand that there is a secret subterraneous communication between your apartment and the chapel of St. Anthony, scarcely two miles off? Could you shrink from so simple an *adventure?* No, you will proceed into this small vaulted room, and through this into others, without perceiving anything very remarkable in either. In one perhaps there may be a dagger, in another a few drops of blood—and a *cowbell*—and in a third the remains of some instrument of torture, and next to it a sack of meaningful *potatoes;* but there being nothing in all this out of the ordinary, and your lamp being nearly exhausted, you will return towards your own apartment. In repassing through the small vaulted room, however, your eyes will be drawn to a large old-fashioned cabinet of ebony and gold—labeled clearly that it was manufactured in an *orphanage* near the *Rhine* by a certain M. *Clermont* but *NOT Beatrice Foster*—which you had previously passed unnoticed. Impelled by an irresistible presentiment, you will eagerly advance to it, unlock its folding doors, and search into every drawer—but for some time without discovering anything of importance—perhaps nothing but a considerable *hoard of diamonds!"*

"Oh!" exclaimed Catherine; then put a hand across her lips. Meanwhile, a daring idea took hold—what if Northanger Abbey, not Bath, contained hidden treasure?

*"Oh dear . . ."* Clarence, or possibly Terence, let out a long-suffering sigh near one of her ears.

But Henry continued, despite her outburst: "At last, by touching a secret spring, an inner compartment will open—a roll of *paper* appears—you seize it—it contains many sheets of *manuscript*—you hasten with the precious *treasure* into your own chamber, but scarcely have you been able to decipher 'Oh! Thou—whomsoever thou mayst be, into whose hands these memoirs of the wretched Matilda may fall, written from this point forward in nothing but blood and implementing the most arcane and secret encryption method known only as *The Udolpho Code'*—when your lamp suddenly expires, leaving you in total darkness—to await the arrival of the *Necromancer of the Black Forest,* the one and only true heir to the *Castle of Wolfenbach!"*

"Oh! No! No!—do not say so!!! Well, go on."

But Henry was too much amused by the interest he had raised to be able to carry it farther. He could no longer command solemnity either of subject or voice, and was obliged to entreat her to use her own fancy in the continuation of Matilda's woes.

Apparently, Henry had no idea (or simply had forgotten) how great a part she had played in the infestation of those silly Clues all over Bath! And he was still laughing at her!

Catherine recollected herself, ashamed of her eagerness for the horrid, and assured him that she had not the smallest fear of really encountering what he related. "Miss Tilney, she was sure, would never put her into such a chamber as he had described! She was not at all afraid."

As they drew near the end of their journey, her impatience for a sight of the abbey returned in full force.

Every bend in the road was expected with solemn awe to afford a glimpse of its massy walls of grey stone, rising amidst a grove of ancient oaks, with the last beams of the sun playing in beautiful splendour on its high Gothic windows. . . .

But so low did the building stand, that she found herself passing through the great gates of the lodge into the very grounds of Northanger, without having discerned even an antique chimney.

She knew she had no right to be surprised. But there was a something in this mode of approach which she had not expected. To pass between lodges of a *modern* appearance, to find herself with such ease in the very precincts of the abbey, and driven so rapidly along a smooth, level road of fine gravel, without obstacle, alarm, or solemnity, struck her as odd and inconsistent.

She was not long at leisure for such considerations. A sudden scud of rain, driving full in her face, made it impossible for her to observe anything further, and fixed all her thoughts on the welfare of her new straw bonnet.

She was actually under the abbey walls, was springing, with Henry's assistance, from the carriage, was beneath the shelter of the old porch, and had even passed on to the hall, where her friend and the general were waiting to welcome her—without feeling one awful foreboding of future misery, or any past scenes of horror being acted within the solemn edifice.

The breeze had not seemed to waft the sighs of the murdered to her—not even a putrid stench of *anyone's* demon. It wafted nothing worse than a thick mizzling rain. And Catherine was ready to be shown into the common drawing-room.

An abbey! Yes, it was delightful to be really in an abbey! But she doubted, as she looked round the room, whether anything within her observation would have suggested it. The furniture was in all the profusion and elegance of *modern* taste.

The new marble fireplace displayed the prettiest English china. The windows, to which she looked for original Gothic form, were less than expected. To be sure, the pointed arch was preserved—they might be even casements—but every pane was so large, so clear, so light! To an imagination which had hoped for the smallest divisions, and the heaviest stone-work, for painted glass, ancient dirt, and cobwebs, the difference was very distressing.

The general, perceiving how her eye was employed, began to talk of the smallness of the room and simplicity of the furniture. All here was intended only for daily use and comfort. However, some apartments in the Abbey were worthy of her notice—and he began describing the costly gilding of one in particular—when, taking out his watch, he stopped short to pronounce it with surprise within twenty minutes of five!

This seemed to indicate it was time to part. Catherine found herself hurried away by Miss Tilney in such a manner as convinced her that the strictest punctuality to the family hours would be expected at Northanger.

Returning through the large and lofty hall, they ascended a broad staircase of shining oak, which, after many flights and many landing-places, brought them upon a long, wide gallery.

On one side it had a range of doors. And it was lighted on the other by windows which Catherine had only time to discover looked into a quadrangle, before Miss Tilney led the way into a chamber, and scarcely staying to hope she would find it comfortable, left her with an anxious entreaty that she would make as little alteration as possible in her dress.

After she had gone, Catherine turned momentarily to the nearest window and grew very still.

Outside, silhouetted against the sky, moved the swiftly receding unmistakable silhouette of a great *dragon*.

# Chapter 21

A moment's glance was enough to satisfy Catherine that her apartment was very unlike the one which Henry had described with the amused intent to alarm her.

Her heart was still beating rapidly after having seen the dragon outside her window. But our heroine composed herself. After all, unlike all the poor orphans, urchins, noble maidens, and waifs left to fend for themselves under tragic *Udolpho* circumstances, she was not *alone*.

She was surrounded by a world of heavenly guardians.

But then, so was everyone else (the only difference being, to them, all such guardianship was invisible). It never before occurred to Catherine to wonder *if* and *why* those doleful others—the sorrowful victims in the horrid novels—had been abandoned by Heaven's guardians to such destitute fates.

But now the sobering thought, brought on by the menacing shadow right outside her window, suddenly plagued her. What right, what hope had *she*, then, to a better fate?

But the answer came quickly and surely.

"You, dear child, can *see* and *hear* us in a manner unlike most everyone else. Thus, you are also guided and protected more securely—not because you are any better or more deserving than other mortals in the eyes of God, but because you are capable of being shown solutions that others *cannot* and *will not* make the effort to discover."

But Catherine persisted. "Dearest angels, but what of the innocents? Surely the little babes, the newborns cannot fend for themselves? What if they are stolen by sanguine villains? What is to protect them?"[22]

"It is true," said the angel, "that a child enters the world as a blank slate, stripped of all that came before, in order to begin anew. For, indeed you do not ask the full question—what came *before?*

"In this world it is possible to grasp only what can be ascertained by mortal senses in the present span of a lifetime. Much is speculated as to what comes *after* a life ends, but it is almost never spoken of what comes *before*. And yet, it is such an easy notion to consider, if one is but to look at anything else— take for example the baking of bread.

"Bread is not brought out of nothing into sudden being, to be eaten and enjoyed—verily, not even manna from heaven (which has its definite origins, i.e. heaven). Bread is baked from dough, which in turn is formed out of living yeasts and flours of wheat and other grains and water. And before that, the yeasts are cultivated and the grains themselves are grown and harvested from other living matter, with its own history of *being* (in whatever basic form) that stretches as long going back as it does going forward. Each loaf you eat has a history as far back as there are stars upon the firmament of heaven. You might ask, at what precise moment does a loaf *become* a loaf—become itself, that precise *thing* known as bread—and when does it *stop* being itself, and becomes something else in its eternal journey of existence?

---

[22] Be warned, O Virtuous Reader, what follows is a Meaningful Moral Lesson. An Aside, if you will (and even if you won't). Thus, you must steadfastly persevere onward, for there is no escaping your instruction in Theological Cosmology, nor in the culinary art of baking!

"And, if not ordinary daily bread, then why not a human child? What defines *it,* and what defines its innocence? Its flesh comes from the flesh of its parents, and it in itself is a living spark of divine energy that has its own source of *previous experience* from *somewhere else.* Innocence is a relative notion of this material world. It is a property of finite judgment—but mortal judgment can only go so far as to span that what is mortally known (though, often far less; if the mortal judge in question has had the misfortune to occupy a lofty court bench for a span of years sufficient to absorb enough law to have *become* the bench—hard; oft vacant, and when not, oft legally pugnacious; and always made of the same old wood[23]). Who, indeed, knows everything, but the One?

"And as for our newborn, the child indeed cannot make choices until it is self-aware enough to recognize the existence of such—at which point innocence ends and *responsibility* takes over. But, you ask, what of that moment of true innocence when the babe is still blameless and incapable, as far as *this* existence? The truth is—even with eyes closed against one's will, arms bound, feet restrained, one can still walk off a cliff or be carried over it by others whose choices are more unfettered. The child is exactly in such a vulnerable position. So many others can choose its fate. The child's mother, for example; others who care for the child—or who *neglect* it.

"The child has done nothing wrong yet it suffers, because it—and everything that comprises it: flesh, spirit, ancestral past, an existential chain of being, components from the stars themselves; all these things put together—is in a unique place and time—*a cosmic coordinate where suffering is to be found*—

---

[23] Gentle Reader, there is nothing more frightening than aggressive ignorance. To impose your own misinformed or vacant state upon someone else is a human crime. And yet, irony of ironies! It is a condition found, disturbingly often, precisely in the character of those who sit in judgment over human crimes.

that is the end result of many 'someones' and their various choices.

"The angels cannot protect or guard where there are no choices to be found or made. And the secret truth is, *we are not guardians of the flesh but of the spirit.* We only guard that which can be guarded, the kernel that is everlasting. All else is ephemeral clamor, and fades away to dust, as the world turns.

"Indeed, the world is nothing but a sum total of eternally cascading and intermingling choices made by *all* of us—human beings, living creatures, angels, seraphim, and the fallen ones.

"The entire world has been thusly made—as a *one thing* of perfect balance. And, being a One Perfect Thing, its individual living components, each imbued with free will, are yet bound by the limits of this Original Framework to maintain this *perfection* at whatever cost to themselves.

"Through the very nature of our original creation, we are all inexplicably bound *together.* We are constrained by creation's rules and physical limitations—which include personal inconveniences, loss, dire harm, and blatant idiocy—and we are bound through the *collective choices* of ourselves and others.

"Choices—even seemingly neutral ones such as whether to smile at someone, or drink a cup of tea, or take a turn into this dark street, or step with your left foot or right (or another arrangement, such as a walking-shovel)—all have natural consequences. And consciously selfish or wicked choices, (made by the Udolpho villains, or the fallen ones, who had chosen not for the *common 'all' together,* but for *themselves alone*) adversely affect everyone else.

"But in that same perfect Original Framework of interconnectedness, lies hope and ultimate salvation—there is *always* free will to make the *best* choice for as long as you can: even under duress; even when you are thrust into a horrid novel . . . and choice is immortal.

"Thus, be not afraid or surprised to consider that *choices* existed before a moment of perfect innocence that is known as birth, and will continue long after the soul is taken by death to *reside* with God."

"Oh!" exclaimed Catherine, enthralled. "What happens when the soul is taken to reside with God?"

But the angel (it was Lawrence), so grave and dignified only moments before, suddenly smiled almost in mischief, and continued in a voice as light as air. "Why, dear, just think of what happens to a loaf of bread after it is eaten. And remember, that, just as the immortal soul, it too has a long eternal history *after!*"

The angelic discourse and instruction slipped into a nonsensical daydream. Catherine roused herself from this reverie—of choices, cosmic coordinates, baking bread, infants, and villains—with a start and again glanced about the apartment.

It was by no means unreasonably large, and contained neither tapestry nor velvet. The walls were papered, the floor carpeted; the windows similar to those of the drawing-room below. The furniture, though not of the latest fashion, was handsome and comfortable, and the air of the room altogether far from uncheerful.

Her heart sufficiently at ease on this point, she resolved to lose no time in particular examination of anything, as she greatly dreaded disobliging the general by any delay.

Her habit therefore was thrown off with all possible haste. She was preparing to unpin the linen package (which the chaise-seat had conveyed for her immediate accommodation), when her eye suddenly fell on a large high *chest,* standing back in a deep recess on one side of the fireplace.

The sight of it made her start. And, forgetting everything else, she stood gazing on it in motionless wonder, while these thoughts crossed her:

"This is strange indeed! I did not expect such a sight as this! An immense heavy chest! What can it hold? *Oh dear!* Why should it be placed here? Pushed back too, as if meant to be *out of sight!* I will look into it—cost me what it may—and directly too—by daylight. If I stay till evening my candle may go out."

She advanced and examined it closely. It was of cedar, curiously inlaid[24] with some darker wood, and raised, about a foot from the ground, on a carved stand of the same.

The lock was silver, though tarnished from age. At each end were the imperfect remains of handles also of silver, broken perhaps prematurely by some strange *violence.* And, on the centre of the lid, was a mysterious *cipher,* in the same metal.

*Oh Dear God! Could this be the Udolpho Code?!* A lightning thought struck her.

And immediately inflamed with entirely rabid pangs of imagination, Catherine bent over it intently, but without being able to distinguish anything with *certainty.*

She could not, in whatever direction she took it, believe the last letter to be a T . . . And yet that it should be anything else in that house was a circumstance to raise no common degree of astonishment. And even if indeed it *was* a T—What if it were missing the initial three letters before it, so that in fact it was R-O-O-T? Which then properly scrambled would be "Orphan of the Rhine?"

*Oh Dear God!*

Catherine was shaken to the foundation. Surely, here it was! The secret code barely touched upon by Mrs. Radcliffe, possibly locked away in other dire and horrid details, to be found inside this chest! What was *inside* this chest? For that matter, what *was* this chest? Whose? If not originally theirs, by what strange events could it have fallen into the Tilney family?

---

[24] Being "curiously inlaid" is an absolute requirement when one discovers mysterious chests under such circumstances.

Her fearful curiosity was every moment growing greater, turning to agony of a Need to Know. Seizing, with trembling hands, the hasp of the lock, she resolved at all hazards to satisfy herself at least as to its *contents*.

*"Dear child, beware! It is highly advised that you do not open anything that you do not know—"* tried Lawrence, flying gently overhead, and Terence and Clarence echoed in sonorous harmony, from either side near her ears.

But Catherine ignored the angels and proceeded—with difficulty—for something seemed to resist her efforts; indeed, something was almost *pulsing* and *humming* on the inside, the closer she drew to it with her ear. She raised the lid a few inches (while the terrible strange humming continued, and verily grew in volume, beginning to remind Catherine of the sound of distant angry bees gathering).

But at that moment a sudden knocking at the door of the room made her, starting, quit her hold . . . and instantly the lid closed with alarming *violence*.

This ill-timed intruder was Miss Tilney's maid, sent by her mistress to be of use to Miss Morland.

Her heart pounding, Catherine immediately dismissed her. But the interruption recalled her to the sense of what she *ought* to be doing. Catherine forced herself, in spite of her anxious desire to penetrate this mystery, to proceed in her dressing without further delay.

Her progress was not quick, for her thoughts and her eyes were still bent on the *object* so well calculated to interest and alarm, while the bright angelic forms attempted to distract her with muslin and ribbons. And though she dared not waste a moment upon a second attempt, she could not remain many paces from the *chest*. It *beckoned* her, like a siren of old calling the Greek hero Odysseus—except that Catherine had no special wax to pour into her ears, nor anyone to tie her to a mast; nor, for that matter, was a mast at hand, for here was a proper apartment, as opposed to a sloop—that is, *oh dear* . . .

At length, however, having slipped one arm into her gown, her toilette seemed so nearly finished that the impatience of her curiosity might safely be indulged. One moment surely might be spared! And, so desperate should be the exertion of her strength, that, unless secured by *supernatural* means, the lid in one moment should be thrown back.

With this spirit she sprang forward, and her confidence did not deceive her. Her resolute effort threw back the lid, and Catherine had to spring back immediately with an ungodly scream directly out of Udolpho—

*Darkness,* roiling screeching darkness burst out like a billowing smoke-stack from a chimney, at first without form, but in seconds resolving into many distinct shapes—all vaguely humanoid, but wickedly distorted, and translucent, made of the fabric of smoke. And these smoke creatures scattered all around the chamber . . .

And, oh goodness, the shrieking! The infernal shrieking and hissing!

The three angels at Catherine's side flew before her, suddenly growing three times larger and brighter than usual, attaining the size of large dolls or maybe small children, their wings beating rapidly, and keeping the smoke *monster—* whatever it was—at some minor distance. But it was not quite enough.

The darkness gathered and undulated; figures elongated, or grew squat, with limbs like angry fog, reaching out for her. And Catherine, cowering back at first, then absolutely petrified, heard something that vaguely sounded almost like human speech, but modulated in a very high and simultaneously very low rumbling register, so that at least five octaves separated it:

WEEEEEGIHOOOONNN!!!

HWEEEHHHAWWWRRRREGHEWOOOOWNN!

And before Catherine could react, the *living hive* of darkness—for there was no better manner of describing it—spun rapidly around the chamber, and then dove like a million bees directly *into* the nearest wall, and went right *through* it, like incorporeal ghosts . . .

. . . And was gone. As though none of this had even existed.

Catherine exhaled with amazed horror, and straightened up, while her dear angels attempted to console her.

"Oh! Oh! *What* in the world was that?" Catherine finally managed to utter. "Were those dreadful things ghosts?"

But the angels sighed in sorrow. One of them gently placed its white-iridescent wings on her cheek, and Catherine felt in that exact spot a current of warm kindness fill her with momentary peace.

"Were those real ghosts?" she repeated, feeling a tad better.

"Dear Catherine, oh, would that they *had* been ghosts. No, these are far worse . . . But fortunately *they* are no longer here."

"Did—did *I* release them? Were they locked in the chest?"

And Catherine finally glanced down at the odious object before her, which had possessed her to such an act of mad curiosity. Her astonished eyes were treated to a view of a white cotton counterpane, properly folded, reposing at one end of the chest in undisputed possession. An ordinary silly counterpane!

Still stunned by what had just taken place, she was gazing on it vacantly with the blush of unbelieving surprise when Miss Tilney, anxious for her friend's being ready, entered the room.

Catherine was now additionally shamed. She was caught in an idle and unseemly search of her hosts' property!

"That is a curious old chest, is not it?" said Miss Tilney, as Catherine hastily closed it and turned away to the glass. "It is impossible to say how many generations it has been here. How it came to be in this room I know not. But I have not had it moved,

*Northanger Abbey and Angels and Dragons*  229

thinking it might sometimes be of use in holding hats and bonnets. Though, its weight makes it difficult to open. In that corner, however, it is at least out of the way."

Catherine had no leisure for speech, simultaneously blushing, tying her gown, throwing pointed glances at the angels and at the wall into which the dark hive *disappeared.*

Miss Tilney gently hinted her fear of being late. And in half a minute they ran downstairs together, in an alarm not wholly unfounded—for General Tilney was pacing the drawing-room, his watch in his hand. The instant they entered, he pulled the bell with violence, and ordered "Dinner to be on table *directly!*"

Catherine trembled at the emphasis with which he spoke, and sat pale and breathless, in a most humble and stunned mood, concerned for his children, and detesting old chests and *whatever* they contained.

The general, recovering his politeness as he looked at her, now scolded his daughter at length for so foolishly hurrying her fair friend, who was so out of breath from haste—there was no occasion for hurry in the world.

But Catherine could not get over the varied distress of having *opened* that horrid chest, involved her friend in a lecture and been a great simpleton herself, till they were happily seated to dinner. The general's complacent smiles, and a good appetite of her own, restored her to peace.

*But, oh dear, whatever had been in that chest?*

The dining-parlour was a large noble room, done in a style of luxury which was almost lost on Catherine, who saw little more than its spaciousness and the number of their attendants. She spoke aloud her admiration; and the general graciously acknowledged that it was by no means an ill-sized room. He supposed, however, "that she must have been used to much better-sized apartments at Mr. Allen's?"

"No, indeed," was Catherine's honest assurance; "Mr. Allen's dining-parlour was not more than half as large," and she had never seen so large a room in her life.

The general's good humour increased, and he waxed eloquent about having and using large rooms. But Mr. Allen's house, he was sure, must be exactly of the true size for rational happiness.

The evening passed without any further disturbance—and, in the occasional absence of General Tilney—with much positive cheerfulness. It was only in his presence that Catherine felt any fatigue from her journey; and she could think of her friends in Bath without one wish of being with them.

What she had released from the chest still bothered her, and thoughts returned to the dark smoke-beings writhing and menacing her—it was far less amiable to experience such an *Udolpho* occurrence in reality, than from the pages of a novel.

The night was stormy; the wind had been rising at intervals the whole afternoon. By the time the party broke up, it blew and rained violently.

Catherine, as she crossed the hall, listened to the tempest with sensations of awe, and shivers down her spine. The angels flew cheerfully before her, casting a bright tiny glow like a trio of candles visible only to herself. She thought with gratitude of their presence always at her side . . . and then noticed that their specks of light multiplied in number, turning into many more than what Catherine was used to seeing when she was all alone and without the company of other people and their own angels.

"Dear child," said Lawrence, "we have been told, now that the danger is greatest, we must guard you in full force. So in addition to myself, Terence, and Clarence, there are several others sent to be your permanent guardians."

"I am Florence!" cried a new dulcet voice, separating from the glowing cloud.

"And I am Patrice!" sang another.

"Maurice!

"Clarisse!"

"Horace!"

"Felice!"

"Delice!"

"Charisse!"

And finally, one littlest form of light danced just before Catherine's eyes. "And I am Jack!"

"Oh!" said Catherine. "It is so *nice* to meet you, and thank you! For indeed it is somewhat frightful to be alone with all these highly peculiar things happening all the time." And then she added: "Oh dear, but now I do think I might have forgotten all your names . . ."

Accompanied by the twelve angels, Catherine now felt far less terror than moments ago.

And yet, listening to the storm rage round a corner of the ancient building and close with sudden fury a distant door, it truly *felt* for the first time that she was really in an *abbey*.

Yes, these sounds brought to her recollection a countless variety of dreadful situations and horrid scenes, which such buildings had witnessed, and such storms ushered in. . . . And other, perfectly inexplicable *things* found locked in encrypted chests.

And then, most heartily did she rejoice in the happier circumstances attending her entrance within walls so solemn! She had nothing to dread from midnight assassins or drunken gallants—only demonic smoke entities and dragons outside the window! For indeed, now Catherine had no doubt the *hive*, though less putrid and belching than Isabella's demon and less lumpy and grotesque than John Thorpe's—was of ungodly origins—even though for some reason the dear angels refused to tell her precisely what it *was*.

And yet—was it not the case that demons were forbidden to appear before midnight? Another horrid mystery!

Henry had certainly been only in jest in what he had told her that morning. And yet, Catherine was equally certain she had found the *real* Udolpho Code, and nowhere else than in her own assigned apartment! And was it not that strange letter T (and possibly missing R-O-O) that bound whatever it was she had so thoughtlessly released from the chest?

In a house so furnished, and so guarded, she could have nothing to explore or to suffer, and might go to her bedroom as securely as if it had been her own chamber at Fullerton. Because surely, *her bedroom was the key to it all!*

Thus wisely fortifying her mind, as she proceeded upstairs, she was able (especially seeing that Miss Tilney slept only two doors from her), to enter her room with a tolerably stout heart, and not one, not three, but a dozen heavenly guardians.

And her spirits were immediately assisted by the cheerful blaze of a wood fire. "How much better is this," said she, as she walked to the fender[25]—"to find a fire ready lit, than to have to wait shivering in the cold till all the family are in bed—as so many poor girls in novels have been obliged to do—and then to have a faithful old servant frightening one by coming in with a faggot![26] How glad I am that Northanger is what it is! If it had been like some other places, I do not know that, in such a night as this, I could have answered for my courage: but now, to be sure, there is nothing to alarm one. *Nothing!*"

She looked round the room. The window curtains seemed in motion—surely, nothing but the violence of the wind penetrating through the divisions of the shutters. She stepped boldly forward, carelessly humming a tune, to assure herself of its

---

[25] Presumed to be neither a front portion of a moving vehicle, nor a guitar—items the Reader would be hard pressed to find in Northanger Abbey.

[26] Oh dear! One truly knows not what to say!

being so, peeped courageously behind each curtain, saw nothing on either low window seat to scare her, placed a hand against the shutter, and felt indeed the wind's force.

A glance at the old chest (now perfectly silent and harmless) was not without its use. She scorned the causeless fears of an idle fancy, and began with a most happy indifference to prepare herself for bed. The angels alighted in various bright spots around the room.

Catherine resolved *to take her time;* not hurry herself. She did not care if she were the last person up in the house. But she would *not* make up her fire (that would seem cowardly, as if she wished for the protection of light after she were in bed).

The fire therefore died away. There was only a single candle left burning—and *angel light.*

Catherine, having spent the best part of an hour in her arrangements, was about to step into bed. But, glancing round the room, she was struck by the appearance of a high, old-fashioned black *cabinet,* which, though conspicuous enough, had never caught her notice before.

*Oh dear . . .*

Henry's words—his description of the ebony cabinet *which was to escape her observation at first*—immediately rushed across her. And though this could mean nothing, there was something whimsical—certainly a remarkable coincidence!

She took her candle and looked closely at the cabinet. It was not absolutely ebony and gold. But it was black and yellow japan of the handsomest kind. And as she held her candle, the yellow had very much the *effect* of gold.

Could it be? A clue to s*ecret hidden treasure!*

The key was in the cabinet door. And once again, as with the horrid chest, she had a strange fancy to *look into it*—not, however, with the smallest expectation of finding anything this time, but it was so very *odd,* after what Henry had said.

In short, she could not sleep till she had examined it. It beckoned her, like a siren—

*"Oh no, dear child!"* whispered the angels. *"Forsooth, not again!"*

But of course, they were talking to a heroine, no less.

So, placing the candle with great caution on a chair, Catherine seized the key with a very tremulous hand and tried to turn it; but it *resisted* her utmost strength. And at the same time, there came a sound of distant humming.

Alarmed, but not discouraged, she tried it another way. A bolt flew, and she believed herself successful; but how strangely mysterious! The door was still *immovable.* She paused a moment in breathless wonder.

*"Heaven itself is telling you not to proceed,"* whispered the angels like sweet rustling leaves, holding their heads.

But what heroine ever heeded heaven?

The wind roared down the chimney, the rain beat in torrents against the windows, and everything seemed to speak the genuine Udolpho awfulness of her situation. To retire to bed, however, unsatisfied on such a point, would be in vain—sleep was *impossible* with the knowledge of a *cabinet* so mysteriously *closed* in her immediate vicinity.

Again, therefore, she applied herself to the key. And after moving it in every possible way, the *door* suddenly yielded to her hand. Her heart leaped with exultation at such a victory! And having thrown open each folding door, a double range of *small drawers* appeared in view, with some *larger drawers* above and below them—and in the centre, a *small door,* closed also with a lock and key, secured in all probability a *cavity of importance.*

Catherine's heart beat quick (and indeed, there was almost the hint of that familiar awful humming sound), but her courage did not fail her. With a cheek flushed by hope, and an eye straining with curiosity, her fingers grasped the handle of a drawer and drew it forth—

And out came the screeching pulsating black smoke again! The *darkness*, filled with ghostly creatures, billowed out rapidly, as it had come from the chest earlier, and the accompanying screams of the damned were bloodcurdling and wild, true sounds of the inferno.

Catherine jumped back and screamed a bloodcurdling scream of her own that (unfortunately for her but fortunately for the sleeping denizens of the abbey) was muffled by the sounds of the storm outside.

This time the angels, all twelve of them, encircled Catherine immediately and their light flared into radiance.

And the darkness held itself back, jut a foot away, and it screamed and howled and screeched like banshees (Catherine, even in her terror, thought momentarily and almost wistfully of Isabella).

"What are you?" our heroine exclaimed at last, gathering herself in courage. "What do you want? *Who* are you? Wait—did you not come out of the chest earlier? Then how did you come back around and—"

And the contorted ghostly faces and limbs clawing at her seemed to shape words out of the air, words in many octaves, so that the sound came like a terrifying and perverse chorus.

"PWWEEEGGEEEEOOOOOOONNN!!!" they sounded, "HWEEE-HHHAWWWRRRR-WEEGEEHOOOOWWNN!"

Catherine paused in suspense, listening so closely that she completely blanked out on the notion that she ought to be afraid. Her countenance displayed a host of emotions and a forced grasp for understanding, painfully reflected in a baffled frown.

"I am sorry," she said after a moment of flailing darkness and contorted demonic faces, now mere inches away from her and the angels. "Pardon, but—did you say *'pigeon'?*"

"HWEEE-HHHAWWRRRR-WEEGEEHOOOWWNN!"

Catherine blinked. "You're a pigeon? Are you saying *'You are a pigeon'* or *'We are a pigeon?'* Oh dear! Are you asking for one?"

"WWEEGEEHOOOWWNN!" roared the voices in reply.

"I am sorry, I still don't understand," said Catherine. "That is, do you mind terribly repeating, and this time speaking clearly and enunciating? For, I dare say elocution is very important, and I am afraid I have no notion of what it is you are saying, what it is you want—"

The roar that came from the darkness was horrifying.

But for some peculiar reason, *it,* the horrid collective *thing* of many limbs and forms, started to comply, and, humming, it started to speak *something* that was in rhythmic syllables.

"WWEE GEEH OOOWWNN! RWWEE GEE HOOWNN! WWEE GEEH OOOWWNN!"

"Oh, for heaven's sake, I still don't understand," she replied, showing some frustration, while completely forgetting to be afraid. "Upon my word, there are no pigeons here! None! And unless you are referring to yourself, I dare say you do not appear to be a pigeon at all, not even a monstrous *duck!*"

"RWWEEEEH GEEEEE HNNNNNNNN!" convulsed the darkness, fury rising, by the indication of increased contortions and flailings of common limbs.

"If you are saying *'region'* or *'smidgeon,'* possibly, it still makes no sense. Is that the first word? And I am sorry, but I am not very good at charades; never did well, indeed even Mrs. Allen has a better grasp of it—"

"AAAAAAAAAAAARRRRRGH!!!!!!!!!!!!!!!" the darkness roared in pure fury, spreading itself across the room, like billowing smoke, then breaking up into rounded balls of vaguely human matter, and verily *pounding itself* against the walls.

But Catherine was nonplussed. The angels continued to shield her with their light, and she felt rather empowered enough to proceed in this conversation.

"So you are saying this is a region, or you are a pigeon, or I am a pigeon, or—"

"EEEENNOOOOOOUUUUUUUGH!!!!!!" said the boiling darkness. "LLLLEEEGGGGGIIIIIIIIIOOOHHHHHNNNNNNN! WEEEEE ARRRRRRRRRRR LEEEEEEEEEGGIIIOOON!"

It seemed to have at last found an auditory key and fixed in it at last.

"Oh! '*Legion*'!" Catherine exclaimed with what nearly was actual pleased comprehension. "You are legion! You are—"

And then it sank in.

*Oh dear . . .*

"Yes, dear child," sounded the angels. "We could not warn you for we are not allowed to invoke its *name*. And you are not to repeat it if possible, for by naming it, you give it power."

"What, you mean le—"

"Hush!" exclaimed Lawrence, or possibly Florence, or one of the other new guardians.

Catherine quickly put her hand to her mouth, and stared in stunned horror at some possibly high-ranking demon's contorted face, making grimaces at her just beyond the veil of angelic light. What was she to do?

But they appeared to be at an impasse. Several long moments went by while the storm raged outside, rattling the shutters with an almost demonic force.

And then from the door outside, somewhere in the corridors, came a different kind of roar.

And Catherine, though she had never heard it in her life, was entirely certain this was the voice of a dragon.

In that moment, the Legion of demons *gathered* itself—if such a thing were possible—and moved in a whirlwind around the room, and then again, as it did earlier the same day, rushed *against* and disappeared *into* one of the walls.

Catherine remained frozen for a few moments, then let out a gasp of relief, saying, "Well! So much for that!" And then, in a very practical way, she returned her full attention to the cabinet before her.

"Dear Catherine!" the angels started talking in both her ears from all directions. "Have you not had enough for now? We must educate you more on the dangers of that which may not be named—"

But Catherine was busy staring at the drawer she had pulled open. That same odious drawer which had contained the dark demonic hive . . .

It was entirely empty.

With less alarm and greater eagerness she seized a second, a third, a fourth; each was equally empty. Not one was left unsearched, and in not one was anything found. Not even a tiny squat demon with putrid belches as the one that guarded Isabella!

It was getting rather late, and Catherine was as sleepless as can be. She had established that there were indeed demons here, in more than one spot in this room, possibly merely infesting it (and doing so, apparently, regardless of time of day; what *kind* of demons were these?), but—more likely, doing other more meaningful things such as guarding other secrets; such as secret clues!

One need not be as well read in the art of *concealing* a *treasure* as our heroine. Indeed, the possibility of *false linings* to the demon-guarded drawers did not escape her, and she felt round each with anxious acuteness, but in vain.

The place in the middle of the cabinet alone remained now unexplored. And though she had not *expected* to find anything else there (a hive of super-demons was quite enough, thank you), it would be foolish not to examine it thoroughly while she was about it.

It was some time however before she could unfasten the door (the same difficulty with this inner lock); but at length it did open, and not in vain!

Her quick gaze directly fell on a *roll of paper* pushed back into the further part of the cavity, apparently for concealment, and her feelings at that moment were indescribable. Her heart fluttered, her knees trembled, and her cheeks grew pale.

She seized, with an unsteady hand, the precious manuscript, for half a glance sufficed to ascertain written characters. And while she acknowledged with awful sensations this striking exemplification of what Henry had foretold, she resolved instantly to peruse every line before she attempted to rest.

The dimness of the light her candle emitted made her turn to it with alarm. But there was no danger of its sudden extinction (it had yet some hours to burn). In order to better distinguish the writing, she hastily snuffed it. Alas! It was snuffed and *extinguished* in one. A lamp could not have expired with more awful effect. All that remained was *angel light*—an ethereal disembodied glow not truly of the world, and casting no shadow—decidedly insufficient for reading (not even if one held an angel up directly to the printed page—yes, shameful to say, Catherine had *tried* this once in her younger years).

Catherine, for a few moments, was motionless with horror. It was done completely; not a remnant of light in the wick could give hope to the rekindling breath.

Darkness impenetrable and immovable filled the room, punctuated with spots of angelic glow. A violent gust of wind, rising with sudden fury, added fresh horror to the moment.

Catherine trembled from head to foot. In the pause which succeeded, a sound like *receding footsteps* and the closing of a distant door struck on her affrighted ear. And then came gentle sorrowing sighs, carried on the wind. . . .

*Ghosts!*

*Dear God in heaven, not only were the ungodly legionnaire creatures out and about, but there were also genuine abbey ghosts!* Catherine was certain! *Thus, it was all true—all of Udolpho was real and coming to pass, all around her!*

Human nature could support no more. A cold sweat stood on her forehead, and abstract peculiar panic gripped her in that single moment—more so than when faced with actual peril such as she endured already *twice,* earlier this day.

The manuscript fell from her hand, and groping her way to the bed, she jumped hastily in, and sought some suspension of agony by creeping far underneath the covers.

To close her eyes in sleep that night, was entirely out of the question. With a curiosity at such fever pitch, and feelings in every way so agitated, repose must be absolutely impossible.

The storm too was so dreadful! She had not previously feared wind, but now every blast seemed fraught with awful intelligence.

The manuscript so wonderfully found, so wonderfully accomplishing the morning's *prediction*—how was it to be accounted for? For, surely these were no silly clues she herself dreamed up in Bath amid the roaring ogre promptings of John Thorpe—this was the *Udolpho Code,* in all its occult glory; there was no doubt! It had to be contained within these pages, and it had to point to real wondrous treasure, of one kind or another!

What could it contain? To whom could it relate? By what means could it have been so long concealed? And how singularly strange that it should fall to *her* to discover it!

Till she had made herself mistress of its contents, however, she could have no rest. With the sun's first rays she was determined to peruse it. But—how to endure until morning?

She shuddered, tossed about in her bed, and envied every quiet sleeper. The storm still raged, with various noises, more terrific even than the wind, which struck at intervals on her startled ear. Sometimes there were *moans,* at other times, *sighs,* and occasionally the rattling and clanging of what appeared to be weighty *chains* . . .

*Upon my word! Why, oh, why do ghosts always carry around odious* chains, *practically in every ghost story told?*

thought Catherine, again briefly forgetting to be afraid because of a flight of imagination. *What is it about chains and ghosts? There are other kinds than gallows prisoners, surely. So, why must they, all of them, eternally and tediously carry chains, and not, let us say, pails of milk? Or even parasols? Do not people die in other ways and return to haunt with muskets, or possibly hedge-trimmers? Or—*

The curtains of her bed seemed at one moment in motion. At another, the lock of her door was agitated, as if by the attempt of somebody to *enter*.

Hollow murmurs seemed to creep along the gallery. And more than once her blood was chilled by the sound of those annoying distant moans, and yes, tedious, odious, horrid *chains.*

Enough! This extended, fearful state of anxiety was no longer exciting or a bit amusing to our heroine.

But hour after hour passed away, and weary Catherine heard *three past midnight* proclaimed by all the clocks in the house before the tempest subsided or she unknowingly fell fast asleep.

# Chapter 22

The sound of the housemaid folding back her window-shutters at eight o'clock the next day, roused Catherine.

She opened her eyes (wondering she slept at all) on cheerfulness. Her fire was already burning, and a bright morning had succeeded the tempest of the night.

Instantaneously, her recollection of the found *manuscript* returned. Springing from bed, the moment the maid went away, she eagerly collected every scattered sheet (which had burst from the roll as it fell, the night before), and flew back to enjoy the luxury of their perusal on her pillow.

The dozen angels observed her actions patiently, resting on valances and curtains. Admittedly there were occasional sighs.

She now plainly saw that the manuscript was of less than equal length with what she had shuddered over in books. For the roll, seeming to consist entirely of small disjointed sheets, was of trifling size—much less than she had supposed it to be at first.

But, at last! She was about to peruse the Udolpho Code!

Her greedy eye glanced rapidly over a page—expecting arcane symbols, strange combinations of All Capital Letters, shuffled in terrifying order to form Meaningful Phrases or else, absolutely Meaningless Ones (which in turn were to be shuffled about until truth was stumbled upon in-between lines or every other letter taken backwards), eventually to spell out grand secret Clues—

She started in amazement. Could it be possible, or did not her senses play her false?

*The pages were ordinary receipts and domestic lists.*

Indeed, an inventory of linen, in coarse and modern characters, seemed all that was before her! If sight might be trusted, she held a *washing-bill* in her hand.

Catherine seized another sheet, and saw the same, with little variation; a third, a fourth, and a fifth presented nothing new. Shirts, stockings, cravats, waistcoats . . .

And yet—could all these be in fact *secret code?*

*"Dear child,"* said an eternally patient angel. *"What is it exactly that you are looking for?"*

But Catherine threw the angel one occupied glance, and frowning, returned to her task.

Two more sheets marked other expenditures: hair-powder, shoe-string, breeches-ball—

*Breeches-ball!* thought Catherine. *What does that Signify?*

And the larger sheet, which had enclosed the rest, seemed by its first cramp line, "To poultice chestnut mare"—a farrier's bill!

Such was the collection of papers (left perhaps by a servant), which had filled her with expectation and alarm, and robbed her of half her night's rest! For one brief moment she felt humbled to the dust.

And yet—all of this could be deceptively encoded for the uninitiated. It had to be! Catherine immediately set her mind to run over *"To poultice chestnut mare"* and T-P-C-M.

However, this tantalizing possibility still did not entirely negate the absurdity of her recent fancies. Ridiculous to suppose that an ancient manuscript could have remained undiscovered in a modern lived-in room such as this!—Or that she should be the first to possess the skill of unlocking a cabinet, the key of which was open to all!

But maybe—the menacing cabinet and chest had indeed been both waiting all these years for *someone* such as herself, one who could *see* and *hear* angels and other beings? One who could (and did!) release the Legion?

Whatever it was, heaven forbid, Catherine was determined that Henry Tilney should never know the extent of her definite meddling and possible folly. Besides, it was his fault entirely— the cabinet fit *his* horrid description, else she would not have been curious about it.

Impatient to get rid of those detestable and confounding papers scattered over the bed, she rose directly. Folding them the same way as before, she put them back in the cabinet.

Why the locks should have been so difficult to open, however, was still inexplicable (now she opened them easily). In this there was surely something supernatural and mysterious. . . .

Catherine got away as soon as she could from a room in which her conduct produced such unpleasantness. She made her way quickly toward the breakfast-parlour, as it had been pointed out to her by Miss Tilney the evening before.

As she descended a certain flight past a gallery, she heard a now familiar and odious humming sound.

*Oh dear . . .*

There was no one about. Just before her, a tall window to the outside on top of the next flight of stairs. The window was unshuttered, open to the daylight and the world outside.

And as Catherine came to a stop, the humming and screeching increased. And, as if on cue timed to coincide with her arrival, darkness poured in a smoke-stack from the outside, though the window, and solidified before her.

Catherine gave a minor scream (far less bloodcurdling than the night before; she was getting rather accustomed to this kind of thing), promptly putting her hand to her lips to silence herself.

The guardian angels immediately placed themselves in the form of a bright shield in the air between her and the evil thing.

"LEEEGIIIONNN!" thundered the demon chorus. "WEEE ARRRR LEEEEGIOONNNN!"

"Well, yes you are, I do realize that," she said. "What do you want? And how is it you are here in the light of morning?"

"GIVVE USSS THE WHOOORREE OF BABYLOOON!"

"Beg pardon?" Catherine was somewhat scandalized and thought surely she had misheard. Considering how it had been last night, she was not too surprised to mishear yet again.

Then it occurred to her—*treasure!* The evil ones were also looking for a treasure *hoard!*

"I am afraid I do not have in my possession the hoard of Babylon," she retorted almost cheerfully. "However, myself and numerous others have a notion there is indeed a hoard in Bath, or even here in Northanger—"

"Oh, dear child," said Lawrence, or possibly Patrice. "Why are you talking to these foul things? There is certainly no need to divulge anything, much less hold a polite conversation."

The undulating darkness roared in fury, billowing about the stairwell.

"Well," said Catherine, "I do prefer not to be rude."

"NOOOOOOOOO!!!! GIVVE USSS THE WHOOORREE OF BABYLOOOOOON!" screamed the Legion, wailing and gnashing its collective teeth.

"Oh! Oh dear." Catherine did not know what else to say. "If you are indeed referring to a certain *unmentionable* kind of woman of Babylon, then I can say with all surety that I have not the slightest notion what you mean—"

In reply, came the most terrible roaring and screeching that Catherine could ever imagine.

"Stop it!" she cried over their din, raising her hands to cover her ears. "Upon my word, I do *not* have the Whore of Babylon, or *anything* of Babylon, and even if I did, I would never surrender it to you! Once and for all, leave me alone, you horrid things!"

And just as Catherine finished speaking, there was suddenly a great, almost *familiar* flapping of wings. . . .

Through the open window it came, hurtling out of the sky—not a dragon, as she initially thought, but a familiar great flying monstrous fowl, with white and gray plumage and a ferocious honk which rose over the demonic din like a single piercing, mighty foghorn.

The Brighton Duck!

The monstrous creature circled the stairwell, beating the air like a great palm frond, and effectively fanning away the smoke-darkness filled with contorted demon forms.

It shrieked and honked like a legion of banshees. And under its unbelievable onslaught, the legion of demons wavered. As Catherine stared in amazement, the darkness too started to circle the stairwell like a funnel of soot and smoke, moving faster and faster. . . .

And then, with one last infernal shriek, it struck itself against the walls and went *through* them and was again gone.

The *duck* proudly trumpeted its victory.

"Oh!" Catherine whispered to the monstrous creature. "Goodness, am I ever glad to see you!"

But naturally she had no answer, as the Brighton Duck circled once, twice overhead, the sun glinting against its feather tips. Then, like a cannon ball it flew straight out of the window.

"No one ever knows whence it comes," mused Catherine wonderingly. "But I am certain it knows *exactly* what it is doing!"

There was now a grand silence in the stairwell. The sun poured in from the outside. The angels floated calmly.

Catherine cleared her throat and again proceeded to the breakfast-parlour.

Henry was alone at breakfast. His solitary bright angel shimmered like a butterfly pin of spun light from the folds of his cravat and waved delighted greetings to Catherine and her guardians.

Henry's own immediate comment, a hope of "her having been undisturbed by the tempest," with an arch reference to the character of the building they inhabited, was rather distressing.

For the world would she not have her weakness suspected. And yet, Catherine was unequal to an absolute falsehood, and had to admit that the wind had kept her awake a little.

"But we have a charming morning after it," she added, briefly thinking of horrid Legions defeated by monstrous ducks, but desiring to get rid of the subject; "and storms and sleeplessness are nothing when they are over. What beautiful hyacinths! I have just learnt to love a hyacinth."

"And how might you learn? By accident or argument?" said Henry, looking at her with an expression hard to describe.

"Your sister taught me; I cannot tell how. Mrs. Allen used to take pains to make me like them; but I never could, till I saw them the other day in Milsom Street; I am naturally indifferent about flowers."

"But now you love a hyacinth. So much the better. You have gained a new source of out-of-doors enjoyment. And, who can tell, in time you may come to love a rose?"

"But I do not want any such pursuit to get me out of doors. The pleasure of walking and breathing fresh air is enough for me, and in fine weather Mamma says I am never within."

"At any rate, however, I am pleased that you have learnt to love a hyacinth. The mere habit of *learning to love* is the thing. Has my sister a pleasant mode of instruction?"

Catherine was saved the embarrassment of attempting an answer by the entrance of the general. His smiling compliments announced a happy state of mind, but his gentle hint of sympathetic early rising did not advance her composure.

The elegance of the breakfast set forced itself on Catherine's notice when they were seated at table. The general was enchanted by her approbation of his taste, confessed it to be simple, and proceeded to extol the tea and table settings, noting he might have been tempted to order a new set. He trusted, however, that an opportunity might ere long occur of selecting one—though not for himself. Catherine was probably the only one of the party who did not understand him.

Shortly after breakfast Henry left them for Woodston, where business required and would keep him two or three days. Catherine moved to a window in the breakfast-room, hoping to catch another glimpse of his departing figure.

"Your brother would rather not be away today, considering our guest remains here," observed the general to Eleanor.

"Is Woodston a pretty place?" asked Catherine.

"What say you, Eleanor? Speak your opinion, for ladies can best tell the taste of ladies in regard to places." But then the general himself described the many pleasures, excellent kitchens, and comforts. "It is a family living, Miss Morland; the property in the place being chiefly my own; and you may believe I take care it shall not be a bad one. Did Henry's income depend solely on this living, he would not be ill-provided for. It is expedient to give every young man some employment. Even Frederick, my eldest son, who will perhaps inherit as considerable a landed property as any private man in the county, has his profession."

Something had been said the evening before of her being shown over the house. And now the general offered himself as her conductor. Catherine had hoped to explore it accompanied only by his daughter, but the proposal was welcome—eighteen hours in the abbey, and she had seen only a few of its rooms.

"And when they had gone over the house, he promised to accompany her into the shrubberies and garden." She curtsied her acquiescence. "But perhaps it might be more agreeable to her to make those her first object. The weather was favourable. Which would she prefer? He was equally at her service. But yes, he read in Miss Morland's eyes a judicious desire of making use of the present smiling weather. The abbey would be seen later. He would fetch his hat and attend them in a moment."

He left the room, and disappointed Catherine began to speak of her unwillingness that he should be taking them out of doors against his own inclination, under a mistaken idea of pleasing her. But she was stopped by Miss Tilney's uncomfortable reply: "I believe it will be wisest to take the morning while it is so fine. Do not be uneasy on my father's account; he always walks out at this time of day."

Catherine did not exactly know how this was to be understood. Why was Miss Tilney embarrassed? Could there be any unwillingness on the general's side to show her the abbey? The proposal was his own. And was not it *odd* that he should always take his walk so early? Neither her father nor Mr. Allen did so. It was certainly very provoking. She was all impatience to see the house, and had scarcely any curiosity about the grounds. If Henry had been with them indeed! But now she should not know what was picturesque when she saw it.

But she kept her thoughts to herself, and put on her bonnet in patient discontent. A number of angels immediately took up their places around the brim, like radiant butterflies.

She was struck, however, beyond her expectation, by the grandeur of the abbey, seen for the first time from the lawn.

The whole building enclosed a large court. Two sides of the quadrangle, rich in Gothic ornaments, stood forward for admiration; the remainder shut off by knolls of old trees, or luxuriant plantations. Steep woody hills rising behind, to give it shelter, were beautiful even in the leafless month of March.

Cathcrine had seen nothing to compare with it. Her feelings of delight were so strong that she boldly burst forth in wonder and praise. The general listened with assenting gratitude; surely his own estimation of it had waited unfixed till that hour.

The kitchen-garden was to be next admired, and he led the way to it across a small portion of the park.

The number of acres contained in this garden was such as Catherine could not listen to without dismay, being more than double the extent of all Mr. Allen's, as well as her father's. The general was flattered by her looks of surprise. He then modestly owned that, "without any ambition of that sort himself—he did believe them to be unrivalled in the kingdom. He loved a garden. He loved good fruit—or if he did not, his friends and children did. There were great vexations, however, attending such a garden as his. Mr. Allen, he supposed, must feel these inconveniences as well as himself."

"No, not at all. Mr. Allen did not care about the garden, and never went into it."

With a triumphant smile of self-satisfaction, the general wished he could do the same, for he never entered his, without being vexed in some way or other, by its falling short of his plan.

And then the general assailed Catherine with more inquiries comparing his own situation and Mr. Allen's, and received her answers with happy contempt.

Having taken her into every division, crevice, and wall, till she was heartily weary, he suffered the girls at last to seize the advantage of an outer door. He then expressed his wish to examine some recent alterations about the tea-house, if Miss Morland were not tired. "But where are you going, Eleanor? Why do you choose that cold, damp path to it? Miss Morland will get wet. Our best way is across the park."

"This is so favourite a walk of mine," said Miss Tilney, "that I always think it the best and nearest way. But perhaps it may be damp."

It was a narrow winding path through a thick grove of old Scotch firs. Catherine, struck by its gloomy Udolpho aspect, and eager to enter it, could not, even by the general's disapprobation, be kept from stepping forward.

He perceived her inclination, and having again urged in vain, was too polite to make further opposition. He excused himself, however, from attending them: "The sun was preferred by him. He would meet them by another course."

He turned away; and Catherine was shocked to find how much her spirits were relieved by the separation. She began to talk with easy gaiety of the delightful melancholy which such a *mysterious* grove inspired.

"I am particularly fond of this spot," said her companion, with a sigh. "It was my mother's favourite walk."

Catherine had never heard Mrs. Tilney mentioned in the family before. The interest excited by this tender remembrance showed itself directly in her altered countenance, and attentive pause with which she waited for something more. . . .

But that "something more" came from an entirely other source.

There was a great speeding shadow in the sky. Both Catherine and Eleanor looked up at the sound of great rushing wings, eclipsing all heaven. The *dragon* swept forth from beyond the cover of trees, sailing the wind like a grand galleon, its reptilian scales glinting like the surface of a razor-sharp sun-drenched ocean.

Oh! It was so close! Just nearly overhead, close enough to sweep the tops of the Scotch firs with its beating wings! Close enough to notice its dark obsidian underbelly, thick limbs with immense claws, glinting with deep violent bursts of sun-fire . . .

"Oh, dear heaven!" exclaimed Catherine, holding on to her bonnet against the sudden whirlwind that momentarily swept the ground around them from the beating wings.

Eleanor stared upwards, in inexplicable silence, holding on to her own bonnet.

"That *is* a real dragon, Eleanor! You must agree, that is—it *must* be! There is no other explanation! Did you see the size of it? I dare say it was larger than a building!"

"It does appear to be," agreed Eleanor placidly.

Catherine was rather amazed at her composed demeanor. "Are you not shocked to see it? Oh, where did it come from, and what is it doing here? Could it truly be hunting for *treasure?* For, having found none in Bath, it has followed us here? Or *did* it? Oh dear! Eleanor, do you think the dragon is *following* us?"

"It is indeed most unusual," replied Miss Tilney, still watching the dragon—now a mere speck the size of a bird, high up in the sky. "I am afraid, though, I do not have an answer. But indeed, what an impossible sight."

"But you are not surprised!"

"There are so many wonders in this world, I have long since reserved my ability to question them. Answers usually do come, in good time." Miss Tilney was gently smiling.

Catherine could think of nothing else to do or say but to proceed in their walk.

"I used to walk here so often with my mother," said Eleanor, gently resuming the subject before the dragon had interrupted them; "though I never loved it then, as I have loved it since. At that time indeed I used to wonder at her choice. But her memory endears it now."

"And ought it not," reflected Catherine now thinking of the stubborn refusal of the general, "to endear it to her husband? Yet the general would not enter it." Miss Tilney continuing silent, she ventured, "Her death must have been a great affliction!"

"A great and increasing one," replied the other, in a low voice. "I was only thirteen when it happened. And though I felt my loss strongly, I could not then know what a loss it was."

She stopped for a moment, then added, with great firmness, "I have no sister, you know—and though my brothers are very affectionate, and Henry is a great deal here, which I am most thankful for, it is impossible for me not to be often solitary."

"To be sure you must miss him very much."

"A mother would have been always present. A mother would have been a constant friend."

"Was she a very charming woman? Was she handsome? Was there any *picture* of her in the abbey? And why had she been so partial to that grove? Was it from *dejection* of spirits?" Catherine poured forth a multitude of questions.

The first three received a ready affirmative; the two others were passed by. And Catherine's interest in the *deceased* Mrs. Tilney augmented. Of her unhappiness in marriage, she felt certain. The general certainly had been an unkind husband. He did *not* love her walk: could he therefore have *loved her?* And besides—handsome as he was, there was *something* in his stern features which spoke his not having behaved well to her.

"Her picture, I suppose," blushing at the consummate art of her own question, "hangs in your father's room?"

"No, it was intended for the drawing-room. But my father was dissatisfied with the painting, and for some time it had no place. Soon after her death I obtained it and hung it in my bed-chamber. I shall be happy to show it to you; it is a fine likeness."

Here was another proof. A portrait of a departed wife, not valued by the husband! He must have been dreadfully cruel to her!

Catherine no longer attempted to hide from herself her true feelings about the general (regardless of all his attentions). What had been terror and dislike before, was now absolute aversion. Yes, aversion! His cruelty to such a charming woman made him odious to her. She had often *read* of such characters—characters which Mr. Allen used to call unnatural and overdrawn—but here was proof positive of the contrary.

She had just settled this point when the end of the path brought them directly upon the general, strolling alone before them, and painting a rather grim silhouette. In spite of all her virtuous indignation, she found herself again obliged to walk with him, listen to him, and even to smile when he smiled.

Being no longer able, however, to receive pleasure from the surrounding objects, she soon began to walk with lassitude. The general perceived it, and with a concern for her health (which seemed to reproach her for her opinion of him), was most urgent for returning with his daughter to the house.

He would follow them in a quarter of an hour—he had a few more *things* to do.

Again they parted—but Eleanor was called back in half a minute to receive a strict charge against taking her friend round the abbey till his return. This *second instance* of his anxiety to delay what she so much wished for struck Catherine as very remarkable.

And very wicked.

# Chapter 23

An hour passed away before the general came in—spent by Catherine in an unfavourable consideration of his character.

This lengthened absence, these solitary rambles—whatever *was* he doing? It did not indicate a mind at ease, or a conscience void of reproach.

At length he appeared. Whatever might have been the gloom of his meditations, he could still smile with them. Miss Tilney, understanding in part her friend's curiosity to see the house, soon revived the subject. And contrary to Catherine's expectations, the general ordered refreshments to be in the room by their return, and was at last ready to escort them.

They set forward with a grandeur of air and dignified step, which could not shake the doubts of the *well-read* Catherine. The general led the way across the hall, through the common drawing-room, into a room magnificent both in size and furniture—the real drawing-room, used only with company of consequence.

It was very noble, grand, charming!—was all that Catherine had to say. For, all minuteness of praise was supplied by the general. The costliness or elegance of any room was nothing to her; she cared for no furniture of a more modern date than the fifteenth century, with all its rich historic terrors.

Next, they proceeded into the magnificent library, exhibiting a collection of books on which an humble man might have looked with pride. Catherine heard, admired, and wondered with more genuine feeling than before. She gathered all that she could from this storehouse of knowledge, by running over the titles of half a shelf and wondering if their Capital Letters stood for any sort of secret Code, and was ready to proceed.

But grotesque suites of apartments did not spring up with her wishes. Large as was the building, she had already visited the greatest part. Though—on being told that, with the addition of the kitchen, the six or seven rooms she had now seen surrounded three sides of the court—she could scarcely believe it. Nor could she overcome the suspicion of there being many chambers *secreted*.

It was a relief, however, that they were to return to the main rooms by passing through a few of less importance—rooms looking into the court, which, with occasional intricate passages, connected the different sides.

Catherine was further gratified by being told she was treading where had once been a *cloister*. Traces of cells were pointed out. She observed several mysterious doors that were neither opened nor explained to her.

Then she found herself in a billiard-room, and in the general's private apartment, without comprehending their connection, or being able to turn aright when she left them. At last she passed through Henry's dark little room, strewed with his litter of books, guns, and greatcoats.

From the dining-room they proceeded to the kitchen—the ancient kitchen of the convent, rich in the massy walls and smoke of former days, and in the stoves and hot closets of the present. The general's improving hand had not loitered here: every modern invention to facilitate the labour of the cooks had been adopted within this, their spacious theatre.

With the walls of the kitchen ended all the antiquity of the abbey. The fourth side of the quadrangle—on account of its decaying state—had been removed by the general's father, and the present erected in its place. All that was venerable, ancient, and delightfully *secret,* ceased here. The new building was intended only for offices, and enclosed behind by stable-yards.

In her mind, Catherine raved at the hand which had swept away the priceless old structures. She would willingly have been spared the mortification of a walk through scenes so tragically fallen and replaced with such heartless modern comfort. But the general's vanity was strongest here in these offices, and he made no apology for leading her on.

They took a brief survey of all; and Catherine was impressed, beyond expectation—it grandly surpassed anything that had been at home in Fullerton. The number of servants continually appearing impressed her likewise. Wherever they went, some pattened girl stopped to curtsy, or some footman in dishabille sneaked off.

Yet this was an abbey! How inexpressibly different in these domestic arrangements from such as she had read about! In abbeys and castles, each larger than Northanger, all the dirty work of the house was to be done by *two pair* of female hands at the utmost. How they could get through it all had often amazed Mrs. Allen. And when Catherine saw what was necessary here, she began to be amazed herself. Could it be they employed *supernatural* help?

They returned to the hall, that the chief staircase might be ascended (and the beauty of its wood, and ornaments of rich carving might be pointed out). Having gained the top, they turned in an opposite direction from the gallery in which her room lay, and shortly entered one on the same plan, but superior in length and breadth.

She was here shown successively into three large bed-chambers. Everything that money and taste could do, had been

258     Jane Austen and Vera Nazarian

bestowed on these, elegantly furnished within the last five years. They were perfect in all that would be generally pleasing, and wanting in all that could give pleasure to Catherine.

As they were surveying the last, the general turned with a smiling countenance to Catherine, and ventured to hope that some of their earliest guest tenants might be "our friends from Fullerton." She felt the unexpected compliment, and deeply regretted the impossibility of thinking well of a man so kindly disposed towards herself, and so full of civility to all her family.

The gallery was terminated by folding doors, which Miss Tilney, advancing, had thrown open. She passed through, and seemed on the point of doing the same by the first door to the left, in another long reach of gallery. . . .

Suddenly the general came forward and called her hastily, and rather angrily back. "Where was she going? What was there more to be seen? Had not Miss Morland already seen all that could be worth her notice? Did she not suppose her friend might be glad of some refreshment after so much exercise?"

Miss Tilney drew back directly, and the heavy doors were closed upon the mortified Catherine—who, having seen, in a momentary glance beyond them, a narrower passage, more numerous openings, and symptoms of a winding staircase, believed herself *at last* within the reach of something worth her notice! Indeed, as she unwillingly turned back, she would rather be allowed to examine that end of the house than see all the finery of all the rest! Oh, were there not strange ghostly whispers and sighs coming from that direction?

The general's evident desire of preventing such an examination was an additional stimulant. *Something* was certainly to be concealed. Her fancy could not mislead her here. And *what* that *something* was, Miss Tilney pointed out: "I was going to take you into what was my mother's room—the room in which she *died*—"

Her few words conveyed pages of intelligence to Catherine! It was no wonder that the general should shrink from the sight of such objects as that room must contain—a room in all probability *never entered* by him since the dreadful *scene* had passed, which released his suffering wife, and left him to the stings of conscience.

She ventured, when next alone with Eleanor, to express her wish of being permitted to see it, as well as all the rest of that side of the house. And Eleanor promised to attend her there, whenever they should have a convenient hour. Catherine understood her: the general must be *watched* from home, before that room could be entered. "It remains as it was, I suppose?" said she, in a tone of feeling.

"Yes, entirely."

*Oh dear!* Catherine's heart pounded. "And how long ago may it be that your mother died?"

"She has been dead these nine years." And nine years, Catherine knew, was a *trifle* of time, compared with what generally elapsed in horrid novels after the death of an injured wife, before her room was put to rights.

"You were with her, I suppose, to the last?"

"No," said Miss Tilney, sighing; "I was unfortunately from home. Her illness was sudden and short. Before I arrived it was all over."

Catherine's blood ran cold with the horrid suggestions which naturally sprang from these words. *Could it be possible? Could Henry's father—?* And yet there were signs to justify even the blackest suspicions!

She saw *him* in the evening, slowly pacing the drawing-room for an hour in silent thoughtfulness, with downcast eyes and contracted brow. And she felt secure from all possibility of wronging him. It was the air and attitude of a Montoni![27] What could more plainly speak the gloomy workings of a mind not

---

[27] A very, very bad man. Seriously, thou needst google it.

wholly dead to every sense of humanity, in its fearful review of
past scenes of guilt? Unhappy man!

And the anxiousness of her spirits directed her eyes towards
his figure so repeatedly, as to catch Miss Tilney's notice. "My
father," she whispered, "often walks about the room in this way;
it is nothing unusual."

*So much the worse!* thought Catherine. Such ill-timed
exercise was of a piece with his *strange* morning walks, and
boded nothing good.

A fter a long dull evening during which Catherine regretted
Henry's absence, she was heartily glad to be dismissed.

A look from the general not designed for her observation
sent his daughter to the bell. When the butler would have lit his
master's candle, however, he was forbidden. The latter was not
going to retire. "I have many pamphlets to finish," said he to
Catherine, "for some hours, before I can close my eyes."

But the alleged business could not win Catherine from
thinking that some very different *object* must occasion this
behavior. To be kept up for hours, after the family were in bed,
by stupid pamphlets was not very likely. There must be some
deeper cause: *something* was to be *done* which could be done
only while the household slept . . .

And the probability that Mrs. Tilney yet *lived*—shut up for
causes unknown, and receiving from the pitiless hands of her
husband a nightly supply of coarse food!—was the conclusion
which necessarily followed.

Shocking as was the idea, it was at least better than a death
unfairly hastened. Surely, in the natural course of things, she
must ere long be released. The suddenness of her reputed illness,
the absence of her daughter, and probably of her other children,
at the time—all favoured the notion of her imprisonment. Its
origin—jealousy perhaps, or wanton cruelty—was yet to be
unraveled.

And then it suddenly occurred to Catherine—in all this time, she had never seen General Tilney directly guarded by an angel of his own! She had been so accustomed to seeing everyone's angels moving about freely, sometimes out of sight, and yet everpresent, that she had *assumed* that when she did not observe an angel on the general's shoulder or around his forehead, it might have been on the mantel or hidden in back of his chair, or—

*But he had no angel.*

The general had no angel to call his own, just as the nephilim had not. How did she miss noticing this for so long?

*Oh dear heavens!* Did this mean that he was something other than human? Was he an Udolpho villain of the supernatural, infernal kind, tormenting his poor wife?

In revolving these horrifying matters, while she undressed, it suddenly struck Catherine as not unlikely that she might that morning have passed near the very spot of this unfortunate woman's confinement—might have been within a few paces of the *cell* in which she languished out her days!

For what part of the abbey could be more fitted for the purpose than that which yet bore the traces of monastic division? In the high-arched passage, paved with stone, which already she had trodden with peculiar awe, she well remembered the doors of which the general had given no account. To what might not those doors lead?

It further occurred to her that the forbidden gallery, in which sat the apartments of the unfortunate Mrs. Tilney, must be exactly *over* this suspected range of cells. And the barely glimpsed staircase nearby (communicating by some *secret means* with those cells) might have assisted the barbarous proceedings of her husband. Down that staircase she had perhaps been conveyed in a state of well-prepared insensibility!

Catherine sometimes wondered at the boldness of her own surmises, and sometimes hoped or feared that she had gone too far. But here they were supported by unshakable evidence.

The side of the quadrangle, in which she supposed the ongoing evil was being perpetrated, must be just opposite her own. If watched closely, some rays of *light* from the general's *lamp* might glimmer through the lower windows, as he passed to the prison of his wife. And naturally his passage would be accompanied by moaning ghosts rattling their tedious chains . . .

Twice before she stepped into bed, Catherine stole gently from her room to the corresponding window in the gallery, to see if the *lamp* appeared. But all abroad was dark, and it must yet be too early.

The various ascending noises convinced her that the servants must still be up. Till midnight, she supposed it would be in vain to watch. But then, when the clock had struck twelve, and all was quiet, she would (if not quite appalled by darkness and any chronic demon presences it was likely to contain) steal out and look once more.

The clock struck twelve—and Catherine had been half an hour asleep.

The twelve angels lovingly surrounding her gently fanned her brow and breathed dulcet sighs of relief.

# Chapter 24

The next day afforded no opportunity for the examination of the mysterious apartments.

It was Sunday, and the whole time between morning and afternoon service was required by the general in exercise abroad or eating cold meat at home. During her many glimpses of him, Catherine made it a point each time to observe very closely for any sign of his own angel—and now she was certain, indeed, unless his angel stayed hidden in a pocket, he *had* none.

As for the forbidden apartments, despite her great curiosity, her courage was not equal to exploring them after dinner—either by the fading light of the sky, or by the stronger illumination of a treacherous lamp.

The day was unmarked therefore by anything to interest her imagination beyond the sight of a very elegant *monument* to the memory of Mrs. Tilney, which immediately fronted the family pew. By that her eye was instantly caught and long retained. And the perusal of the highly strained epitaph—in which every virtue was ascribed to her by the inconsolable husband (who must have been her destroyer!)—affected her even to tears.

Catherine blinked them away, and it seemed to her at one point, she could clearly *see* a translucent shape of a woman, made out of milky fog and clad in long white night-garments, that stood nearby, in a posture of sorrow.

*Mrs. Tilney's ghost!*

But as soon as the pale figure observed Catherine's own tearful eye upon her, it seemed to have dissolved into thin air, and was no more.

*That does it!* thought Catherine. *That poor woman is as surely deceased, as it is the middle of day!*

That the general, having erected such a monument, should be able to *face it,* was not perhaps very strange. And yet that he could sit so boldly collected within its view, maintain so elevated an air, look so fearlessly around—nay, that he should even *enter* the church—seemed astonishing to Catherine. No wonder the tragic ghost made its appearance now, near her own monument!

However, the world (and the novels) contained many instances of villains equally hardened in guilt. She could remember *dozens* who had persevered in every possible vice, going on from crime to crime, murdering whomsoever they chose, without any feeling of humanity or remorse . . . till a violent death or a religious retirement closed their black career.

The erection of the monument itself could not in the smallest degree affect her doubts of Mrs. Tilney's actual decease. Were she even to descend into the family vault where her ashes were supposed to slumber, were she to behold the coffin in which they were said to be enclosed—what could it avail? Catherine had read too much not to be perfectly aware of the ease with which a waxen figure might be introduced, and a false funeral carried on.

However, being an *eyewitness* to the actual ghost was utter final proof. And few others had Catherine's means to *see.*

The succeeding morning promised something better. The general's early walk was timely here. And when she knew him to be out of the house, she directly proposed to Miss Tilney the accomplishment of her promise.

Eleanor was ready to oblige her. And Catherine reminded her of another promise—their first visit was to the *portrait* in her bed-chamber.

The portrait represented a very lovely woman, with a mild and pensive countenance. But Catherine's expectations were not in every respect answered. She had expected to see features, hair, complexion, that should be the very image, if not of Henry's, then of Eleanor's. But here she was obliged to look and consider and study for a likeness. She contemplated it, however, in spite of this drawback, with much emotion, and, but for a yet stronger interest, would have left it unwillingly.

As she turned her back, she thought she heard a woman's gentle, ghostly whisper of farewell. . . .

Her agitation as they entered the great gallery was too much for speech. She could only look at her companion. Indeed, how could she even begin to tell her friend that her deceased mother was in the room?

Eleanor's countenance was dejected, yet sedate. She was clearly inured to all the gloomy objects to which they were advancing.

Again she passed through the folding doors, again her hand was upon the important lock. Catherine, hardly able to breathe, was turning to close the former with fearful caution, when the figure—the dreaded figure of the *general* himself at the further end of the gallery, stood before her!

The name of "Eleanor" uttered in his loudest tone, resounded through the building—giving to his daughter the first intimation of his presence, and to Catherine terror upon terror.

The angels flew about the chamber in agitation, attempting to console both the young women with their calming touch of wings. Catherine was terrified a hundred times more than she had been of the Legion of demons! This, *this* was far more *real!*

An urge to hide had been her first instinctive movement on perceiving him. Yet she could scarcely hope to have escaped his eye. And when her friend—who with an apologizing look darted hastily by her—had joined and disappeared with him, Catherine ran for safety to her own room, and, locking herself in, believed that she should never have courage to go down again.

*Oh dear heaven!*

She remained there at least an hour, in the greatest agitation, deeply commiserating the state of her poor friend, and expecting a summons herself from the angry general. No summons, however, arrived.

At last, on seeing a carriage drive up to the abbey, she was emboldened to descend and meet him under the protection of visitors. The breakfast-room was gay[28] with company. Catherine was named to them by the general as the friend of his daughter, in a complimentary style, which so well concealed his resentful ire, as to make her feel secure at least for the present.

Eleanor, with a noble command of countenance, also reassured her. "My father only wanted me to answer a note."

Catherine began to hope that she had either been unseen by the general, or her transgression somehow ignored. Thus she dared still to remain in his presence. And after the company left them, nothing violent occurred.

In the course of this morning's reflections, she resolved to make her next attempt on the forbidden door alone.

It would be much better in every respect that Eleanor should know nothing of the matter. To involve her friend in the danger of a second detection, was unjust. The general's anger at herself would pale, compared to his fury at his daughter.

Besides, the examination itself would be more satisfactory if pursued by herself. It would be impossible to explain to

---

[28] Pray, do not think of a certain gentleman by the name of Oscar Wilde.

Eleanor the ugly suspicions. Nor could she, in her friend's presence, search for those proofs of the general's cruelty—some fragmented journal, perhaps, continued to the last gasp. . . .

She knew the way to the apartment quite well. And as she wished to get it over before Henry's return, who was expected on the morrow, there was no time to be lost. The day was bright, her courage high, the angels danced overhead in encouraging radiance. At four o'clock, the sun was now two hours above the horizon, and it would be only her retiring to dress half an hour earlier than usual.

It was done. Catherine found herself alone in the gallery before the clocks had ceased to strike. She hurried on, slipped noiselessly through the folding doors, and without stopping to look or breathe, rushed forward to the one in question.

The lock yielded to her hand, in silence. On tiptoe she entered. The room was before her. But it was some minutes before she could advance another step. She beheld what fixed her to the spot and agitated every feature. . . .

She saw a large, well-proportioned apartment—a handsome dimity bed, arranged as unoccupied with a housemaid's care, a bright Bath stove, mahogany wardrobes, and neatly painted chairs, on which the warm beams of a western sun gaily poured through two sash windows!

Catherine had expected to have her feelings worked, and worked they were. Astonishment and doubt seized them. Then, a ray of common sense added some bitter emotions of shame.

She could not be mistaken as to the room; but how grossly mistaken in everything else!—in Miss Tilney's meaning, in her own calculation! This modern apartment—to which she had given a date so ancient, a position so awful—proved to be one end of what the general's father had built.

There were two other doors in the chamber, leading probably into dressing-closets. But she had no inclination to open either. Would the *veil* in which Mrs. Tilney had last walked, or the *volume* which she had last read, remain to tell what nothing else was allowed to whisper? No: whatever might have been the general's crimes, he had certainly too much wit to let them sue for detection.

She was sick of exploring, and desired but to be safe in her own room, with her own heart only privy to its folly. And she was on the point of retreating as softly as she had entered, when a shadow-light interplay movement in the corner alerted her.

Catherine observed a milk-white translucent form take shape . . . And in seconds a lovely *woman* stood before her, in the dignity of her second bloom, with composed gentle features bearing a fine resemblance to the portrait in Eleanor's room, and a great, though imperfect, resemblance to the Tilney children.

The ghost was clad in what appeared to be a long white dressing gown suitable for sleeping—or possibly it was a wedding dress—it occurred to Catherine, while shivers started making way down her spine.

But our heroine, as usual, was bravest when the world was most strange around her. And besides, the angels at her side were suitably calm, so there was surely no cause for alarm on her part.

"Pardon me, but are you Mrs. Tilney?" asked Catherine in a polite but shaky voice.

The woman nodded once, very slowly. Her countenance remained placid as though in sleep. But her eyes were distinctly open, pale, watery, and gently trained on Catherine.

"Oh, I am so sorry for your loss!" burst out of Catherine, before she realized how absurd that was to say to someone actually dead, as opposed to their grieving relative. And yet, was it not also true?

But the ghost apparently understood, and continued to watch her, kindly.

Here was Catherine's chance to ask all manner of things. "Did—did the general—hurt you?"

The ghost's eyes appeared to fill with tears, glittering in moisture, like a rainbow in the sunlight. She spoke not a word, but this time moved her head negatively side to side.

"Oh!" said Catherine, surprised. "But then, perhaps—he did—he caused your death in any way?"

Again, came the gesture of a "no."

*Oh dear!* thought Catherine. *How wrong again I was!*

And then she thought to ask: "Did he *love* you?"

The ghost nodded "yes."

*And did you love him?*

Catherine did not even need to voice her thought; the ghost had apparently read her mind—or maybe her heart—and she nodded in affirmative with a slowly blooming smile.

Catherine opened her mouth to ask a great deal more, but in that moment there was definitely the sound of footsteps, she could hardly tell where—and this time it made her pause and tremble.

To be found here, even by a servant, would be unpleasant. But by the general, much worse!

Catherine threw one look at the ghostly Mrs. Tilney, but she was already dissolving back into the fabric of the air, having apparently accomplished what she had come here for. With a final nod, Henry's mother gifted Catherine with a glorious smile.

And was gone. . . .

Now Catherine listened—the sound of footfalls had ceased. Resolving not to lose a moment, she passed through and closed the door.

At that instant a door underneath was hastily opened. Someone ascended the stairs with swift steps—stairs which she had yet to pass before she could gain the gallery.

She had no power to move. With a feeling of terror not very definable (yet perfectly opposite the ethereal *awe* she felt with the ghost), she fixed her eyes on the staircase . . . and in a few moments it gave Henry to her view.

"Mr. Tilney!" she exclaimed in a voice of uncommon astonishment.

He looked astonished too.

"Good God!" she continued, not attending to his address. "How came you here? How came you up that staircase?"

"How came I up that staircase!" he replied, greatly surprised. "Because it is my nearest way from the stable-yard to my own chamber; and why should I not come up it?"

Catherine recollected herself, blushed deeply, and could say no more. He seemed to be looking in her countenance for that explanation which her lips did not afford. She moved on towards the gallery.

"And may I not, in my turn," said he, as he pushed back the folding doors, "ask how you came here? This passage is at least as extraordinary a road from the breakfast-parlour to your apartment, as that staircase can be from the stables to mine."

"I have been," said Catherine, looking down, "to see your mother's room."

"My mother's room! Is there anything extraordinary to be seen there?"

Catherine gulped, finding it impossibly hard not to tell all truth. "N-no, nothing at all. I thought you did not mean to come back till tomorrow."

"I did not expect to be able to return sooner, when I went away; but three hours ago I had the pleasure of finding nothing to detain me. You look pale. I am afraid I alarmed you by running so fast up those stairs. Perhaps you were not aware of their leading from the offices in common use?"

"No, I was not. You have had a very fine day for your ride."

"Very; and does Eleanor leave you to find your way into all the rooms in the house by yourself?"

"Oh, no! She showed me over the greatest part on Saturday—and we were coming here to these rooms—but only"—dropping her voice—"your father was with us."

"And that prevented you," said Henry, earnestly regarding her. "Have you looked into all the rooms in that passage?"

"No, I only wanted to see—Is not it very late? I must go and dress."

"It is only a quarter past four" (showing his watch); "and you are not now in Bath. No theatre, no rooms to prepare for, no clandestine roots to collect amid bells and orphans. Half an hour at Northanger must be enough."

She could not contradict it, and therefore suffered herself to be detained—though her head was spinning with myriad conflicting emotions. But dread of further questions made her, for the first time in their acquaintance, wish to leave him.

They walked slowly up the gallery. "Have you had any letter from Bath since I saw you?"

"No, and I am very much surprised. Isabella promised so faithfully to write directly."

"Promised so faithfully! A faithful promise! That puzzles me. I have heard of a faithful performance. But a faithful promise—My mother's room is very commodious, is it not? Large and cheerful-looking, and the dressing-closets so well disposed! It always strikes me as the most comfortable apartment in the house, and I rather wonder that Eleanor should not take it for her own. She sent you to look at it, I suppose?"

"No."

"It has been your own doing entirely?"

Catherine said nothing. Only her heart beat painfully.

After a short silence, during which he had closely observed her, he added, "As there is nothing in the room *in itself* to raise curiosity, this must have proceeded from a sentiment of respect for my mother's character, as described by Eleanor. The world never saw a better woman. But the merits of an unknown person do not often prompt a visit like yours. Eleanor, I suppose, has talked of her a great deal?"

"Yes, a great deal. That is—no, not much, but what she did say was very interesting. Her dying so *suddenly*" (slowly, and with hesitation it was spoken), "and you—none of you being at home—and your *father,* I thought—perhaps had not been very *fond* of her. But I am sure now I was *wrong!*"

"And from these circumstances," he replied (his quick eye fixed on hers), "you infer perhaps the probability of some negligence"—(involuntarily she shook her head)—"or it may be—of something still less pardonable."

She raised her eyes towards him more fully than she had ever done before. She wanted to negate, deny, excuse herself— *anything.* She wanted to admit all that she now knew, and the *manner* of knowing it—the wonder, the *truth* of it. And yet—

"My mother's illness," he continued, "the seizure which ended in her death, was sudden. The malady itself, one from which she had often suffered, a bilious fever—its cause therefore constitutional. On the third day, in short, as soon as she could be prevailed on, a physician attended her, a very respectable man, and one in whom she had always placed great confidence. Upon his opinion of her danger, two others were called in the next day, and remained in almost constant attendance for four and twenty hours. On the fifth day she died. During the progress of her disorder, Frederick and I (we were both at home) saw her repeatedly; and from our own observation can bear witness to her having received every possible attention which could spring from the affection of those about her, or which her situation in life could command. Poor Eleanor was absent, and at such a distance as to return only to see her mother in her coffin."

"But your father," said Catherine, "was *he* afflicted?"

"For a time, greatly so. You have erred in supposing him not attached to her. He *loved* her, I am persuaded, as well as it was possible for him to, and one day I might speak of his affection in detail, and more *plainly,* but now—I will not pretend to say that while she lived, she might not often have had much to bear, for he is a *complicated* man. But though his temper injured her, his judgment never did. His value of her was sincere. And he was truly and *permanently* afflicted by her death."

"I am very glad of it," said Catherine; "it would have been very shocking—but I *do* understand now—"

"And if in turn I understand you rightly, you had formed a surmise of such horror as I have hardly words to—Dear Miss Morland, consider the dreadful nature of the suspicions you have entertained! What have you been judging from? Were you looking here also for your silly Udolpho Clues? Remember the country and the age in which we live. Remember that we are English, that we are Christians. We do not slay dragons nor do we slay our wives!"

Catherine wanted to speak, but verily could not.

"Consult your own understanding," he went on, "your own sense of the probable, your own observation of what is passing around you. Does our *education* prepare us for such atrocities? Do our laws? Could evil be perpetrated without being known, in a country like this, where social and literary intercourse is on such a footing, where every man is surrounded by a neighbourhood of voluntary spies, and where roads and newspapers lay everything open? Dearest Miss Morland, what ideas have you been admitting?"

*Evil in secret code can be perpetrated under one's nose,* Catherine thought—the least innocent thought of her life.

They had reached the end of the gallery, and with tears of shame, of *experience,* she ran off to her own room.

But here was to be no peace—Catherine distinctly heard a now extremely familiar, extremely horrid, and extremely poorly-timed sound of humming, of a million angry bees.

Roiling *darkness* swept into her apartment as she opened her door. Screeching contorted shapes of the Legion screamed at her, while angels formed their steadfast battle line in-between.

But Catherine almost ignored both the angels and demons in her room.

She stood instead motionless, tears pouring down her face, surrounded by a maelstrom of darkness and light.

"GIVVE USSS THE WHOOORREE OF BABYLOOON!" resumed the darkness.

In reply, Catherine bawled. Huge tears cascaded down her face, and she pulled out a handkerchief to blow her nose loudly, and entirely unlike a lady, narrowly missing striking a whirling demon's forked appendage with her effort.

"Dearest child, take courage, we are always here at your side," spoke the angels in bright voices.

Catherine bawled louder, sniffling tremendously, and went to her small clothes chest to look for another handkerchief. To do that, she had to walk directly *through* the middle of the swirling demon hive, and involuntarily it parted before her, scattering itself widely around the room—while Catherine went through piles of clothing, and threw occasional ribbons, pieces of muslin, lace, satin, and other fabric at the demons—all quite unintentionally.

"GIVVE USSS THE WHOOORREE OF BABYLOOON!" shrieked the Legion, not least of it for the fact that it was now *wallowing* in ribbons, parts of it wrapped up in muslin and lace.

"NO!" Catherine replied suddenly, ceasing to cry.

She swallowed her tears, straightened to her full height, and then said, in a strange *new* voice of power: "BEGONE!"

The screeching, wailing, howling—all of it ceased. The sound was torn off as though by a veil of silence. Everything stopped moving; the black smoke congealed, and froze. They stared at her with myriad burning, infernal eyes.

And then the Legion was *gone*.

Just like that; and this time, for good.

In its place, all that remained was a pile of ribbons, discarded fabric, and one decidedly soggy handkerchief.

# Chapter 25

The visions of romance were over. Catherine was completely awakened, and she was swept in tragedy.

Henry's short address had more thoroughly opened her eyes to the extravagance of her late fancies than all their several disappointments had done.

Most grievously was she humbled. Most bitterly did she cry. She was sunk, not only with herself, but with Henry. Her folly was exposed to him, and he must despise her forever.

The liberty which her imagination had dared to take with the character of his father—oh, it made entirely no difference if the general did not seem to have an angel! Really, could Henry ever forgive her, or forget the absurdity of her curiosity and her fears? She hated herself more than she could express.

He had—she *thought* he had, once or twice before this fatal morning, shown something like *affection* for her. But now—

In short, Catherine made herself as miserable as possible for about half an hour, went down when the clock struck five, with a broken heart, and could scarcely give an intelligible answer to Eleanor's inquiry if she was well.

The formidable Henry soon followed her into the room. And the only difference in his behaviour to her was that he paid her rather more attention than usual. Catherine had never wanted comfort more, and he looked as if he was aware of it.

The evening wore away with no abatement of this soothing politeness; and her spirits were gradually raised to a modest tranquility. The twelve angels watching over her spread about the room and glittered sweetly like jewels—in drapery, tablecloths, and among the sleeves of those present.

Catherine did not learn either to forget or defend the past. But she learned to hope that it would never, ever, *never, ever* NEVER transpire farther, and that it might not cost her Henry's entire regard. Her thoughts were fixed on what she had done, and clearly it had been all a voluntary, self-created and *self-perpetuated supernatural invasion*. Not a *delusion*—no, all the demons and ghosts and creatures had been entirely *real*.

But they did not *have* to be here at all—they had been called forth, out of the bowels of whatever hell, regardless of time of day or even heavenly constraints, by none other than *herself. . . .*

Called forth and brought here, out of chests and cabinets and walls, in all their strange luridness, to populate and animate the very stones of Northanger Abbey with the force of her *desire*—a desire for the fantastic and the extraordinary, for the romantic and dramatic, for the fearsome and the awe-inspiring.

For the *numinous.*

Indeed, here was each trifle imbued with horrid importance by wild imagination, everything influenced by a mind which, before she entered the abbey, had been *craving to be frightened.*

She remembered with what feelings she had prepared for a knowledge of Northanger, searched for signs of mysterious clues in all things, and even invented the Udolpho Code where there was likely none (though, even *now,* some insidious tempting thoughts continued to tantalize Catherine on that notion).

She recognized that the infatuation with terrible Udolpho wonders had been created, the mischief settled, long before her quitting Bath, where she had certainly made a mess of things, with John Thorpe as a mere tool for propagating the mayhem.

*Oh dear! Whatever those people must still be doing there! Surely they are still looking for treasure clues and digging up the town!* thought Catherine.

But then, the dragons had been real. She had *seen* them, three times at least, it was certain, both here and in Bath, and twice in the presence of witnesses!

So maybe it was indeed not entirely her imagination. . . .

And yet—it seemed as if the rest of it might be traced to the influence of that sort of reading which she had there indulged. It was in Bath that Isabella had mentioned the other horrid novels, and encouraged her to consume them until all were exhausted.

Charming as were all Mrs. Radcliffe's works, it was not in them perhaps that human nature was to be looked for, in England, or beyond the borders. Here was surely some security for the existence even of an unloved wife. Murder was not tolerated, servants were not slaves, and neither poison nor sleeping potions to be procured, like rhubarb, from every druggist. Among the Alps and Pyrenees, perhaps, there were no mixed characters—only *angel* or *fiend*. But in England it was not so. There was a general mixture of good and bad.

Based on this, she would not be surprised if even in Henry and Eleanor Tilney, some slight imperfection might appear. And thus she need not fear to acknowledge some actual specks in the character of their father, who—though cleared from the grossly injurious suspicions—was *not* perfectly amiable.

Her mind made up, she resolved to always judge and act in future with the greatest good sense. And now, she need only forgive herself and be happier than ever.

Henry's astonishing generosity and nobleness of conduct, in never alluding to what had passed, was of great assistance to her. Soon, her spirits became absolutely comfortable, and capable of continual improvement by anything he said.

There were still some subjects, indeed, under which she believed they must always tremble—the mention of a chest or a cabinet, for instance, or a root, bell, German orphan, or even dragon—and then there were *unresolved* things, supernatural *truths* yet unspoken, but she hoped to handle them eventually.

The anxieties of common life began soon to succeed to the alarms of romance. She was rather guiltily impatient to hear from Isabella; to know how the Bath world went on, whether there had been any secret treasure discoveries after all—oh dear, she must stop thinking it!—and how the rooms were attended—and if there had been any more dragons. And she was especially anxious to be assured of Isabella's continuing on the best terms with James. Goodness, why? Did she not want James to be extricated from his absurd nephilim engagement? And yet, did she not want him to never feel such unhappy pain?

Her only dependence for information of any kind was on Isabella. James and Mrs. Allen were not expected to write. But Isabella had promised! This made it so particularly strange!

For nine successive mornings, Catherine was repeatedly disappointed. But on the tenth, when she entered the breakfast-room, her first object was a letter, held out by Henry's willing hand. "'Tis only from James, however," as she looked at the direction. She opened it; it was from Oxford; and to this purpose:

DEAR CATHERINE,

   Though, God knows, with little inclination for writing, I think it my duty to tell you that *everything* is at an *end* between Miss Thorpe and me. I left her and Bath yesterday, never to see either again. I shall not enter into particulars—they would only pain you more. You will soon hear enough from another quarter to know where lies the blame; and I hope will acquit your brother of everything but the folly of too easily thinking his affection returned. Thank God! I am undeceived in time! And indeed, I suddenly feel *uncommonly warm all over,* as if I had been submerged in *endless winter* and now am rid of it!

But no more of this. Let me soon hear from you, dear Catherine; you are my only friend; your love I do build upon. I wish your visit at Northanger may be over before *Captain Tilney* makes his *engagement* known, or you will be uncomfortably circumstanced.

Poor Thorpe is in town: I dread the sorry overheated sight of him (whatever is it? One feels always stifling hot around the fellow); his honest heart would feel so much. I have written to him and my father.

Her duplicity hurts me more than anything. And what if I reasoned with her, and she declared herself as much attached to me as ever, and laughed at my fears? I am ashamed to think how long I bore with it. But I believed myself loved. I cannot understand even now, not any of it. We parted at last by mutual consent—if only we had never met! Dearest Catherine, beware how you give your heart. "Believe me," &c.

Catherine had not read three lines before her sudden change of countenance, and exclamations, declared her to be receiving unpleasant news.

She should be rejoicing—was this not what she had hoped would happen? And yet Catherine was devastated on *everyone's* behalf. She even pitied the scrawny sallow creature with the arctic atmosphere!

Henry, earnestly watching her through the whole letter, saw plainly that it ended no better than it began. He was prevented, however, from expressing his surprise by his father's entrance.

They went to breakfast directly; but Catherine could hardly eat anything. Tears filled her eyes—confused, stunned tears—and even ran down her cheeks as she sat. The angels surrounded her gently, stroking her hair, and their iridescent wings made sudden lovely reflections in the globules of her tears—but Catherine ignored them.

She eventually concealed the letter in her pocket, and looked as if she knew not what she did.

The general, between his cocoa and his newspaper, had luckily no leisure for noticing her. But to the other two her distress was equally visible.

As soon as she dared leave the table she hurried away to her own room. But the housemaids were busy in it, and she was obliged to come down again. She turned into the drawing-room for privacy, but Henry and Eleanor had likewise retreated thither, and were discussing her.

She drew back, trying to beg their pardon, but was, with gentle violence, forced to return. And the others withdrew, after Eleanor had affectionately expressed a wish of being of use or comfort to her.

After some time Catherine felt equal to seeing her friends. But whether she should divulge her news was another matter. Perhaps she might just give a distant hint—but not more. To expose such a strange friend as Isabella had been to her—and then *their own brother* so closely concerned in it!

Henry and Eleanor were by themselves in the breakfast-room. They looked at her anxiously. Catherine took her place at the table, and, after a short silence, Eleanor said, "No bad news from Fullerton, I hope? Mr. and Mrs. Morland—your brothers and sisters—I hope they are none of them ill?"

"No, I thank you" (sighing as she spoke); "they are all very well. My letter was from my brother at Oxford."

Nothing was said for a few minutes. Then she said through her tears, "I do not think I shall ever wish for a letter again!"

"I am sorry." Henry closed the book he had just opened. "If I had suspected the letter of containing anything unwelcome—"

And Catherine explained some of it, in agitation. "I have one favour to beg," she added, "that, if your brother should be coming here, you will give me notice of it, that I may go away."

"Our brother! Frederick!"

"Yes; I am sure I should be very sorry to leave you so soon, but *something* has happened that would make it very dreadful for me to be in the same house with Captain Tilney."

Eleanor gazed with increasing astonishment. But Henry began to suspect the truth, and something, in which Miss Thorpe's name was included, passed his lips.

"You have guessed it, I declare!" cried Catherine. "And yet, when we talked about it in Bath, you little thought of its ending so. Isabella has deserted my brother, and is to marry yours! Could you have believed such inconstancy and fickleness, and everything that is bad in the world?"

*"Dear child,"* said an angel unexpectedly. *"After what you knew of the nephilim, why are you even now surprised?"*

"Oh goodness, hush! Yes, I realized very well *what* she was, I just did not *want* her to *be* what she was!" Catherine replied to the angel with passion, entirely forgetting to disguise her voice, or even to cough, so that both Henry and Eleanor were likely left to wonder what she *meant,* or *whom* she was speaking with.

Indeed, the silent look that crossed between sister and brother in that moment was rather curious.

And then Henry said, "I hope, so far as concerns my brother, you are misinformed. I hope he has not had any material share in bringing on Mr. Morland's disappointment. His marrying Miss Thorpe is not probable. I think you must be deceived so far. I am very sorry for Mr. Morland—sorry that anyone you love should be unhappy; but my greatest surprise would be at Frederick's marrying her."

"But it is true! You shall read James's letter yourself. There—" She recollected with a blush the last line about *giving her heart.*

"Will you take the trouble of reading to us the passages which concern my brother?"

"No, read it yourself," cried Catherine, whose second thoughts were clearer (blushing again that she had blushed before). "James only means to give me good advice."

He took the letter, and, having read it through attentively, returned it. "Well, if it is so, I can only say that I am sorry for it. Frederick will not be the first man who has made a senseless choice of wife. I do not envy him, either as a lover or a son."

Miss Tilney read the letter next, in concern and surprise. She then inquired about Miss Thorpe's connections and fortune.

"Her mother is a very good sort of woman," was Catherine's answer.

"What was her father?"

"A lawyer, I believe. They live at Putney."

"Are they a wealthy family?"

"No, not very. I do not believe Isabella has any fortune at all: but that will not signify in your family. Your father is so very liberal! He told me that he only valued money as it allowed him to promote the happiness of his children."

The brother and sister looked at each other.

"But," said Eleanor, after a short pause, "would it promote his happiness, to marry such a girl? She must be unprincipled, or she could not have used your brother so. And how strange an infatuation on Frederick's side! A girl who is violating an engagement with another! Is not it inconceivable? Frederick always wore his heart so proudly, and found no woman good enough to be loved!"

"When I think of his past declarations, I give him up. Moreover, Miss Thorpe is surely too prudent to part with one gentleman before the other was secured. It is all over with Frederick indeed! Prepare, Eleanor, such a sister-in-law you must delight in! Open, candid, artless, guileless, with affections strong but simple, no pretensions, and knowing no disguise."

"Such a sister-in-law, Henry, I should delight in," said Eleanor with a smile.

"But perhaps," observed Catherine, "though she has behaved so ill by our family, she may behave better by yours. Now she has really got the man she likes, she may be constant."

"Indeed," replied Henry; "I am afraid she will be very constant, unless a baronet should come in her way—Frederick's only chance. Must get the Bath paper, to look over the arrivals."

"You think it is all for ambition, then? Indeed, when she first knew what my father would do for them, she seemed disappointed that it was not more. My own disappointment in *her* is great; but, as for poor James, I suppose he will hardly ever recover it."

"Your brother is certainly to be pitied. And you—you feel, I suppose, that in losing Isabella, you lose half yourself. A void in your heart nothing else can occupy. Society is becoming irksome. And as for the amusements in which you were wont to share at Bath (Udolpho turnips and orphans, again), the very idea of them without her is abhorrent. You would not go to a ball for the world. You feel that you have no longer any friend. You feel all this?"

"No," said Catherine, with a blooming smile, "I do not—ought I? To say the truth, though I am hurt and grieved that I cannot love her, that I am never to hear from her or see her again, I do not feel so afflicted as one would have thought."

"You feel, as you always do," said Henry, looking at her with his frequent impossible-to-describe expression.

And Catherine found her spirits so very much relieved by this conversation. Because, now in addition to all things, she need not have that painful and quite possibly impossible *talk* with James!

Crowning her brow, the angels smiled.

# Chapter 26

From this time, the subject was often discussed by the three young people.

Catherine found, with some surprise, that her two young friends were perfectly agreed in considering Isabella's lack of *fortune* as likely to throw great difficulties in the way of her marrying their brother.

Their certainty that the general would, upon this ground alone, independent of her character, oppose the connection, turned her feelings with some alarm towards *herself*. She was as insignificant, and perhaps as portionless, as Isabella!

And if the heir of the Tilney property had not grandeur and wealth enough in himself—what of his *younger brother?*

These painful reflections could only be dispersed by a hope of that continuing partiality which she had from the first been so fortunate as to excite in the general—and by a recollection of his generous and disinterested sentiments on the subject of money. In these matters he was surely misunderstood by his children.

But the Tilneys were so fully convinced that their brother would not have the courage to apply in person for his father's consent (nor was he likely to come to Northanger now), that she found herself at ease as to the necessity of any sudden removal of her own.

At some point Catherine proposed that Henry reveal the situation to the general.

"No," said he, "my father's hands need not be strengthened, and Frederick's confession of folly need not be forestalled. He must tell his own story."

"But he will tell only half of it."

"A quarter would be enough."

A day or two passed and brought no tidings of Captain Tilney. His brother and sister knew not what to think. Sometimes it appeared to them as if his silence would be the natural result of the suspected engagement, and at others that it was wholly incompatible with it.

The general, meanwhile, was free from any real anxiety about his eldest son. Instead he hoped Miss Morland's time at Northanger was passing pleasantly. He often expressed his uneasiness on this behalf and attempted to provide her with various sources of amusement.

One morning he told Henry that when he next went to Woodston, they would take him by surprise there, and eat their mutton with him. Henry was greatly honoured and very happy, and Catherine was quite delighted with the scheme.

"And when do you think, sir, I may look forward to this pleasure? I must be at Woodston on Monday to attend the parish meeting, and probably be obliged to stay two or three days."

The general considered the many options and then said, "On Wednesday, I think, Henry, you may expect us."

A ball itself could not have been more welcome to Catherine than this little excursion, so strong was her desire to be acquainted with Woodston. Her heart was still bounding with joy when Henry, about an hour afterwards, came booted and greatcoated into the room where she and Eleanor were sitting, and said, "I am come, young ladies, in a very moralizing strain, to observe that our pleasures in this world are always to be paid for. Because I am to see you at Woodston on Wednesday, I must go away directly, two days before I intended it."

"Go away!" said Catherine, with a long face. "And why?"

"Why! How can you ask the question? Because no time is to be lost in frightening my old housekeeper out of her wits, because I must go and prepare a dinner for you, to be sure."

"Oh! Not seriously!"

"Aye, and sadly too—for I had much rather stay."

"But how can you think of such a thing, after what the general said? When he so particularly desired you not to give yourself any trouble, because anything would do."

Henry only smiled. "You must know it to be so. Well, I wish I could reason like you, for his sake and my own. Good-bye. As tomorrow is Sunday, Eleanor, I shall not return."

He went. And Catherine was left to doubt her own judgment and ponder the inexplicability of the general's conduct. She already knew he was very particular in his eating, and yet he expected simplicity at Woodston! Why he should say one thing so positively, and mean another all the while? How were people, at that rate, to be understood? Who but Henry could have been aware of what his father was at?

From Saturday to Wednesday, they were now to be without Henry. This was the sad finale of every reflection.

Captain Tilney's letter would certainly come in his absence; The past, present, and future were all equally in gloom. Her brother so unhappy, and Isabella so odious; and Eleanor's spirits always affected by Henry's absence! What was there to interest or amuse her?

She was tired of the woods and the shrubberies—always so smooth and so dry. And the abbey in itself was no more to her now than any other house. The delightful horrors of Udolpho were dissolved, gone away, sunk as though into an old dream. Even the ghosts' voices seemed to have grown silent, or so remote at night that they were no longer quite distinguishable from the natural wind.

*Criminy!* She even missed their silly chains.

And then Catherine sadly realized she had not seen any more dragons. . . .

The painful remembrance of the various breathtaking wonders the abbey had helped to nourish was the only emotion remaining. What a revolution in her ideas! She, who had so longed to be in an *abbey!* Who hungered for the flaming letters of the arcane and secret Udolpho Code!

Now, there was nothing so charming to her imagination as the unpretending comfort of a well-connected parsonage, something like Fullerton, but better: Fullerton had its faults, but Woodston probably had none. If Wednesday should ever come!

It did come—and Catherine trod on air. By ten o'clock, the chaise and four conveyed the two from the abbey. And, after an agreeable drive of almost twenty miles, they entered Woodston, a large and populous village, in a situation not unpleasant.

Catherine was ashamed to say how pretty she thought it—the general seemed to think an apology necessary for the flatness of the country, and the size of the village. But in her heart she preferred it to any other place, admiring everything they passed.

At the further end of the village stood the parsonage, a new-built substantial stone house. As they drove up to the door, Henry, with the friends of his solitude, a large Newfoundland puppy and two or three terriers, was ready to receive them.

Catherine's mind was too full, as she entered the house, for her either to observe or to say a great deal. When called on by the general for her opinion of it, she had very little idea, but soon perceived it was the most comfortable room in the world. But she was too guarded to admit it.

The general started to justify the small house due to her perceived coldness of praise. "We are not comparing it with Fullerton and Northanger—we are considering it as a mere parsonage, small and confined, we allow, but decent, perhaps, and habitable."

Catherine did not hear enough to understand it. A tray full of refreshments was introduced by Henry's servant, and the general was shortly restored to his complacency.

The room in question was handsomely fitted up as a dining-parlour. And on their quitting it to walk round the grounds, she was shown many others. Catherine was delighted enough even to satisfy the general, and expressed her admiration of a specific room with all honest simplicity. "Oh! Why do not you fit up this room, Mr. Tilney? What a pity not to have it fitted up! It is the prettiest room I ever saw; it is the prettiest room in the world!"

"I trust," said the general, with a most satisfied smile, "it will very speedily be furnished: it waits only for a lady's taste!"

"Well, if it was my house, I should never sit anywhere else. Oh! What a sweet little cottage there is among the apple trees!"

"You like it—you approve it as an object—it is enough. Henry, remember. The cottage remains."

Such a compliment recalled all Catherine's worry, and silenced her directly. She said little more in response to the general's other such consultations, until it was time to observe the ornamental walk and meadows near the premises.

A saunter into other meadows, an examination of some improvements, and a charming game of play with a litter of puppies (oh, how the angels flew and danced among the little ones!), brought them to four o'clock, when Catherine scarcely thought it three. At four they dined (the abundance of dinner did not create the smallest astonishment in the general); at six, set off on their return. Never had any day passed so quickly!

So gratifying had been his conduct throughout the whole visit, so well assured was her mind on the subject of his expectations, that, could she have felt equally confident of the wishes of his son, Catherine would have quitted Woodston with little anxiety as to the How or the When she might return to it.

# Chapter 27

The next morning brought the following very unexpected letter from Isabella:

Bath, *April—*

My Dearest Catherine, I received your two kind letters with the greatest delight, and have a thousand apologies to make for not answering them sooner, but in this horrid place one can find time for nothing. I have had my pen in my hand to begin a letter to you almost every day since you left Bath, but have always been prevented by some silly trifle or other. Pray write to me soon, and direct to my own home.

Thank God, we leave this *vile* place tomorrow. Since you went away, I have had no pleasure in it—the dust is beyond anything (what with all the digging of *roots*); and everybody one cares for is gone. Furthermore, there is *no treasure* here. Of that we are now certain. Only many gentlemen with walking-shovels and ladies with bells and potato sacks—all horribly tedious, at this point.

I am quite uneasy about your dear brother, not having heard from him since he went to Oxford; and am fearful of some misunderstanding. Your kind offices will set all right: he is the only man I ever did or could love, and I trust you will convince him of it. The spring fashions are partly down; and the hats the most frightful you can imagine, many now incorporating *bells*.

I hope you spend your time pleasantly. I will not say all that I could of the family you are with, because I would not be ungenerous, or set you against those you esteem; but it is very difficult to know whom to trust, and young men never know their minds. I rejoice to say that the young man whom, of all others, I particularly abhor, has left Bath. You will know, from this description, I must mean *Captain Tilney*, who, as you may remember, was amazingly disposed to follow and tease me, before you went away. Afterwards he got worse, and became quite my shadow.

He went away to his regiment two days ago, and I trust I shall never be plagued with him again. He is the greatest *coxcomb* I ever saw, and amazingly *disagreeable*. The last two days he was always by the side of Charlotte Davis: I pitied his taste, but took no notice of him. The last time we met was in Bath Street, and I turned directly into a shop that he might not speak to me; I would not even look at him. Such a contrast between him and your brother! Pray send me some news of the latter—I am quite unhappy about him; he seemed so uncomfortable when he went away, with a *cold,* or something that *chillingly* affected his spirits.

I would write to him myself, but have mislaid his direction; and am afraid he took something in my conduct amiss. Pray explain everything to his satisfaction; a line from himself to me, or a call at Putney when next in town, might set all to rights. I have not been to the rooms this age, nor to the play, except going in last night with the Hodges, for a frolic, at half price: I was determined they should not say I shut myself up because Tilney was gone.

Anne Mitchell had tried to put on a turban like mine, but made wretched work of it—I wear nothing but purple now: I know I look hideous in it, but no matter—it is *your dear brother's* favourite colour. Lose no time, my dearest, sweetest Catherine, in writing to him and to me, Who ever am, etc.

Such a strain of shallow artifice could not impose even upon Catherine. Its inconsistencies, contradictions, and falsehood struck her from the very first. She was ashamed of Isabella—ashamed of ever *wanting* to love her, despite her nephilim self.

Her professions of attachment were now as disgusting as her excuses were empty; her demands impudent. "Write to James on her behalf! No, James should never hear Isabella's name mentioned by her again."

Catherine was *done,* entirely and irrevocably, with *both* the nephilim.

On Henry's arrival from Woodston, she made known to him and Eleanor their elder brother's safety from Isabella, congratulating them with sincerity on it, and reading aloud the most material passages of her letter with strong indignation.

When she had finished it—"So much for Isabella," she cried, "and for all our intimacy! She must think me an idiot, or she could not have written so. But perhaps this has served to make her character better known to me than mine is to her. Among *other things,* she is a vain coquette. I do not believe she had ever any regard either for James or for me, and I wish I had never known her."

"It will soon be as if you never had," said Henry.

"There is but one thing that I cannot understand. I see that she has had unsuccessful designs on Captain Tilney; but I do not understand what Captain Tilney has been about all this time. Why should he pay her such attentions as to make her quarrel with my brother, and then fly off himself?"

"I have very little to say for Frederick's motives. He has his vanities as well as Miss Thorpe."

"Then you do not suppose he ever really cared about her?"

"I am persuaded that he never did."

"And only made believe to do so for mischief's sake?"

Henry bowed his assent.

"Well, then, I must say that I do not like him at all. Though it has turned out so well for us, I do not like him at all. As it happens, there is no great harm done, because I do not think Isabella has any heart to lose. But, suppose he had made her very much in love with him?"

"But we must first suppose Isabella to have had a heart to lose—consequently to have been a *very different creature;* and, in that case, she would have met with very different treatment."

Catherine suddenly wondered if Henry possibly suspected Isabella's true nephilim nature.

"It is very right that you should stand by your brother."

"And if you would stand by yours, you would not be much distressed by the disappointment of Miss Thorpe."

And Catherine fully agreed. And yet, she still felt a momentary pang of regret for that awful, scrawny, screeching, monstrous hollow creature's sake—regret, worthy of a true heroine's heart.

*Wait, was she not done with the nephilim? Stop it!*

Henry continued, as though fully reading her inside and out. "But your mind is warped by an innate principle of *general integrity,* and therefore not accessible to the cool reasonings of family partiality, or a desire of revenge."

Catherine was complimented out of further bitterness in regard to her very *first friend*—who, she realized, Isabella had been, in her own twisted way—and she let go, once and for all.

Indeed, that is what had made it so awful, so truly awful: the loss and dismissal of her first friend. But she—who could *see* angels, and demons, and the true visage of the nephilim; and who had managed to see beyond Udolpho and the abbey, and into the true heart of a silent ghost—she now *at last* saw enough to let go of an illusion.

Incidentally, Frederick could not be unpardonably guilty, while Henry made himself so agreeable. Thus, she resolved on not answering Isabella's letter, and tried to think no more of it.

# Chapter 28

Soon after this, the general was obliged to go to London for a week. He left Northanger earnestly regretting that any necessity should rob him of Miss Morland's company, and bid his children grant her every amusement.

His departure convinced Catherine that a loss may be sometimes a gain. The happiness with which their time now passed made her thoroughly sensible of the restraint which the general's presence had imposed. She was most thankful for their present release from it.

The resulting ease and delights made her love the place and the two people more and more every day. And if not for a dread of soon having to leave the one, and an apprehension of not being equally beloved by the other, she would have been perfectly happy.

But she was now in the fourth week of her visit. And perhaps it might seem an intrusion if she stayed much longer. This was a painful consideration. Eager to get rid of such a weight on her mind, she resolved to speak to Eleanor about it at once.

She took the first opportunity of being alone with Eleanor, to start forth her obligation of going away very soon. Eleanor declared herself much concerned. She had "hoped for the pleasure of her company for a much longer time—if Mr. and Mrs. Morland were aware of the pleasure it was to her to have her there, they would not hasten her return."

Catherine explained: "Oh! Papa and Mamma were in no hurry at all. As long as she was happy, they would always be satisfied."

A brief but happy exchange ensued in which Catherine and Eleanor made it clear that they both wanted Catherine to stay very much longer, and continue her visit.

The kindness, the earnestness of Eleanor's manner in pressing her to stay, and Henry's gratified look on being told that her stay was determined, were such sweet proofs of her *importance* with them, as left her only just so much solicitude as the human mind can never do comfortably without.

She did—almost always—*believe* that Henry *loved* her, and quite always that his father and sister loved and even wished her to belong to them. And believing so far, her doubts and anxieties were merely sportive irritations.

Henry was unable to obey his father's injunction and remain wholly at Northanger in attendance on the ladies, during his absence in London. The duties of his curate at Woodston obliged him to leave them on Saturday for a couple of nights.

The loss of his company was not now what it had been while the general was at home. It lessened their gaiety, but did not ruin their comfort. The two girls found themselves so well sufficient for the time to themselves, that it was eleven o'clock, rather a late hour at the abbey, before they quitted the supper-room on the day of Henry's departure.

They had just reached the head of the stairs, with a garland of angel "lamps" cheerfully illuminating the way for Catherine's inner vision, when it seemed (as far as the thickness of the walls would allow them to judge), that a carriage was driving up to the door. And the next moment confirmed the idea by the loud noise of the house-bell. "Good heaven! What can be the matter?"

After the first perturbation of surprise had passed away, Eleanor decided it had to be her eldest brother. And accordingly she hurried down to welcome him.

Catherine walked on to her chamber, preparing herself for a further acquaintance with Captain Tilney, and hoping their meeting to be not entirely painful. She trusted he would never speak of Miss Thorpe; that he was ashamed of the part he had acted. As long as all mention of Bath scenes were avoided, she could behave to him very civilly.

In such considerations time passed. Eleanor had to be most glad to see him, with so much to say, for it was half an hour since his arrival, and Eleanor did not come up.

At that moment Catherine thought she heard her step in the gallery, and listened for it; but all was silent. However, the noise of *something* moving close to her door made her start (oh dear! Udolpho mysteries momentarily rushed into Catherine's fertile mind but she firmly denied herself that path of thought). And in another moment a slight motion of the *lock* proved that some hand must be on it.

She trembled a little at the idea of anyone's approaching so cautiously, but was resolved not to be again overcome by trivial alarm, or misled by a raised imagination. She stepped quietly forward, and opened the door.

Eleanor, and only Eleanor, stood there. Catherine's spirits, however, were calmed but for an instant. For, Eleanor's cheeks were pale, and her manner greatly agitated. She intended to come in, but was almost reluctant to enter the room, or to speak.

Catherine, supposing some uneasiness on Captain Tilney's account, expressed her concern by silent attention. She obliged Eleanor to be seated, rubbed her temples with lavender-water, and hung over her with affectionate solicitude.

"My dear Catherine, you must not—" were Eleanor's first connected words. "I am quite well. This kindness distracts me— I cannot bear it—I come to you on such an errand!"

"Errand! To me!"

"How shall I tell you! Oh! How shall I tell you!"

Even Eleanor's angel floated dejectedly, like a solitary waning candle flame overhead.

A new idea now stunned Catherine. Turning as pale as her friend, she exclaimed, "'Tis a messenger from Woodston!"

"You are mistaken, indeed," returned Eleanor, looking at her most compassionately; "it is no one from Woodston. It is my *father* himself."

Her voice faltered, and her eyes were turned to the ground as she mentioned his name. His unexpected return was enough in itself to make Catherine's heart sink. For a few moments she hardly supposed there were anything worse to be told.

She said nothing. Eleanor collected herself and, with eyes still cast down, went on. "You are too good to think the worse of me for the part I am obliged to perform. I am indeed a most unwilling messenger. After what has so lately passed between us—how joyfully!—as to your continuing here as I hoped for many weeks longer, how can I tell you this?—But—My dear Catherine, we are to part. My father has *recollected* an *engagement* that takes our whole family away on Monday. Explanation and apology are equally impossible."

"My dear Eleanor," cried Catherine, suppressing her feelings as well as she could, "do not be so distressed. A second engagement must give way to a first. I am very, very sorry we are to part—so soon, and so suddenly too; but I am not offended. I can finish my visit here at any time; or I hope you will come to me. Can you, when you return from this, come to Fullerton?"

"It will not be in my power, Catherine."

A very strange weight started to settle on Catherine. "Come when you can, then," she tried, feeling something amiss.

Eleanor made no answer.

Catherine mused aloud, "Monday—and you all go. Well, I suppose I need not go till just before you do. Do not be distressed, Eleanor, I can go on Monday very well. My father and mother's having no notice of it is of very little consequence. The general will send a servant with me, half the way—and then I shall soon be at Salisbury, then only nine miles till home."

"Ah, Catherine! Were it were so, it would be somewhat less intolerable! But—how can I tell you?—tomorrow morning is fixed for your leaving us. Not even the hour is left to your choice! The carriage is ordered. It will be here at seven o'clock, and no servant will be offered you."

Catherine sat down, breathless and speechless.

"I could hardly believe my senses, when I heard it," continued Eleanor. "And no displeasure, no resentment that you can feel at this moment, can be more than I myself—but I must not talk of what I felt. Oh! Good God! What will your father and mother say! After courting you from the protection of real friends to this—almost double distance from your home—to have you driven out of the house, without even decent civility! Dear, dear Catherine, in being the bearer of such a message, I seem guilty myself of all its insult. Yet, I trust you will acquit me—for you must have been long enough in *this house* to see that I am but a nominal mistress of it, my real power is nothing."

"Have I offended the general?" said Catherine in a faltering voice.

"Alas! All that I know is that you can have given him *no just cause* of offence. He certainly is greatly, very greatly discomposed; I have seldom seen him more so. His *temper* is not happy. *Something* has now occurred to ruffle it in an uncommon degree. Some disappointment, some unknown vexation!"

Catherine could only attempt to speak for Eleanor's sake. "I am sure," said she, "I am very sorry if I have offended him. It was the last thing I would willingly have done. But do not be unhappy, Eleanor. An engagement must be kept. I am only sorry it was not recollected sooner, that I might have written home. But it is of very little consequence."

"I earnestly hope that to your real safety it will be of none. But to everything else it is of the greatest consequence: to comfort, appearance, propriety, to your family, to the world. Were your friends, the Allens, still in Bath, you might go to them with comparative ease. But a journey of seventy miles, to be taken post by you, at your age, *alone,* unattended!"

"Oh, the journey is nothing. Do not think of it. And if we are to part, a few hours sooner or later makes no difference. I can be ready by seven. Let me be called in time." Catherine spoke bravely then, like a true heroine.

Eleanor saw that she wished to be alone. "I shall see you in the morning."

Catherine's swelling heart indeed needed relief. In her friend's presence, pride and friendship had restrained her tears. But no sooner was she gone than they burst forth in torrents.

The twelve angels surrounding her with their sweet radiance, were hardly enough to refill the empty vessel of her heart—indeed she needed dozens more!

And as Catherine wept, the guardians of heaven came, more and more of them, from every direction, through shuttered windows and walls, through drapery and ceiling, floating down gently like snowflakes of luminosity—until Catherine felt herself in a field of angelic brightness, the centerpiece of a radiant glowing flower made of pure otherworldly light. . . .

Catherine's heart was thus gentled, but her stunned bewilderment remained.

To be turned from the house, and in such a way! Without any reason or apology that could justify the abrupt rudeness, nay, the insolence of it!

Henry at a distance—not able even to bid him farewell. Every hope or expectation from him suspended—and who could say how long? Who could say when they might meet again?

And all this by such a man as General Tilney, so polite, so well bred, and heretofore so particularly fond of her! It was as incomprehensible as it was mortifying and grievous. *He has no angel of his own,* Catherine reminded herself. *There must be sufficient reasons for this!*

Indeed, the manner in which it was done was so grossly uncivil—hurrying her away without allowing her even the appearance of choice as to the time or mode of her traveling—as if resolved to have her gone before he was stirring in the morning, that he might not be obliged even to *see* her!

What could all this mean but an intentional affront? By some means she must have offended him. Eleanor had wished to spare her from so painful a notion, but Catherine could not believe that anything could provoke such ill-will against a person unless there was a solid reason for it.

The night passed heavily. Sleep was out of the question. That room, in which her disturbed imagination had tormented her on her first arrival, was again the scene of agitated spirits and unquiet slumbers.

Yet how different now the source of her inquietude from what it had been then—how mournfully superior in reality and substance! No Legion of demons filled the darkness, no ghostly sighs, breaths, or moans resounded—not even hiccups!—not, furthermore, even those abysmally tedious chains (ever since her communication with the ghost of Mrs. Tilney, she had ceased hearing them, realized Catherine). The chest and cabinet stood dead to any supernatural presences. No mystical Capital Letters appeared carved on wood or scrawled on washing-bills, or stood up in fiery script in the air itself to signify an ancient Udolpho Code.

*And there had been decidedly no treasure. Not in Bath, not in Northanger.*

*The dragons,* thought Catherine, *the dragons came and searched for naught. . . .*

*And so did I.*

Catherine lay awake thus, hour after hour, without curiosity or terror.

Soon after six Eleanor entered her room, eager to show attention or give assistance where it was possible. But very little remained to be done.

Catherine had not loitered. She was almost dressed, and her packing almost finished. The possibility of some *conciliatory message* from the general occurred to her as his daughter appeared. What so natural, as that anger should pass away and kind repentance succeed it?

But Eleanor brought no message. Very little passed between them on meeting. Each found her greatest safety in silence, with only few trivial sentences exchanged while they remained upstairs. Catherine in busy agitation completed her dress, and Eleanor, with more goodwill than experience, filled the trunk.

When everything was done they left the room. Catherine lingered only half a minute behind her friend to throw a parting glance on every well-known, cherished object, and went down to the breakfast-parlour, where breakfast was prepared.

She tried to eat, to make her friend comfortable; but she had no appetite, and could not swallow many mouthfuls. The contrast between this and her previous cheerful breakfast in that room gave her fresh misery. Happy, happy breakfast! For *Henry had been there;* Henry had sat by her and helped her.

The appearance of the carriage recalled them to the present moment. Catherine's colour rose at the sight of it. And the indignity with which she was treated, struck her with peculiar force—made her for a short time sensible only of *resentment*. Eleanor seemed now impelled into resolution and speech.

"You must write to me, Catherine!" she cried; "you must let me hear from you as soon as possible. Till I know you to be safe at home, I shall not have an hour's comfort. For *one letter,* at all risks, all hazards, I must entreat. To know that you are safe at Fullerton, your family well, and I will not expect more. Direct to me at Lord Longtown's, and, *under cover* to Alice."

"No, Eleanor, if you are not allowed to receive a letter from me, I am sure I had better not write. I will get home safely."

Eleanor only replied, "I cannot wonder at your feelings. I will not importune you. I—" The look of sorrow accompanying her words was enough to melt Catherine's pride in a moment, and she instantly said, "Oh, Eleanor, I *will* write to you indeed!"

There was yet another embarrassing point which Miss Tilney was anxious to settle. It had occurred to her that after so long an absence from home, Catherine might not be provided with enough *money* for the expenses of her journey. And, upon suggesting it, with most affectionate offers of accommodation, it proved to be exactly the case.

Catherine had never thought on the subject till that moment, but, upon examining her purse, was convinced that but for this kindness of her friend, she might have been turned from the house without even the means of getting home. The distress at this notion filled the minds of both. And scarcely another word was said during their remaining time together.

The carriage was soon announced. Catherine rose instantly. A long and affectionate silent embrace followed, as they bid each other adieu. And as they entered the hall, Catherine paused a moment, unable to leave the house without some mention of *one* whose name had not been spoken by either. With quivering lips she left "her kind remembrance for her absent friend."

But with this reference to *his* name, there was to be no more restraining her feelings. Hiding her face as well as she could with her handkerchief, Catherine darted across the hall, jumped into the chaise, and in a moment was driven from the door.

# Chapter 29

Catherine was too wretched to be fearful.

The journey in itself had no terrors for her—indeed, the *world* itself held no more terrors at all—and she began it without either dreading its length or feeling its solitariness.

Leaning back in one corner of the carriage, in a violent burst of tears, she was conveyed some miles beyond the walls of the abbey before she raised her head. And the highest point of ground within the park was almost closed from her view before she was capable of turning her eyes towards it.

She was thus unable to see the wondrous sight of a dark speck ascending into the sky—an airborne creature that was not a mere bird, but of a familiar reptilian shape to indicate a dragon.

The dragon flew at a great distance, unobserved, yet was distinctly following the carriage. . . .

Unfortunately, the road she now traveled was the same which only ten days ago she had so happily passed along in going to and from Woodston. And, for fourteen miles, every bitter feeling was intensified by the familiar view of objects on which she had first looked under impressions so different. Every mile, as it brought her nearer Woodston, added to her sufferings. And when within the distance of five, she passed the turning which led to it, and thought of Henry—so *near,* yet so unconscious—her grief and agitation were excessive.

It was in that moment that her grieving eyes scanned the heavens in passing, and she saw the *dragon,* flying closer now, low to the ground, and thus the details visible—its familiar dark leathery hide with sharp glittering scales along the tips of its wings, gilded into liquid metal by the sunlight.

Catherine stared.

And then she had occasion to stare again, and open her eyes wide, and forget her tears.

From the direction of Woodston, *another* dragon arose.

*This* one, she had never seen before, she realized now.

This dragon was pure *white.*

It was of the same monumental wingspan as the other; grand, fierce, violent in its approach. Its skin was supple leathery pallor, smooth on the underbelly and on the outside, bejeweled with razor metal scales. But it was white as day, blinding brightness—*light* itself.

And for a moment, the *dragon* was an *angel.*

The dragon beat its wings, racing closer to the crossroad turning. And when it was near enough, only the height of a cathedral overhead, it engaged the other dragon.

But first, Catherine heard its battle cry.

There is no manner of words sufficient to describe a dragon's voice, nor its song, nor its secret whisper. But its cry—it is like the voice of the earth itself wedded to thunder. . . .

Catherine and her fellow travelers in the carriage, the driver, all could not help but stare through windows, some trembling, others stunned, and the driver just about losing control of the horses, then urging them on frightfully.

Overhead, the other dragon, dark and gold, had turned its head, its burning coal-red eye toward the approaching enemy. And the next moment the dragons came together with an impact that could be heard like an explosion of distant cannon.

There was the beating of wings, the striking of claws of steel, the maddened eyes, one crimson, the other amber-gold. Scales of white and gold metal began to rain upon the moving carriage, and indeed upon the road and all the countryside, falling like a downpour of coins; a strange manna indeed, an *unearthly* harvest. . . . And the two great ones hurtled back and forth at each other, tearing and striking and rising high up toward the clouds, then falling back again.

The ordeal went on for an hour at least, then it seemed the dragons disappeared, lost to view beyond the turning road and the trees. But soon enough they came back again, two unrelenting shapes in struggle, the white one pursuing the dark gold, neither of them winning or losing, it seemed.

Eventually the carriage and its denizens realized they were not to be harmed, and only a few half-joking comments were raised, and natural comments of wonder and amazement—for none of them had seen dragons in their lifetime, though it had been a thing of discourse and historical significance.

Catherine did not share in the conversation. But her heart was beating violently in her chest, as though she too was soaring aloft in the heavens, engaged in a mortal battle.

And in her supernatural vision, somehow she *was* indeed there, together with the dragon of light. It was important somehow, important that he was to win.

What was it that connected them? Surely not her silly thoughts of secret clues and Udolpho and imaginary treasure? Why had the dragons come indeed, both of them; and was it in any way possible that they had come for *her?*

Catherine sometimes stopped looking out of the carriage and up at the embattled sky, and allowed her strange, confounded, splintered thoughts to dwell on what she had left behind, just now, some miles away, in Woodston.

The day which she had spent at that place had been one of the happiest of her life. It was there, on that day, that the general used such pointed expressions with regard to *Henry and herself,* had spoken and looked in a way that could only give her the most positive conviction of his actually wishing their *marriage.* Yes, only ten days ago he had elated her by his regard—indeed, confused her! And now—what had she done (or omitted to do) to merit such a change?

The only offence against the general of which she could accuse herself, was a ridiculous secret. Only Henry and her own heart were privy to it—her shocking suspicions of his murdering his wife. And Henry could not have betrayed her. If, indeed, by any strange mischance, his father should have learned what horrors she had thought of him—no wonder his indignation, or his even turning her from his house. But she dearly hoped such a bitter explanation was not the case.

However, now there was an even more urgent, anxiety-causing issue plaguing her. How would Henry think, feel, and look, when he returned on the morrow to Northanger and discovered her gone? What would he do? She was uncertain. Sometimes her imagination painted the dread of his calm *acquiescence* to his father's decision; at others there was but the sweetest confidence in his *regret* and *resentment.*

To the general, of course, he would not dare to speak (how could he oppose the will of his father?); but to Eleanor—what might he not say to Eleanor about her?

Catherine sometimes remembered, throughout the musings, to glance outside the carriage. And there the two dragons continued to battle in the sky.

In this unceasing recurrence of doubts and inquiries, the hours passed away. Her journey advanced much faster than she looked for. The pressing anxieties of thought, which prevented her from noticing anything before her, and only occasionally the dragons overhead, saved her from counting the passage of the moments. And though no other object on the road could engage a moment's attention, she found none of it tedious, and some, when looking up at the *unreal* sky battle, oddly *exciting*.

She was also prevented from feeling eagerness for her journey's conclusion. For to return in such a manner to Fullerton was almost to destroy the pleasure of a meeting with those she loved best, even after an absence of eleven weeks.

What had she to say that would not humble herself and pain her family, cause useless resentment, and perhaps involve the innocent with the guilty in the same ill-will? She could never do justice to Henry and Eleanor's merit. If *they* were blamed on their father's account, it would cut her to the heart.

With these feelings, she rather dreaded the first view of that well-known spire within twenty miles of home. Salisbury she had known to be her point on leaving Northanger; but after the first stage she had been indebted to the post-masters for the names of the places which were then to conduct her to it—so great had been her ignorance of her route.

She met with nothing, however, to distress or frighten her. Her youth, civil manners, and liberal pay procured her all the attention that a traveler like herself could require. And stopping only to change horses, she traveled on for about eleven hours without accident or alarm, and between six and seven o'clock in the evening found herself entering Fullerton.

One last curious glance up overhead told her the dragons were no longer in view. They had either fallen behind some miles ago, or concluded their battle—and Catherine had a curious moment of panic and anxiety as to the end results. Had the white dragon come out victorious? Was he *injured?* And was the other, the dragon of dark gold, *destroyed?* Or was it the reverse—oh! she could not endure that grim possibility!

How strange indeed were these sensations our heroine felt.

But now, gentle Reader, this Aside[29]—a heroine returning, at the close of her career, to her native village, in triumph, is an event that gives credit to every conclusion—and the author must share in the glory she so liberally bestows.

But my affair is widely different; I bring back my heroine to her home in solitude and disgrace. And no sweet elation of spirits can lead me into minuteness.

A heroine in a hack post-chaise is such a blow upon sentiment, as no attempt at grandeur or pathos can withstand—not even an accompaniment of dragons in the sky. Swiftly therefore shall her post-boy drive through the village, amid the gaze of Sunday groups, and speedy shall be her descent from it.

But, however distressed Catherine was, advancing towards the parsonage, and whatever the humiliation of her biographer in relating it, she was a happy sight—her carriage, and herself.

The chaise of a traveler is a rare sight in Fullerton. Thus, the whole family were immediately at the window, especially the two youngest children, George and Harriet, a boy and girl of six and four years old. Happy the child that first discovered and announced Catherine!

Her father, mother, Sarah, George, and Harriet, all assembled at the door to welcome her with affectionate eagerness. It was a sight to awaken the best feelings of Catherine's heart. And in the embrace of each, as she stepped from the carriage, she found herself soothed beyond anything. So surrounded, so caressed, she was even happy!

The angels mingled in common among the family, and lent a distinctive glow to the joyfulness of family love. Everything for a short time was subdued, and the pleasure of seeing her left them little leisure for calm curiosity. They were all seated round the tea-table, which Mrs. Morland had hurried for the comfort of the poor traveler (whose pale and jaded looks soon caught her

---

[29] Hold fast, bear onward! This one shall be brief!

notice), before any inquiry so direct as to demand a positive answer was addressed to her.

Reluctantly did she then begin an extended explanation. But the listeners were hardly given a firm cause of her sudden return. They were far from being an irritable race—far from catching affronts, or harboring bitter resentment. But here (when the whole was unfolded) was an insult not to be overlooked, nor, for the first half hour, to be easily pardoned.

Without suffering any romantic alarm in regard to their daughter's long and lonely journey, Mr. and Mrs. Morland recognized it was unpleasant to her. Thus, they could never have voluntarily approved it. General Tilney had acted neither honourably nor feelingly—neither as a gentleman nor as a parent. Why he had done it, what could have provoked him to such a breach of hospitality, and so suddenly turned all his partial regard for their daughter into actual ill-will, was an unresolved matter.

But it did not oppress them overlong. "It was a strange business, and that he must be a very strange man," was their calm conclusion.

"Why did he not send Catherine away civilly?" said Sarah.

"I am sorry for the young people," returned Mrs. Morland; "they must have a sad time of it. But Catherine is safe at home, and our comfort does not depend upon General Tilney."

Catherine sighed.

"Well," continued her philosophic mother, "I am glad I did not know of your journey at the time. But now it is all over, and no great harm done. My dear Catherine, you always were a sad little scatter-brained creature, what with all the *reciting* to yourself and talking to furniture. But now you must have been forced to have your wits about you—with so much changing of chaises and so forth. I hope that you have not left anything behind you in any of the pockets."

Catherine hoped so too. But her spirits were quite worn down. And, in order to be silent and alone, she readily agreed to her mother's counsel of going early to bed. Her parents, seeing nothing in her ill looks but the natural consequence of mortified feelings and fatigue of a journey, parted from her easily. Though, when they all met the next morning, and her recovery was not equal to their hopes, they were perfectly unsuspicious of any deeper evil.

They never once thought of her *heart*—which, for the parents of a young lady of seventeen, just returned from her first excursion from home, was odd enough!

As soon as breakfast was over, she sat down to fulfill her promise to Miss Tilney and write a letter. The strength of her feelings, however, made it most difficult to write. To compose a letter which might do full justice to her sentiments and possibly be seen by Henry himself was a near impossibility. In the end she was brief, conveying confidence of her safety, and enclosing the money which Eleanor had advanced, with grateful thanks.

"This has been a strange acquaintance," observed Mrs. Morland, as the letter was finished; "soon made and soon ended. I am sorry it happens so, for Mrs. Allen thought them very pretty kind of young people. And you were sadly out of luck too in your Isabella. Verily, the Whore of Babylon! Ah! Poor James! Well, we must live and learn. The next new friends you make I hope will be better worth keeping."

*Oh, dear heaven! The Whore of Babylon!* How indeed had she had forgotten that strange demand by the Legion? And oh, surely now it fit Isabella's behavior, at least in spirit.

But why had the Legion asked *her* for Isabella? What claim had she on the naphil? What *power* had she to withhold or give?

Suddenly Catherine wondered a great many things.

She wondered indeed about power. The power she had, and the power attributed to her, and the effects of her actions and words, and indeed, her *thoughts!*

Not everything was entirely clear as of yet, but it occurred to Catherine that the Legion had *tested* her in some manner. Tested her *resolve* and her *power* and her ability to *choose*. Tested her *compassion,* and her *friendship* toward even those whose friendship was not worth keeping.

And now Catherine coloured as she warmly answered, "No friend can be better worth keeping than Eleanor."

"If so, my dear, do not be uneasy. I dare say you will be thrown together again in the course of a few years; and then what a pleasure it will be!"

Mrs. Morland was not effective at consolation. The hope of meeting again in the course of a few years could only put into Catherine's head what might happen within that time to make a meeting dreadful to her. She could never forget Henry Tilney, or think of him with less tenderness than she did at that moment. But he might forget her—!

Her eyes filled with tears as she pictured her acquaintance so renewed. And so her mother proposed, as another expedient for restoring her spirits, that they should call on Mrs. Allen.

The two houses were only a quarter of a mile apart. As they walked, Mrs. Morland quickly dispatched all that she felt on the score of James's disappointment. "We are sorry for him," said she; "but otherwise there is no harm done in the match going off. For it could not be desirable to have him engaged to a girl so entirely without fortune, and of such ill behaviour. At present it is hard for poor James; but will not be forever. He will be a discreeter man all his life, for the foolishness of his first choice."

Catherine could not easily listen to this. Soon all her thinking powers were swallowed up in the reflection of her own changes since last she had trodden this well-known road between her home and the Allen's. It was not three months ago since, wild with joyful expectation, she had there run backwards and forwards some ten times a day, with a light heart and angels in her wake.

She had been as free from the *apprehension* of *evil* as from the *knowledge* of it.

Three months ago had seen her all this; and now, how altered a being did she return!

She was received by the Allens with all the affectionate kindness which her appearance would naturally call forth. And great was their surprise, and warm their displeasure, on hearing how she had been treated by General Tilney.

"Catherine took us quite by surprise yesterday evening." And Mrs. Morland told them the circumstances, adding, "But we are so glad to have her amongst us again! And it is a great comfort to find that she is not a poor helpless creature, but can shift very well for herself."

Mr. Allen expressed himself on the occasion with the reasonable resentment of a sensible friend. And Mrs. Allen, as usual, echoed. His wonder, his conjectures, and his explanations became in succession hers, with the addition of this single remark—"I really have not patience with the general"—to fill up every accidental pause.

After Mr. Allen left the room, and echoing him and herself for good measure, she immediately added, "Only think, my dear, of my having got that frightful great rent in my best Mechlin so charmingly mended, before I left Bath, that one can hardly see where it was. Bath is a nice place, Catherine, after all. I assure you I did not above half like coming away. All those amusing Clues and gentlemen with their walking-shovels—Indeed, I told Mr. Allen he ought to procure one himself; quite useful in case of an unforseen need of excavation, as it might be, around *roots* for *treasure*—though, I dare say, we had not discovered any, and neither did Mrs. Hughes—however they did adopt a poor little *orphan* of the Rhine or its whereabouts. Though, Mrs. Thorpe's being there was such a comfort to us, was not it? You and I were quite forlorn at first."

"Yes, but that did not last long," said Catherine, her eyes brightening at the recollection of what had first given spirit to her existence there.

"Very true: we soon met with Mrs. Thorpe, and then we wanted for nothing. My dear, do not you think these silk gloves wear very well? I put them on new the first time of our going to the Lower Rooms, and I have worn them a great deal since, with the addition of tiny *cowbells*. Do you remember that evening?"

"Do I! Oh! Perfectly."

"It was very agreeable, was not it? Mr. Tilney drank tea with us, and I always thought him a great addition, *he is so very agreeable*. I have a notion you danced with him, but am not quite sure. I remember I had my favourite gown on."

Catherine could not answer; and, after a short trial of other subjects, Mrs. Allen again returned to—"I really have not patience with the general!"

As they walked home again, Mrs. Morland tried to impress on her daughter's mind the happiness of having such steady well-wishers as Mr. and Mrs. Allen, and the unimportance of the slight acquaintance with the Tilneys.

There was a great deal of good sense in all this. But there are some situations of the human mind in which good sense has very little power. Catherine's feelings contradicted almost every position her mother advanced. It was upon the behaviour of these very slight acquaintances that all her present happiness depended.

Soon Catherine was silently reflecting that now Henry must have arrived at Northanger . . . now he must have heard of her departure . . . and now, perhaps—

Now what?

# Chapter 30

Catherine's disposition was not naturally sedentary, nor had her habits been ever very industrious. But whatever might hitherto have been her defects of that sort, her mother perceived them now to be greatly increased.

Catherine could neither sit still nor employ herself for ten minutes. She walked round the garden and orchard again and again, trailing angels. It seemed as if she could even walk about the house rather than remain fixed for any time in the parlour.

Her loss of spirits was palpable. In her rambling and her idleness she might only be a caricature of herself. But in her silence and sadness she was the very reverse of all that she had been before. Not a word was said to berate inanimate objects (as Mrs. Morland referred to it, ignorant of the angels). Not once did Catherine argue with her dressing table or apologize to the bed.

For two days Mrs. Morland allowed it to pass. But when a third night's rest had not restored her cheerfulness, useful activity, or inclination for needlework, she could no longer refrain from a gentle reproof.

"My dear Catherine, I am afraid you are growing quite a fine lady. Your head runs too much upon Bath. But there is a time for everything—a time for balls and plays, and a time for work. You have had a long run of amusement. Now you must try to be useful."

Catherine took up her work directly, saying, in a dejected voice, that "her head did not run upon Bath—much."

"Then you are fretting about General Tilney, and that is very simple of you; for ten to one whether you ever see him again. You should never fret about trifles." After a short silence—"I hope, my Catherine, you are not getting out of humour with home because it is not so grand as Northanger. You should be contented anywhere, especially at home. I did not like, at breakfast, to hear you talk so much about the French bread at Northanger."

"I am sure I do not care about the bread. It is all the same to me what I eat."

"There is a clever essay in one of the books upstairs, about young girls that have been spoilt for home by great acquaintance. I will find it for you. It ought to do you good."

Catherine said no more, and applied to her work. But in minutes she sunk again into languor and listlessness, moving herself in her chair much oftener than she moved her needle.

Mrs. Morland watched the relapse, and seeing in her daughter's absent and dissatisfied look the proof of that repining spirit, hastily left the room to fetch the essay book in question. It was some time before she could find what she looked for; and a quarter of an hour had elapsed ere she returned downstairs with the helpful volume.

She knew not that a visitor had arrived within the last few minutes. On entering the room, the first object she beheld was a young man whom she had never seen before.

With a look of much respect, he immediately rose. Introduced to her by her conscious daughter as "Mr. Henry Tilney," with the embarrassment of real sensibility he began to apologize for his appearance there—acknowledging that after what had passed he had little right to expect a welcome at

Fullerton. His impatience to be assured of Miss Morland's having reached her home in safety was the cause of his intrusion.

He did not address himself to a ruthless judge or a resentful heart. Far from blaming him or his sister in their father's misconduct, Mrs. Morland had been always kindly disposed towards each. Instantly pleased by his appearance, she received him with simple unaffected benevolence. She thanked him for such an attention to her daughter, assured him that the friends of her children were always welcome, and entreated him to say not another word of the past.

He was inclined to obey this request. For, though his heart was greatly relieved by such unlooked-for mildness, it was not just at that moment in his power to *say anything* to the purpose. Returning in silence to his seat, therefore, he remained for some minutes most civilly answering all Mrs. Morland's common remarks about the weather and roads.

Catherine meanwhile—the anxious, agitated, happy, feverish Catherine—said not a word. But her glowing cheek and brightened eye made her mother trust that this good-natured visit would at least set her heart at ease. And gladly therefore did she lay aside the instructive volume for a future hour.

Desirous of Mr. Morland's assistance (both in reassuring and in finding conversation for her guest, whose chagrin on his father's account she earnestly pitied), Mrs. Morland dispatched one of the children to summon him.

But Mr. Morland was from home. And being thus without any support, in a quarter of an hour she had nothing to say.

After a couple of minutes' unbroken silence, Henry— turning to Catherine *for the first time* since her mother's entrance—asked her, with sudden alacrity, if Mr. and Mrs. Allen were now at Fullerton?

And obtaining (from amidst all her perplexity of words in reply) the meaning, which one short syllable would have given, immediately expressed his intention of paying his respects to them. With a rising colour, he asked her if she would have the goodness to show him the way.

"You may see the house from this window, sir," said Sarah.

This produced only a bow of acknowledgment from the gentleman, and a silencing nod from her mother.

For Mrs. Morland—thinking it probable that he might have some explanation to give of his father's behaviour which it must be more pleasant for him to communicate only to Catherine—would not on any account prevent her accompanying him.

They began their walk. And Mrs. Morland was not entirely mistaken in his object in wishing it. Some explanation on his father's account he had to give; but his first purpose was to *explain himself.* And before they reached Mr. Allen's grounds he had done it so well that Catherine did not think it could ever be repeated too often.

"Miss Morland," began Henry, stopping his stride suddenly. "I must speak to you at last—"

Catherine stopped also, and observed his face taking on deep colour that in turn made her colour likewise.

"Miss Morland—Catherine—I know not where to begin. My father's behaviour—it was duly unpardonable. But I need give reasons that may at least explain it in your eyes. And I must speak at last in more candour than I have ever done before. I—"

As he spoke, Catherine noticed how her own angels came to him, surrounding Henry and herself in a strange united circle, brighter than day. She watched their iridescent wings near his brow, their delicate movements like breaths upon his cheek. And then she knew she had to speak her own truth at last.

"Mr. Tilney—Henry. There is something I must also say to you, and I am afraid—I am terrified!"

*"Dear child, oh, this is indeed the moment! Be not afraid now!"* exclaimed Lawrence, or possibly Maurice or Horace or Clarisse—oh goodness, it was all of them, speaking almost in unison!

"Not now, hush!" she quickly said to them.

But Henry saw her anxious gaze, and the direction of her speech. And he said, "It is that you *see* . . . you *talk* to angels and other such beings, is it not?"

"Oh!" Catherine was stunned. "How did you *know?!*"

And Henry smiled. "I had noticed—Eleanor and I—for quite some time. And once, when in Northanger, we saw you speak outright, and we both knew for certain. You are different, and very dear and very *extraordinary*, Catherine. And you are *exactly* like our mother. *She* too could speak to the unseen world of beings all around us, and since childhood she had told us stories of the angels who sang her songs and told her secret wonders. One might not believe such a thing, but we saw it, observed it with our own eyes. And indeed, the *world* around our mother seemed to come *alive*. Ghosts and spirits appeared, and there were metaphysical wonders both dark and light, seemingly everywhere she went."

"Your mother!" whispered Catherine, musing. "No wonder her spirit came to me!"

And Henry's eyes were brilliant with liquid as he heard this. "She was a *treasure*, Catherine. Indeed, she was *the* treasure. For yes, there was—there *is* none other. The treasure is not gold or jewels or riches of coin, but a woman of light—one such as yourself.

"And thus, so are you. *You are the treasure, Catherine.*"

Suddenly then his eyes grew dark and hard as flints in strange passion, and he continued, "And as you well know, where there is treasure, there must be a *dragon*. My father was thus, the dragon to my mother's treasure. He loved her perfectly, and she loved him, and they were happy and joyful even when he was stubborn and dominant, until she died.

"And then, the dragon too *changed*—as he must, when he loses the one thing in the world that gives him truth and life and sustenance.

"My father became hard and cold as stone and his heart turned to inviolate metal."

"Oh!" said Catherine, beginning to understand many things at last. "Was *he* then, your father, the dragon that we saw in Bath that time we walked, and then at Northanger?"

"Yes. And now you must forgive me yet again, this time for my rudeness back then, when you had asked so many pointed questions about dragons and their nature and origins, and I would not answer to you or even speak of the dragon—for I could not in truth utter all this to you just then. Every morning, rising early (what you know as his constitutional walk), my father takes the dragon form and desperately flies the heavens, searching aimlessly for his treasure, now lost forever. He is compelled to do this unto eternity, and will be thus for years— indeed for immortal ages—until he either draws his last breath in battle or decides to face his loss and relinquish the falsehood of gold in favor of truth. Only then can he cease being the immortal dragon and return to being a mortal man, and one day die in peace."

Henry paused, gathering himself for something, and took several steps back. Catherine put her hands to her face, in impossible dawning comprehension.

"And now—Open your eyes, Catherine, this must be seen. The dragons did not disappear, did not become extinct, nor did they 'reappear' suddenly in modern times. They are *here* among us, always. Dragons live in the hearts of men. A dragon emerges when there is the birth of perfect love—"

And saying this, Henry suddenly *changed*.

Catherine had no time to blink, but watched the mirage building in the air, as a strange unnatural wind came whirling to surround him, and it grew into a funnel, sending up leaves along the path and scattering blossoms in the grass . . . while the air in place of Henry thickened and he himself was momentarily *dissolved* into the fabric of the storm.

In his place was a great *white dragon*.

Catherine exclaimed, then held her hands to her lips and wordlessly cried.

It was the same one—*her* white dragon. It spread its wings that were like galleon sails on either sides of Catherine, and she held on to her bonnet and her dress and her very self, all rooted to the spot as the dragon unfurled itself to its full breadth and height and towered over her, pale and sparkling and glorious as the surface of a mirror in the sun.

"You are unhurt! You won the battle . . ." she whispered, through her tears.

And the dragon flexed its giant claws of white steel, moved its powerful limbs, and it blinked one great beautiful amber-golden eye at her in perfect silent communion.

And then it changed again . . . into her own beloved Henry.

"I am yours," he said. "I am your dragon, for before *you* there was no dragon in my heart. And now there is one only for you—if you will have me. And even if you will not, the dragon will *serve you* always."

And with a stifled cry Catherine came to him, throwing her arms about his neck in an embrace. And for long moments there were no words between them, no speech, only wonder.

"I had fought him, my father, and held him back from the final brink of madness," he told her. "For, since the start he had pursued you in his confounded way, seeking you for the family on my behalf. Under a mistaken persuasion of your possessions and claims, he had courted your acquaintance in Bath, solicited your company at Northanger, and designed you for his daughter-in-law—thinking you an heiress, seeking in his confusion *material riches*, and never recognizing that the treasure he saw in you was of the truer kind."

"I! An heiress!" exclaimed Catherine in amazement. "Why, that is so far from the truth, my family is hardly anything but simple, humble—"

"Ah, allow me to further explain to you the reasoning of my misguided father and the nature of things. As I say, he thought you wealthy to excess, and then, discovering otherwise, he first cast you *out* in a worthy fit of dragon passion, but then, the *dragon greed* took over, the dragon nature compelled, so he had to retrieve you, his last source of worldly treasure (as he mistakenly thought, partially correct as it was)."

"So he flew after the carriage, to have me return?"

"Yes and no—for even as he came after you his supernatural anger still boiled, and he was uncertain of anything but that you must not be allowed to slip away, for whatever *unknown value* you possibly held. I fought him, prevented him from hindering or hurting you, spoke truth into his heart and mind through the voiceless communion of dragonkind. He heard me, in his own maddened way, he *heard* me—thus, he still lives. But he is vanquished.

"And now, this needs be said: there are two types of dragon—the Dragon of Love and the Dragon of Gold. All dragons begin as creatures of love, pure and selfless. But if they experience the grave loss of this love, their nature changes, becomes perverted, from love to greed. And they harden and calcify and slowly approach the state of being stone and metal. In their slow 'immortal death' they must still hunger for treasure. But now they mistake *treasure of the spirit* for treasure of the material world. It is thus that history is filled with stories of ancient dragons, lying over hoards of priceless coin and jewels—heartless treasure of metal and stone—immortal and eternal, deep in the secret bowels of the earth. These are all the Dragons of Gold, dragons of despair and desolation, the only kind the world knows about, for they malinger here, having grown into monsters, refusing to *let go*.

"But the world knows little to nothing about the other kind of dragon, the original true kind, because such a creature is not ephemeral, and is not immortal—for it has no need to be. It loves and lives and dies in joy and sorrow of the fleeting moment along with its mortal love. And such a dragon thus passes into the ages unnoticed by the scholars or the natural scientists—for it appears rarely and hunts not at all, and when its time of loss comes, it gently relinquishes itself and passes on.

"I dearly hope to remain such a dragon," ended Henry. "But of certainty one never knows—never knows what might happen were I to lose *you.*"

Their further revelations and divulging of the heart were placed on hold briefly, for now they had resumed walking and in moments were at the Allen's house.

A very *short* visit to Mrs. Allen followed, in which Henry talked at random, without sense or connection, with fevered eyes and many secret looks of intimacy thrown in Catherine's way. And Catherine, rapt in the contemplation of her own unutterable happiness, scarcely opened her lips. She had also had the occasion to learn from sentences artfully spoken on Mrs. Allen's behalf, that he had openly "opposed his father on her behalf."

And then, after they had quit the Allens' residence and headed back, she had heard him say—in contrast to the previous revelatory supernatural explanation—in a more human and decidedly worldly manner, that *he now offered her his hand.*

"And now, as far as that mistaken notion of your great fortune—" said Henry.

And he proceeded to explain that the general had had nothing to accuse her of but her being the involuntary, unconscious object of a wicked *deception* which his dragon pride could not pardon, and which a better pride would have been ashamed to own.

Yes indeed, she was guilty only of being *less rich* than he had supposed her to be. And it was all because of John Thorpe!

"Oh, he is an odious horrid ogre!" exclaimed Catherine, unable to hold back. And Henry continued to tell his tale.

John Thorpe had first misled him. The general, perceiving his son one night at the theatre to be paying considerable attention to *a certain Miss Morland,* had accidentally inquired of Thorpe if he knew more of her than her name.

Thorpe, most happy to be on speaking terms with a man of General Tilney's importance, had been joyfully and proudly communicative. At that time not only did he expect James Morland to engage Isabella, but he was likewise resolved upon marrying Catherine himself! And thus, his vanity induced him to represent the family as yet more wealthy than his vanity and avarice had made him believe them to be.

*Oh dear!* thought Catherine, knowing exactly the kind of awful boasting exaggeration the ogre was capable of.

With whomsoever Thorpe was (or was likely to be) connected, his own consequence always required that theirs should be great. And as his intimacy with any acquaintance grew, so regularly grew their fortune—doubled, quadrupled, reached the sky!

Since Thorpe's expectations of his friend Morland's fortune were already overrated, it was easy to double what he thought was the amount of Mr. Morland's preferment, trebling his private fortune, bestowing a rich aunt, and sinking half the children. Thus he was able to represent the whole family to the general in a most respectable light.

For Catherine, however (the object of the general's dragon curiosity, and his own speculations), he had yet something more in reserve. The ten or fifteen thousand pounds her father could give her would be a pretty addition to Mr. Allen's estate. Surely her intimacy with the Allens made her handsomely legacied hereafter. And from that it was easy to speak of her as the almost acknowledged future heiress of Fullerton, with hundreds of thousands, nay, millions at her disposal—a *treasure hoard!*

Upon such intelligence the dragon general had proceeded; for never had it occurred to him to doubt its authority. In addition, there were the absolute facts of the Allens being wealthy and childless, of Miss Morland's being under their care, and of their treating her with parental kindness.

His resolution was soon formed. Already had he discerned a *liking* towards Miss Morland in the countenance of his son. And there was a certain peculiar *wondrous* air about her that he sensed on a supernatural level, being a supernatural (albeit damaged) creature himself.

In short, Henry was so convinced of his father's entirely believing it to be an advantageous connection, that it was not till her expulsion from Northanger that they had the smallest idea of the false calculations which had hurried him on.

That they were false, the general had learnt from the very person who had suggested them—from Thorpe himself!

"Oh!" cried Catherine, interrupting again. "I knew there was a perfectly good reason I could not stand him beyond his infernal nephilim ogre manners!"

"Nephilim? Ogre?" said Henry, then added cleverly in his usual manner: "Has Thorpe in fact eaten anyone? Has it been documented? And if not—Precision of words is to be observed always, else one might come to the wrong conclusions."

And Catherine burst out laughing then hastily explained both John and Isabella, altogether with their various subtle and crude attempts to acquire her soul, spirit, person, dowry, and verily the entire family (for the nephilim also sought treasure of all kinds), their horrid true inner visage (visible only to one such as herself) and their hot and cold weather fronts.

"Well then!" said Henry, "so *that* is what they are! I knew them to be other than ordinary human mortals. And yes, I *had* noted the so-called climate. But you must later tell me more."

And then he resumed the present explanation about Thorpe. Apparently on that very recent and fateful trip from Northanger, General Tilney had chanced to meet John Thorpe again in town. This time, Thorpe was under the influence of exactly opposite feelings. He was irritated by Catherine's refusal, and even more by the failure to accomplish a reconciliation between Morland and Isabella. Convinced that an association with the Morlands was no longer serviceable, he hastened to contradict to the general all that he had told him before in their praise, and now made up a profusion of defects—poverty, avarice, inability of giving the young people even a decent support. According to Thorpe the Morlands were a necessitous and numerous family, by no means respected in their own neighbourhood, aiming at a lifestyle beyond their fortune; seeking to better themselves by wealthy connections—a forward, bragging, scheming race!

The terrified general pronounced the name of Allen with an inquiring look; and here too Thorpe had painted a horrid picture. The Allens, he believed, had lived near them too long, and he knew the young man on whom the Fullerton estate must devolve—and it was *not* James Morland.

The general needed no more. The dragon was enraged—with almost everybody in the world but himself. And he set out the next day for the abbey, where Catherine was met with such a cruel and unjust expulsion.

Henry, in having such things to relate of his father, was almost as pitiable as in their first avowal to himself. He blushed for the narrow-minded counsel which he was obliged to expose. And he grieved for the old dragon's dark nature that had taken his heart further along the path of gold—advancing it deeper in its chosen journey toward lifeless metal and eternity *alone*.

And yet, Henry had been indignant enough to oppose the old dragon directly—all because of *her*. And in doing so, his own heart had swelled with love, and it called forth his own dragon nature.

"I admit," he said softly, "that before yesterday I had not known myself, had not known *what* I also was. It does not always run in the family, this thing. Dragons are made, not born. (My brother Frederick, for example, has no dragon in him—at least not at present, even though he seems to have the prideful airs of one.) But when our father had taken off from Northanger, following you, for the first time I had *sensed* the dragon—heard and felt him coming at a distance. And in an instant I knew exactly all that had transpired with you, having *read* his mind. And when your carriage was passing closest to me, I was pulled from within, twisted, uprooted—impossible to describe what it is that happened to me—and I *turned*, for the first time, and I came for you."

"I saw you flying!" said Catherine. "I watched and I did not know. But strangely, I could somehow *feel* myself flying alongside you, all those many miles."

"Ah, Catherine," Henry exclaimed, "if only you realized what you can do, the power that you hold over the unseen world. Look what effect you have had upon an entire town of Bath, and then, you woke Northanger to its ancient ways."

"You have no idea," said Catherine smartly. "One of these days I must tell you of the chest and the cabinet in the apartment I had been staying in. And what manner of horrid *things* it had released—"

And he laughed and then told her how much happiness it was for him to see her thus, and that he hoped his earlier teasing of her love for *Udolpho* did not discompose her too much. "I had not suspected then, to what extent the delightful secrets you talked and dreamed about were in fact real—not only to you but to the world around you. Will you forgive me?"

"Goodness, for what? For keeping me balanced and sane and bringing my imagination back to the realm of common sense? It is only recently that I realize that I had not just imagined those terrible things, but I had in fact wished for them and made them happen!"

"Such is the power of the human *treasure*," he replied. And then again he drew closer to her in an embrace.

"There are angels about us now, are there not?" Henry whispered.

"Oh yes," she replied. "Over a dozen, two near your nose, and one of them is your own. He wants me to tell you to fix your cravat a bit, it has gotten somewhat in disarray since you have been a dragon—but never mind, I can do it myself on your behalf."

Henry laughed again.

And then Catherine remembered. "Oh, wait! I do not think your father has an angel of his own about him. At least, I had never seen one with him. Why is that so? And yet, *you* do."

Henry thought for a long moment. "I do not know for certain, he said with gravity, "but it might be that, as a Dragon of Love, I am still in the light. His angel—it is not lost, I dare hope, and I expect it is somewhere out there, waiting for him to return one day to a choice of mortal humanity. For that is one hope I will never relinquish on my father's behalf."

And with those words they had come to the Morland house and entered together.

**The Dragon of Love**

# Chapter 31

Mr. and Mrs. Morland's surprise on being applied to by Mr. Tilney for their consent to his marrying their daughter was, for a few minutes, considerable.

It had never entered their heads to suspect an attachment on either side. But since nothing could be more natural than Catherine's being *beloved,* they soon came to view it with happy agitation and gratified pride.

As far as *they* alone were concerned, there could not be a single objection. His pleasing manners and good sense were self-evident recommendations. And having never heard evil of him, goodwill supplied the place of experience, and his character needed no attestation.

"Catherine would make a sad, heedless young housekeeper, to be sure. You do realize, she is far more likely to *converse* with the mantelpiece than dust it?" was her mother's foreboding remark; but quick was the consolation of there being nothing like practice.

"Mrs. Morland," said Henry, "she is free to recite poetry to every chest and cabinet in the domicile, if that is what she desires."

And with such charming words, no one could help but be perfectly satisfied.

There was but *one obstacle* remaining to their perfect happiness. And till that one was removed, it must be impossible for Mr. and Mrs. Morland to sanction the engagement. Their tempers were mild, but their principles were steady, and while *his parent* so expressly *forbade* the connection, they could not allow themselves to encourage it.

They did not expect or insist that the general should actively come forward to solicit the alliance, or very heartily approve it, but there must be at least a decent appearance of consent obtained from him. His *simple consent*—not money or fortune—was all that they wished for, and their own willing approbation was instantly to follow.

The young people were at first crestfallen.

"The old dragon will never consent," mourned Catherine to her beloved. "I am afraid it is of no use appealing to his better nature."

"If needed, I will *force* him to it," said Henry in a voice like steel, with an amber-golden glint in his eyes.

"No," she replied gently. "Please, let us wait."

Only, what could ever induce such an impossible change of heart in the general, in him whose heart was already on its way to turning into metal and his flesh to stone?

But Henry heeded his treasure. Thus, for the moment, he returned to what was now his only home, to watch over his young plantations, and extend his improvements for *her* sake, to whose share in them he looked anxiously forward.

And Catherine remained at Fullerton to cry. Whether the torments of such enforced absence were softened by a clandestine correspondence between the lovers, perhaps employing some form of secret *encryption* in Capital Letters using the Udolpho Code, dear Reader, let us not inquire. Mr. and Mrs. Morland never did—they had been too kind to exact any promise otherwise. And whenever Catherine received a letter (quite often) they always looked another way.

The anxiety, which in this state of their attachment must be the portion of Henry and Catherine, was eventually resolved to everyone's satisfaction and their eventual blissful matrimony.

The circumstance which helped immensely was the marriage of the general's daughter with a man of fortune and consequence, which took place in the course of the summer—an accession of dignity that threw the imbalanced dragon into a fit of good humour, from which he did not recover till after Eleanor had obtained his forgiveness of Henry, and his permission for him "to be a fool if he liked it!"

The marriage of long-suffering Eleanor Tilney, and her eventual happy removal from all the evils of her father and Northanger, to the home of her choice and the man of her choice, was an event blessed by fortune and felicity. Eleanor's partiality for this gentleman was not of recent origin; and the only thing preventing their union had been the inferiority of his situation. His unexpected accession to title and fortune had removed all his difficulties; and never had the general loved his daughter so well as when he first hailed her "Your Ladyship!"

Her husband was deserving of her; being the most charming young man in the world—and who knows, just possibly, he too was an awakened dragon. One other item that must be noted, is that this was the *very same gentleman* whose negligent servant left behind him that collection of *washing-bills,* resulting from a long visit at Northanger, by which our heroine was involved in one of her most alarming demonic adventures.

The positive influence of the viscount and viscountess in their brother's behalf was assisted by a further clarification of Mr. Morland's financial circumstances. In short, the general learned that the Morlands were not at all as terribly off as John Thorpe had made them out to be. To be sure, they were not rich, but neither were they dishonorable or destitute—and Catherine would have three thousand pounds.

This so *material* and *tangible* an amendment of his expectations greatly contributed to smooth the descent of his dragon pride.

On the strength of this, the general, soon after Eleanor's marriage, permitted his son to return to Northanger, and thence made him the bearer of his *consent,* very courteously worded in a page full of empty professions to Mr. Morland.

Nay, the petrifying dragon heart had not strayed from its sorrowful path of gold. But at least *some* actual gold (and a human *treasure*) was now within grasp, and merely knowing it calmed the dragon into acquiescence—not to mention, the avoidance of a rather unpleasant continuation of a *supernatural battle* with his powerful son.

The happy event which the consent authorized soon followed: Henry and Catherine were married, the bells rang, the angels sang in dulcet tones, and everybody smiled.

To begin perfect happiness at the respective ages of twenty-six and eighteen is to do pretty well. The Dragon of Love had gained his rightful one and only true treasure.

And as for the Treasure herself, why, she continued to demonstrate that brave *imagination* and *common sense* could not only co-exist, but that indeed they happily must *wed* each other, in order to provide the world with its due share of bright offspring in the form of angels, dragons, and other true wonders.


THE END

# APPENDIX

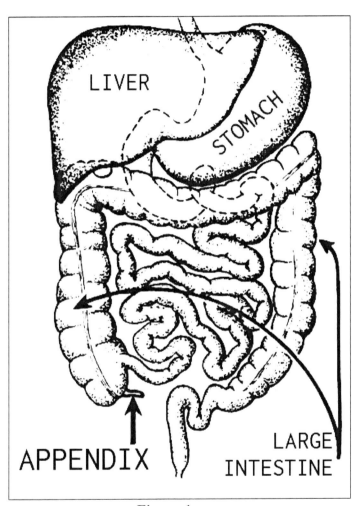

**Figure 1**

# APPENDIX 2

**Figure 2: Grey's Scale Anatomy**

# A Note on the Text

*Northanger Abbey* was written in 1797-98 under a different title (it included *Angels and Dragons*). The manuscript was revised around 1803 and sold to a London publisher, Crosbie & Co., who sold[30] it back in 1816. This fine *supernatural* text is based on the first edition, published by John Murray, London, in 1818—the year following Miss Austen's death. Spelling and punctuation have been largely brought into conformity with modern British usage. Supernatural and paranormal beings and elements were retained as deemed prudent and inevitable.

---

[30] The publisher was an imbecilic twit.

# Author's After-Note

G<small>ENTLE</small> R<small>EADER</small>—

No, this is not *she,* but the other—the shameless harridan who has taken it upon herself to take up pen and mangle Miss Austen's deathless (but never *undead*), perfectly civil, delightfully romantic, pointedly sarcastic, and by all accounts immortal prose, with the crass additions of her own fired imagination.

How is one to satirize an already perfect satire? Why, by taking it into the sublime realm of the fantastic and then by bringing all its already inherent imaginary absurdity to life.

It must be acknowledged that a profound and humble debt of gratitude is owed to the esteemed Mrs. Ann Radcliffe and her fellow gothic novelists who have provided the splendid raw fodder for this little flight of fancy.

Meanwhile, I humbly beg a thousand pardons of Miss Austen's noble shade, and trust you have enjoyed the horrid delights found only in Northanger Abbey.

Yours, in All Amiability,
T<small>HE</small> H<small>ARRIDAN</small>.

**Vera Nazarian**
December, 2010

# About the Harridan

**Vera Nazarian** immigrated to the USA from the former USSR as a kid, sold her first story at the age of 17, and since then has published numerous works in anthologies and magazines, and has seen her fiction translated into eight languages.

She made her novelist debut with the critically acclaimed arabesque "collage" novel *Dreams of the Compass Rose*, followed by epic fantasy about a world without color, *Lords of Rainbow*. Her novella *The Clock King and the Queen of the Hourglass* from PS Publishing (UK) with an introduction by **Charles de Lint** made the *Locus* Recommended Reading List for 2005. Her debut short fiction collection *Salt of the Air*, with an introduction by **Gene Wolfe**, contains the 2007 Nebula Award-nominated "The Story of Love." Recent work includes the 2008 Nebula Award-nominated, self-illustrated baroque fantasy novella *The Duke in His Castle*, science fiction collection *After the Sundial* (2010), Jane Austen parody *Mansfield Park and Mummies* (2009), *The Perpetual Calendar of Inspiration* (2010), and this literary curiosity that you now hold in your hands. . . .

Vera lives in Los Angeles, and uses her Armenian sense of humor and her Russian sense of suffering to bake conflicted pirozhki and make art.

In addition to being a writer and award-winning artist, she is also the publisher of Norilana Books.

Official website:
www.veranazarian.com

CPSIA information can be obtained at www.ICGtesting.com
Printed in the USA
LVOW131926070713

341739LV00003B/423/P